The Runaway

Katie Flynn has lived for many years in the north-west. A compulsive writer, she started with short stories and articles and many of her early stories were broadcast on Radio Merseyside. She decided to write her Liverpool series after hearing the reminiscences of family members about life in the city in the early years of the twentieth century. For many years she has had to cope with ME, but has continued to write. She also writes as Judith Saxton.

Katie Flynn

The Runaway

arrow books

Published by Arrow Books in 2012

11

First published in Great Britain in 2012 by
Arrow Books
The Random House Group Limited
20 Vauxhall Bridge Road, London, SW1V 2SA

www.randomhouse.co.uk

Addresses for companies within The Random House Group Limited can be found at:
www.randomhouse.co.uk/offices.htm

The Random House Group Limited Reg. No. 954009

A CIP catalogue record for this book
is available from the British Library

Penguin Random House is committed to a sustainable future for
our business, our readers and our planet. This book is made from
Forest Stewardship Council® certified paper.

Printed and bound in Great Britain by Clays Ltd, Elcograf S.p.A.

Typeset in Palatino by Palimpsest Book Production Limited,
Falkirk, Stirlingshire

For Holly Pemberton, who leapt into the breach and saved the day. Thanks Holly!

Dear Reader,

I first had the idea for *The Runaway* when a mental picture of Sandra and Beryl in *The Liver Birds* came into my head. In *The Runaway* Dana is Irish and a dreamer, but Polly is very much the down-to-earth Scouser, and when she makes up her mind to resolve her friend's troubles, she dives in feet first, dragging her hapless friend Ernie along with her, regardless of his wishes.

I loved writing about Castletara – no I shan't tell you where it is in reality – and hope that the differences between Dana's background and Polly's make the story more interesting for you; certainly they did for the writer!

Love

Katie Flynn

Prologue

Castletara, 1928

Dana was deeply asleep, did not even hear the light tap upon her bedroom door, but woke when a hand grasped her shoulder and a voice hissed in her ear: 'Wake up, you eejit! I thought as how you were going to wake me, and here you are fathoms deep and me waitin' for as long as I dared before I decided to fetch you. Come on, come on! We've got to be at the well by midnight, or there's no point in us going at all.'

Dana sat up, still groggy with sleep, and rubbed her eyes. She began to ask if it was morning and then remembered. The previous day had been her thirteenth birthday and during the wonderful party, at which almost all the pupils at the village school had been present, she and Con had heard about Mrs O'Connor's well for the first time.

"Tis a magic well, a wishing well,' one of the girls had said. "Tis blessed by the fairy folk, or so my granny told me. She says if you go to the O'Connor well at midnight, when the moon's at the full, bow to it three times and then ask it to grant you a favour, it will do so. She said it'll show you the face of the feller you're goin' to marry, or something o' that sort.'

'Tell you who's goin' to win the three thirty, or come

1

out on top in the Grand National?' one of the listening boys had put in, his mouth curving into a mocking smile. 'Or where to put your crosses on the football coupon so's you win a fortune? You girls! As if it mattered who you marry!'

The girl who had been telling the tale had flushed angrily. 'I've not finished yet,' she had said sharply. And it 'ud matter to you if you weren't goin' to marry at all, because then, when you looked into the well water, you'd see nothin' but a ghastly skellington, leerin' at you. So I guess you'd be too scared to try it, Micky, because wit' a great conk like yours it 'ud be the skull you'd see for sure.'

This remark had caused much amusement and the subject had been allowed to drop but later, when everyone had gone home, Con and Dana had sat side by side on the mossy wooden gate which led to the home pasture talking over the story of Mrs O'Connor's fairy well. 'I don't believe a word of it,' Dana had said stoutly. 'I've never heard Mammy or Daddy talk about it, not even when they've been tellin' tall tales. What about you, Con? Has Mr Devlin ever mentioned it?'

Con had shaken his head. 'No, but my dad isn't at all superstitious. If he mentioned it at all it would be to say 'twas rubbish. Anyway, in earlier times they'd probably have called Mrs O'Connor a witch.' He had chuckled. 'Her nose and her chin damn near touch, so they do. But I tell you what; it would be a bit of a laugh to test it out for ourselves. 'Tis full moon tonight and there'll not be a cloud in the sky, I reckon, because your daddy says we're in for a spell of good weather and he's usually right. What do you say? Are you on?' He had grinned at Dana, his dark, lively face alight with mischief, and Dana had grinned back. To go adventuring with Con, who was a whole year older than herself and a great deal braver, was her idea of heaven. It would make her thirteenth birthday very special indeed.

'Course I'm on,' she had said accordingly. ''Tis a fair walk to the O'Connors' place so we'd best set out at eleven o' clock. I'll come and get you as soon as I wake.'

So now, in the shivery, chancy light of the full moon – for there were some small clouds in the sky despite Donovan McBride's weather forecast – the two young people set off. Despite her intention to prove to Con that she feared nothing, Dana clutched his arm, trying very hard to be brave when they plunged into the little lane which would lead them to the well and was in deep shadow, but mostly shutting her eyes and simply hoping that Con would not notice.

They reached the well at last and stared up at the moon, waiting for a wispy, scudding cloud to pass before bending over the brick parapet. 'C'mon, fairies, show us how good you are at tellin' the future,' Con said, taking Dana's hand and giving it a squeeze. 'Who's goin' to win the Grand National, eh? We're not asking much of the fairy folk, and we could do wit' the money, so we could.'

But the water in the well remained infuriatingly unresponsive, though Dana was so glad that neither of them saw a skeleton that she forgave the fairies for their ticklish ways, and presently Con hauled the wooden bucket up on to the brickwork and they both had a drink of the sweet, cool water before gently lowering it into the depths once more. Then they watched as the ripples gradually calmed, leaving a perfect mirror below them.

'Well, that was a waste of time,' Con grumbled as they set off for home once more. 'The only reflection I saw in the water was us – you and me – wit' not a word about football pools or the Grand National. I was goin' to tell the fellers at school how we'd heard a mysterious voice, sort of gargling, you know, and it had told us the future . . .'

But Dana was chilly, and beginning to think longingly of her bed. She tugged impatiently on her companion's hand. 'Shut up and walk a bit quicker,' she said. 'It's icy cold so it is, and we did see *something*, even if it was only us.'

Chapter One

'Mind your perishin' backs, you gairls, 'cos I'm a-coming through!'

Caitlin and Dana, washing up in the kitchens of the Willows restaurant, shrank against the big stone sinks as Mrs Haggerty, the cook, squeezed past them, giving Dana a sharp jab with her elbow as she did so.

'Ouch!' Dana said, but she said it quietly so that only Caitlin could hear. It was no use antagonising Mrs Haggerty, who detested both girls anyway, because despite her name she disliked the Irish and saw to it that Dana and Caitlin always got the most unpopular jobs.

But perhaps she had heard; at any rate she paused in her onward rush – she was carrying a pile of clean plates over to the bain-marie to be filled – and nudged Caitlin. 'You! Gerron wi' them cups an' saucers; there's some folk like a cuppa when they's ate me good food.' She turned to Dana. 'You! Gerrin the veggie scullery an' start peelin' spuds for tomorrer. There's a full sack want doin' an' you ain't much good for owt else.'

'Right you are, Mrs H,' Dana said as politely as she could. 'Only shouldn't I finish here first? I don't think Caitlin can lift the metal baskets out of the boiling water without someone to give a hand.'

The cook scowled. 'Polly can help her; you ain't gerrin' out o' spud bashin' that easy,' she said, and gave a snort of laughter. 'Move!'

Dana would have liked to point out that Polly Smith was small and frail, and new to kitchen work, but bit the words back. She had no desire to see Polly become the next worker on the cook's hate list. The younger girl was eager to please and, on hearing her name, came over to the sink at a run. 'Yes, Miz Haggerty?' she said brightly. 'What'll I do? I heered you call me.'

Mrs Haggerty was explaining how one lifted the big metal racks out of the boiling water as Dana headed for the vegetable scullery. It was a horrid, dank little room: a brick-built and brick-floored extension, unplastered and unpainted, with a knee-level sink the very sight of which made Dana's long spine shrink with horror. She was tall and slim and because of that low sink particularly hated spud peeling. There was an ancient machine in one corner of the scullery, called the rumbler by the staff, which was the nearest thing to an automatic potato peeler the Willows possessed apart from me, Dana thought bitterly. It looked a little like a concrete mixer, with a big bowl for the potatoes and a handle on the side. One filled the bucket with spuds, added water, closed the lid and began to turn the handle vigorously. It was hard work, but nowhere near as tedious as peeling by hand, nor unfortunately as thorough. Mrs Haggerty hated it, and because of the rumbling noise the wretched thing made Dana dared not even think of employing it. Instead, with a sigh, she fitted the big plug in the sink, turned on the brass tap and began throwing potatoes into the water.

She was well into her task when two of the other kitchen workers, Ernie and Sam, entered the room behind her. Ernie had been out on an errand for Mrs H, who had run short of cooking apples – pork was on the menu today – and had now drawn his pal into the malodorous little scullery for a quiet chat.

Dana, peeling the potatoes, grinned to herself. Usually their talk was of girls, football or food, but now it seemed that Ernie had picked up some interesting gossip. 'You know old Squab-nose, the butcher on Heyworth?' he asked in a low voice. 'I call to mind you sayin' weeks back that he were headin' for the high jump. Well, he's been and gone and done a moonlight; left the place in a terrible state. I seen it wi' me own eyes, though I got the story from a neighbour none too sorry to see him go. Seems the old bugger had a grudge agin his landlord so he ordered up as usual – offal mainly – then he closed all the winders, put a note on the door sayin' he'd gone on his holidays and jimmied off, owin' a month's rent. They say the stench made some delicate souls throw up, to say nothin' o' the bleedin' bluebottles what come to the feast.' Ernie laughed. 'Reckon that'll mean another empty shop, 'cos Mr Thwaite's the landlord and everyone knows he's mean as hell. Apparently he opened the door, staggered back as a million bluebottles come tearin' out, then slammed the door shut, goin' blue in the face. He said he weren't responsible for the pong, nor the flies, and he'd leave it to the next tenant to clear up.'

'Only who'll take it on in a state like that?' Sam said gleefully. 'It weren't as though old Squab-nose were ever good at his trade, and once that modern butcher's shop set up only half a dozen doors away his customers left

7

in a body.' He cackled. 'Wonder where the old devil's gone?'

'Somewhere Thwaite will never think of lookin',' Ernie said, forgetting to keep his voice low. He became aware that Dana was staring at him with open interest. He reached out and gave her cheek an affectionate pat. 'D'you hear that, Dee? Old Joshua Rayner's scarpered. Want to start up in the butchery business?' He chuckled hoarsely. 'There'll be a butcher's shop going beggin' once all the bluebottles is dead and Thwaite's managed to persuade someone to take the rotten meat off of his hands.'

When she and Caitlin had first come to work at the Willows they had resented the Liverpudlians' habit of shortening names, but had finally given up protesting and Dana now answered to Dee, when pressed. 'Is it a lock-up?' she said. 'Me and Caitlin are looking for a room to share . . . we're still at the YWCA, which is cheap and cheerful but crowded, and Heyworth Street isn't all that far from here.'

Sam shrugged, but Ernie considered the question seriously. 'I dunno whether it's a lock-up but I squinted through the winder – between the dead bluebottles, y'know – and it's like most small shops: the bit the customers see, with a long wooden counter, then a door at the back which were wide open, showin' another room, a storeroom I guess. There's stairs leadin' upwards in the storeroom, I remember that much, so I reckon there'll be some sort of flat above. But you'd not want a whole flat, not on what this job pays; you'd be after a room, some-where real cheap, with a gas ring to boil a kettle and a bucket for your water. Old Squab-nose would have had runnin' water, a yard for his bins, electricity, mebbe – oh, all sorts.'

Dana's shoulders drooped. 'You're right, of course . . .' she began, then brightened. 'But if it was really cheap we might get together with two or three other girls to help pay the rent. There's always adverts in the *Echo* for girls wanting a flat-share. If we got in first . . .'

Sam grinned. 'Wharrabout you two startin' up in the butchery business? If you promised to clean the place up for free, Thwaite might let you have the flat and the shop for what they calls a peppercorn rent. I can just see you an' Caitlin in blue and white striped aprons, hatchets in hand and blood up to your elbows as you butcher some poor innocent joint o' meat.'

Dana sighed and turned back to the sink. She scooped up a handful of dirty water and threw it at the two lads, who guffawed and might have retaliated had not a woman's large form appeared in the doorway. 'Did you get them apples?' Mrs H barked. 'Sam, what the devil are you doin' in here when we's up to our eyes in hungry customers? Gerrout of it the pair of you and let Ginger gerron wi' them spuds.'

Dana slanted a malevolent glance over her shoulder and began to say that she had not stopped peeling spuds for one moment and did not mean to answer to Ginger as well as Dee, but Mrs H was already turning away, leaving Dana to her task and her thoughts, which were pretty chaotic. She and Caitlin were always on the lookout for affordable accommodation, but though they had now been earning at the restaurant for nearly six months they were always pipped at the post by people who had local friends or relatives to apply on their behalf for any decent room or flat which came on the market, whereas Dana and Caitlin had left all their friends and relatives in Ireland. However, judging by what Ernie had said, this particular property had only recently become vacant, and folk might not realise that the flat above would also be available.

Dana chopped a quantity of peeled potatoes into pan-sized pieces and carried them through to the kitchen. As soon as she saw her, the cook gave an evil grin, snatched the pan of potatoes and turned to address Ernie and Sam. 'Ernie, peel them apples; Sam, start choppin' the mutton for tomorrer's special. I'm makin' Lancashire hotpot . . .' she looked over at Dana, standing near the sink, 'which is why I want *all* that sack of spuds peeled, not just a few. Off you go, Ginger.'

For the next two hours the kitchen was a hell of heat and bustle as cooks cooked, waitresses waited and Mrs Haggerty generally harassed her staff. By mid-afternoon, however, Mrs Haggerty had put all the food that would not keep a further day into two large tureens and divided the staff into two sittings, deliberately separating Dana and Caitlin – who would be acting as waitress to customers drifting in for a late snack lunch or early tea – because she knew they liked to be together.

Dana, who was longing to pass on Ernie's interesting gossip, pulled a face as Caitlin hurried past her and hissed that she had news to impart. There was no chance to exchange more than a few words, however, before Caitlin, having shed her calico overall and donned the white frilly pinafore, white cuffs and trim little cap of a waitress, set off for the dining rooms. Dana grinned to herself as she saw the neat manoeuvre which her friend executed as she passed Mr Lionel, the restaurant owner, in the doorway. Her friend was beautiful, with dark hair, eyes so deep a blue that they might have been described as violet, and rosy lips. Her skin was creamy, her figure perfection – and Mr Lionel, well known for being a bottom pincher, liked to stand just inside the swing doors which divided the kitchen from the dining rooms so he could fondle the rear of any pretty waitress. Caitlin's quick swerve as she passed him was to dodge his wandering hands, though it was so neatly done that Dana doubted if Mr Lionel was aware of it. Caitlin was always threatening to jab Mr Lionel in the stomach or tread on his toes – by accident on purpose – as she slithered past, but of course she had never done any such thing. Jobs were scarce, even ill-paid and demanding jobs like this one, and though at present they were lodged at the YWCA, Dana and Caitlin's ambition was to find a room which they could share at a price they could afford. Anything, in fact, which would get them out of the YWCA.

By the time they left the Willows, a fine drizzle was falling. The girls headed for their tram stop and Dana, bursting with her news, felt quite cross with her friend for talking non-stop about her new admirer, a man in his thirties she rather thought, not precisely handsome but fascinating and attractive, who had asked her to accompany him to a dinner dance the following Saturday and had tipped her a whole quid when she had agreed to go. Indeed, by the time they reached the tram queue Dana's impatience had got the better of her and she fairly snapped at Caitlin when her friend began to tell her all over again how attentive her new admirer had become.

'Shut up and *listen*, will you?' she demanded hotly as they shuffled nearer the head of the queue, for it was a busy time of day and the conductors were only accepting the first half-dozen would-be passengers. 'I was in the vegetable scullery . . .'

The story, however, did not bring a sparkle to those big, dark blue eyes, or a smile to those rosy lips. Caitlin stared. 'A *butcher's* shop?' she said incredulously. 'Why ever should we be interested in a butcher's shop? We want somewhere to live decently, with a bit of privacy; I thought we'd agreed on that if nothing else.'

'Hey, we agree on most things, so we do,' Dana objected, knowing that she sounded hurt and not caring. She *was* hurt, dammit! 'And you aren't listening, Caitlin. It's not the perishin' shop we're interested in, of course it isn't, but the flat above. According to Ernie, the landlord – his name's Thwaite – is a stingy blighter who won't even clean the shop up, and the last tenant left a month ago. But they only discovered he'd gone today, which might mean . . .'

'Oh, I see,' Caitlin said, but she spoke dreamily. 'I know I've told you time out of mind that I never wanted to get involved wit' a man again, but a rich one . . . well, that's different.'

'It sure is,' Dana said with a chuckle. 'Caitlin Flannagan, you little gold-digger! Are you trying to tell me that you'd marry a midden for muck, as the saying goes? Because if so, I don't believe you. You've had admirers by the score ever since we arrived in Liverpool. Half the boys at the YMCA are in love with you and you're always telling me that when you're waitressing the young men fight to be on one of your tables and leave you good tips. Just remember, there'll have to be a payback for that quid, even if it's only a lot of kissing and cuddling. How do you feel about that, eh?'

Caitlin smiled guiltily and a dimple peeped in her left cheek. 'I suppose I'll have to put up with it since I guess I'll get married one day; I don't intend to wait on tables or peel spuds for the rest of my life,' she said. 'When I left Dublin to come across the sea, I t'ought I'd get a job as a mannequin in one of the big stores, Lewis's or Blackler's, or perhaps as a saleslady in gowns. No one ever told me that finding a job in Liverpool would be as difficult as it was in Dublin, mebbe worse; if I'd known I'd end up skivvying . . .'

Dana sighed. She and Caitlin had met on the ferry and had immediately seen the advantage of knowing someone when starting life in a big city for the first time. Dana, deeply unhappy and hurt by the circumstances which had caused her to flee her native land, had volunteered very little information about her past; indeed, now that she was on strange ground, she tried never to think of the home she had left. When she had decided to leave she had told herself, perhaps rather melodramatically, that she was slamming the door on her past, and had done so, but Caitlin had not been so reticent. Within a week of entering the YWCA and getting jobs at the Willows as kitchen workers, Dana knew that her new friend had fled her comfortable home and loving family because the young man she had meant to marry had been and gone and wed another.

'The shame of it,' Caitlin had moaned. 'And to make

matters worse, it were my own young sister Patricia his fancy settled on. She asked me to be bridesmaid so I waited till the wedding day and lit out, leaving her a note to say I'd better things to do than dance attendance on a girl three years younger than myself. And I just hope I ruined the wedding for them,' she had added with unusual bitterness.

Dana had truly sympathised, but as time went on she had begun to suspect that there were two sides to this story and the side Caitlin had imparted was probably biased to say the least.

Oddly enough, Caitlin had simply accepted that Dana had left home to try to repair the family fortunes without asking one question, though her eyes had brimmed with easy, sympathetic tears when Dana had explained that the necessity to earn her own living was caused by the death of her father. 'You poor thing, alanna,' Caitlin had said. 'And you've no brothers nor sisters? We'll make our fortunes in spite of everything, though. I'm sure of it.'

Now, standing at the tram stop, Dana began to suggest that the two of them should not go straight back to the YWCA but should visit the landlord of the flat on Heyworth Street. 'Someone's bound to know his address and Thwaite isn't a common name,' she said. 'Oh, be a sport, Caitlin my love! You're not going to this dinner dance until Saturday, so you've almost three days to prepare yourself.'

Caitlin pulled a face. 'It's a new dance dress I'll be needing,' she pointed out. 'It'll take all my savings, but if James – that's his name, James Mortimer – sees me in my best, perhaps there will be other invitations.' She flung an arm round her friend's neck as the tram drew up beside them. 'Look, I'll come wit' you when I've found my dress, and when I marry my duke I'll find you someone even richer, someone with a stately home and heaps of servants. Maybe you'll employ the Hag as your head cook and order her about, like she orders you. What d'you say to that?'

Behind the two girls in the queue for the tram, Polly and Myra, who also worked in the Willows kitchens, listened avidly as Caitlin and Dana chatted. 'If I looked like Kay, I wouldn't work in any old kitchens,' Polly said in a low voice. 'Come to that, if I were Dee – Dana, I mean – I'd ask to be put on waitressing occasionally. It ain't fair that her pal gets all the tips.'

Myra sniggered. 'Dee wouldn't get no tips, not wi' that bright ginger fuzz she calls hair, an' the white eyelashes and eyebrows,' she pointed out. 'To say nothin' of havin' a figure like a stick.'

'Ye-es, but she's got . . . wotsit . . . you know what I mean,' Polly said. 'I admit she ain't pretty exactly, but she's got . . . oh, I dunno what to call it, but I bet she'd get tips awright.'

There was a pause whilst Myra appeared to consider her friend's words, but when she spoke it was to change the subject. 'What's all this about a butcher's shop? You don't get girls workin' for butchers as a rule, 'cos it's rare hard work; you need to be strong to heft the carcasses out of the lorries and into the shop.'

Polly giggled. She was a small fair-haired girl, skinny as a rake but beginning to put on flesh due, the head cook boasted, to the excellent meals she gave her staff.

Polly, who had been brought up in an orphanage, acknowledged the truth of this, for though the food varied there was always plenty of it. Soggy cabbage, overcooked potatoes, gristly meat and cold pudding, but it was all food. She thought about Myra's last remark. 'A *butcher's* shop? Wharron earth are you on about? Oh, I remember. It weren't old Rayner's shop they were talkin' about, it were the flat above. They were sayin' – or Dee was at any rate – that they might be able to rent it if they could find another couple of girls to share the expense.' She sighed wistfully. 'Wish we could move in and share. Ooh, wouldn't it be wonderful, Myra? If only we could! But I'm on the very lowest wage old Lionel pays, so no chance of savin' up. If only I could grow a few inches taller! Mr Lionel did suggest I might waitress at teatime when the trays ain't so heavy, but Mrs Lionel said she'd be prosecuted for employing child labour and it's not been mentioned since.'

'Well, I think you and me should apply for waitress work anyway . . .' Myra was beginning when the tram clattered up beside them and the queue began to edge forward. The girls just managed to follow Dana and Caitlin on board before the conductor shot his hand out to prevent anyone else from ascending the platform.

'Just room for a littl'un,' he said cheerfully. 'Shove up, ladies and gents all.'

Polly obeyed, squeezing past several strap-hanging passengers until she was once again near enough to overhear the older girls' conversation, but Myra, both taller and more robust than her friend, was unable to follow suit. Too small to strap hang comfortably, Polly

16

was glad of the opportunity to listen once more, since it took her mind off her aching arm. She heard Dee trying to persuade Caitlin to accompany her in her search for the landlord, and when at last the ginger-haired girl was successful Polly had hard work not to cheer.

The conductor rang his bell and bawled the name of her stop, and she began to push her way past the other passengers again, a quick glance over her shoulder telling her that the two older girls were getting off as well. Myra, she knew, would remain aboard for another three stops. Suddenly, she decided that instead of going straight to the girls' home, which was where she was billeted until she was old enough to find accommodation for herself, she would follow Dana and Caitlin and have a look at this butcher's shop for herself. She was on the pavement first and turned as the two older girls alighted, Caitlin talking animatedly whilst Dee listened and interjected a word now and then. Polly smiled at them and was pleased when Dee said: 'How're you doing, Polly?' She thought it kind of the older girl to remember her name, for she had only been at the Dining Rooms for a few weeks and so far had spent most of her time alone in the vegetable scullery, knocking earth off spuds, chopping the tops off carrots and removing caterpillars and similar bugs from the cosy homes they had made for themselves in the big pale green cabbages.

She dropped behind Dee and Caitlin and presently found herself approaching a dingy shop frontage with the words *J. T. Rayner, Family Butcher* in faded lettering above the dirty bow window. The older girls went right up to the glass and peered inside but Polly, afraid of being accused of nosy parkering, hung back until Dana

17

and Caitlin, after some conversation which Polly was too far away to hear, suddenly dived into the newspaper and tobacconist's shop next door. Hastily Polly scooted the few yards which separated her from the butcher's window and had her nose actually pressed to the glass when the older girls emerged, scrutinising a piece of paper and pointing up the road. Polly was debating whether to follow them when a tram passed and drew up at a stop a little way ahead. Dana and Caitlin began to run and the conductor, about to ring his bell, swung out on the pole and yelled to the girls to hurry because he and his driver had their timetable to consider.

Polly made no attempt to climb aboard, looking pointedly the other way as she neared the tram; she had no pennies to spare, nor any idea of her fellow workers' eventual destination. As soon as the vehicle had trundled out of sight, however, she returned to the butcher's shop. Even from outside she fancied she could smell the whiff of bad meat and it was easy to guess at the state of the whole place after only a cursory glance. As Ernie had said, it was thick with bluebottles, the sawdust on the floor churned up and filthy, the long wooden counter bloodstained. Through the open door which led into the back room, Polly could see not only the disgusting state of the place but the stairs which she guessed must lead to the flat above. She could not see the back door, and was standing on tiptoe in an effort to improve her view when somebody jabbed something hard between her shoulder blades and a voice growled: 'Stick 'em up!'

Polly jumped guiltily, then swung round, having recognised Ernie's voice. 'Leave off!' she commanded wrathfully. 'Stick 'em up yourself! Who do you think you are, perishin' Tom Mix?'

'Nah, he's old hat; I'm Gary Cooper I am,' Ernie said. He cocked his cap to one side and affected an American drawl. 'Who's you spyin' on, sister? Or is you thinkin' of takin' old Squab-nose's shop on?' He chuckled hoarsely. 'Or d'you mean to offer old Thwaite a few dollars for them pesky bluebottles?' He dropped the phoney accent and dived a hand into the pocket of his shabby jacket, producing a crumpled paper bag. 'Want a pear drop? Old Clegg, what cleans down when the Dining Rooms is shut, give me a threepenny joe for fetching his pipe tobacco.'

'I don't mind if I do,' Polly said, taking a sweet and tucking it comfortably into her cheek. 'Thanks, Ernie. And now I'm off home or I'll miss me supper.'

Having acquired Mr Thwaite's address from the obliging tobacconist, Dana had thought that it would be a simple matter to call on the landlord and ask him whether he would rent the flat above the butcher's shop. However, it was more than a month before she and Caitlin managed to find him at home when they called. After so many fruitless attempts to catch him it was not really surprising that Caitlin wanted to give up, but on this occasion, just before they turned away, Dana cocked an ear and grabbed her friend's arm, for she had heard footsteps approaching the door from the other side. Presently it creaked open and a small, grey-haired man in his shirtsleeves stood staring at them whilst his jaws worked rhythmically; clearly he was eating his supper. It was almost eight thirty, for a helpful neighbour had advised them to 'Try later, young ladies, say half past eight or nine o'clock. Mr Thwaite collects his rents evenings, when folks is home after their day's work. Or you might catch him come midday. His housekeeper cooks him a good dinner and he's usually home between noon and two o'clock.'

The girls were always at work lunchtimes, but now the helpful neighbour's advice was proving to be correct, for the small man chewed, swallowed, and then snapped: 'Yes?' in such an unfriendly tone that Caitlin stepped back, blinking.

Dana, however, was made of sterner stuff. 'Mr Thwaite?' she said. 'I wonder if we might have a word; it's about some premises which we believe you own. If we might come in for a moment . . .'

As she spoke, she moved forward, and since Caitlin hastily followed suit the small man was forced to step back. After a moment's hesitation, he ushered them through a doorway into a small parlour where he clicked on the light, saying suspiciously as he did so: 'I'm sure I don't know that any of my premises would interest young ladies . . . are you summat to do with the sanitary inspector? Because if so—'

'No, no,' Dana said hastily. 'We were told you owned Rayner's butcher shop, and the flat above it. It's the flat which interests us. We've been told your rents are reasonable . . .' behind her back she crossed her fingers since, truth to tell, they had heard nothing good about either Mr Thwaite or his properties, 'and as we understand it Mr Rayner moved out a month ago.'

'Yes, I own Rayner's shop,' Mr Thwaite admitted. 'And I won't deny it's for rent. It's a grand little property, in a good trading position. Mr Rayner's retired, seeing as how he's made his pile there, but what would you young ladies want with a butcher's shop? I've never let property to a woman, save hairdressers, and most of them is backed by a feller.'

'It isn't the shop we want but the flat above,' Dana said eagerly. 'If the rent was right, we'd undertake to clean the shop for you. If it was spotless, with fresh paint and clean sawdust on the floor, I'm sure someone else would take it as – as a lock-up . . .'

Mr Thwaite pulled his narrow lips into a sneer. 'So you don't want the shop at all?' he said disagreeably. 'Then we won't waste any more of each other's time. Good day to you.'

He ushered them out of the parlour, but even as he opened the front door, jerking his head at the two girls, Dana spoke again. 'If you let us rent the flat and someone else took the shop, then you'd be getting double rent,' she said craftily. 'That sounds like good business sense to me, Mr Thwaite.'

The landlord snorted. 'Forget it,' he said harshly. 'I don't do business wi' children.' And before they could even think of a crushing retort, they found themselves out on the pavement with the door slamming shut behind them.

Dana stamped her foot. 'Horrible, mean little miser,' she raged. 'He wasn't even prepared to listen, let alone show us over the flat. Oh, Caitlin, I've never wished I was a man before, but I wish it now. He'd have listened to a man, and if he was rude, like he was to us, a man would have punched him on the nose.'

Caitlin giggled. 'You're daft, you are,' she said affectionately. 'Tell you what, shall I have a word with James?

21

At least he could find out how much old Thwaite is asking for the rent of the flat and the shop. He might even persuade the old devil to show him round. If it's a three-bedroom, or even a two, we could easily find enough girls to make a flat-share a real possibility.'

'It seems such a cheek,' Dana said. 'I've never met him, remember; he might be willing to help you, but not me. We're total strangers, after all.'

Caitlin put her head on one side, considering her friend's remark, then brightened. 'You're right, of course; if he is to help us, and I do believe he can, then the sooner you and he meet the better. You'll like him, I know you will, and he'll like you.' She turned a somewhat doubtful gaze upon her friend. 'He's different from any other man I've ever gone out with. He's . . . oh, I can't describe him, but I'm sure you'll like each other. Tell you what. I've asked him to meet me outside the Grafton during the first interval tomorrow, so you can come outside as well. I'll introduce you and explain the problem with Mr Thwaite, and I'm sure he'll help us.'

Dana agreed to this rather reluctantly. During the time she and Caitlin had known each other, she had met at least half a dozen of Caitlin's boyfriends, all of whom had been in their mid-twenties, extremely handsome and quite well off: not the sort of young men to make much impression upon Mr Thwaite. But Caitlin was insistent that James Mortimer was different, so more for the sake of peace than anything else Dana agreed to the meeting.

The following evening, she and Caitlin donned their party dresses, then set off for the ballroom with their dancing pumps in paper carriers. At the first interval, when everyone else was queuing for a glass of orangeade and a couple of Marie biscuits, Caitlin dragged Dana out of the ballroom, both girls having had their wrists stamped to ensure free readmittance when the interval was over.

Outside, the stars and moon blazed down from a dark sky and Dana wished she had retrieved her coat from the cloakroom, for it was distinctly chilly. The pavement was quite crowded, predominantly with young men, several of whom looked at her friend with interest and one might, she supposed, be James Mortimer, unsure of whom to approach in the tricky lamplight.

'There he is!' Caitlin said as a young man came towards them. He was tall, slim and blond, and Dana's heart sank. It was just as she had supposed: this man would make about as much impression upon Mr Thwaite as she and Caitlin had done. Oh, he might have money, but she guessed that Mr Thwaite would want more than that before he parted with any information, let alone considered renting his property to someone.

'Dana, this is my friend, Mr James Mortimer. James, this is Miss Dana McBride; I told you about her when we first met.'

Dana stared, but as Mr James Mortimer held out his hand she automatically placed her own in it. The fair young man had walked straight past them; clearly, he was nothing to do with Caitlin. The man whose hand grasped hers so firmly was a very different kettle of fish. He was in his mid to late thirties, squat and powerful, with broad shoulders and a crop of dark curly hair, silvering at the temples. He was dark-eyed and olive-skinned and he emanated a sort of ruthless power to which Caitlin was clearly not immune. The fact that he was an inch or so shorter than Dana herself was surprising, but he did not seem at all worried by his lack of inches; in fact when Caitlin had introduced him and he had put out his hand, his eyes had met Dana's squarely as though they were of a height.

'How do you do, Miss McBride,' he said formally. His voice had a suspicion of a cockney twang, and as his dark eyes flickered over her Dana realised that he was sizing her up, trying to probe beneath her very ordinary appearance to the young woman beneath. Without meaning to do so, she realised she was bristling; what a cheek! But then he gave her a lopsided grin, and suddenly she saw why he had attracted her notoriously fussy friend. He was neither tall, blond nor handsome, but he had something . . . and she was in no doubt that if he chose to espouse their cause he would at least get the information they wanted from Mr Thwaite.

But what about his relationship with Caitlin? As Dana watched her friend telling him what the landlord had said, she found herself hoping guiltily that it was just a passing phase, and he would move on. She was truly fond of the other girl but was forced to admit, if only to herself, that Caitlin was not clever. Beautiful, yes, bright and bouncy, good company, but not clever. And she rather thought that this powerful, fascinating man would demand more than looks from his future wife.

But the bell which announced that the interval was over sounded at this point and Mr Mortimer said he would accompany them into the ballroom provided that they would both give him a dance. 'We'll discuss your business with this Thwaite when the dance is over,' he said, taking Caitlin's arm in a proprietorial fashion. 'I'm not much of a dancer, but I enjoy watching others.'

Dana, smiling and nodding, wondered if he was married; at his age it was quite possible. She put the point to Caitlin whilst Mr Mortimer – she could not think of him as James – deposited his coat in the cloakroom, but her friend shook her head. 'He said he's been too busy building up his business to think about marriage,' she said. 'But now he truly believes I'm the girl he's been looking for all his life.' She sighed dramatically. 'He's ever so kind. He's a real man, not like the boys I've been going about with.'

'True,' Dana said. Mr Mortimer was clearly a man of the world, with considerable experience of business matters, she guessed.

'Look, if you agree I'll do as I suggested and ask him to see Mr Thwaite for us and find out everything we want to know about Rayner's flat,' Caitlin said. 'He'll know just what questions to ask and whether old Thwaite was telling the truth or lying like – like a flat fish.'

'But would he do it?' Dana asked doubtfully. She did not think Mr Mortimer would dance to any tune but his own, but Caitlin disagreed.

'He's what they call a property developer,' she explained. 'He's come to Liverpool because he says the Depression is bound to end soon. Right now, he's searching for cheap, run-down properties which he'll make good and sell when the Depression's over. Then he'll be able to charge two or three times what he paid . . . he's very shrewd, Dana. So you see he knows a great deal about small businesses, flats and cheap housing, and if I ask him I'm sure he'll see Mr Thwaite for us.'

'Well, there's no harm in asking,' Dana said, still doubtfully, but she was beginning to believe that her friend was right; if this strange, dark-avised man wanted to smooth their path she was sure he could do so. But she thought he would have to be watched. His expression gave nothing away, and though his eyes showed admiration when they rested on Caitlin, she felt he would be a bad person to cross. Already she could see that her friend would be putty in his hands.

When the dance ended Caitlin explained what they needed from him, and he agreed to help at once.

'I'll make an appointment to see the landlord in the course of the next few days,' he said. 'As soon as I've got the information you want I'll be in touch.'

The girls thanked him, Caitlin more effusively than Dana, and they parted. As they undressed for bed, Caitlin leaned across and nudged her friend. 'Our days at the YW are numbered,' she whispered jubilantly. 'Oh, I'm sure we're going to be renting that flat in no time!'

Polly had formed the habit of trying to leave the Willows at the same time as Dana and Caitlin, for the two girls fascinated her. She loved their voices, which had only the slightest trace of an Irish accent, she thought Caitlin the most beautiful girl she had ever seen and Dana was undoubtedly both clever and kind. When they were working near each other Dana always included her in any conversation, and if the boys were rude Dana could twist their remarks so that it was they who seemed foolish. It never occurred to Polly, when she did her best to stand or sit near the two Irish girls, that she was eavesdropping; indeed, she did not know the meaning of the word. If people wanted to exchange secrets they would whisper them, she thought, but Caitlin in particular had a very clear and carrying voice, which was how Polly had come to learn that the girls were off to the Grafton that evening. Intrigued, she gathered that they had found themselves a feller, one with enough money and influence to interfere on their behalf over that dirty little butcher's shop in which they seemed so strangely interested, and they were going to talk to him about it that very night. Unable to resist the chance to find out more, she hung around outside the Grafton for a good fifteen minutes during the first interval, trying to distinguish the two girls in the crowd and taking a good deal of cheek from nasty girls who suggested 'she were tryin' to pick up a feller' and from rude boys saying the same thing, though less politely. Disheartened, she was just beginning to walk towards the nearest tram stop when she saw them coming towards her. Caitlin was hanging on the arm of a short, curly-headed man whilst Dana, looking embarrassed, brought up the rear.

Polly had a good long look at the fellow. He was dark-haired and dark-skinned, with what she thought of as a foreign look about him; a dangerous look. I wouldn't trust him any further than I could throw him, Polly thought. He's a real smoothie – just the sort of fellow mams tell their daughters to avoid. And he's old enough to be Caitlin's father. Wharrever are they thinking of?

Polly sighed as the tram she wanted drew up beside her. It was none of her business, of course, she thought as she jumped aboard, and she doubted very much if either girl would listen to advice from someone so much younger than they. But I've had more experience of bad

27

'uns than they have, she thought ruefully, handing the conductor her fare, and it will certainly make life more interesting watching how they deal with him. Settling back in her seat, however, she could not help musing that she might even be able to help them one of these fine days. Satisfied, she began to wonder what she should have for her supper.

'Psst!' Dana, once more up to her elbows in water and potatoes, turned her head sharply as someone entered the scullery behind her. It was Ernie, looking portentous. 'I gorra message for you from your pal,' he said in thrilling tones. 'She says her feller has been an' gone an' done whatever it were you wanted 'im to . . .' He gave a snigger, then straightened up hastily as Dana's cupped hand withdrew from the water in a threatening manner. 'Awright, awright, keep your hair on! Caitlin says this feller will meet the pair of you out of work when the Willows closes, so's you can talk business. She would ha' telled you herself, but —'

'Ernie Frost! Wharrever d'you think you're doin'? If you're thinkin' to help young Ginger wi' them spuds, you can think again. Unless you want to miss your dinner, of course.' Dana knew Mrs Haggerty's voice so well that she had not turned away from the sink, but now she heard herself addressed. 'Done them spuds yet, Ginger? If so, fill a pan and bring it through, and you can be on first dinner. I might even let you sit next to that other bogtrotter, since I'll grant you that you've worked well today.'

Dana, splashing peeled potatoes into a big pan of water, turned an astonished face towards the head cook, wondering what was up now. Mrs Haggerty never praised anyone, and saved her nastiest comments for anyone with the misfortune to be Irish. This was odd, because Mrs Haggerty had to be Irish herself with a name like that. Everyone in the kitchen knew that 'Mrs' was a courtesy title; Clara Haggerty she had been at her birth, and Clara Haggerty she had remained ever since.

So now Dana, clutching her pan of potatoes, approached the big woman almost blocking the narrow doorway rather warily. Past experience told her that the cook was quite capable of jabbing her in the ribs or squashing her against the doorpost if she was in one of her more spiteful moods. Accordingly, she slowed as she reached the doorway, but the cook stood aside, leaving Dana a clear passageway past her, and as the two women's eyes met she spoke again, her tone pleasanter than Dana had ever known it. 'Mrs Lionel has been doin' sums. She says we're sellin' twice as many Specials as t'other meals on the menu. Specials is cheaper, see, and folk are watchin' the pennies. So she wants to lose two kitchen workers.' She paused, as though waiting for Dana's reaction, but Dana merely folded her lips and kept her face as expressionless as possible. If she were for the high jump . . . the elbow . . . the little brown envelope . . . then she would not give Mrs Haggerty the satisfaction of showing how horrified she felt.

'Well? Ain't you a-goin' to ax me who's gettin' their cards at the end o' the week? Ain't you interested?'

The pan of potatoes seemed to be growing heavier by the minute. Dana stood the pan down on the nearest surface, but continued to say nothing; what was the point? She did not think Mr Lionel would agree to

29

Caitlin's being sacked because she was popular with customers when waiting on, but she herself . . .

Mrs Haggerty sighed; she was clearly getting tired of her little game. 'I told 'im I needed every one of you, and if he tried to reduce me staff he'd find even the sale of his Specials would shrink,' she said. 'An' I'll give you this, Ginger, you're a bleedin' hard worker. You never complain and you've not lost a day through sickness, not even when you had that shockin' cold last February. And now put them spuds on the stove and get yourself sat down for first dinners.'

Dana was so relieved that she actually beamed at the cook. 'Thanks, Mrs Haggerty,' she said, sliding into the chair next to Caitlin's. The meal in front of her – scrag end stew and dumplings – both looked and smelt pretty good, but before she had taken a mouthful she dug Caitlin in the ribs. 'What's up?' she hissed. 'Ernie said your feller – I take it he means Mr Mortimer – is going to meet us out of work. Does that mean he's managed to persuade old Thwaite to let us rent the flat? If so, I take back all the rude things I've been thinking about the sort of man who takes up with a girl half his age.'

'Oh, you're just jealous,' Caitlin said, helping herself to another dumpling from the tureen in the middle of the table, 'and James isn't old, he's just mature. I expect you're right though and he's got round old Thwaite somehow; he's a businessman and knows what's what. Oh, I don't know how I shall get through this afternoon!'

Mr Mortimer picked the girls up from work in a taxi and took them straight to the butcher's shop in Heyworth

Street. The last time Dana had seen the shop it had been through a haze of bluebottles and dirt-smeared glass and the faint stench of bad meat had seemed to hang in the air, so now, as Mr Mortimer selected a large key and thrust it into the lock, she drew back a little, but though a number of bluebottles charged gleefully past them into the open air someone – Mr Thwaite presumably – had done some clearing up. The filthy sawdust had been removed from the stained floorboards and the disgusting offal had disappeared. Even the butchery counter had been cleaned and Dana breathed in the smell of carbolic soap and bleach with relief. Anything, she told herself, was better than the stench of rotten meat.

'In you go, young ladies,' Mr Mortimer said.

He followed them into the shop and looked from one face to the other but Dana held her peace, leaving it to Caitlin to exclaim: 'Well, you must have impressed Mr Thwaite, James, because it's nowhere near as bad as it was five or six weeks ago.' She giggled. 'Dana and I offered to clean the shop for him if he would let us rent the flat, but since he doesn't know it's us I suppose he got someone else to do it.'

'I paid a couple of lads to get rid of the worst of the filth,' Mr Mortimer said briefly. 'After I'd spoken to Thwaite, of course. I couldn't ask two young ladies to face what I faced on my first visit.'

'That was kind,' Caitlin said appreciatively. 'But can we go up to the flat now, please? We aren't at all interested in the shop, you know.'

Mr Mortimer gave Caitlin an indulgent glance but did not move, merely closing and locking the shop door, remarking as he did so that they did not want to find themselves entertaining half the neighbourhood. Then he turned to Dana. 'Well, Miss McBride? Can you see any reason why Thwaite would not even consider renting the flat without the shop? I guess this is your first visit, but I should've thought . . .'

'I'm beginning to realise,' Dana said in a hollow voice. 'Oh, Caitlin, what fools we've been! I hadn't thought, because we could see so little through that dreadful, disgusting window . . .'

'Whatever are you talking about?' Caitlin said, frowning at her friend. 'I can't see why we shouldn't rent the flat – if it's fairly cheap, of course. If you're so clever, Dana McBride, just tell me what's wrong with that?'

'Oh, Caitlin, use your loaf,' Dana said impatiently. 'How are you going to get to the flat? Can you fly?'

'No, of course I can't,' Caitlin said, frowning more than ever. 'There're stairs in the storeroom which must lead up to the flat, I suppose.' She turned to Mr Mortimer. 'Why should we need to fly when there are stairs? What's wrong with them, pray?'

Dana interrupted before the man could reply. 'Don't you see, dearest Caitlin? The only way to reach the flat is through the storeroom. No trader worth his salt would let a couple of girls – or a couple of men for that matter – traipse through his premises whilst he was trying to conduct his business. And then, when the shop was closed, we would have to have access! If we weren't honest, it would be an open invitation to a thief.' She sighed deeply. 'Oh, dammit, why ever didn't we *think*? I'm sorry, Mr Mortimer, to have wasted your time; I can only plead that I was carried away by the prospect of moving out of the YWCA.'

As she spoke, she turned her apologetic gaze upon Mr Mortimer and saw once again why Caitlin seemed so fond of him, though she herself was still wary, still suspicious that beneath the frank manner was a deviousness he had not yet revealed. But now he was smiling at her friend, and when he noticed she was looking at him he straightened his face. 'It's all right, Miss McBride, you've not wasted my time,' he said soothingly. 'Thwaite and myself had a long discussion, after which I had a chat with my – my man of business, and I think we've arrived at a solution. But we'd best take a look at the flat before I put my suggestion to you.'

He headed for the storeroom door and stood to one side, gesturing to the girls to precede him, and it was as he said 'Youth before beauty' that once again Dana recognised the twang in his voice as the buried remnants of a cockney accent. So you may have made your pile, you may even be a property developer like you say, but to my way of thinking you're just a cockney barrer boy what's made good, she thought rather nastily, following Caitlin up the stairs. I just hope you didn't get out of London one jump ahead of the coppers!

She was still wondering about Mr James Mortimer when she reached the head of the stairs and stood in the tiny hallway, looking around her. Two doors, both closed . . . but Caitlin was pushing open the nearest and the girls and their companion stepped into a tiny living room with a sizeable window through which they could see out into Heyworth Street. Dana swept the room with a practised eye. No furniture, no carpets or linoleum, but the floorboards were only dusty, not filthy, and there was room for a table, a sofa, and a couple of easy chairs. Yes, it would suit them, if they could find a way of reaching the upper floor without trespassing upon the property of whoever took the shop.

'Awright?'

Once more, Mr Mortimer's accent grated, but Dana merely nodded her head. 'Small, but possible,' she said. She pointed to another door. 'What's through there?'

'Kitchen,' Mr Mortimer said. He crossed the room and held open the door. 'Small, too . . . take a look.'

This time there was linoleum on the floor, a sink with wooden draining boards and some shelving. The window overlooked the back yard, and Dana could see a shed, which she took to be the privy, below. She said as much and Mr Mortimer nodded, his dark eyes narrowing. 'Oh aye, but you'd not expect indoor plumbing in a flat this size.' He laughed. 'You can't afford to be picky.' He crossed the kitchen and the living room, then flung open the other door in the small hallway. 'Bedroom; only one, I'm afraid, but you're used to sharin', since you're at the YW.'

'Oh yes, we don't mind sharing,' Caitlin said quickly. 'And it's a lovely flat; but why bother to come up if the landlord won't let the place separately?'

'Because we've reached a compromise, me and your landlord. If you'll undertake to clean the place thoroughly, and that means redecorate, make good anything which needs doing – it needs rewiring, for a start – then he'll let you have the place rent-free for the first three months. For the next three months he'll charge a small rent, and you will have to find a trader willing to take on the butcher's shop itself, without the storeroom at the back, because you'll need that for access.'

34

There was a long silence whilst both girls grappled with what Mr Mortimer had said, and then Caitlin spoke. 'But it doesn't make sense,' she said slowly. 'Mr Thwaite wouldn't even consider us as tenants, and this way he'd be dependent on us not only to make good his property but to find a suitable tenant for the butcher's shop. Why should he do that, James?'

There was a pregnant pause before the man spoke and then he gave a rueful grin and took Caitlin's hand. 'Good girl; you've got a head on them pretty shoulders,' he said, and Dana noticed that now he was beginning to relax the cockney twang was more in evidence than ever. 'I'd better come clean. When we met I said I were a property developer. Well, that's what I mean to be one day, but at present I'm what you might call on the fringe of the industry, having to box clever wi' my cash. I didn't tell old Thwaite that, of course, but—'

'Does he know you're acting on behalf of a couple of girls who know nothing about renting shops, let alone cleaning and decorating and so on?' Dana cut in. 'I dare say you found Mr Thwaite more willing to talk business with a man than he was with us, but it was plain he didn't mean to be landlord to a couple of females . . .'

James Mortimer interrupted her without apology. 'Shut your face,' he said rudely, then gave her his lopsided grin. 'Sorry, sorry . . . I had hoped . . . but I can see I'll have to let you have the whole story. I've bought the perishin' shop, flat and all, which means I'm your landlord.'

There was an astonished silence, broken by Dana once more. 'But why are you letting *us* take on the flat? What's different about us?'

This time he answered promptly and, Dana thought, honestly.

'You done me a real favour, Miss McBride, even if you didn't realise it. I've been having trouble finding suitable property for sale at a price I could afford. In normal circumstances Thwaite would have had the place cleaned up and made good before offering it for sale, but because it was truly foul he kept putting it off, letting it get worse and worse. When I came on the scene, before he'd had a chance to do a quick spit an' polish job on it, I acted disgusted – well, I was – said I'd inform the authorities that the place was a health hazard, offered to take it off his hands for a song . . . and he jumped at it. So you see, I'm grateful.'

'And when the three months is up, will you help us to find a suitable person to rent the shop?' Caitlin asked slowly. 'Because I'm sure Dana and I would be far too trusting and probably never get the rent . . .'

Dana laughed and gave her friend a shove. 'You're daft, you are,' she said affectionately. 'If Mr Mortimer is now our landlord, everything's different. Isn't that so, Mr Mortimer?'

James Mortimer nodded. 'Well, not everything; you will still have the property rent-free for the first three months, starting in a few days when the sale's gone through, and I shall still expect you to clean, decorate and so on. The obvious solution to both my problem and yours is for you to take on the shop as well as the flat. Of course, if you feel no desire to own and run your own business, then I suppose I'll have to help you to rent out the butcher's shop, but surely you must have skills of various sorts? All young women knit and sew, and cook of course. Remember, if you were to take on the shop yourselves, then you could use the storeroom and your profit would easily pay the rent I should ask; indeed you could double the size of the shop.' He smiled coaxingly at Caitlin. 'Wouldn't you like to own your own little business? Say you sold knitting wools, patterns, embroidery silks . . . oh, I don't know, but I expect you do! And then there's confectionery . . . homemade toffee, fudge, sticks of rock even . . .'

'Come come, Mr Mortimer, let us be practical,' Dana cut in, seeing the doubtful look on her friend's face. 'Such shops would need to be stocked, and I can't see any reputable bank lending money to a couple of girls like Caitlin and myself. There's a Depression on, as the government keep reminding us, and besides, if you sold knitting wool you would be expected to have samples – jerseys, matinée jackets, socks and gloves even – on show. I'm a rotten knitter and can't embroider for love nor money, and even though I dare say I could whip up some home-made fudge and toffee, I couldn't do it on a commercial scale without staff, and heaps of ingredients.' She looked wistfully round the tiny hall in which they were standing. 'It's awfully good of you, Mr Mortimer, but running our own business just isn't on the cards unless we can find a wealthy backer. In fact I've just realised that we shall have to furnish the flat, which will take every penny we possess. We shall have to continue working at the Dining Rooms too, so the improvements to the property will have to be done during the evenings and on Sundays . . .'

James Mortimer made an impatient gesture. 'I'll find you a couple of cheap beds and mebbe a Primus stove,' he said. 'But look, girls, I've not come up the Thames on a biscuit, you know. You come from Ireland, but you can't kid me that your families are poor as church mice. You neither of you speak with even a touch of the brogue and though I've only known you a few weeks, Caitlin, it's clear you're well educated.' He turned to Dana. 'And no doubt you are the same, Miss McBride. I'm self-taught I am, dragged myself up by my bootlaces, but I can recognise quality when I see it. What about a loan from your families? It isn't as though you would be asking them to give money, but to invest in a venture which I'm sure could be a real success.'

Dana shook her head decidedly. 'I've explained to Caitlin that after my father's death things at home became difficult. I couldn't possibly expect my mother to help me,' she said briefly. She turned to her friend. 'What about you, Caitlin? I know you more or less ran away, but that's about all I do know. Any chance of a loan from your people?'

'Shouldn't think so,' Caitlin mumbled, and then brightened. 'But I've an uncle who might come across. He spoiled me rotten when I was a kid. He might lend me some money, just so's he could tell the rest of the family we were in touch, 'cos I'd have to give him my address, otherwise he couldn't send money, could he?'

'Well there you are then,' Mr Mortimer said triumphantly. 'I mean to pay for the cleaning, repairs and decoration, but you'd have to furnish the flat yourselves. If you decided to go at the end of three months, you could take the furniture with you . . .'

'But not the painting and decorating, nor the rewiring,' Dana reminded him sharply. 'I no longer wonder why you are willing to let us rent the flat, Mr Mortimer; it's very much in your interest to do so.'

Mr Mortimer began to bluster, to say that he was presenting them with a grand opportunity, but then he caught Caitlin's eye and gave a reluctant laugh instead. 'Well, all right, maybe I shan't do too badly out of it,' he admitted. 'Tell you what, if you did decide to take on the shop, I'd arrange a loan – a proper bank loan – so that you could buy at least some of the stock you'd need; the rest you should be able to finance yourselves with the help of your families, because I can't believe blood relatives would turn down such pretty, clever girls.'

'I wouldn't even ask,' Dana said stiffly. How dare this man suggest that she and Caitlin might sink their pride and beg for money! But Caitlin was saying enthusiastically that they could buy second-hand, that they only *really* needed the beds which dear James had already said he would supply, that she did have a little money saved up from her wages at the Willows . . .

'Oh please, Dana; I'm longing to have a place of my own so I am,' she wheedled. 'I'll write to my uncle this very day . . .'

'I give up,' Dana said loudly and crossly. 'Very well, we'll take on the flat and start cleaning and repainting here – and in the shop of course – this weekend.' She turned to Caitlin. 'And if it all goes horribly wrong at least we shall still have our jobs at the Dining Rooms.'

'And three months living in the flat rent-free,' Caitlin reminded her. 'And I wouldn't mind selling knitting wool and embroidery silks . . . it wouldn't take up much room . . .'

'Right; let's shake on it,' Mr Mortimer said briskly,

holding out a square, capable hand. 'And you must call me James, Miss McBride, since we are partners now.'

'Huh!' said Dana, but she said it quietly, too quietly for either of the others, already heading for the stairs, to hear. And though she had little faith in Mr Mortimer's plans or promises, she was aware of a thrill of excitement at the thought of moving into the flat and perhaps starting up their own business in the shop beneath. Life, she told herself, would at least be interesting over the next three months.

Chapter Two

Dana was perched precariously on the top of a ladder, carefully whitewashing the ceiling of the butcher's shop, when the door opened and a man came cautiously in. 'Hello, James. Come to see how we're getting on? Well, you might as well make yourself useful and pass me that paint pot, 'cos this one's running dry,' Dana said cheerfully. She still regarded James Mortimer with suspicion, but got along with him better, thinking that his affection for Caitlin was genuine and that he accepted her presence without finding fault . . . he could scarcely do so, she thought, since she was working so hard on his property.

Two months had passed since the momentous day when they had agreed to move into the flat above the shop when it was ready for occupation. Now that she knew James Mortimer better, she was able to appreciate his good qualities – his sharp mind and quick reactions – though she chided him from time to time over what she thought of as his sharp business practices. She knew he had got tenders for work which they could not tackle themselves and had heard the tradesmen grumbling that he never paid the agreed price, always finding an excuse for reducing the sums quoted.

However, to Caitlin and herself he behaved in an exemplary fashion. They had agreed to take a lump sum for the work they did on both shop and flat, and to do him credit he never asked them where the money had gone, or how much Caitlin had managed to persuade her rich uncle to hand over. Dana knew of course and was daily grateful for Uncle Seamus's generosity. Uncle Seamus was childless and had made a great deal of money out of a lucky investment in South African gold mines. Now, he seemed to consider his niece's suggestion that he might put money into whatever venture she decided to undertake as a sensible proposition, which might well make them both a little richer.

You're a grand lass so you are, he had written in his spiky, old-fashioned hand. *I'm happy to be able to help you but shall expect regular reports on how you're doing once you start trading. As you know, I'm a betting man, willing to put my money on anything which looks as though it might make me a good return. I shall come over to England next spring for to watch the Grand National and have a bet or two, so I shall be sure to visit Heyworth Street and see how my little niece is doing.*

But it was still only July, so there was plenty of time to get the place respectable before Uncle Seamus so much as left Ireland, far less arrived on their doorstep.

Now, Dana gestured to a number of paint pots standing on the butchery counter. In the fullness of time, this counter would be replaced by a modern one, either glass-topped to display the goods inside or with a shiny mahogany surface, but for now they preferred that any mess should land on the old counter. 'I don't know which one you want,' James said, prising the lids off tins and peering in at the contents. 'This one is undercoat – it says so on the lid – and this one's hard gloss; does one hard gloss a ceiling?'

Dana gave a crow of laughter. 'No, of course not. The whitewash is in the big tin, on the very end of the counter,' she said gaily. She had lost all her fear of offending James and despite his occasional attacks of 'I'm the boss!' she now treated him much as she did Caitlin, or indeed Ernie at the Dining Rooms, for both girls still slogged away at the Willows, working on the Heyworth Street property evenings and weekends. The rewiring was done and the plumber would come next week to pipe water up to the flat. At present the only supply was in the storeroom so if they decided to let the shop to someone else they would have to have further work done. But already the girls had practically given up all thought of renting out; with James's help, they would start their own business just as soon as the work on the shop was finished. They even meant to have an electric heater over the sink in the flat, a very modern contrivance, which would save them having to boil kettles whenever they needed hot water.

'There you are.' James handed up the big tin of white-wash and relieved Dana of the empty one. He looked round approvingly. 'Sensible to leave the ceiling till last and a good thing you wrapped your head in that length of muslin, otherwise you'd be a ravishin' blonde instead of a ravishin' redhead.' He laughed at his own joke. 'Still quarrellin' over what sort of shop to start?'

'We never quarrel, we just discuss,' Dana said placidly, beginning to stroke the paint on to the ceiling once more. 'And I don't know why you think doing the ceiling in

43

here will be the last job – the last painting job I mean – because you're wrong. The entire shop has to be left until the electrician has finished and I'm only doing the ceiling because the plumber has sworn neither he nor his mate will need to touch it when they start the pipework.'

'Well, whatever you do, you do well,' James said tactfully. 'How's work at the Willows going; any more talk of sackings?'

'Not so far,' Dana said cautiously, but she had noticed that as the weather grew more clement sales of hot dinners declined. Now that Caitlin had become a full-time waitress after one of the girls left – as Mr Lionel had said, she just about doubled her salary with tips – Dana waited on occasionally, and could not help noticing that men who, in the winter and spring, had ordered either the day's Special or some other hot meal quite often decided on sandwiches or filled rolls now, though salads were still mainly ordered by their female customers.

She said as much to James, adding that she and Caitlin were taking the next Sunday off in order to follow the advice they had been given by the owner of the tobacconist's next door. 'Look for a gap in the market, gairls,' Mrs Ramsbottom had said. 'See what shops there ain't on Heyworth, then look into fillin' the gap. Tek a walk on a weekend wi' a notebook, writin' down what each one sells, and you'll be surprised why no one's ever thought of sellin' . . . oh, wharrever ain't there, if you get me drift.'

The girls had talked it over and decided that the older woman was right; so this very weekend they would walk the length of Heyworth and maybe several side streets and see what wasn't already there. Bakers and confectioners abounded, as did greengrocers and the ubiquitous corner shops, but Dana could not remember seeing a wool shop and Caitlin still thought a nice tea room would do well.

'We've learned an awful lot about catering by working at the Willows,' she urged. 'Oh, I'm not saying we should do full meals and that, but we could manage tea, coffee and snacks without any retraining.'

Dana however was doubtful. 'What do we do with food we can't sell? I mean we'd have to buy in biscuits and scones and teacakes and stuff, and we'd have to get a stove to toast things and probably a big urn to heat water for the drinks,' she pointed out. 'I agree we wouldn't need a counter, which would give us a bit more room, but I don't think we could get more than four tables in the place without it looking crowded and uncomfortable, and that would never do. Now wool and embroidery silks and stuff like that doesn't go bad if it isn't sold immediately. Still, we've not taken Mrs Ramsbottom's advice yet; I think "wait and see" should be our motto. We've got another month to go before we have to start paying rent.'

Caitlin sniffed. 'I think James was being very unfair when he said we couldn't move into the flat until we've decided what sort of business we mean to run, or whether we're going to rent the shop out,' she said resentfully. 'We could have saved quite a lot of money if we weren't at the YW . . .'

Dana chuckled. 'He's shrewd as they come, your friend James,' she said. 'If he hadn't insisted that we have to make up our minds about the shop before moving into the flat, we'd still be dithering.'

Caitlin pulled a face, then giggled. 'We *are* still dithering,' she pointed out. 'Tell you what, Dana, let's say we walk up and down Heyworth first thing Sunday morning, and make up our minds for definite by noon. Then when James arrives to take us out for a bite to eat we'll tell him what we've decided, give in our notice at the YW and move into the flat straight away.'

Rather to James's amusement, the girls' tour of the neighbourhood had revealed neither café nor wool shop in Heyworth Street or its surroundings, but when they had contacted suppliers both girls had realised at once that setting up as purveyors of haberdashery was out of the question. Even stocking a small shop with such items as wool, silks and cottons, let alone fancy collars, strips of broderie anglaise and knitting needles in every possible size, would be beyond them; even if they could have managed the outlay, unless they began to sell immediately, and in large quantities, they would rapidly come to grief.

A nice little tea room, on the other hand, was a distinct possibility. True, the shop was on the small side, but if they did away with the counter and kept all the supplies in the storeroom, James thought that they should be able to lay sixteen covers and this made economic sense. Dana worried about the scones and little cakes not selling, but the mark-up was sufficient to allow for a certain amount of 'dead stock', and anyway, the girls could always reduce their prices at the end of each day just to cover what each item had cost them. Yes, his Caitlin was right: a teashop was almost certainly their best bet. Thinking it over afterwards, Dana began to suspect that James had always meant them to go into catering. Everything else he had suggested had been fraught with difficulties, so in the end they had settled for a tea room, thinking it was their own choice, whereas in fact it was what James Mortimer had intended all along.

So James set off to bargain with local bakers and confectioners, assuring them that a steady sale, at a reasonable price, to the new tea room – they planned to call it Cathy's Place – was better than having to dispose of unwanted goods at the end of their trading day.

Now it was decided at last, the girls began to plan simple menus and bought a second-hand electric cooker which would stand in the storeroom – which would now become the tea room's kitchen – so that they might toast bread and teacakes, and warm through such items as scones and sausage rolls. Caitlin had told James that they had looked wistfully at a magnificent urn, but for the time being they had simply purchased a very large kettle with which to make cups of tea, coffee and cocoa, as required.

James had bowed to the girls' superior knowledge regarding the decoration of the tea room, though he had pulled a doubtful face over the plain deal tables with their square tops. But in this instance at least, Dana had proved right. The room, shorn of its counter, was square – fourteen feet by fourteen feet – and though round tables might have been prettier, they would have wasted space. Also, square tablecloths were considerably cheaper than round ones, and in the event of a party of ladies numbering more than four wanting to sit together, square tables could be pushed end to end to accommodate them.

The night before the café was due to open, James took

both girls to the Adelphi for dinner, telling them jubilantly that they would rapidly become the proprietors of their own successful business. 'I want to be able to pay Uncle Seamus back,' Caitlin said, dimpling at James. 'Not that he expects it, and he'll probably insist that the money he gave me was a present, but it would be nice to offer, don't you think?'

James did not agree; to his way of thinking, an investment was just that, and though this Uncle Seamus might be entitled to a share in the profits when the tea room was thriving – even beginning to expand – he thought it would be downright foolish to pay back money whilst they might still be having to work very hard just to take a small wage from the profits.

The girls were understandably nervous at first, picking at their food, but he jollied them along with stories of successes achieved by people no older or more experienced than themselves, and when he finally deposited them outside Cathy's Place he knew that their nervous fears had been calmed, for the moment at any rate.

Next morning, James was tempted to go straight round to the tea room, but decided this would be unfair. The girls would be busy, taking delivery of stock, chalking an A board which they would stand outside on the pavement, and deciding which items would draw in most customers. Instead, he sat at the table in his boarding house eating toast and drinking strong tea, and when his landlady came into the room and handed him his post he was glad he had not abandoned his breakfast, for the very first letter on the pile was from his old friend and one-time partner, Jack Ewing. Good old Jack. The two men had never lost touch and still wrote regularly, though they were now miles apart. Smiling in pleasant anticipation, James slit open the long blue envelope.

Polly had been sad when Dana and Caitlin had left the Willows, but she had continued her admiring surveillance, occasionally forgoing her evening meal at the girls' home and getting off the tram halfway up Heyworth Street to check on progress in the butcher's shop. Though now it was no longer a butcher's shop, but a tea room with a neat green fascia board upon which was written, in curly script, *Cathy's Place*.

Polly had longed to offer help with the cleaning and redecorating, but she was frightened of the man who seemed to be in charge. The girls called him James and they did not seem to be in awe of him. Polly herself was scared stiff of Mr Lionel and made more mistakes when his eye was upon her than at any other time, so she thought it was a good thing that Dana and Caitlin seemed to be at ease in the presence of this James.

And today they were to open for the first time and Polly was determined to be there; to be their first customer if she could manage it. She and Ernie travelled to work on the same tram, so she waited at the stop and grabbed Ernie's arm as soon as he appeared. 'Ern! Can you tell the Hag that I been took bad wi' a sore stomach? Say I were sick all night and don't want no one else to gerrit. Say—'

'What's all this about?' Ernie said suspiciously. 'There ain't nothin' wrong wi' you, queen. You look as fit as a perishin' flea.'

'Well, I am,' Polly acknowledged. 'But I've got business to look to. Oh, Ern, be a sport an' tell her I'm feelin' mortal bad but I'll be in as soon as I feels more like meself. Are you on? Only I dare not risk losin' me job, and you know what Mr Lionel is when the Hag complains about one o' us.'

'Awright, I'll do it if you'll just leggo me arm so's I can get on this bleedin' tram,' Ernie said pugnaciously as one rumbled to a halt beside them. 'Only you're to tell me wharrit's all about when you do come in, agreed?'

'Agreed,' Polly said thankfully. 'You're a pal, Ernie Frost.'

She stood back to let the queue of people climb aboard the tram, then waved to Ernie until the vehicle was out of sight. Only then did she turn round and head for Cathy's Place. When she reached it, there was considerable bustle going on. The door was open and tradesmen were going in bearing full trays of various bakery goods. Polly knew the man from Sample's and gave him a tight little grin when he smiled at her. Sample's made the best iced buns in Liverpool and whenever she had a penny to spare Polly bought herself one. So now she felt justified in saying cheerfully: 'Mornin', Mr Reggie! What time's this place opening for business then?'

Reggie jerked his thumb at the A board. 'Ten a.m. to six p.m., it says there,' he informed her. 'Mind, as it's their first day, they might open early, see what sort of trade they have. Why not nip in and ask if they'll do you a cup of tea and a round of toast? Or they might be doing a Special, seeing as it's their first day.'

'I might; only I got shopping to do,' Polly said untruthfully. She wondered what tea and toast would cost and stuck her hand into the pocket of her jacket, checking the pennies; there were four of them, but for the time being at least she would simply look. She had seen someone at the back of the tea room and when she had come forward a ray of sunlight had lit up her bright hair: Dana!

But the stream of suppliers had now dwindled and she could see through the window that the girls were setting out their wares. Dana was laying tablecloths and putting a tiny bunch of flowers in a little blue vase upon each, whilst Caitlin piled scones into one pyramid and teacakes in another, then placed both beneath glass bells on the shelf which ran along the back wall. They had had the doorway between kitchen and tea room enlarged, and through the double doors, which had been pinned back whilst they took in the deliveries, Polly could see a Maid Saver upon which were stacked plates, cups and saucers and little bowls which, Polly supposed, would presently be filled with sugar, jam, butter, or anything else the customers might require. For a moment she hesitated, longing to go in but fearing to find herself very much in the way.

She was turning back towards the tram stop when Dana came out, apparently to resite the A board, and spotted her. 'Morning, Polly; how nice to see a familiar face,' she said cheerfully. 'What do you think? It's our first day, but of course Monday is when most folk do their washing so we don't expect to get crowded. I'd offer you a cuppa but the kettle hasn't boiled yet . . . in fact, I don't think we've even put it on the stove.'

Polly was about to say that she had shopping to do but would call in on her way back when Dana's hand flew to her mouth. 'Gracious, did you hear that? It's the church clock striking nine. Oh, Polly, you're going to be in awful trouble! Get yourself on to the next tram, girl; no one knows better than me what Mrs Haggerty can be like when she's cross!'

Polly took her courage in both hands. 'I've took a day off because I'm thinkin' of changin' me job,' she said, and felt heat invade her cheeks as she spoke. 'I – I suppose you and C-Caitlin aren't needin' a waitress? Someone small what could nip atwixt the tables without so much as brushin' agin 'em? I know I haven't done much wait-ressin', but I'd learn quick, and as to kitchen work, I knows that like the back of me hand. I'm rare good at peelin' veggies, gratin' carrots, makin' soup—'

Dana interrupted at once, though she smiled very kindly. 'Oh, Poll, I wish we could employ someone; it's going to be really tough with only the two of us. But we've spent all the money Mr Mortimer paid us for cleaning up his property and we've only just managed to scrape up enough to pay the bakers and the greengro-cers and so on. To be truthful . . .' she lowered her voice so that Polly had to get closer to hear what she was saying, 'if we don't make money in our very first week, we shan't be able to pay ourselves anything and we'll be hard put to it to meet our bills. Oh, Poll, I *am* sorry.'

Polly conjured up a grin. 'It don't matter. No harm in askin', is there?' she said, speaking as chirpily as she could. 'I'm on me way to Everton Library to borry a book. If you ain't rushed off your feet when I come back, I'll pop in for that cuppa.'

Dana returned to the tea room and immediately forgot all about Polly, though she had spoken the truth when she had said they could do with another pair of hands.

As it was, the girls had agreed that for the time being at least they would be kitchen workers, waitresses, cooks and the takers of money; in fact, each would do whatever was needed at the time.

At first their customers came mainly out of curiosity and to slake their thirst with pots of tea. Naturally, both Dana and Caitlin tried to tempt them with a display of cakes and scones, but no one succumbed. Still, it was early days. They knew from their experience at the Willows that customers followed one another, a little like sheep following a shepherd, so that when one said she'd try a scone others would follow suit. Even so, it was a sad couple who faced each other across the ancient till at six o'clock that evening, when they finally put up the shutters and swung the *Open* sign to read *Closed*.

'We haven't taken enough money to reorder scones for tomorrow. I did think we might pop today's batch into the oven, put it on a low heat and let customers think they were newly baked, but since most people know Sample's scones when they see them I suppose that wouldn't work. Oh, whatever will James say when we show him the till roll?' Caitlin mourned. 'He's meeting us here at half past six, to give us time to clear up.'

'I expect he'll guess that Mondays aren't good trading days,' Dana said comfortingly. 'If we've not done better by the end of the week, he might indeed be upset, but I'm sure things will improve, especially if you smile, Caitlin.'

And half an hour later, Dana was proved right. James came in, cast a desultory look at the till roll and said: 'Well done! Oh, I can see from your faces that you think you've done badly because you only sold cups of tea, but think of it like this. Every person who came into the tea room today and drank tea looked around her and undoubtedly liked what she saw. I don't know if you realise, but you sold one hundred and forty cups, so now you have a hundred and forty satisfied customers.'

Dana interrupted without compunction. 'How do you know they were satisfied customers?' she asked pugnaciously. 'For all we know, they might go off and tell their friends the tea was too weak or too strong. They might say they didn't have a scone because we charge twice as much as they would have to pay if they bought it straight from Sample's. They might say our chairs were uncomfortable . . .'

'Did they?' James Mortimer said challengingly. 'Did you have one customer complaint? Did someone break a tooth on a Sample's scone, or have hot tea spilt into her lap? Come along now, let's hear the worst. Where's the complaints book? I suppose you had to start one if your customers were so dissatisfied.'

Despite herself, Dana felt a smile curl her lips, and catching Caitlin's eye she saw that her friend, too, was trying to stifle her amusement. 'All right, you've got a point; no one complained,' she admitted. 'In fact several people – the ones who bought pots of tea and not just cups – asked for more hot water. I suppose that's quite a good sign.'

'And I had to go up to the dairy for more milk,' Caitlin said eagerly. 'The trouble is I think we over-bought; we were careful with bread, not knowing how much toast we would sell, but we honestly believed the scones would go like hot cakes. When we were working at the Willows, the women who came in for a sit down and a cuppa after their shopping nearly always asked for a scone. It was the men who went for toast, but there aren't many offices round here so we thought our customers would mainly be women and we thought—'

James Mortimer cut across her ruthlessly. 'Don't make excuses, because they ain't necessary,' he said sharply. 'I'm telling you you've done well; at least as well as I expected, and I know a good deal more about the catering business than you'd credit. We'll sell these scones off cheap tomorrow, even cheaper than what we bought them for from Samples.' He gave her the benefit of his most engaging grin. 'What attracts a customer to scones and cakes is the smell of baking. Tomorrow I want you and Dana to come in at nine o'clock and make a batch of fresh scones. I guess there's ordinary scones and what they call rich ones, and I want you to make the richer sort; put plenty of sultanas into the mix, and more sugar, maybe? Anyway, make 'em good, real special.'

Dana remembered her mother making scones for special occasions and being allowed to scrape the bowl out. 'Mammy used an egg instead of water to bind the flour and shortening and all that,' she said eagerly. 'She made the best scones in the whole of Ireland. I know the recipe and could whip up a couple of dozen in no time.'

James Mortimer nodded his approval, then gave Caitlin's shoulders a squeeze. 'See?' he said, grinning and pointing at Dana. 'You've got a partner who knows what's what. But don't forget the importance of the smell of baking. Your customers can go along to Samples and buy themselves a scone any time, but they can't have a cup of tea with it, nor a sit down . . .'

'And it won't be buttered, or have jam on,' Caitlin finished for him. 'Oh, James, you've cheered me up no end. I was thinking you'd be upset and cross and want to close us down. Wasn't I foolish?'

'No, no; it's just that you're new to the business. You'll soon grow accustomed and get to know your customers' likes and dislikes. Before long you'll be able to predict how many scones or slices of toast you will sell on a rainy day and how many when the sun is bouncing off the pavement. Now come along. You're much too tired to cook so I'll take you out to Lyons Corner House and buy you a slap-up supper. How does that appeal?'

Dana and Caitlin beamed at him, then Dana rushed across to the customers' coat rack and took down her jacket and Caitlin's. 'We've had nothing to eat all day because we were so anxious,' she said, unlocking the door. 'Come along, Caitlin. It'll be grand to be waited on for a change!'

As time passed, it was soon clear to both girls that James Mortimer knew what he was doing. His prophecy regarding the tea drinkers had proved correct, and soon Dana was coming down to the storeroom kitchen by eight o'clock in order to bake her scones. At the end of the first month, they invested in a larger and much more modern cooker, and also an electric toaster which could toast two slices of bread simultaneously, a great help when they were busy.

Caitlin was keen to have cushions made for the rather unyielding wooden chairs they had bought, but James had shaken his head. 'No, we don't want customers lingering after they've had their tea and toast or whatever,' he had said firmly. 'We want them to eat and drink up and then go, leaving space for more customers. If we make them too comfortable they'll linger and lingerers pay nothing.'

Both girls realised that they could learn a good deal from James Mortimer, though there were some business practices which both Dana and Caitlin absolutely refused to use. He had told them to scrape burnt toast, to use margarine instead of butter, to cut down on the richness of the scones Dana baked each morning now they had plenty of customers, and to buy cheap cuts of meat when they began to make sandwiches for the lunchtime trade.

'If we take advice like that, James, we'll end up losing our good customers and our good reputation, and have to rely on folk whose only priority is cheapness,' Dana had told him. 'At present, we always buy Sample's best white bread, which is so delicious that it scarcely needs butter or jam, but if we began to present the customers with the really cheap stuff . . .'

James Mortimer had flung up his hands in a gesture of defeat. He had been grinning. 'You learn fast, ladies,' he had said. 'I won't interfere with what you're doing, at least until your six months is up. Then we'll take a long, hard look at prices, profits and so on, and decide whether to expand, find somewhere better suited to our business . . .'

The girls had cried out at this. 'It's not your business, James, it's ours,' Dana pointed out. 'We pay you rent; we've kept our side of the bargain, getting the place immaculate and keeping it so. We're happy to take your advice when we're not sure of our way forward, but further than that we aren't prepared to go.'

To say that James looked startled was an understatement, Dana reminded Caitlin now, as they cleared the tea room after a particularly successful day's trading. 'He still thinks of Cathy's Place as his baby, but it's not, you know. We pay the rent he asks, do all the work, keep the books . . . well, I admit his advice has come in handy, but sometimes he gets quite the wrong end of the stick, and then we go our own way and so far we've been proved right. No customer complaints, no brickbats, lots of back-patting, no bills we can't meet . . .'

'Oh, all right, we're perfect,' Caitlin said rather crossly. 'But if it hadn't been for James . . .'

'I don't deny we couldn't have done it without him,' Dana said quickly. 'But we've worked hard and now we're reaping our reward and I don't see why he should preen himself. Look at the flat, for instance. He had no hand in that, did he?'

The flat was indeed the girls' pride and joy. They had not rushed into furnishing it with whatever was cheap, but at first had managed with two battered wooden chairs, an ancient cooker and a couple of truckle beds. They had had a blanket and a pillow each, but such luxuries as sheets and pillowcases had had to come later.

Now, however, halfway through September, the flat was as fully furnished as they felt necessary. The living room boasted an elegant three-piece suite in cream-coloured velveteen, a nest of occasional tables, a large walnutwood wireless set and a square of dark blue carpet patterned with roses and curtains to match. It was here that the girls relaxed, listening to the wireless and playing music on Caitlin's Dansette record player.

They did not have guests often, being too tired after

each long day's work. James was by far their most frequent visitor and he often came to help rather than to be entertained. Though Dana was perfectly capable of keeping the books, he liked to look them over and analyse each day's sales. Profit fascinated him and he was full of ideas by which they could increase their turnover. But since much of his advice involved things like having two sets of books, one for the authorities to read and one which the girls should keep well out of sight, they treated it with a mixture of amusement and scorn, and though he had told them that one had to be one jump ahead in business and that practices which might seem a trifle sharp to their innocent minds were actually in common use amongst their competitors, the girls had remained firm.

'If you want cheating tenants, remember that it isn't just the public and the authorities which such people cheat, but landlords,' Dana had told him severely. She had been paying bills – Sample's, Mr Gregg the butcher, old Mrs Platt who made delicious jams – and now she waved him away impatiently, for he was standing at her shoulder, peering at the figures as she filled them in. 'Do go away, James; you're putting me off my stroke.'

James had backed down on that occasion but it worried Dana that her friend might embrace his values rather than her own. She realised that, since she and Caitlin were partners, both of them would be held equally responsible for doctored books or misleading figures, and decided she really must have a word with Caitlin.

So as soon as James had left, Dana tackled her friend on the subject. She had thought that Caitlin might become indignant, even refuse to listen, for it was clear that her friend not only admired James but was more than half in love with him. And the feeling may well be reciprocated, Dana told herself somewhat uneasily. However, everything should be all right. Caitlin's as honest as the day – she's been brought up as strictly as I have myself – and I'm sure she won't let James persuade her into bad ways.

Time passed, and by October the two girls realised that they were now running a very successful little business. James wanted them to expand, but so far the girls had resisted change. Why should they saddle themselves with complications such as bigger premises, paid staff and a whole new way of life, when they were so happy with the present arrangements? So despite his urging, James's suggestions of expansion had fallen on deaf ears.

The girls had just cleared up and closed one extremely busy Saturday when James came thundering up the stairs two at a time and burst into the flat. 'I've got a proposition for you,' he said, and threw down a bulging file on their small kitchen table. 'See if you can resist this, ladies!'

'I'm too tired for much resistance,' Caitlin said, but she sat down opposite him and gestured to Dana to do likewise. 'What is it now, James? You keep having brilliant ideas, or you say they're brilliant, but we're run off our feet as it is, without you plotting to get us yet more customers!'

'Ah, but this time it's not just air-dreaming,' James said, tapping the file. 'I've had a fellow round to take a look at the tea room and he says he could do a complete conversion and so on in a month, maybe six weeks. He's experienced in such things, I can tell you, got all the figures at his fingertips . . .'

'You talked it over with this "fellow" without so much as consulting us?' Dana interrupted incredulously, though she was not really at all surprised. James was often high-handed, and she had seen him only the previous day sitting at one of the window tables with a large fat man in a smart business suit whose spiky grey hair stood up like a cock's comb on his round, bullet head. He and James had been deep in conversation, and Dana would not have dreamed of interrupting what had been clearly a business meeting. Thinking back, she remembered that James had gestured around him several times, pointing to a plan lying on the table half covered by teacups, saucers and plates bearing the crumbs of the scones they had devoured. He often brought business contacts into the café; Dana had thought nothing of it until now. She cleared her throat. 'I'd better point out that I saw you in the café yesterday, so I take it that it wasn't just tea and scones you and your fat friend were discussing. Really, James, didn't it occur to you that it would have been good manners to introduce him to either Caitlin or myself? We don't own the place, of course, but we are your tenants and must deserve some consideration!'

If she had hoped to discompose him, however, she was disappointed. He flashed her a big, self-confident grin then leaned across the table, meaning to chuck her under the chin. Dana dodged, though she said nothing. She had long ago realised that James automatically patronised women, convinced that the entire female race was inferior to the male. 'Good manners? What's them?' he said cockily. 'I'm a plain man, me.' His eyes met Dana's and she caught a flicker of something – was it humour?

61

– in his glance, but then he transferred his gaze from herself to Caitlin and Dana took back her unvoiced criticism, because his whole face changed when his eyes met those of her friend. If he really does love her, Dana told herself, I'd better listen to his latest hare-brained scheme before I tell him we're not going to play.

'Ready? Then pin back your lugholes . . .'

This time, the scheme was not just to rearrange the tea room to give them a couple of extra tables, or to move to bigger premises; this time it was to tear the café apart. The wall between the café itself and the storeroom would come down, a window would be made in the rear wall to give the place more natural light, and their dear little flat would be gutted and turned into a modern kitchen.

'And where are we supposed to live?' Dana asked sarcastically. 'In the outside privy?'

She expected James to be confounded by the question, but he grinned even more broadly. 'I've bought a flat over the cycle shop in Wentworth Street, only a couple of hundred yards or so from here,' he said triumphantly. 'If you agree to the conversion you can live there rent-free for three months. Because of the upheaval, we'll say – for a while at least – that it's one of the perks of the job. How's that for good manners?'

Dana could not help laughing, but Caitlin gave a little squeal of excitement and began to exclaim, then glanced at her friend. 'Oh, but what are we to do whilst the place is being altered?' she asked. 'And we've not even seen the Wentworth Street flat yet; we might hate it.'

'You'll love it,' James said positively. 'It's got its own private staircase, leading from the yard to the front hall, so you won't have to go into the shop at all. Wentworth

Street is a lot quieter than Heyworth, and just think how nice it will be to be able to lock the door of the café and walk away from work as other people do.'

'You make it sound very tempting, but I should need to know a lot more before agreeing to such a radical change,' Dana said coolly. 'For a start, it would mean closing the café for several weeks, if not months . . .'

James interrupted at once. 'No, no, I've thought of that. Herbie Porter says he'll do the work in four to six weeks, from start to finish. You won't need to close the café for long, because he'll try to do the messiest work on Sundays whenever possible.' He delved into his file and produced a number of typewritten sheets. 'Sign here, ladies, and I'll arrange a meeting between Herbie, you and me. Obviously I'd like you to capitalise on the Christmas rush, but when that's over Porter will start converting the property and improving it as well.'

He pushed the forms enticingly towards Caitlin, but when her friend would have seized the pen Dana shook her head. 'No you don't, alanna,' she said firmly. 'There are several things to be done first.' She ticked them off on her fingers. 'One, we must examine the costings for this work and see precisely how long it's likely to take; two, we want to know how it will affect our rent. At the moment we pay our way comfortably, but in larger premises we would need to employ staff and increase our supplies. Three, I suppose we would have to offer hot meals as well and that would mean not just waitresses but also a professional cook and a commercial stove, both of which cost money. And four, there's this flat you speak of; you may say we'll love it, but I prefer to make my own decisions on such matters – as does Caitlin, of course,' she added guiltily, suddenly aware that she was sounding just as high-handed as James. 'Well? Answers please, Mr Mortimer!'

James heaved a deep, dramatic sigh. 'I can't tell you the exact cost, but you needn't worry about that since I intend to pay for everything. As for your rent, it will stay the same for the first three months that the restaurant is open, because though I am sure your turnover and there-fore your profit will increase dramatically you're quite right, you will have added expenses. And of course you must approve the flat, so we'll go there right away.' He stood up, tucked the file under his arm and produced a bunch of keys. 'Wait till you see your new abode!'

Chapter Three

Dana was always wary of James and his bright ideas, though she could not have said why, but on this occasion at least, it seemed that she need have no worries. Once Christmas was over – they had enjoyed fantastic business as the holiday approached – they were able to concentrate on the work being done to the tea room and the flat above. They had met Mr Porter and thought his assessment of the work which needed doing was probably correct. Despite her initial dislike of the scheme, Dana had examined the carefully drawn up plans of how the restaurant would look and thought them most attractive, and the new flat was just as nice as James had promised.

The kitchen was delightful, with every modern convenience already in place, and the small living room had a wide window overlooking the street, with a padded window seat and gleaming brocade curtains. It also had a telephone, an almost unheard of luxury, though James told them he had had it installed because they might need to be in touch with the restaurant, and they would also find it useful to be able to put in an order by telephone to those of their suppliers who were connected. 'It's on a party line with the one which is being installed in the restaurant,' he explained, 'so when one of you is in the flat and the other at work you can have a chat.' But the main attraction of the new flat was the bathroom and lavatory; not having to traipse down to the public baths on Margaret Street or to go outside to the privy on rainy nights was delightful.

Today, Caitlin had gone round to Sample's to discuss with the chief baker how much bread they would need once the new restaurant was up and running. Dana was at the flat, awaiting the delivery of a couple of single beds. They had been sleeping on truckle beds in Heyworth Street, but had decided they deserved a bit of comfort now they had a larger bedroom.

When the doorbell rang she hurried for the stairs . . . then realised that the bell was still ringing and, smiling ruefully, retraced her steps. It was the telephone, of course; they would have to invest in a new doorbell, one with a different ring, or she and Caitlin would waste time galloping to the head of their outside staircase when they could have been comfortably ensconced in the warmth of the flat, listening to whoever had rung them.

Re-entering the living room, Dana grabbed the receiver and put it to her ear, her mouth opening to tell Caitlin – it was bound to be Caitlin – that she was still awaiting the arrival of their new beds. Then she stopped short and sank down on the nearest chair, the telephone still pressed to her ear. Neither of the voices she could hear was Caitlin's. One voice belonged to James, the other to a stranger. Dana was about to replace the receiver when she heard her own name. She continued to listen, feeling her face grow cold with shock. She was eavesdropping, of course, but . . .

The conversation finished, the two men replaced their receivers and Dana, after the briefest of pauses, did likewise. Then she brushed away the wretched tears which had begun to form in her eyes. But what to do, what to do? First, she must contact Caitlin, tell her . . . oh, tell her plainly what she had overheard. She took the telephone receiver off its cradle, then hesitated. No, she needed to talk to her friend in private, and she was not the only person who might pick up a telephone and hear something she was not supposed to know.

It was an icy cold, rainy January day, but Dana did not even pause to throw a coat around her shoulders before bolting out of the flat. She was halfway down the metal stair when her heel caught and she pitched forward. She had a confused picture of the world turning . . . then something hit her smartly on the back of the head and darkness descended.

'I wonder if I ought to give Dana a ring,' Caitlin said as she and James supervised the closing of the restaurant. Jess, the Saturday girl, had just said goodnight to their last customer, and James had gone back into the tea room to turn the *Open* sign to *Closed* and to shoot the bolts across. Despite the fact that the conversion of the store-room was not yet fully completed, the restaurant was doing tremendously well. Of course, as James was so fond of pointing out, the customers, being Liverpudlians, took a lively interest in every change as it was made, and did not hesitate to give their opinion of such changes with great frankness.

'You'll be purrin' your perishin' prices up I've no doubt,' old Mrs Harrow had remarked gloomily earlier in the day. 'Someone's gorra pay for them nice new tables and I don't reckon that winder come cheap.'

Caitlin had been unable to suppress a guilty grin. The window overlooked the back yard, not a pretty sight with its dustbins, crumbling wall and the door to the jigger hanging by one hinge and in need of fresh paint. According to James and Mr Porter, a nice net curtain would solve the problem of the view, but Caitlin had discussed it with Dana and they had decided that on this issue they would be firm. '*Not* a net curtain, nor a lace one; we want stained glass,' Caitlin had said firmly, though she was still rather in awe of Mr Porter and guessed that he would try to overrule her. Indeed, both he and James had blustered when they discovered the price of using stained glass on such a large window, but the girls had been determined.

'A net curtain is an invitation to any customer to lift it up and take a peek,' Dana had said frostily. 'As for nailing the curtain to the window frame, that's downright cheapskate. Folk will think we've something to hide.'

James had chuckled. 'You've got a point,' he had admitted. 'So go round to Boyle's, the glass merchants, and choose the cheapest on offer, and tell him I want it fitted right away, else I might change my mind.'

So Dana and Caitlin had gone to the glass merchants and chosen some beautiful stained glass, and Dana told Mr Boyle that if he dared to tell Mr Mortimer he could have had frosted glass for a fraction of the price, she would personally murder him.

Mr Boyle had laughed. 'I've knocked me price down as low as it'll go, and what you've bought is a deal better'n frosted. Don't you worrit yourself, queen; your

68

boss's gettin' a bargain and he's well known for likin' a bargain.'

Now Caitlin raised her brows as James came towards her and repeated her question. 'James, I asked you if I ought to give Dana a ring; she's not rung me at all today. It looks as though the furniture people haven't arrived . . . but since we've closed I might as well go straight home and find out what's going on for myself.'

'Oh, but I thought we'd go for a bite to eat first,' James said hopefully. 'You and I hardly ever get a chance to be by ourselves. Anyone would think you and Dana were a pair of Siamese twins who could never be torn apart.'

Caitlin gave a breathless little laugh. 'You keep telling us you're a businessman, so you should understand that Dana and I aren't simply friends, but business partners as well,' she reminded him. A thought struck her and she turned towards him, her eyes widening. 'Oh, I know what's happened! I heard the telephone ring earlier, but I was busy with a customer and Jess answered it – it must have been Dana telephoning to say the beds had arrived. I wonder why Jess didn't tell me? But we really have been rushed off our feet – I expect it went out of her head.'

Agreeing, James opened the door and flinched back as rain blew in. He was already clad in coat and hat and now he unfurled a large umbrella and held it over Caitlin's head. 'Off we go, then!'

They locked up and left the building, heads lowered and umbrella held before them, but when James turned to the right Caitlin pulled on his arm. 'Wherever are you off to? Wentworth Street . . .' she pointed, 'is that way!'

'As if I didn't know!' James said mockingly. 'But I said I'd take you for a bite to eat.'

'Well, yes, but I'll have to go back to the flat first,' Caitlin insisted. 'It may not have been Dana on the phone earlier, perhaps she's still waiting. I really can't just walk away from her. If only I'd thought, we could have telephoned from the tea room and she could have met us somewhere.'

James gave a dramatic groan, tilted his hat to the back of his Brylcreemed head and pretended to tear his hair. 'There you go again!' he said bitterly. 'If we telephone, or go back to the flat, Dana will take it for granted that she's coming out with us. Oh, come on, Caitlin, be a sport. We can take Dana out some other time . . .' he blinked rainwater out of his eyes and gave Caitlin's arm a little shake, 'and next time it will be the Adelphi; how about that for a bribe?'

Caitlin was tempted, but insisted that they should return to the flat. They hurried down the jigger, crossed the slippery cobbles and headed for the metal stair, James telling Caitlin firmly to remain where she was whilst he climbed the flight. 'If the beds have arrived, I'll tell her to meet us at Joe Lyons; no point in us hanging around waiting for her,' he said. 'And if the beds haven't arrived, I'll explain that you and I will get a snack somewhere . . . and we'll all go out to dinner at the Adelphi tomorrow, because by then I'll have some news to impart.'

'That sounds exciting . . .' Caitlin began, but found she was addressing empty air; James was already halfway up the staircase.

She saw him raise his hand to knock, hesitate, then press the bell. He waited a few seconds, then came down, a frown on his brow. 'She's gone out,' he said in a rather aggrieved tone. 'Did she have any plans once the beds had arrived? But she's definitely not in. There were no lights on, so far as I could see, and the door's locked.'

Caitlin thought carefully. 'She's been meaning to go back to the Willows to have a chat to the girls we knew when we worked there,' she said. 'We'll be needing extra staff once the conversion is complete and Dana thought it would be nice to employ people we already know. I wonder if she went there?'

James took her arm once more. 'No point in wondering; we might as well grab ourselves a bite to eat. I'm sure we'll find there's some logical explanation.' They left the yard and were heading back up the jigger when a voice hailed them.

'Miss, miss? My dear, you'll be wonderin' what's happened to your pal.'

Caitlin swung round. A little fat woman in a stained floral overall was waddling after them, and when they stopped she panted up beside them, casting a nervous glance at James before turning to Caitlin. Caitlin recognised her as a neighbour who had watched with interest on the previous day as she and Dana had carried a kitchen chair each across the yard and up the metal stair. She had introduced herself and offered help, but the girls had assured her that they could manage and had noted with amusement that she had withdrawn only as far as her own yard, whence she could watch proceedings without appearing to do so.

'Oh, good afternoon, Mrs . . . Robbins, wasn't it? I'm so sorry, I didn't quite catch . . . did you say you'd seen my friend? She seems to have gone out.'

'They come for her near on an hour ago, queen, and took her off . . . the ambulance men, I mean. She must ha' fell down them perishin' stairs; they're that slippery in the rain. I heered the motor turn into the jigger and come round to see wharr I could do.'

'My God!' Caitlin said, grabbing James's arm in a vice-like grip. 'Oh, poor Dana. Which hospital, Mrs Robbins? We must go to her at once.'

'It'll be the Stanley, I dare say,' Mrs Robbins said. 'One o' the fellers in the ambulance was me nephew by marriage, an' he works there. Your pal were unconscious . . . ever so pale she looked, white as milk, poor gal. I heered one o' the men say somethin' about her leg, and then a bump on her noggin . . . he reckoned she were concussed. Me nephew said she were wet to the skin an' deathly cold, so they thought she'd been lyin' there some time.'

'Right, we'll get off then,' James said, speaking for the first time since Mrs Robbins had appeared. 'I wonder who called the ambulance?'

'Oh, it were Mrs D'Arcy, from the post office,' Mrs Robbins said at once. 'I don't reckon she were the one who found her, 'xactly, 'cos that were some feller from Ginsberg's furniture shop on the Scotty. He ran to the post office 'cos they've gorra telephone . . .'

But already James and Caitlin were hurrying up the jigger, Caitlin calling over her shoulder that they were much obliged and would tell Mrs Robbins what had happened as soon as they knew themselves.

They were shown on to the ward by a brisk little nurse who patted Caitlin's hand consolingly and said there was very little wrong with her friend apart from a bump on the head and a suspected fracture of the tibia. Seeing Caitlin's puzzled look, she explained that the tibia was just a medical name for the shin bone. 'She won't be able to work until it's begun to knit . . . but don't you worry, my dear, the doctors aren't certain that it's broken. They'll do some more investigations when she comes round, which should be later this evening.'

At James's insistence they had an interview with the doctor who was handling Dana's case. He was young and friendly and very reassuring. 'If the leg is broken, it's not a bad break, more like a crack, so she should be able to get around on crutches once it's plastered,' he told them. 'The bump on the head wouldn't have been serious had she been discovered earlier, but the men who brought her in said she must have been lying on the cobbles in the rain for long enough to become dangerously cold. As you can see, we wrapped her up in every blanket we could lay our hands on and she'll remain so wrapped until her colour begins to return. I'm sure if you come back tomorrow she'll be sitting up and taking nourishment, but for the moment she just needs quiet and warmth.'

Caitlin would have liked to remain with her friend, but James thought this ridiculous. 'She's in the best possible hands, and since you aren't a nurse or a doctor there's no way you can be of assistance,' he said. 'Making yourself ill through not eating your supper will scarcely help Dana. Tell you what, we'll go out and have that meal I promised you and come back in an hour. Will that satisfy you?'

Caitlin looked at Dana's white face and motionless body, with the cage over her left leg to keep the bedclothes from rubbing against it. Then she sighed, leaned over the bed and kissed her friend's cheek. 'We're going to get something to eat, but we'll be back before you know it,' she whispered. Turning away, she tucked her hand into James's arm. 'Come along then. Now that I come to think of it, I could eat a horse!'

Polly had continued to take an interest in the two girls. She still neither liked nor trusted the dark man whose name she now knew to be James Mortimer, but she told herself she was prejudiced because he had removed the girls she so admired from her workplace. It must have been his influence which had allowed Dana and Caitlin to start their tea room. She had never actually gone into Cathy's Place since the first day, but she had grown friendly with one of the waitresses so had been told all about the wonderful new restaurant which would be opened in the New Year. The young woman had explained to Polly that the flat above the tea room had been converted into marvellously modern kitchens and Dana and Caitlin had moved to a place in Wentworth Street. Polly was pleased; she often walked that way when visiting friends so was able to look up at the windows of the flat above the cycle shop and imagine the girls within. In fact, she had been heading for Wentworth Street when an ambulance, bell ringing and headlights blazing, had rushed past her. A couple of days later she learned from her waitress friend that the vehicle had been on its way to pick up the injured Dana. Horrified, she went straight to the hospital as soon as she finished work, and was actually sitting by the bed holding Dana's hand and murmuring words of comfort when a hand descended on to her shoulder and a harsh voice spoke in her ear. 'Who the devil are you? I know I've seen you somewhere before, but you've got no right to be here.'

Polly jumped guiltily to her feet as the man's hand left her shoulder. 'I'm – I'm a friend, that's all,' she stammered. 'Me and Dana – and Caitlin, of course – used to work together . . .'

Her explanation was rudely interrupted. 'I know! You're that kid who's been hanging around the restaurant, trying to nose out what's going on. Well you can clear out right now, do you hear me? Miss McBride is very ill, so it's family only. Understand?'

Polly stared up into the dark and threatening face scowling down at her. 'But – but Dana don't have no relatives, not in England,' she stammered. 'She's from some place in Ireland. Her dad's dead . . .'

But this only seemed to inflame Mr James Mortimer more. 'Never you mind about her relatives. Don't go thinking you can butter up to the McBrides by telling them Dana's in hospital,' he said harshly. 'Just get out of here and don't come back, or I'll tell the staff you're a troublemaker and they mustn't let you near their patient.'

Polly began to protest, to say that she would never do anything to hurt the girl lying so pale and still in her hospital bed, but James Mortimer caught her by the shoulders and almost ran her out of the ward. 'I'm warning you . . .' he began, just as they reached the swing doors and Polly saw Caitlin coming towards them. As James Mortimer thrust her through the doors and into the corridor she tried to say that Caitlin would vouch for her, but before she could so much as open her mouth the man spoke. 'Darling, I thought we were going to meet in the hospital foyer so we could see Dana together,' he said. 'I've just been telling this – this young person that Dana's too ill for other visitors.'

'Is she?' Caitlin's eyes lit on Polly and a frown creased her beautiful brow. 'Oh, hello. Were you visiting Dana as well? You were at the Willows at the same time as us, but I'm afraid I can't remember your name.' She gave Polly a distracted smile, then linked her arm in James Mortimer's. 'Come along, dearest.'

The two of them disappeared into the ward but not before the man had given Polly the sort of look which turned her blood to ice. It was clear that if he found her there again he would do something really unpleasant. But I shall visit, Polly told herself, crossing the hospital foyer and going out through the swing doors. Only I'll make bleedin' sure that I do so when Mr Wonderful Mortimer is otherwise engaged.

Dana was dreaming. She was back in the yard behind the cycle shop; she felt the rain pattering on her face and the hardness of the cobbles against her back. She was cold, colder than she had ever been; in fact so cold that numbness was creeping up her body. When the numbness reaches my heart I'll be dead and I don't *want* to die, she found herself thinking. They'll be so distressed if I die and I'll be no use to anyone. How will poor Caitlin manage with the restaurant still not finished? I simply must move, try to sit up, call for help!

She turned her head a little and a sharp pain stabbed from the back of her neck to the top of her head, making her wince and long to cry out, but when she opened her mouth no sound emerged and rain fell in. She moved her head again, more cautiously this time, and the pain arrowed through her, from her neck to the back of her eyes, and did not stop for some seconds after she had frozen into immobility once more.

Later, she could not tell how much, she opened her eyes, but saw only the grey sky above and the steadily falling rain. Then there was darkness, and a voice she did not know saying words she could not recognise; they might have been in a foreign language for all she could tell.

Later still, she woke again to a rocking motion, and to hear another unknown voice saying something about concussion. She tried to open her eyes, to speak, but her lids seemed glued shut and her mouth would not obey her command to open. Terror seized her. Where was she? *Who* was she?

Then the dream changed and she could feel sunshine warm on her body, and knew she was lying on grass, with someone shouting, footsteps thundering over the turf towards her. A new voice spoke and now she understood every word, even realised that the speaker was worried half to death. Daddy! It was her own dear daddy, on his knees beside her, patting her cheek, begging her to wake up. She tried to open her eyes, to say she was quite all right and didn't he always say she was so full of mischief that when she fell over she bounced like a ball? But when she tried to speak all that came out was a little miaow, like a kitten, and Daddy was shouting for Mammy, sending Conan Devlin off to find her because 'Dee may be hurt real bad, Con.'

Dee? Oh, yes, she was Dee. Her mind wandered. Her father had christened her Dana because he had wanted a son, and Dana was a little bit like Daniel, the name they would have chosen had she been a boy. Her mother's choice had been Elizabeth so she was Dana Elizabeth McBride, but no one ever called her that except her mother, who only did so when she was very cross.

Dana gave a little smile, thinking how inappropriate the name Elizabeth would have been. She was such a tomboy, so good with the horses, such a companion to her daddy, that Donovan McBride was wont to boast that she was better than any son could have been, better in every way, and wasn't he the lucky feller to have such a child?

But now his worry forced her to reassure him, for she could never bear to see him unhappy. 'Daddy?' she said, her voice coming out rather high and frail-sounding.

But that one word made her father say: 'T'ank God, t'ank God,' whilst Con, who was the only son of Donovan McBride's partner and her best pal, said gruffly that Mrs McBride was on her way and oughtn't they to get Dee off the wet grass and into her own bed?

'I'm all right so I am,' Dana said, trying to sound offhand, proud even, but her voice let her down by coming out squeaky and thin. 'I don't want me bed, Daddy . . . only there was rain . . . I'm warm now, but I was mortal cold . . .'

'You bumped your little noggin, Dee,' her mother said, her voice reassuring, and Dana knew she must be looking poorly for her mother liked to use her proper name, Dana, and rarely called her tomboy daughter Dee. 'Daddy will carry you up to your room and we'll get Dr Cassidy to give you the once-over. Your leg looks as though it was doubled under you as you fell.'

Dana opened her eyes and saw her father's strong, narrow face looming over her, his dark brown eyes anxious, a lock of red hair falling across his forehead. But when he saw her looking up at him the anxious look fled and he grinned reassuringly. 'Aren't you the naughty one? How many times have I told you not to ride the horses when they've just been let out into the new pastures? The grass is sweet, and full of sugar, so it goes to their heads like champagne, and even your own little Flame cavorts and bucks and wants to pretend he's a circus pony. I suppose he threw you? Or was it the strawberry roan? You've longed to get your leg over him for many a day, and he's grassed up and full of himself right now. Was it that 'un?'

Dana considered agreeing, but despite being only six years old she knew that lies will always find you out, so she shook her head as her parent lifted her off the grass and began to carry her towards the crumbling castle which was her home. 'No, Daddy, it weren't Flame, nor the roan,' she confessed. 'It were the grey stallion, the one you call Thunderer. I fell off when he slipped on the mud by the paddock gate.'

'Thunderer? You rode me best stallion, and him wit'out so much as a halter?' Donovan was so surprised that he nearly dropped her. He slowed his pace as they entered the house, where he carried her across the kitchen and up the spiral stair which led directly to her room. 'It's to be hoped you've not broke both his knees, you imp of Satan.' He gave her a little shake. 'Your mammy's away with a message for Dr Cassidy . . .' he began as he pushed open the door of her room, 'and when he comes, young lady, you must be lying flat in your bed so he can examine

79

you and tell us what mischief you've done to yourself this time.' With the words he sidled into the small, eight-sided tower room and dumped her, though carefully, upon her bed. 'Stay just there. I'm off to check on Thunderer; your mammy will be up as soon as she gets back. If she knew you'd been aboard Thunderer she'd marmalise the pair of us. That horse is a divil on legs; how many times have I told you not to go near him? And mind, you spalpeen, that if you've harmed a hair of his hide I'll see to it that you don't ride for a month.'

She reared up in bed, indignation making her forget her hurts for a moment, but he had turned away and she lay back again, conscious that she would be glad of some time alone, for her head felt addled and strange. She had a dim memory of cold rain on her face coming down steadily from grey skies, of cobbles beneath her body and an ache in her heart for . . . what? For Castletara and her daddy and mammy, for the dear familiarity of her beloved home?

Oh, but it must have been a dream, that cold rain and those grey skies; a nightmare, more likely. Best forget it, put it right out of her mind. She would concentrate on the reality around her instead. She moved her head slowly, taking in every detail of her small bedroom. Because it was in one of the towers it had eight sides, like a threepenny bit, with two long, narrow lancet windows overlooking the rolling meadows of her father's land and the distant blue of the mountains. Beneath one window was a small bookcase containing a grosh of books, many about horses, others typical children's classics: everything E. Nesbit and Patricia Lynch had ever written, *The Wind in the Willows* by Kenneth Grahame and many others, all old friends. Then there was a chest of drawers in which she folded her clean clothes when they were ironed and neat, and a rail for her skirts, jodhpurs and jerseys. On one wall were paintings of the surrounding countryside – her mother dabbled in watercolours – and on another a picture of Flame, head up to show the curve of his neck and his creamy mane, which brought the tears to Dana's eyes. If her daddy were to forbid her to ride her pony . . .

Quickly, she forced her mind to change direction. Her head still felt muzzy and strange, and she sighed and shifted uncomfortably in the bed. I love Castletara, even though Mammy says 'tis crumblin' away from neglect, but like my daddy I t'ink the fields and the meadows, the woods and the lake and the mountains, are more important than any house, no matter how old it may be. And horses are most important of all, because my daddy is the best horse breeder in Ireland, so he is, and when he puts up a horse for sale or to stud the fellers come from miles around, even the Irish tinkers, though Daddy won't sell to them and when they're in the neighbourhood he brings the horses in and locks the stables. Tinkers' animals get more kicks than kisses, Daddy says – even their donkeys look as though they never had a decent mouthful of food – but some of the tinks can whisper horses. Horses have little brains, poor t'ings, and will follow a whisperer even if it means leaving grand pastures for the hard life on the road. Daddy won't let the tinkers get so much as a sniff of Castletara's animals.

But despite assuring her mother, when she came carefully up the stairs carrying a nice hot cup of tea, that she was fine so she was, by the time Dr Cassidy arrived Dana was bone weary and ached all over. The doctor was an old friend and examined her carefully before telling her that she should remain quietly in bed for several days. He said her leg had what he called a green fracture, which would mend with rest, quiet and good food, and he decided on a light splint, with bandages, to hold it in position.

Dana gritted her teeth and bit her lip stoically and endured, but when the job was done she was glad to hitch herself down the bed, to thank her mother for another cup of tea which she felt too sick to drink, and to agree to have the windows curtained so that she might try to sleep.

Next time she woke, it was pitch dark and she hurt so much that she was unable to suppress a few tears. But this was not the first time she had been thrown from a horse or had a crack on the head, and, despite her few years, past experience told her that the pain would ease if she gave it a chance. Dr Cassidy had said he would loosen the bandages if the splint still hurt when he visited the next day, but if possible he wanted to avoid sending her to hospital to have her leg put in a plaster cast. It was a long way to the nearest town, and he thought that being jolted over the rough Irish roads would probably widen the crack in her bone besides giving her a most uncomfortable journey.

The six-year-old Dana had never been in hospital – never spent a night away from Castletara – and had no desire to experience such a horrid fate. She knew nothing of plaster casts but could not imagine them to be less painful than splints and bandages, so she had done her best to remain cheerful as Dr Cassidy 'tidied her up', as he put it, and saved her tears for when she was alone. Presently, she slept.

'She's still slightly concussed,' the doctor told Caitlin and James when they visited Dana next day. 'A trifle out of sorts as well. But it's good that she's drunk a cup of tea and tried to sit up. Go through to her, and don't be surprised if she's a little confused.'

'Right,' James said. He took Caitlin's arm in a masterful manner. 'Come along. I'm sure, if she can drink a cup of tea, she'll be able to tell us just what happened.'

They reached Dana's bed, smiling. But Caitlin felt her smile freeze on her lips when her friend looked up at her, then past her, then sighed and switched her gaze to the far end of the ward as though she was still waiting for someone she knew to appear.

'Dana?' Caitlin's voice was almost frightened. 'The doctor says . . .'

Dana's eyes flickered over her, then over James, before returning to gaze thoughtfully towards the doors at the far end of the ward. She did not speak at all.

James stepped forward. 'Don't you know your friends when they come a-visiting?' he said, and Caitlin realised that his tone was meant to be jokey, light-hearted, but it came out tense, almost bullying. 'Come on, Dana, here's Caitlin been worried out of her life and you don't even say hello.'

Dana frowned. 'I'm sorry, I don't think I know either of you,' she said slowly. 'What did you say your name was? And mine? I – I don't seem to know who I am . . . well, not my name, at any rate.'

83

There was a long stool by Dana's bed; Caitlin sat down on it with a thump. 'You've had concussion, Dana,' she said slowly and clearly. 'But surely you must know who you are! Everyone knows who they are.'

'Do they?' Dana's voice was verging on the aggressive. 'Then let's pretend we've just met for the first time. Give me your name and perhaps the sound of it will awaken something in my head.'

Caitlin cast a frightened look at James, then turned back to Dana. 'You're pretending, aren't you?' she said, trying to sound as light and jokey as she believed James had done and failing quite as miserably. 'I'm Caitlin Flannagan, your partner in the tea room we started a few months back. We met on the ferry from Ireland and palled up. I was running away from – from an unhappy affair and you were leaving Ireland to make your fortune.' She sighed as the other girl's face remained blank. 'Dana? You're not even *trying* to remember! Your father had died and there was no more money, which was why you took the ferry to Liverpool. You simply *must* remember!'

Dana compressed her lips but said nothing for a moment. Then she pointed at James. 'Who's he?'

'This is James Mortimer, who rents the tea room to us, as well as our dear little flat . . . oh, Dana, you're frightening me. You're Dana McBride and we run Cathy's Place together.'

'Oh,' Dana said blankly. 'But if you'll excuse me asking, how do I know you're telling the truth? I believe someone hit me over the head and knocked me down.' She turned an impersonal glance on Caitlin. 'I don't suppose it was you, because you look a respectable kind of girl, but it might well have been him.' She pointed an accusing finger towards James. 'He looks capable of all sorts of skulduggery.'

Caitlin felt her face flame with annoyance; how dared Dana insult James! But she knew nothing about concussion or memory loss and if Dana really neither recognised them nor knew who she was herself, she could scarcely be blamed for thinking that James, with his tough, aggressive appearance, could be the person who had hit her over the head.

But when she looked at James he was grinning and did not seem in the least offended by Dana's accusation. 'So far as we know, you weren't hit by anyone. You fell down a flight of stairs, cracking your head on the bottom one and breaking your leg as you fell,' he said. 'No one was about, and you lay in the rain for a long time. Naturally enough it made you ill, so perhaps that's why you've lost your memory. But the doctor is sure it will return in a couple of days. And now, dear Dana, if you'll excuse us, Caitlin and I must go back to the tea room. It's being converted into a proper restaurant, but I don't suppose you remember that?'

Caitlin looked hopefully at her friend's face, but Dana's expression remained politely blank. Sighing, she followed James out of the ward.

After the two visitors had left, Dana lay back against her pillows and tried very hard to remember who she was. She supposed she must accept that she was Dana McBride, that this hospital was situated in Liverpool and that the girl, Caitlin, was her partner. Though why it should have occurred to either of them to start a tea room she could not imagine.

She had the feeling that the city was alien to her. She believed she was a country girl, and since Caitlin had told her that she had come from Ireland she supposed that this at least must be the truth. But she was getting tired; no doubt her memory would return in its own good time. The doctor had told her not to worry, but anyone would worry if they woke up in a strange hospital bed with one leg in plaster, a bump the size of a hen's egg on the back of her skull and absolutely no recollection of who she was. 'Get plenty of rest and above all don't worry,' the young doctor had said. Well, all she could do was obey his instructions and for the time being at least accept what the girl, Caitlin, had told her, and hope that her memory would soon return.

As she settled herself, a nurse in a blue striped dress came rustling up the ward and stopped by her bed. Hesitantly, Dana said, 'Nurse, could you find me a mirror? If I saw my own face . . .'

The nurse beamed at her. 'What a good idea,' she said cheerfully. 'I'll fetch one at once. I gather from Sister that the sight of your friends didn't do the trick? Oh well, I suppose it was too much to expect. I'll just see to Mrs Stevens and then I'll fetch you that mirror.'

Moments later, Dana gazed into a cheap little mirror and found that she was astonished by the face reflected therein. Hair the bright orange of carrots and curly as – as a pig's tail. A face smothered in freckles and eyes green as bottle-glass with white lashes and brows. Not a pretty sight, but . . . She grinned at her reflection, then lowered the mirror, suddenly almost frightened. The person she had just seen reflected was a stranger! Not me; I'm – I'm not like that, she thought confusedly. I didn't think I was pretty, exactly, but . . . that orange hair! I've seen better-looking cats, she thought, and realised even as it entered her mind that somewhere in her life was a large ginger cat with green eyes and a bottle-brush tail . . .

'Well, queen? Aren't you a nice-lookin' gairl, then?' The nurse's voice was cheery. She laughed. 'Reckernise yerself, do you? Well, I can assure you that the gairl in that mirror and the gairl in the bed is both Dana McBride. How did you get on with your pal, eh? Know her, did you? And the feller?'

Dana gave a little shiver. Thinking back she realised that Caitlin's companion gave her the creeps. He had seemed straightforward enough, as though he wanted her to regain her memory, but suddenly she was sure he wanted nothing of the sort. She did not know why she felt that, but decided that for the time being at least she would continue to regard Mr James Mortimer with a good deal of suspicion. Caitlin, on the other hand, seemed a nice enough girl; perhaps if she could get her alone she might also get some answers. The only trouble was that right now she could not think of any question she ought to ask.

'Well? Can I have me mirror back now, or do you want to freeze on to it for a bit?' The nurse's rosy young face suddenly broke into a broad smile. 'Want to ax it some questions?' She giggled again. *Mirror, mirror on the wall, who is the fairest of them all?'* she quoted.

Dana laughed with her but handed back the mirror. 'I always was plain as a pikestaff,' she said ruefully, then wondered what had made her say that. But the nurse was moving away from the bed, going over to another patient whose wildly waving hand indicated her urgent need for a bedpan. Dana slid down the bed, abruptly realising that she was worn out. Even talking to her visitors – she could not call them friends – had taken all her strength. Now she would take the doctor's advice and rest. Soon, she slept.

When Dana had been in hospital for a week, James invited Caitlin out for a meal. He had been hinting that there was something he wanted to tell her and Caitlin had hoped he meant to reveal his feelings, for his attentions had become more marked ever since Dana's accident. So after their daily visit to the hospital James told Caitlin that he had booked a table at the Adelphi and did not intend to take no for an answer. 'For a whole week I've been trying to get you to myself,' he grumbled. 'First of all, you've spent every spare moment trying to help Dana to get her memory back. Then you've been fussing round the tea room – or restaurant I should say – trying to persuade the men to get the work finished so that the place can reopen. But now it's my turn. I want to tell you – but no, I won't say another word until we're seated at the table.'

'Sounds nice,' Caitlin said. 'Dana's getting better every time we visit, don't you think? She doesn't mind talking about the tea room – restaurant, I mean – though she still looks puzzled when we try to tell her about the improvements. She'd never heard of a dumb waiter – think of that, dear James!'

James grinned. 'Neither had you, before I told you I was having one put in,' he reminded her.

'Oh well, that was ages ago,' Caitlin said airily. 'I've learned a lot lately. 'The only thing that worries me is that although the restaurant belongs to Dana and me, the staff you've employed will know much more than either of us about catering, particularly about hot food. Oh, I know they served hot food at the Willows, but we just did as we were told when we worked there. Now it's different because we shall be telling other people what to do; people who'll probably know ten times more than we do.'

She spoke as James, a hand on her elbow, was guiding her across the large, softly lit dining room and James shushed her rather peremptorily. 'No talking until we're seated,' he said, pulling out her chair and then taking his place opposite her. 'Ah, here comes the waiter; we'll order, then talk.'

As soon as the man left with their order, James's hands shot across the table and seized Caitlin's. 'I guess you know I want you to marry me,' he said gruffly. 'I'm a plain man and I've been far too busy making my way in the world to consider marriage until now. You're very young and I didn't want to hurry you, but something has happened which changes things. I'm going abroad, dearest Caitlin, and I desperately want to take you with me. I'd like us to marry here – I've got a special licence – but if we can't fit it in, we might have to marry in America; would you object to that?'

Caitlin stared at him, for a moment unable to say a word, and when she did speak her voice shook. 'Oh, James, aren't you taking rather a lot for granted? You've not said you love me, nor why you have to go to America, and you've bought a special licence without even mentioning marriage until now. I'd love to be married, but how can I possibly go off with you and leave Dana, still in hospital, still not knowing who she is? She couldn't possibly manage the restaurant in her present state; even if I was there, things would be very difficult.' She heaved a sigh. 'I wish to God we'd never made the place so big. All we wanted to do was run a nice little tea room, selling tea, coffee and a few snacks. Then you came along with your big ideas, never taking into account the fact that we were just a couple of girls trying to make a living. And now you mean to swan off to the States, with me tucked under your arm like a trophy, leaving Dana to try to control staff who are total strangers and a business we neither of us ever truly wanted – oh, James, how could you?'

James looked stunned, and Caitlin thought that he had never for one moment considered that she might not jump at his handsome offer. But whilst he was still staring at her, a dark and angry look in his eyes, another thought struck her. 'Why are you going to America? According to what you've told me, you're doing awfully well right here in Liverpool. And how will you collect the rents on the property you own in London, and here, when you'll have to cross an ocean to get your money?'

She half expected James to get totally furious, for she knew he hated having to explain himself, but though he sighed wearily he began to answer her pleasantly enough. 'I don't believe I've ever mentioned it before, but when I first started my London business I was in partnership with a feller called Jack Ewing. To tell the truth, we were at school together, and though I knew he was a sharp operator I also knew he'd never cheat me. We started off with a market stall on Petticoat Lane, selling antiques.' He grinned reminiscently. 'I well remember Jack and me making wormholes with an old pair of compasses in a chest of drawers which we told the customer had been made in the time of Queen Anne. He was a Yank – the customer, I mean – and believed whatever he was told, poor sap.

'But there's money to be made in genuine antiques,' he added hastily, no doubt seeing the dismay on Caitlin's face. 'And we soon got into the way of it. Only then we began to buy property, and got up the noses of some cockney gangs . . . we had to sell up and clear out. We split the money and Jack went off to the States whilst I came up to Liverpool, not being too keen to risk every penny I possessed in a strange country. I started buying property up here and did all right, but I don't have Jack's flair. He didn't just buy property, he took on corner sites and turned them, one by one, into milk bars or soda fountains. He's doing brilliantly in New York, but wants to expand. Only for that he needs a partner, since he can't be in two places at once, and that means it's got to be someone who will not only put money into the business but will be totally trustworthy. He asked me weeks ago to consider joining him, but first I had to get together a pretty sizeable sum—'

'If that's the case, then why on earth did you sink so much of your capital in our restaurant?' Caitlin interrupted. 'And you've bought the flat! Oh dear, I wish I understood financial affairs, but I'm afraid I don't.' She brightened. 'Or have you still got enough of your London money left to buy into the partnership?'

James glanced away from her, as though he had no wish to answer her question. 'Where has that bloody waiter gone?' he said resentfully. 'When I order a meal

I expect it to arrive pronto.' And then, seeing Caitlin's eyes still fixed upon him, he spoke once more. 'I've laid out a good deal lately, what with the restaurant and your flat,' he told her. 'However, I've managed to get a buyer for some of my property, which should enable me to raise the necessary.'

Caitlin stared; some feminine intuition told her that he wouldn't have kept putting off speaking to her had he only had good news – marriage plans – to impart. 'Are you trying to tell me you've had to sell our dear little flat?' she said slowly; and then, as light dawned: 'Oh my God, James! You've sold the restaurant! But it's ours – mine and Dana's. Oh, James, how could you?'

'Well, I didn't have much choice,' James said, sounding rather pleased than otherwise, Caitlin realised resentfully. He grinned at her. 'What a clever girl my future wife is, and I thought her just a pretty – well, a beautiful – face! I can see you and I are heading for a fantastic future in the States, little Caitlin!'

But Caitlin knew when she was being patronised and longed for Dana and her quick wits and sharp tongue; Dana would know what to do! James was talking again. 'You see, darling, the restaurant and your smart little flat are easily my best investments and, to be honest, I never thought you and Dana could make a go of the place once it had been enlarged and modernised. You wouldn't have been able to afford the rent, let alone staff salaries . . .'

'But it's *ours*!' Caitlin wailed, feeling tears well up and trickle down her cheeks. Gulping, she tried to speak calmly. 'Cathy's Place was our own little tea room and we were making a go of it, doing well! How could you turn it into a restaurant and then sell it over our heads?

Indeed, how *can* you do so? I'm sure such a thing is illegal! We could take you to court, demand that you give it back . . .'

James wagged a sorrowful head, but Caitlin could see the gleam of wicked amusement in his dark, unfathomable eyes and felt sure he was enjoying her helplessness. 'No use, my dear girl; remember all those papers you signed? You agreed that I should be your business manager and could take decisions on your behalf . . . well, I've received an excellent offer from Mr Porter and the money will be paid into my bank account within the next few days. Everything's signed and sealed; all you've got to do is agree.'

'But I won't agree,' Caitlin said tremulously. 'And what about Dana? She doesn't say much, except that she's beginning to remember things, but she won't agree to your cheating us out of our home and our tea room.'

'Yes, Dana was a big drawback, but her losing her memory couldn't have come at a better moment . . . sorry for her though I am, of course—'

'Oh yes, I can see how sorry you are,' Caitlin said. She jumped to her feet. 'I'm going to see Dana; she'll find a way out of this disgusting tangle. And I wouldn't marry you if you were the last man on earth, so put that in your pipe and smoke it!'

She whipped round, then felt herself grabbed and shaken as though she was a naughty child. Then, in front of all the other diners, James slammed her into her seat and placed both hands on her shoulders, making escape impossible. 'You're going nowhere,' he said rather breathlessly. 'And don't you dare try to walk out on me when I've just ordered our meal! Can't you understand what

I've been saying, you little halfwit? Dana can't do anything, any more than you can. I've secured her future by making it a condition of sale that she shall be employed in the restaurant – good of me, ain't it? And you, darling Caitlin, will be marrying me and coming to the New World to seek your fortune.' He leaned across the table and tried to kiss the tip of her nose, but she jerked her head away. Irritated, he seized her chin and planted a hard kiss on her mouth. 'You're a lucky girl,' he said rather breathlessly. 'A new life, a new country and a man of vision to share it with!'

Caitlin was still fighting tears as the waiter, his face expressionless but his eyes knowing, put their plates down before them. Another waiter, hovering, began to revolve a bottle of wine preparatory to pouring it into their glasses, and Caitlin decided that to make a scene would help neither herself nor Dana. Besides, she realised that she was genuinely frightened of James Mortimer.

As soon as the waiters left, she decided she had better pretend to accept James's proposal of marriage. She wiped her eyes and began to ask him about the new restaurant. She even touched on the possibility of Dana's being given money to start up a tea room once more, but James, apparently believing that she was now totally compliant, shook his head. 'Think of the difficulties you had before you met me,' he pointed out. 'No one would rent property to a couple of girls; it was only myself who decided to take a chance. No, my dear. If you stay in Liverpool it will be to work for someone else, whereas if you come to the States with me the world is your oyster.'

'That is a bloody silly saying,' Caitlin said, suddenly tiring of his attitude. 'Do you know, I've quite lost my appetite?' and with the words, a sudden rage filled her. She picked up her plate with its burden of roast chicken, stuffing and vegetables and flung it straight into her companion's face. James, with food running down his cheeks, jumped to his feet, clearly about to exact revenge, but Caitlin was too quick for him. She was out of the restaurant and running along the pavement before he had taken more than a couple of steps in her direction, and glancing back she saw that his efforts to follow her were being frustrated by the waiter, who was holding his arm and flourishing a bill beneath his nose – a nose which was dripping with gravy.

Caitlin giggled. Where had she got her courage from? She realised she had always been rather afraid of James, but tonight his behaviour, his whole attitude, had caught her on the raw. He had cheated her and lied to her and pretended to be in love with her, but now she knew the truth. She dared not even consider returning to the flat, because he was in such a rage that he might easily become violent and he was a good deal stronger – and nastier – than herself, so rather than cross swords with him again she would sleep on the pavement, or go back to the YWCA and beg them to give her a bed for the night.

Then she remembered her friend. She had said she would go to the hospital and spill the beans, get Dana's advice, and now she would actually do so. James would not dare to storm into a hospital ward and start bullying her. Caitlin saw a tram draw up ahead of her and ran like a hare. Dana would know what to do!

Dana was practising on her crutches, because the staff had said she might go home next day provided she could

95

walk the length of the corridor without stopping or falling over. They were not worried that her memory refused to come out of hiding and said that such things could occur after a spell of concussion, but Caitlin, when she had visited earlier in the evening, had been sure that the sight of their 'lovely little flat', as she put it, would instantly bring everything racing back.

Dana was not so sure, but she knew that being with Caitlin would help her to regain her wretched memory at some point. In a way she dreaded her re-entry into the normal world, but with Caitlin beside her it would be less frightening. The restaurant, however, she viewed with very real fear. If she could not remember how to do such simple tasks as making a cup of tea or baking a scone, how on earth would she behave in a smart restaurant, with staff asking her what they should do? When Caitlin had grumbled that the workmen were taking their time and James should remind them that with every day Cathy's Place remained closed they were all – apart from the construction workers, she supposed – losing money, Dana could only be thankful. Caitlin had warned that the customers who had gone elsewhere might not return, but James had pointed out that the clientele who would come to the restaurant would not be the people who had popped into the tea room for a cup of tea and a bun, and Dana supposed he was right.

She just wished, though, that Caitlin would visit her without dragging James along, for she could not like the man and was pretty sure the feeling was mutual. James pretended friendship, interest, concern, but when he did not know he was being observed Dana sometimes caught a look on his face that made her distinctly uneasy. She thought that he was jealous of Caitlin's affection for herself and would have sacked her had he been in a position to do so. Caitlin had assured her that she, Dana, had been very much in command when they had run Cathy's Place together, but Dana harboured the horrid suspicion that she might have been an expensive luxury and that James, once the place reopened, with many members of staff being experienced caterers, would politely but firmly tell her to go.

She had voiced the thought aloud to her friend when they had visited the hospital lavatories, their one and only chance of a conversation not overheard by James, but Caitlin had reminded her that though James owned the property, the good will in the tea room was theirs and theirs alone. 'And he's no fool; you can't remember, I know, but you were much more . . . oh, more *aware* . . . than me,' she had said. 'You ran things, honest to God you did, alanna. And now stop worrying; one glance round our flat and you'll remember all right.'

So now Dana swung along the corridor on her crutches, stopping occasionally for breath and to exchange a few words with a member of staff or another patient also practising their skill. When the revolving doors in the entrance hall suddenly began to move she did not expect to know the intruder, for visiting time was long over, so she was turning away, executing quite a neat manoeuvre she thought approvingly, when a voice called her name and she glanced over her shoulder to see Caitlin, very red in the face, charging towards her, coatless, hatless, and clearly in a state of considerable perturbation.

'Hello! What's up?' Dana said. 'You look very hot and

bothered. I see you've shed your coat and hat somewhere along the way.'

'Yes – no – oh, we can't talk here. He may have guessed where I've gone,' Caitlin gabbled. 'Let's go back to your ward; he isn't likely to come in there. In fact he won't be allowed to if the staff see him. Come to that, I don't suppose they'd have let me in either, only there aren't many people about. Oh, Dana, do hurry!'

The jerk she gave to Dana's arm nearly had her over. Dana opened her mouth to protest and then saw the frightened look in her friend's eyes as she glanced towards the revolving doors, and decided to say nothing. Caitlin was obviously in the grip of some as yet unexplained fear; she would wait to speak until they were back on the ward.

As soon as they entered the long room, a nurse came up to them, wagging a reproachful finger and reminding them that visiting had finished. Dana opened her mouth to beg that her friend might be allowed to stay for a few moments, but Caitlin cut across her. 'I'm most awfully sorry, nurse, but I really do have to speak to Dana. It's important. And could you make sure that we aren't interrupted by Mr Mortimer? It wouldn't do at all if he were to burst in upon us and discover us exchanging confidences.'

The nurse looked doubtful. 'I really should ask you to leave, Miss Flannagan,' she said. 'As for Mr Mortimer, he most certainly may not enter a women's ward, except at visiting time.' She looked at Dana. 'Is there anything I can do?'

Hastily, Caitlin shook her head. 'No thank you, nurse, but if I stay with Miss McBride here for ten or fifteen minutes it will give Mr Mortimer time to cool down.'

'Oh, I see,' the nurse said, but she still spoke doubtfully. 'I wonder why the receptionist on duty didn't turn you away?'

'She wasn't at her desk,' Caitlin said glibly. 'Thanks very much, nurse. We'll be as quick as we can.'

The nurse made her way back along the ward and the girls perched on Dana's bed. Caitlin began to describe all that had happened that evening, but when she reached the point where she said James was planning to cheat them, Dana slid off the bed with an exclamation. 'Shut up, shut up,' she said, flapping a hand at her friend. 'Oh my God, no wonder James doesn't like me! If you'll just hold your tongue for a moment, I will tell *you* what's been going on. On the day of my accident, the telephone rang in our flat and I picked up the receiver without really thinking, and put it to my ear. Two men were talking about the restaurant – one of them was James and the other, I think, was Herbie Porter. James was saying that when he had cashed the cheque for the money Mr Porter was paying for the restaurant and flat, everything would be settled. He hoped Mr Porter would continue to employ me in the new restaurant – in some menial capacity, I suppose – and as for you, you would be on the way to the United States as his wife!'

Caitlin stared at her, her mouth dropping open. 'You've remembered!' she squeaked. 'Oh, Dana, was that why you fell down the stairs, because you were in such a hurry to tell me we were being cheated?'

Dana put both hands to her head and rumpled her ginger curls. 'I suppose it must have been,' she said slowly. 'Yes, I knew I must get hold of you so we could go to the solicitor, see if we could prevent the sale.' She looked thoughtfully at Caitlin's flushed face. 'So what did James tell you, this evening? The whole story? I take it he did ask you to marry him?'

'Oh, yes, he *asked* me,' Caitlin said bitterly. 'I was so shocked, Dana, that I threw my dinner in his face and lit out while he was still rubbing stuffing out of his eyes.'

Dana stared at her friend with considerable respect. 'You threw your dinner in his face? Oh, Caitlin, you are brave! But where were you? In the flat? Oh, don't say you were in Lyons Corner House!'

'No, we were at the Adelphi,' Caitlin said airily. 'And when James would have followed me, the waiter grabbed him and waved the bill in front of him. I was really grateful because James looked fit to murder, which is why I don't mean to go back to the flat.'

'I don't blame you,' Dana said fervently. 'I've always had a bad feeling about your James, only he was so generous to us at first, buying the butcher's shop and only charging a tiny rent. But I never could trust him. His mouth says one thing whilst his eyes say another, if you understand me.'

'Well I do now, though I took him at face value until this evening,' Caitlin confirmed. 'But what'll we do, Dana? It's a good while since you overheard that telephone conversation – is it too late to stop the sale?'

'I doubt if we could do that, no matter how quickly we acted. Can you see a solicitor taking our side against Mr Porter? I imagine that since it is he who now owns the restaurant, our grievance will be against him rather than James.'

Caitlin sighed. 'I don't know a thing about business, but I know when I'm being cheated and I know by whom,' she said wearily. 'I've not told you yet, but apparently, when we signed all those papers saying that we were agreeable to the improvements being made to the restaurant, we were also signing for James to become our business manager and, when necessary, to take decisions without consulting us. So where does that leave us? He knows no one will rent to us so we can start up in business again – he actually said so, with a smirk. Oh, how I hate that man!'

'So do I, but I don't think you need worry that he'll try to pursue you tonight,' Dana said, after sitting for a moment in frowning thought. 'He won't hang about to find himself embroiled in a legal tangle. I don't say the law would make him retract the sale or give us all the money, but it would certainly insist that he cough up for the goodwill, and possibly for breaching the terms of our lease. So I reckon by the time the banks open tomorrow, he'll have left his flat and be aboard a transatlantic liner, even if he has to sign on as a cabin boy!'

Caitlin laughed and gave her friend an impulsive hug. 'With his pockets stuffed with bank notes,' she said gaily. 'Oh, Dana, nothing seems so terrible now that you've got your memory back! I suppose we could work at the Willows again if the worst came to the worst, but I hope it won't come to that. If I wasn't such a coward I'd go round to his place and insist that I accompany him to the bank tomorrow, so that he can pay me in actual cash for our share of the business, but I *am* a coward, I fear.'

'I tell you what, you could linger outside his flat tomorrow and follow him when he goes out – keeping well back, of course,' Dana said. 'Then when he goes into the bank and begins to draw out his money, you can say you've come for our share.'

'I suppose I could, but I'm just afraid he'd turn round and either murder me or pretend I was planning to steal from him,' Caitlin said gloomily. 'But I'll come to the hospital first thing, and if they'll release you we can both go to his flat and then to Mr Porter at the restaurant.'

'Agreed,' Dana said. 'Yes, that's fine; after all, he can't eat us. You must go home, Caitlin, because you can't sleep on the streets and even the YW won't welcome you at this time of night. Remember there's only one entrance to the flat and James doesn't have a key. Once you're inside, you can slide the bolts across to make doubly sure you're not disturbed. But no matter how much he disliked having food thrown in his face, I don't think James will want to have anything more to do with either of us. You'll be safe in the flat till morning.'

After her friend had left, Dana lay down on her hospital bed, thinking ruefully that her mind was too full to sleep. Presently, almost with a sense of adventure, she began to go over the events that had occurred since she and Caitlin had met and taken up their new lives in Liverpool. Inevitably, thoughts of the tea room and the way they had been treated could not be banished entirely, so she bent her mind to the last thing she remembered before she had had her accident. Yes, everything was there: the pot of tea and the plate of cheese and pickle sandwiches she had made for her lunch. The number of times she had shifted all the furniture one way or another so that the twin beds, when they were delivered, would be able to pass through the kitchen, across the hall and into the bedroom without hindrance. But the beds had not arrived, so when she had heard the telephone bell she had assumed, not unnaturally, that it would be either Caitlin, demanding to know what had happened to their new furniture, or the shop itself apologising for the delay in delivery. Instead, however, she had heard a conversation most definitely not intended for her ears; heard how James and even Mr Porter had plotted against two young girls who had trusted them. She had heard their receivers go down and had almost dropped hers, for her hand had been slippery with perspiration.

But she had known she must contact Caitlin at once; tell her what was being planned. All thoughts of beds and deliveries had flown out of her head. She had fairly erupted out of the kitchen door, heedless of the cold rain which soaked her in seconds. She had felt her foot slip, had tried to grab the metal banister, and then there had been an excruciating pain in her leg and something had hit the back of her head, plunging her into darkness. After that had come a daze of semi-wakening, so that she felt the rain on her face and the cobbles beneath her back. She had grown cold, cold as death, and had drifted into unconsciousness once more, only to wake to see blue skies arching over her and feel the softness of grass beneath her. For a moment she even felt the warmth of the sun on her bare arms, but then she was back on the cobbles with the rain and the pain.

Dana frowned, trying to dismiss her confused recollection of her accident. Green grass? Warmth? Sunshine even? Oh, she must have dreamed the whole. But what pleasure such a dream could bring after so much cruel reality! She cuddled into her hospital pillow and tried to banish thought, memories – the past, in fact. Soon, she slept.

Chapter Four

The sun, peeping through the ill-fitting curtains at the window of Dana's rented room, woke her even before her alarm had gone off. For a moment she lay there, wondering why she felt rather pleased with life. Of course it might be just the sunshine, because although August was not yet over they had had a pretty poor summer. What were she and Caitlin planning to do today? She frowned with the effort of memory. Ever since her accident her mind had seemed sluggish, but her leg, now long out of plaster, was very much better, the muscles stronger and the skin no longer white and wasted. So just what was making her feel almost jolly, if it was not just the sunshine?

Abruptly, her memory kicked in. The girl at the labour exchange had got her an interview later today with the owner of a small tea room, who wanted someone – on a part-time basis, unfortunately – to do just about any job which came to hand. Caitlin had had a few waitressing jobs but had lost them through bad time-keeping, or bursting into tears in front of astonished customers. In fact Dana herself had got pretty fed up with her onetime partner, who had been given to frequent storms of weeping, wailing and gnashing of teeth over James

Mortimer's defection, blaming herself for introducing Mortimer to Dana, though, as Dana was tired of pointing out, had she not done so they would never have opened Cathy's Place.

Today, however, Dana decided she would have to have a serious talk with her partner. To be sure, they had been treated abominably, for James and Mr Porter had signed contracts without so much as mentioning either girl's name, and this meant that they had no claim whatsoever on the restaurant, or the flat.

But Dana decided that today she would tell Caitlin severely that it was pointless crying over spilt milk and warn her that she must put the past behind her and start living for the future. Of course, she had done so many times already and Caitlin always said that she would try to pull herself together, but on this particular day, if Dana got the job at the tea room, she intended to suggest that Caitlin should apply for any waiting on job coming up there in the near future. Caitlin was more than pretty, she was downright beautiful, and if only she would smile and speak cheerfully there was absolutely no reason why she too might not be taken on eventually. Even the half-promise of work might take Caitlin's mind off her misery, which had to be a good thing.

The alarm clock situated between the two beds gave a small despairing tinkle and Dana, frowning, swung her legs off the mattress, put on her slippers and stared hard at the clock's small face. Had she forgotten to wind it up last night? She must not do so again, for most employers these days insisted on their staff being early for work. She swished back the curtains and went across to the other bed, a hand raised to grab Caitlin's shoulder, then stopped short. The bed was empty.

Dana stood rooted to the spot. Her friend was not an early riser, would use anything as an excuse to remain in her bed, so why . . . but then Dana saw, pinned to the pillow, a brown envelope with *Dana McBride* written upon it in Caitlin's rather round and childish hand.

Dana's heart descended into her scuffed slippers. She grabbed the envelope with a shaking hand, tore it open, sat down on her bed and began to read.

Dear Dana,

Oh, I know you're going to be so cross but I can't help it, indeed, indeed I can't. Ever since James left and we lost the restaurant I've been miserable, and I do so hate being unhappy. I didn't tell you, but a couple of weeks ago I wrote to my sister – not the one who stole my feller – and asked her what she thought I should do. The postman brought a letter a week ago, only you'd already gone out, so I read it all by myself. Oh, Dana, Catherine was so wonderful. She said I was to come home right away because I was sorely missed. She sent money for my fare and said Felix O'Hara talked of nothing but how he wished I'd come home, and of course Mammy and Daddy are desperate to get me back. I'm a big coward and always have been so I said nothing to you but just kept wondering what to do for the best. I thought and thought because I knew I'd be letting you down, Dana, if I left, but in the end I made up my mind and I put all my savings in that little blue velvet bag which you admired once and left it for

106

you; it's in the top drawer of the dressing table. Don't be angry with me. As soon as I get home I'll write to let you know I'm safe. Then you can write back and tell me how you're going on.

I wish you'd come back to Ireland with me, but I know you won't. You're so stubborn, Dana, and anyway if I'm honest I know you'll be better off without me. I've not had one decent job since James took off for the States, so I've only managed to pay my share of the rent from the money my uncle gave us and that's running out fast. In fact after I bought my ticket on the ferry I put the rest into the blue velvet bag so I'm penniless! Say you forgive me, darling Dana! You are my best friend but I don't have your strength. I hate being poor. Sorry, sorry, sorry.

Love, Caitlin

Dana felt hot rage welling up in her breast and tore the letter across and across, then thought better of it, and sat holding the pieces in her hand until common sense reasserted itself. After all, she had known for ages that Caitlin was deeply unhappy and longed to return to her home and family. I knew it, but I was just as scared as she was of being poor and having no family behind me, she told herself, as her initial hurt and rage slowly ebbed into a sort of resigned acceptance. I'm not really strong, it's just that I burnt my boats when I left in a way which Caitlin did not. She ran away because it turned out that her lover didn't love her after all. I ran away because I felt everyone had turned against me, as well as against my dearest daddy. I always meant to go back one day, when I had proved that I could manage without them, and perhaps I really will. But that day hasn't come yet and unless I pull myself together right away it never will.

Dana jumped to her feet. So get going, Dana McBride, she told herself. Go for the interview, be as charming as you know how, impress the lady who owns the tea room with your efficiency, be nice to the staff – yes, you can be very charming when you try – and then look round for another part-time job because once you're working six days a week you may actually begin to save towards a place of your own.

The previous evening she had filled a bucket with water and now she washed and then ran into the other room, filled the kettle, lit the Primus, put the kettle over the flame and cut some bread and butter whilst waiting for it to boil. As she ate her breakfast – bread, jam and tea – she reminded herself that Caitlin was right about one thing: she, Dana, would be better off without her friend in many ways. Caitlin's eternal tearful grumbling had been beginning to get her down and the fact that Caitlin had had several quite good jobs but had lost all of them without apparently caring at all had also annoyed her.

But right now she had no time to dwell on the rights and wrongs of Caitlin's flight. Instead she checked her appearance in the mirror, decided she would stand as much chance as anyone else of getting the position and set off towards the tram stop. As she went she wondered just who Felix O'Hara was. When they had first joined forces Caitlin had chattered of the many friends and admirers she had had in Ireland. Dana had stopped listening but now she supposed that Caitlin must have mentioned a Felix but that she, Dana, had stopped attending by the time his name had come up in conversation.

As the tram drew up beside her and Dana hopped aboard it occurred to her that the next few days, or even weeks, would be strange, for she would be entirely alone. Of course if she got the job there would be other people around her all day, but when at home – if you could call two miserable rented rooms home – she would be quite alone in a way she had never been before.

The conductor came to collect her fare and Dana reflected that she would walk home, thus saving tuppence. I shall like being alone, she told herself as the tram swayed and creaked along the busy street. It will be a change, and a change for the better, furthermore. I was fond of Caitlin – we were like sisters – but I could sense that a row was brewing over her determination to feel hard done by. Of course she was absolutely right, we were treated disgracefully by both James Mortimer and Mr Porter, but in one way Caitlin was a good deal luckier than I. When we went to that solicitor to ask if we could get compensation for what we put into the business, he managed to get most of the money her uncle had sent her back on the strength of his letter, which named the sum he was putting into our venture. It was a good thing Caitlin had hung on to it.

Dana sighed. She had never grudged Caitlin the money, but now she realised that it had not been helpful to either of them, because it had meant that her friend did not have to work. She paid her share of the rent out of that money whenever she lost a job, which was often, so perhaps the solicitor had done neither of them a good turn when he had handed back her uncle's investment.

The tram screeched to a halt and Dana got down. She gave the conductor a cheerful smile, but he was busy with his ticket machine and did not notice. Dana set off along the pavement rehearsing what she would say about her previous experience in catering, only first she would have to take the measure of her would-be employer. Some people resented the fact that she had run Cathy's Place; as usual, she had best play it by ear. Squaring her shoulders, Dana began to walk up the hill towards her destination.

The interview was satisfactory and Dana could have got the job, but, regretfully, she had to turn it down. Miss Brown, who owned the café, wanted someone who would stand in for her whenever she had business elsewhere and this meant that Dana would not be able to take on any other sort of work, since Miss Brown expected to be able to call on her at a moment's notice. If the pay had been good it might not have mattered so much, but when Miss Brown told Dana the rates of pay the younger girl realised she could not even make her rent. Regretfully, she told Miss Brown that it was out of the question. She must have either regular hours or an enormous increase in wages.

Miss Brown, who had been charming until then, immediately turned very nasty indeed, claiming that Dana had wasted her whole morning and saying rather spitefully that she had only offered Dana the job out of pity. Dana thought of several sharp retorts but used none of them, telling herself that Miss Brown might one day need someone to fill a full-time post and it would be best if she remembered Dana as someone who accepted defeat gracefully rather than being quick with a sharp retort.

Considerably chastened by this experience, Dana was returning to the tram stop when she saw a blue-painted fascia board with a name written upon it which she recognised. *The Modern*, it said. Dana stopped short, crossed the road and stood outside the café. Sure enough, in the right-hand corner of the big plate glass window was a small, hand-printed notice: *Staff Wanted*.

Dana hesitated. Only the previous week Caitlin had been a waitress at the Modern, but she had left after only three days saying that the proprietor wanted to get blood out of a stone, expected his staff to work like slaves for a pittance, and even tried to take the waitresses' tips if he spied a sixpence or a threepenny joe tucked under a plate, as yet unnoticed by the girl who had served that table.

Dana bent and looked hard at the notice, then smiled to herself. She remembered Caitlin telling her that, because of Mr Gillingham's nasty temper, the card in the window was a permanent fixture. His staff, apart from one or two elderly regulars, were forever leaving, vowing that they would find easier or at any rate more congenial work elsewhere.

As a rule, Dana had been annoyed with Caitlin when she left a job without giving notice, but on the occasion of her leaving the Modern Dana had been in sympathy with her friend. She had called for Caitlin after work a couple of times and had seen how Mr Gillingham had shouted and threatened to reduce wages simply because someone could not carry more than half a dozen of the big dinner plates at any one time.

Still, a job was a job. At least this one would be full-time which would mean she could pay the rent of her two rooms at 5 Temperance Court even if it meant living on bread and jam and cups of weak tea. And then there might be other jobs; one thing often leads to another, and if she could assure a would-be employer that she had stuck conditions at the Modern for some considerable time she might get work that was both better paid and pleasanter; perhaps even as a nippy at Lyons Corner House.

So Dana put on her brightest smile and entered the café. She went straight to the counter, and as soon as the lady in the cash desk turned to her, eyebrows rising, she spoke boldly. 'I come about the advertisement in the window—' she began, and the woman interrupted immediately.

'Oh, aye: Mr Gillingham told me earlier that one o' the waitresses hadn't turned in. I tek it you're used to waiting on? The pay ain't bad . . . But wharr am I thinkin' of?' She got laboriously to her feet and seizing Dana's arm led her through the swing door and into the kitchen.

The proprietor, a short fat man who wheezed as he spoke, turned at their entrance. 'What's this, Annie?' he said breathlessly. 'You know you ain't supposed to bring customers—'

The elderly lady interrupted him. 'She ain't a customer. She's come about the waitressin' job.' She turned to Dana. 'Or was it the kitchen job?'

The proprietor's eyes, which had been roving around the room, fastened upon Dana's face and narrowed. 'Aha!

I s'pose you've come to tell me how she were took ill, which were why she let me down last week,' he said. 'Well you can tell her from me to bleedin' well forget it. Ho yes, I reckernise you, what thinks yourself so smart and grand! Why, I wouldn't have her back, nor I wouldn't have her pal in my café, not if you was to pay me a hundred pound.'

Dana began to reply, cursing her carroty crop which made her so instantly recognisable, but the man cut across her words. 'If she were to come in here this minute wanting her precious job back I'd not tek her on. If you asks me, it were her what walked off with me petty cash, to say nothin' of a whole steak and kidney pie. If I so much as sees her in the street she'll find herself in a prison cell before she's blinked twice. Bleedin' little thief, just because she's pretty as a picture . . .' he glared at Dana, 'which you ain't, bein' plain as a pikestaff and ginger as – as a tomcat,' he added nastily. 'I bleedin' well bet you'd not bring in a single customer. One thing I will say, young Kate had fellers round her like bees round a honey pot, which is always good for business.'

Dana considered arguing, then realised it would get her nowhere and decided on a polite acceptance of his decision. 'You're very right, Mr Gillingham; I certainly don't have my friend Caitlin's allure,' she said pleasantly. 'And of course you're also right, I do have red hair – ginger if you prefer – and am plain as a pikestaff . . .' she looked him critically up and down, 'but you're no oil painting yourself.' She turned quickly to make her escape in case he might decide to try to give her a clip round the ear, for he looked quite angry enough.

Hurrying away, she was tempted to go back to her rooms, but decided that since she needed work she would look around her first. It was a lovely day, with warm sunshine and a gentle breeze, and for some reason her short, sharp encounter with the owner of the Mod, as the customers called it, had given her confidence. He had been hateful, and she had just laughed. Yes, today was a good day to begin searching for work.

When September came, a good deal of Dana's bright optimism had begun to fade, for well-paid work was continuing to elude her. True, she no longer had to draw the dole, for she had various little jobs which together paid her enough to live on. She cleaned the Pitch-Pine pub three days a week – after closing time, of course – and quite enjoyed the work because the barmaids and barmen were friendly and the landlady gave her any unsold sandwiches or pies which she thought would not go another day. Then there was the fish stall in the Great Charlotte Street market. She worked there Fridays and Saturdays, holding down the job without difficulty, for no one else wanted to smell of fish, particularly on a Saturday evening when they were bound for a dance hall or a date at the flicks.

Dana had tried to get waitress or even kitchen work, but, according to employers, business was bad. Folk who normally bought themselves a hot dinner at midday were making do with sandwiches, so the catering trade was suffering. Dana had met a waitress she had known when she worked at the Willows, and the woman had told her that the staff had been asked to accept a cut in wages 'until things were better'.

'But the work's no easier. When someone leaves, old Lionel won't replace 'em; he just expects us to work longer and harder,' she had said and Dana had sighed sympathetically.

'What does the Hag have to say about it?' she had asked, remembering how dictatorial the old cook had been. 'I bet *she* hasn't had to take a cut in wages!'

The other woman had stared. 'Ain't you heard?' she had asked incredulously. 'Old Lionel give her the sack, the old heave-ho. She don't work at the Willows no more, which is another reason why trade's bad, if you want my opinion.'

'What's the new cook like?' Dana had asked, wondering aloud whether she should approach the Dining Rooms now that Mrs Haggerty was no longer in charge, but the waitress had pulled a doubtful face.

'You could try, but Mrs Griffiths is one o' them what's gorra funny old temper,' she had warned. 'Tell you what, pop in of a Saturday, near on closing time. She's sometimes in a better mood when she can see her day off a-comin' up.'

So now it was Saturday and Dana was hurrying home to her rooms. The kitchen of the Willows always smelled of food, but she did not mean to lose the chance of a full-time job because she reeked of fish. Her employer at the Charlotte Street market had been happy to let her leave early for once since there was virtually nothing left on the stall, save for a handful of brown shrimps and a couple of plaice, so she would be able to clean down with only her ten-year-old nephew's assistance. 'And you can take the plaice and the shrimps for your tea tonight,' her employer had added, grinning toothlessly at Dana. 'You're a good lass; see you next Friday!'

Now, Dana pulled the string to bring up the key which unlocked the front door of No. 5. She had the large room on the ground floor, which in happier times had been the kitchen, and a tiny slip of a room not much bigger than a pantry, in which she slept. Now she opened the door, slung her coat and hat on the peg and picked up the large tin bucket beneath the kitchen table. She usually filled it up with water before she left for work, but she had been late waking, so now she carried the bucket into the yard, filled it from the big brass tap and returned to her rooms. She had a quick wash, put on a clean dress, tied back her hair with a blue ribbon and checked her reflection in the small mirror which Caitlin had left behind when she went. Deciding she looked tidy enough to satisfy even Mr Lionel should he be still on the premises, she put her coat and hat back on and left.

As she turned into the Willow's jigger, she began to notice an odd sort of smell. Having sniffed thoughtfully, she decided it must be coming from the restaurant's kitchens. She wrinkled her nose; Mrs Haggerty, old wretch though she was, would never have let the kitchens smell so horrid. Oh, she would not have traced the pong herself, but she would have sent her minions scurrying into every corner until the source of the smell was detected and done away with.

Dana swung along the jigger, pushed open the door into the Willows' yard, then stopped. Someone was emerging from the kitchens, someone small and fair, someone crying bitterly. Dana shrank against the dustbins, not wanting to embarrass the other girl, then recognised her. 'Polly!' she gasped. 'Oh, my dear Polly, whatever has happened? Are you hurt?'

Polly knuckled her eyes, produced a bit of rag from a pocket and blew her nose vigorously, trying to hide her tears as she did so, and keeping her gaze on the ground. 'It ain't nothin',' she said gruffly. 'Who's you, anyway? If Mr Lionel cotched you in his yard, you'd be in dead trouble, like what I am.' She hiccuped pathetically, then raised her tear-drenched eyes to the other girl's face, her mouth rounding with astonishment. 'Dana!' she exclaimed. 'Oh, it's you! But they said as how you and Caitlin had gone back to Ireland!'

'Well, Caitlin has gone back to Ireland, but I'm still here,' Dana said cheerfully. She put her arms round Polly's thin shoulders and gave her a hug. 'Come on, tell me why you're crying like a fountain.'

Polly, whose tears had miraculously stopped flowing, immediately began to weep again. 'She give me the push,' she said bitterly, through her tears. 'Old Ma Griffiths, I mean. She said I were late this mornin' but I weren't, honest to God I weren't . . .'

The tears began to flow more copiously than ever and Dana tightened her hold on the younger girl's shoulders. 'So you've lost your job, but you'll soon find another,' she said. 'It's not the end of the world, Poll. Look at me – I've lost a whole tea room, to say nothing of my best friend, but I'm pulling myself up by my boot straps and mean to start up again one day.'

'But they'll kick me out of me lodgings if I can't pay the rent, and I ain't got no money, norra penny piece,' Polly wailed. 'I axed the old griffin – that's what we call old Ma Griffiths when she ain't listenin', which ain't often – if I could have the wages owed, and she said she wouldn't give me nothin'. But I'm sixteen now, too old for

117

the girls' home, so I moved into these lodgings a fortnight back . . . the woman what runs 'em is a right terror, she'd see me sleep on the street sooner than wait for the dole to come through – if they pays dole to someone my age, that is. Oh, Dana, what'll I do?'

'Well, for a start you can come back with me to my rooms and I'll buy us both fish and chips and we'll share a pot of tea and talk about jobs,' Dana said. 'Would you like that? My rooms aren't much, but . . .'

'I'd love it,' Polly said eagerly. She looked shyly up at Dana. 'I used to watch you and Caitlin through the winder when you had the tea room, and when it was bein' turned into a restaurant I follered you and saw you goin' into a flat on Wentworth Street. Only after a few weeks, when I didn't see you working in the restaurant, I went to the door of the flat to ask how you was gettin' on and a big fat woman in a fancy apron answered. I axed her if she knew where you'd gone, but she just said "Back to Ireland" and shut the door in me face, so a'course I believed her and never looked for you no more.'

'Well, never mind,' Dana said. She sniffed. 'I was going to ask your Mrs Griffiths if she could do with another kitchen worker or a waitress, but if she's in a mood to sack you I doubt she'd consider taking anyone else on. I say, Poll, what's that awful smell? I was just thinking that the Hag would never have stood for it.'

Polly sniffed too, then shook her head. 'I dunno,' she admitted. 'But do let's gerrout of here! The Griffin might pop out o' the kitchen door any minute.'

Dana agreed to this and the two of them hurried out of the yard, along the jigger and on to the main road, but when at last they reached Temperance Court Polly tugged at her companion's arm. 'The smell's bad here, too,' she hissed. 'What've you gorrin your coat pocket, Dana? I *think* the pong's comin' from you!'

Dana was about to refute this calumny indignantly when she plunged a hand into her pocket and felt the paper-wrapped plaice fillets and brown shrimps. Giggling, she told Polly she was sure the fish had been fresh when the stallholder had given it to her, but in the warmth of her pocket it had begun to smell very fishy indeed. And this was soon proved correct when the girls looked behind them and realised they were being closely followed by half a dozen mangy-looking cats. Dana began to laugh, then tossed the fish down on the cobbles. The cats were on it like lightning, and it was with considerably lighter hearts – and in Dana's case pocket – that the two girls entered the house.

Dana unlocked and ushered her unexpected guest inside, where Polly immediately began to admire the room and the way Dana had furnished it. To make it seem more like a living room and less like a kitchen Dana had bought old basket chairs which were quite comfy, and the plain deal table was hidden by a lace cloth. Polly agreed with Dana that it was a pity there was no running water and no electricity or gas laid on, but thought the round blue bowl standing on the side table was ideal for washing up dirty dishes, the paraffin stove would throw out a good heat in winter and candle or lamp light was much prettier – and cheaper – than electricity would have been. Dana had grown fond of her room and was usually glad to be alone in it when her day's work, whatever that might be, was done, but now she found Polly's admiration very heart-warming, and instead of being slightly ashamed of the shifts she had to employ to get a hot meal occasionally she felt proud of her ingenuity.

When she had first come to England she had not been able to cook, but once she and Caitlin had opened the tea room it had been only common sense to bake their own bread, cakes and scones. There had seemed no possibility of baking in this room, however, until she had remembered her mother's camp oven, which they had taken on picnics or shooting parties. It was simply a tin box which would stand over a fire or on top of a paraffin stove, and could be used to bake bread, scones or pies, though one had to watch it carefully for it was a tricky business getting the temperature right.

Polly gazed at the camp oven with awe, as indeed she had gazed at everything: the rag rugs on the floor, the pretty curtains at the window, which had once been an evening dress, sold by Mrs Capper of Paddy's market for two shillings and converted into curtains with much painful labour, for Dana was no seamstress. There were pictures on the walls, and Dana even showed Polly the colourful chamber pot which matched the basin and ewer on the elderly marble-topped washstand and made it unnecessary to go to the outside privy when the rain was tipping down or the cobbles were covered with ice.

'Oh, Dana, you've made it lovely. Ain't you clever?' Polly exclaimed. 'If I ever get a room of me own, I'll do it up just like this one. They never taught us nothing useful at the home, 'cept how to hem sheets and knit squares for blankets.' She walked over to the pictures on the wall. 'Ain't these lovely! Oh, I wish I lived in the country! Where's they of?'

Dana winced. 'Where are the scenes they show, you

mean,' she corrected. 'To be honest, Poll, I don't really know. They might be figments of the artist's imagination, but myself, I think they're real places. They're only prints, of course, but I liked them so much that I bought them with money I should've put in my savings account.'

'Oh, I like them too, and I'm sure they're real places, not figgywotsits,' Polly said, her nose only an inch away from the nearest picture. 'I bet they're all places in Ireland; Ireland's beautiful. We had a teacher when I were in the home what came from Kerry, and he said Ireland was the most beautiful place in the whole world.'

'So it is,' Dana said unguardedly and immediately wished she had not, for it laid her open to Polly's next question.

The younger girl turned away from the pictures and fixed her wide blue gaze on her friend. 'Why *did* you leave, Dana?' she asked curiously. 'Caitlin told everyone that she left because her sister stole her feller, but I never heered you say anything about your home or your fambly.'

'I left because Ireland is a poor country with very little to offer in the way of employment,' Dana said slowly. 'After my father died I had to earn my own living, so I came to Liverpool to find work. The rest is history.'

'Didn't you have no brothers or sisters?' Polly asked, but before Dana could answer the younger girl smacked her own hand and grinned ruefully at her companion. 'Oh, I's real sorry Dana. If you'd have wanted to tell folks, then you'd have done it months ago. Don't you heed me, queen; all Scousers is nosy by nature.'

Dana got to her feet. 'It's all right, but I don't like to think about the past. And now how about those fish 'n' chips? The shop on the corner said *Frying at six*, so I reckon if we go right away we'll be at the head of the queue.'

Later, when the fish and chips were only a memory and the washing up and clearing away had been done, the girls sat in the basket chairs whilst Dana read aloud the job advertisements in that night's *Echo*. After a while, however, Polly sighed and got to her feet. 'It's time I were off,' she said sadly. 'You've done me a power o' good, Dana; thanks ever so. But I'd better see if I can gerra bed in the YW, just for tonight, you know. And on Monday I'll try for some of them jobs you read out an' I made a note of.' She went across the room and took her coat from the hook near the door. 'I'll let you know how I gerron. Cheerio for now.'

Dana opened her mouth to wish Polly luck and say goodbye, and found quite different words emerging. 'Oh, Poll, there's no need for that. I sold Caitlin's bed, I'm afraid, but we could top to toe it in mine if you like. And I do think we should go to your lodgings and explain what's happened to your landlady; no point in her calling out the scuffers to find her missing tenant when you're with me. Then, with tomorrow being Sunday, the two of us can take a walk along all the busiest streets. Most shopkeepers put a card in their window when they want staff, so you never know, we might both get fixed up.'

Polly, halfway into her coat, struggled out of it and flung it on the floor. Then she ran over to Dana, a huge smile breaking out on her small face. 'Oh, Dana, you are good,' she gasped, grabbing her companion's hands and squeezing them so hard that Dana squeaked. 'Ever since Myra left the Willows – she gorra job aboard

122

a transatlantic liner, lucky old Myra – I've not had a girlfriend to tell me troubles to, and though Ernie – d'you remember Ernie? – is a grand pal, it ain't the same somehow.' She hesitated and Dana saw some of the pleasure and excitement drain from her face. 'But are you sure you want to share?' she asked anxiously. 'I knows you shared wi' Caitlin, but she were posh, like what you are. I'm not. I'm nothin'.'

When Dana had first made the suggestion she had done it simply to help the other girl, but now she realised that she missed Caitlin's company more than she had ever allowed herself to admit. She had truly enjoyed Polly's visit and knew life would be a lot more fun if it was shared with another girl. To be sure, she and Caitlin had been of an age and Polly was only just sixteen, but she was streetwise in a way that Dana herself was not. So she smiled reassuringly at her friend, thinking even as she did so that Polly looked more like a twelve-year-old child than a young woman. 'You're certainly *not* nothing; you're a broth of a girl so you are,' she said in a stage Irish accent. 'We'll be pals and partners from this moment on, and if ever we have enough money to start our own tea room I'm sure, together, we'll make a success of it.' She shot out a hand and Polly seized it at once. 'Shake, partner!'

Dana and Polly stayed up far later than either would have done under normal circumstances, but at last they stopped chattering and got into their nightgowns. They had visited Polly's landlady, an unpleasant steely-eyed woman in her fifties, who had actually demanded that Polly should pay her a full week's money since one of her beds would now be unoccupied. But Polly, flushed with the triumph of one who has made her arrangements and need no longer fear sleeping on the streets, would have none of it. 'I paid you a week in advance, so I owes you nothin',' she had said briskly. 'And you'll let that bed by noon tomorrer, Sunday or no Sunday. Just remember, I could've lit out and left you wonderin' whatever had become of me, 'cept me pal here thought it weren't fair on you.'

The landlady would probably have argued, but Dana had seized Polly's skinny little arm and the two of them had headed back to Temperance Court, heedless of the woman's turkeycock gobbling as she shouted abuse after them before banging her door with enough force, Polly said, to break its hinges.

Now, however, safely tucked up at opposite ends of the single bed, with Polly using a cushion for a pillow and Dana feeling all the satisfaction of one who has done a generous act and been thanked for it, the girls snuggled down. 'Oh, Dana, today's the best thing that's ever happened to me, and I thought it were goin' to be the worst,' Polly said ecstatically. 'It makes me think o' somethin' that teacher I told you about used to say.' She clasped her hands and closed her eyes, as though to conjure up the teacher's very words: '*When one door closes, another opens*. Oh, ain't that so true!'

And that, Dana thought long afterwards, was where it all began.

Chapter Five

The dream began at once, the scene instantly recognisable. Dana found herself standing in the wilderness that had once been the rose garden. She glanced around her; great leggy roses, taller than herself, reached for the sky and the sweet scent of them mingled with that of a large rosemary bush which stretched across the weedy bed. Ivy had its stranglehold on once beautiful shrubs and trees, and the gravel paths were green with grass, gold with buttercups and white with daisies. But the wilderness was not her destination; her hand was already on the latch of the green door in the high brick wall which surrounded the McBrides' kitchen garden. She pushed open the door a crack and listened intently, but could hear no sound. Cautiously, she pushed the door wider, smiling to herself as it swung soundlessly beneath her hand. She and Con had oiled the hinges only the previous day so they could nip in and help themselves to a few strawberries or a pod of peas without the betraying shriek which the hinges had previously given. The kitchen garden was old Arthur's pride and joy, so if he was already at work she would offer to give him a hand, but she knew the old man always went along to the house first where her mother would make him tea and a couple of thick bacon sandwiches, saying that at Arthur's age one should never start work on an empty stomach.

Dana had been woken early by the sunshine stealing through a gap in her bedroom curtains and falling across her face, and had crept down the winding spiral stair leading to the kitchen. The room had been quiet and deserted, the gingham curtains still drawn across and the fire in the Aga just a dull glow. In the middle of the table was a loaf of her mother's homemade bread and a pat of butter, and this gave her an idea. She loved radishes, especially the long red and white ones which had a peppery bite of their own, her father always said. If she could just sneak into Arthur's garden she could help herself to a bunch of radishes, go back to the kitchen and make a large and delicious sandwich, well salted, and eat it sitting on the mounting block in the stable yard, waiting for Con to wake up to the new day.

But since the kitchen was empty and her mother was not yet up, Arthur was scarcely likely to be about; she would be pretty safe to push the green door wider yet and enter his territory. She did so, casting a guilty glance around her, and then headed straight for the fruit cage in one corner. She was not here for the fruit, but perhaps she would just take one or two . . . she reached the cage and saw fat, scarlet strawberries glowing amidst their dark green foliage. A blackbird, squeezed against the wire netting with his beak buried deep in a berry, gave a startled squawk and made off at the sight of her. Dana laughed, inserted her fingers through the wire, picked the damaged fruit and tossed it gently along the gravelled path, then watched the blackbird come cautiously down, seize the berry and make off, no doubt to feed his fledglings. Only then did she pluck a fruit for herself and pop it into her mouth. Delicious! But they would have strawberries for tea today so it would not be fair to take more than a couple. She did wonder whether to pick some for Con but decided against it. He was quite capable of stealing his own fruit, she thought with a grin, though Johnny Devlin, Con's father, was a far stricter parent than her own daddy. But perhaps that was because her parents owned Castletara and Johnny Devlin, though Don McBride's partner in the horse breeding business, also acted as his head groom and had the flat above the stables as a part of his wages.

Now that she was in the garden and could see for herself that no one lurked in the raspberry canes or behind the gooseberry bushes, Dana returned to close the green door as softly as she had opened it. Then she headed for the salad bed. Old Arthur was meticulous; worth his weight in gold, her daddy said. The salad bed fairly bristled with different types of lettuce, a cucumber frame, great swags of tomatoes, their colour ranging from palest green to a deep, dramatic scarlet, a whole row of spring onions and, oh bliss, another one of radishes. Dana bent down and began to pull until she held a sizeable bunch. She was wearing her oldest riding breeches and a shirt which had once belonged to her daddy, and found when she tried to cram the radishes into the breeches' pocket that she had picked too many. She top and tailed a couple, rubbed them on the seat of her pants and crammed them into her mouth. Then she twisted the leaves off the rest of the bunch and was looking around for somewhere to hide the evidence when the door in the high brick wall began to open and a voice spoke behind her. Quickly, she threw the radish leaves into the box hedge which surrounded the salad patch and turned as though she were about to leave, whistling a tune beneath her breath. It was not Arthur who entered, however, but Con, and as soon as he saw her he grinned, his dark eyes knowing.

'You rotten thief. I'll tell Arthur who's been after his . . .' his calculating gaze swept over her, 'strawberries. Not the poor blackbirds, which get the blame when someone – no names, no pack drill – manages to get inside the fruit cage, but the young divil herself.'

'Well, you're wrong, Mr Know-all. Mammy's having a strawberry tea for the Ladies' Sewing Circle this afternoon, and I wouldn't risk spoiling that,' Dana said righteously.

'You're a little goody-goody,' Con said automatically. He came over and flicked a hand at her dirt-smeared breeches. 'If not strawberries . . . could it be peas?' His grin became wider. 'I'm partial to a few pods meself; what say we go shares?'

'If I'd been stealing stuff I dare say I'd go shares, but I haven't so much as touched the peas . . .' Dana was beginning, when Con gave a crow of triumph, bent down and fished the loose leaves from the box hedge.

'Radishes!' he shouted. 'Oh, you dirty little beggar, you've been eating 'em with all the muck on 'em! What would Mammy say if she knew her 'ickle precious had been eating earth?'

Dana giggled; she couldn't help it. Trust Con to find her out! Not that he'd dream of telling, she knew that. They were best friends, true pals. Con was older than her by a whole year, but he never used his seniority to boss her about, and when they fought, which even the best of friends do from time to time, she knew he never employed his full strength. But now he was dangling the bunch of leaves tauntingly in front of her nose, not laughing aloud though she knew he was doing so inside. 'Well, tiddler? Are you going to deny it?'

'Oh, ha ha! With you finding the evidence before my very eyes? But radishes . . . well, it's not like stealing fruit, or even peas. Why, we sowed the seed of these radishes six weeks or so back, when Arthur grumbled that we might make ourselves useful for once, and we sowed the lettuce and the spring onion seed too. So I reckon I'm entitled.' She plunged a hand into her pocket and produced the remaining radishes.

'*We* sowed the seed,' Con reminded her at once. 'And *we* can reap the benefit, now they're are full grown.' He took the bunch, divided it into two, then rubbed his own share on his ragged trousers and shoved one into his mouth, speaking thickly through it. 'Fancy a lettuce? Or a nice spring onion?'

'No thanks,' Dana said at once. 'What time is it?'

Con looked surprised, as well he might since neither of them owned a watch and in any case time was only important on weekdays – they both went to the village school – and today was Saturday. 'Dunno. Why, for God's sake?'

'Don't take the name of the Lord in vain,' Dana said automatically. 'Because you said we might fish Lord Prothero's trout stream if he was giving a shooting party to get rid of some of the rabbits. Horrible old man,' she added, without much rancour. 'Why can't he be content with the birds he rears specially to shoot?'

'He says a rabbit shoot keeps the guns up to the mark, otherwise when autumn comes the shot goes pretty wild,' Con said. 'And you must agree rabbits can be a pest when there's so many of 'em.'

Dana shrugged. She did not mean to admit how much she hated the thought of the rabbits being slain because she knew this would only prove to Con that girls were soft. But she often woke at dawn to see, in the pale grey light, twenty or thirty rabbits and their young, nibbling the sweet grass of the great lawn. How dreadful if his lord-ship's shoot were successful and there were no more rabbits to prick up their ears and thump the danger signal when they saw her watching them at her open window.

But Con was looking up at the sky, no doubt judging the height of the sun, deciding more or less what time it was. 'It was seven o'clock when Dad and I had tea and toast for our brekker,' he said thoughtfully. 'I came out quite soon after that; say seven thirty. It's probably around eight or nine o'clock and the guns won't be out before ten. Now look, I've been thinking. If we catch any trout it's no use pretending we got 'em from the lake, because I don't believe I've ever seen trout there. They're in the stream because old Prothero stocks it. So the minute your people – or my father – see us with them they'll know we've been poaching. But if we get a heap of dry wood and some matches – oh, and a fry-pan I suppose – we can eat anything we catch for our dinners and no one the wiser.'

Dana beamed. A picnic! No, more than that: a feast of forbidden fish, and a fire in the woods, which was also forbidden, and Con's company, which was more precious to her than all the rest. 'I'll bring the fry-pan

130

and the matches,' she said at once. 'Oh, Con, won't it be grand!'

'Aye – if no one catches us,' Con said, grinning. 'There's a pile of kindling at the back of the stables for when the weather gets colder and we need a fire, but that's a long way off. Dad won't notice if a bundle of sticks goes missing. But best go and persuade your mam to hand over some bread and cheese and a few pickled onions, just in case the trout won't oblige.'

Dana pouted. 'If I provide the grub and the pan and that, what'll you bring – apart from the kindling, I mean?' she asked aggrievedly. 'It's not fair, Con Devlin.'

'I shall provide me expertise as well as a fishing rod,' Con said at once. 'And remember, if we're caught it's me that'll get a skelping and not yourself. Are you on?'

'Oh, all right,' Dana said with pretended reluctance. 'But you might rob a few fruit from the apple loft, just in case we're specially hungry.'

Con agreed to do so as they sauntered towards the door in the wall which led out of the garden. Sometimes, when her father was boasting about the money he had got from an English milord for 'a sweet little mare wit' a mouth like silk', Dana wondered aloud why some of his money was not spent on Castletara, either on the house itself or on its grounds, but her father would only pinch her chin and give her the same reply. ''Tis the land and the beasts which make the money for us and they care nowt for rose gardens or a few missing slates,' he always assured her. 'I buy the best possible animals, feed and train them and get a rich reward when they enter the sale ring. One day, when you're a woman and not a fractious little girl, Prince Charming will come along and we'll have the castle done up for your wedding, rose garden, banqueting hall and all. I'm saving up, you see, for that great day when I get you off my hands.' And he would laugh uproariously and give her a hug whilst Mammy stood back and smiled and told her not to heed her daddy now, for on the day she wed he'd be weeping like a fountain and thinking up excuses to keep his girl where she belonged, even if it meant having to house Prince Charming at Castletara as well as his only daughter.

'Did you notice how quietly the door opens since we used bicycle oil on it yesterday?' Con said now, bringing her back to earth as he stretched out a hand to lift the latch. 'I bet old Arthur would say 'twas the work of the little people.' He grinned down at her, his dark eyes alight with mischief, a lock of his night-black hair falling across his tanned brow. 'And since it was yourself who applied the oil, tiddler, you could say he was right and it was one of the fairy folk.'

He began to pull the door towards them, gesturing her to go through ahead of him. She did so, telling him that though she might be smaller than he, she could scarcely qualify as one of the little people. But as she stepped through the doorway mist rolled towards her, enveloping the wilderness, the kitchen garden and Castletara, and Con's voice, repeating 'one door opens, opens . . . opens . . .' was the only sound she could hear. Then the whole scene was replaced by the familiar surroundings of Temperance Court, with the grey light of a Liverpool morning sidling in round the edges of Dana's homemade curtains.

For a long moment Dana simply lay in her bed, aware

of Polly still slumbering, aware that she was in her own room, that the dream had been just a dream. She reminded herself that she had slammed the door on her past, but it was impossible to prevent oneself from dreaming. She remembered Polly's last remark before they had settled down for the night, and was sure that this had triggered her own recollection, a memory so clear that she had difficulty in convincing herself that it really was a dream, and that now she must forget all about it and continue with her Liverpool life.

She turned over and peered at the clock. Good heavens, it was near on nine. She would be late, and she could not afford to lose her job with work so hard to find. She was halfway out of the covers when she remembered that today was Sunday, and she and Polly – her new flatmate – had decided to treat themselves to a lie-in. Smiling, she wriggled under the blankets again, reminding herself that a dream meant nothing, was as fictional as a book or a cinema show, and would soon fade. The fact that this one particular dream had seemed so real, had been more like a recollection of something which had really happened, was strange, but nothing to worry about. She had closed the door on her past – no, slammed it – and though she could not prevent herself from dreaming, she could forget such dreams as soon as she woke. Yet she lay in the semi-darkness for another ten minutes, frowning with concentration, trying to work out just why, after almost two years of never letting herself remember Castletara or her life there, the past had decided to force its way into her dreams.

Finally, she shrugged and turned her pillow so that

the cool side lay against her cheek. And, presently, fell deeply asleep.

She did not dream.

Polly, waking as the light strengthened, could not at first remember where on earth she was. She did realise, however, that she was sharing a bed and heaved herself carefully up on one elbow to have a look around. She remembered vaguely that she had left her miserable lodgings, which had been all she could afford, and wondered for a split second if she had been given a room at the YWCA, for as soon as she remembered leaving her lodgings she remembered losing her job and a stab of fear went through her.

But then she saw Dana's flushed face cuddled into her pillow and all her worries fled. She remembered every detail of her good fortune, for now she and Dana were to share these lovely rooms and Dana was going to help her to find a job as soon as the shops and markets opened for business on Monday morning. Polly wriggled cautiously out of bed, checked that Dana still slumbered and padded softly into the other room, and across to the paraffin stove upon which the kettle was balanced. She knew it was full of water – Dana had explained that she always left it full overnight so that she might make herself a cup of tea before setting off for work. Today being Sunday, however, Dana had not set the alarm, so if Polly got going at once she could present her friend and benefactor with a hot cup of tea before the other girl had left her bed.

Hugging herself with delighted anticipation of the treat she had planned, Polly found matches and lit the Primus. As soon as the kettle boiled she made a brew of strong tea, fetched milk from the pantry and poured it into blue Bakelite mugs. She re-entered the bedroom, tiptoed across to where Dana lay, still dead to the world, put both cups on the small table by the head of the bed, and plonked herself down on the covers. 'Wakey, wakey! I've brung you a cup of tea 'cos I've gorra go out. But there's no need for you to come wi' me. I reckon I'll be back by noon, so if you want to stay in bed till then I'll make you some snap when I comes back.'

She stared at Dana's sleeping face and saw her lids flicker up and a frown crease her brow; clearly she was having difficulty in remembering how Polly came to be sitting on the bed in her nightie and offering her hostess a cup of tea. The puzzlement, however, did not last long. A slow smile spread across Dana's face and she sat up and picked up one of the mugs. 'I say, Poll, you're spoiling me,' she said, raising the mug to her lips. She took a hefty swallow then stood the mug down again. 'One and a half sugars, just the way I like it. But why are you up already? I thought we agreed to lie in, since it's Sunday.'

'I suddenly remembered I'd not had a chance to tell Ernie I'd been sacked, nor that I were living wi' you,' she explained. 'He's in a hostel for fellers out on St Domingo's Road, an' I reckon if I goes up there and asks the feller in charge if I can have a word wi' Ernie Frost he'll send me pal out and we can have a bit of a jangle.'

'Who's Ernie Frost?' Dana asked rather blankly. 'Does he work at the Willows? If so, I suppose he's new since my time.'

Polly snorted and took a sip of tea from the mug she was cradling in both hands. 'Honest to God, Dana, it ain't that long since you were working at the Willows!

You can't have forgot old Ernie. He were pals wi' Sammy Higgins. Don't say you can't remember either of 'em!'

Dana chuckled. 'How could I ever forget those two? Old Haggerty was always complaining about them, but I believe she had a soft spot for the one with yellow hair. She used to send him off to buy ingredients if she was running short; the rest of us were so envious! We'd have done anything to escape from the heat of the kitchen for half an hour. Didn't they use to call the one with yellow hair Cheepy Chick?'

Polly nodded, grinning. 'That's Ernie.' She sighed. 'It weren't too bad at the Willows even after the Hag left while Ernie were there, but a few weeks ago Mr Lionel brought in some great brawny feller, a relative of his I reckon, and said that now he had Humphrey he could do wi'out Ernie and Sam. Sam gorra good job – well, a job at any rate – workin' as a street cleaner, but Ernie's still lookin'. He's a bit on the skinny side, gets summat called asthma what makes him wheeze like a grampus if he gets overtired, so employers ain't fallin' over themselves to give him work. But he'll get something, 'cos he's after every job what comes up like a terrier after a rat.'

Dana laughed, drained her mug of tea and lay back against her pillows. 'Well, good for Ernie,' she said rather drowsily. 'And now, since it's Sunday and you don't need me, I'll grab an extra half-hour in bed. See you later!'

Taking the hint, Polly jumped up, heaved her nightdress over her head and had a brief wash. Since it was Sunday and she and Dana had collected her few belongings when they visited her landlady, she went to the bottom two drawers of their clothes chest, which they had agreed should be hers, selected her one and only Sunday dress and her most respectable undies, and proceeded to dress rapidly, noticing with approval that her friend now lay with her back to her, her red head buried in the pillow.

Polly finished dressing, thrust her feet into her thread-bare plimsolls and cleared her throat. 'All done. I's respectable, so you can look now,' she said playfully. 'Mind if I have some bread an' marg afore I goes off? I promise as soon as I get my dole – or a job – I'll hand over some cash for what I've ate an' that.'

'Don't worry, idiot,' Dana said drowsily. 'They say two can live as cheaply as one so now we'll see if it's true. There's jam on the bottom shelf; help yourself.'

Polly went into the other room and cut bread and smeared jam, poured herself another half cup of tea, ate and drank, then took her much patched jacket down from the hook. She popped her head round the bedroom door. 'I'm off now,' she said cheerfully. 'Oh, by the way, did you know you talk in your sleep? Who's Con?'

There was a perceptible pause before Dana said: 'Con? What d'you mean, Polly?'

'You were talkin' in your sleep and you said "Con" three or four times,' Polly said. 'But dreams bein' what they are, I dare say it were just nonsense.'

'That's it,' Dana said at once. 'I didn't know I talked in my sleep, though. Hope you find Ernie. See you later, queen!'

When Polly had gone Dana swung her legs out of bed and went into the other room and over to the window, watching her friend until she had disappeared under the arch of the court and into the road. Then she went over to the table, cut herself a generous wedge of the loaf, spread it thinly with margarine and thickly with jam, and slumped into the nearest chair, beginning to devour the food and wondering whether there was enough tea in the pot to refill her mug. Having ascertained that this was indeed so, she poured another mug of tea, then turned her thoughts rather apprehensively to what Polly had said. It seemed that she, Dana, had talked in her sleep, and talked, furthermore, about the home which she had been determined to forget. So far as she knew she had never done such a thing before, certainly not whilst she and Caitlin had shared a room; or, if she had done so, Caitlin had never mentioned it. But then Caitlin slept like the dead and always had to be shaken awake even after the alarm had shrilled out and Dana herself was ready for the day ahead.

She finished her makeshift breakfast and began methodically to wash and dress. Polly had pulled the curtains back before she left and Dana could see it was a sunny day, the sort of day to be out of doors. I'll go out, walk down to the river, occupy my mind with some-thing other than dreams, she told herself, and twenty minutes later she was locking the door behind her and slipping the key on its string back through the letterbox.

She set out, walking fast, enjoying the exercise, but despite her best efforts her mind refused to obey her command to forget her recent dream. She could not recall ever dreaming of home since her flight; why should it happen now? When she had first woken she had blamed Polly, since her friend had mentioned something about opening and closing doors, and the dream had begun with the door to the kitchen garden opening to let her through. But that was nonsense, really, just her mind trying to justify ignoring her command to forget. The real reason was the fish and chips, eaten at least an hour later than usual, and the excitement of taking Polly in. When at last they had gone to bed she had been unusually relaxed and the dream, seeing this, had sidled into her subconscious.

Dana reached the Pier Head and watched the activity going on all around. What did dreams mean, after all? It didn't even matter that she had talked in her sleep, nor that Polly, overhearing, had been curious, because it wouldn't happen again. She would not allow it. The past was just that, past. Tomorrow she and Polly would go job-hunting, and no doubt return to Temperance Court so worn out that they would sleep like a couple of logs. If they dreamed – if they talked in their sleep – they would be too worn out next day to remember what they had heard.

But it was odd, very odd. Now that she had had time to think, she remembered the incident in the kitchen garden and knew that it had not been just a dream, but a recollection of a time long gone. A happy time. In a way she wished that the dream had not ended so abruptly, for now that she had allowed herself to remember she knew that she and Con had indeed fished the trout stream, though without success. But they had built their fire as dusk crept down and toasted the bread and cheese and spiked the apples Con had robbed on sticks, holding them out to the flames until their rosy skin was split and sweet. Everything had tasted of smoke, but even thinking about it brought the water rushing to her mouth; it had been a wonderful feast, as good as the trout would have been. She could see Con's dark face as he concentrated on adding a piece of dry branch to the fire, and leaned forward to rescue an apple which had just plopped from its stick into the glowing embers.

'Mind yourself, gal, we're comin' through!' A raucous voice brought Dana back to the present with a vengeance. She dodged as two men carrying an enormous sea-chest between them made their way to the floating road, then turned away from the busy scene. She had best get back. She would begin to concoct some sort of meal which she and Polly could share, and this afternoon they would stroll along the Scotty, looking for any vacancies posted in the shop windows for possible employment.

Dana turned away from the fascinating goings-on at the Pier Head and headed for Temperance Court.

Polly set off into the bright morning, singing a song beneath her breath. She had a small, tuneful voice and enjoyed the sound of it, though her command of the words was somewhat shaky. '*Any time you're Lambeth way, any evening, any day, you'll find us all, doin' the Lambeth Walk, oy!*' she carolled. '*Every little Lambeth girl, da da da dee da dee da, you'll find us all, doin' the Lambeth Walk, oy!*'

This lasted her for several blocks, then she changed to something even more cheerful and even more in tune with her mood, which was one of gaiety and optimism. '*Nothing's impossible I have found, for when my chin is on the ground, I pick myself up, dust myself off, start all over again!*'

She was still singing this, and earning a good few smiles and indulgent glances from passers-by, when she reached the tall, almost forbidding hostel where thirty or forty boys and young men, most of whom had not yet managed to find employment, were housed. There were half a dozen steps leading to the brown-painted front door and Polly marched up them, changing her tune to 'Onward Christian soldiers' in deference to the fact that it was Sunday. Since it would not do to antagonise whoever came in answer to her knock, she stopped singing as soon as she heard the clatter of approaching footsteps and put on her most winning smile. The door was opened by a young man in dirty overalls, with a sharp, knowing face whose cheeks and chin were covered in a rash of acne. He was carrying a mop and bucket, and Polly remembered that the occupants took it in turns to brush and mop floors, clean windows, cook and prepare food for the one meal provided, and do other menial tasks, though each was responsible for his own washing and ironing. She smiled ingratiatingly at the young man, who scowled in reply, saying 'Yes? Whadda you want?' in a tone so antagonistic that had she been less anxious to find her pal, Polly might well have mumbled an excuse and fled.

'Oh! I'm that sorry to disturb you on a Sunday, but I'd like to see Mr Ernest Frost, if it's not too much trouble. And if he's in, a'course,' Polly said. 'He's stayin' here . . . I think he's in Blue dormitory,' she added conscientiously.

The young man frowned, then gave Polly a penetrating stare. 'Chick, d'you mean? Little feller wi' yaller hair? Gorra squeaky voice, and legs like pipe cleaners?'

Polly began to swell with righteous wrath at this unkind description of her pal, then subsided. No point getting into a fight with this coarse and unpleasant youth, she told herself, and conjured up the sweet smile which had temporarily deserted her. 'They do call him Chick, but he's really Ernest Frost,' she said. 'And he's staying here, in this house, until . . .'

Behind the sharp-faced one's shoulders she could see a flight of steep, linoleum-covered stairs and a skinny youth with a yellow quiff descending them. Polly, who had stepped back in the face of the door opener's rudeness, stepped forward again. 'It's awright, it's him comin' down the stairs this very minute,' she said eagerly. She leaned forward. 'Ernie! It's me, Polly. Can you come out for a few minutes? I've gorra lot to tell you.'

Ernie jumped the last half-dozen steps and cantered across the hallway, shouldering his way unceremoniously past the young man. ''Scuse me, Spotty,' he said. 'It's me young lady. I done me jobs for the day so I can go out for an hour or so.' He shot through the open doorway, grinning from ear to ear at Polly and ignoring the young man, who was saying frostily that his name was Walter and he'd thank Chick to remember it.

Immensely heartened by her friend's delight at seeing her, Polly said, 'Thanks, Spotty. See you later.' She let Ernie take her hand and together they hurried away from the building. As soon as they were well out of earshot, Ernie stopped and turned to Polly, his whole body seeming to resemble a question mark. 'Well? I come round to the Willows late yesterday, 'cos it were a fine sunny day and I reckoned they'd not shut the doors until every last customer had been fed,' he said. 'But I were wrong – or at any rate you'd gone and no one said anything about news. Don't say the old griffin's made you up to waiting on! I've said time out o' mind that pretty little gals like you can get atween the tables quicker and neater than gals what's all bum and bosom. Has the Griffin – or Mr Lionel for that matter – had a rush o' blood to the head and took you out o' the kitchen?'

By now they were strolling along the pavement heading for the Mersey, and when Polly heard a tram trundling up behind them she seized Ernie's arm and pointed. 'Look, Ern, a tram, and it's bound for the park. What say we jump aboard? I've gorra be back at – at me new lodgings by noon but that's a long way off, and I just fancy flowers an' grass an' that, so's we've summat nice to look at whiles we talk.'

'I'm agreeable, though I'm a bit short of the readies,' Ernie said somewhat doubtfully. 'But I can run to tram rides for two and a cup o' tea at one of the cafés.' He stuck out a hand and the tram screeched to a halt so that the two of them could scramble aboard. Ernie bought two tickets and pushed his companion into a seat, descending heavily on the hard wooden bench himself. 'No use tryin' to talk whilst we're aboard this perishin' noisy vehicle,' he shouted in Polly's ear. 'Leave it until we reach the park.'

Polly agreed, but when they were strolling down the long sloping path towards the lake and the ducks, she found it difficult to begin. She looked sideways at her old pal and saw that he was eyeing her curiously. 'What's up, old gal?' he asked at last. 'Never known you so quiet! Cat got your tongue?'

Polly giggled. 'No-o-o, but it's not so easy to explain as I thought. I'd better begin at the very beginning, with the Griffin sacking me and refusing to pay me for the last week, though I were owed. She said I'd been late comin' in for three days, which were a huge lie, and when the teatime rush eased at around four o'clock she snatched me jacket off the peg and told me I were sacked. I told her and told her that it weren't me who'd been late but one of t'other girls, namin' no names, but she wouldn't listen and out I were slung. So of course I were howlin' and wonderin' what the divil I should do, havin' no money and so on . . .'

'If I'd been there I'd have punched her on the snout, head cook or no head cook,' Ernie said vengefully. 'Wharra wicked woman! But didn't none of the other gals take your side? Wharrabout Teresa, the head waitress? Wharrabout Mr Lionel himself, for God's sake?' He ground his teeth and balled his hands into fists. 'I'll go round there first thing Monday . . .'

'It's awright,' Polly said hastily. 'I've not told you the best part yet! I come out o' the kitchen, bawlin' like a five-year-old . . .'

She proceeded with her story, but when she got to the bit where Dana had taken her home Ernie interrupted. 'Who did you say? That ginger girl what was a pal of the pretty one? What were her name, now? Oh aye, Caitlin. Where was she?'

'I don't know . . . yes I do. She's gone back to Ireland,' Polly said impatiently. 'She's got nothing to do with it! I'm tryin' to tell you it were Dana – Dana McBride – who worked in the Willows a while back.'

'Oh aye?' Ernie gave a disdainful sniff. 'She and t'other one ran that tea room . . . can't remember what they called it . . . and turned it into a real posh restaurant. Come to think, they wasn't like the rest of us at all. The redhead talked all posh and BBC, as I remember.' In what Polly supposed he thought was a refined falsetto, he said, 'Oh, how fraightfully common these kitchen workers are, and we're supposed to work alongside of 'em!' He brightened suddenly as a thought occurred to him and he dropped back into his own voice. 'I say, did she offer you a job? Any chance o' me gettin' work there? I ain't keen on kitchen work, but—'

'Oh, Ernie, don't be such a bleedin' beast! There's no call to be nasty about Dana, as you'll soon realise if you'll just shut up and let me finish,' Polly said, feeling tears rise to her eyes. Why on earth should Ernie start being downright horrid about Dana? He had not disliked her when they had worked together at the Willows. But men, even young ones, were odd creatures, so Polly took out a hanky and blew her nose, then addressed her companion. 'Are you going to listen? She and Caitlin were cheated out of their tea room and then out of the restaurant. Caitlin went back to Ireland and Dana got a room in Temperance Court and a job of some sort, but listen to what happened after the Griffin kicked me out of me job . . .'

She began to tell him how Dana had whisked her away from the Willows and round to her room in the court, but once more she was interrupted.

'I don't see what reason she had for interferin',' Ernie put in. 'I'd ha' seen you right, Poll, honest to God I would.'

'Yes, but Ern, you weren't *there*,' Polly pointed out. 'And Dana was; well, not when the Griffin was bein' horrible but later, when the old divil had throwed me out and I were cryin' in the back yard. Honest, Ern, no one could have been kinder than Dana. She give me a hug and told me to dry me eyes, and then when we were walkin' along the pavement and I smelled a funny smell and we saw the moggies a-follerin' us she made me laugh like anything.'

'So she smells funny, does she?' Ernie asked. He sniffed. 'They say women wi' red hair smells different from the rest of us; I believe it's a sort of foxy smell. And you say the cats noticed and follered? Well, it don't surprise me.' He sniggered. 'Glad I ain't a carrot-top.'

'Ernie Frost, you should be ashamed,' Polly said hotly as they reached the little café and plonked themselves down, side by side, at one of the small tables. 'Dana don't smell – well, only of soap and that – and nor does anyone else wi' red hair. The thing is . . . oh, sorry, miss, I didn't see you there.'

The waitress whipped her pad out of her apron and stared at them, eyebrows lifting. 'Yes, chuck? There's a special offer on a pot o' tea for two and a round of toast and jam. Want that?'

'That'll be grand,' Ernie said, although Polly was thinking that on such a warm day lemonade would have been nice. The waitress scribbled on the page and left them and Polly scowled at her companion.

'I never thought you could be so horrible, especially when the person you're being horrible about were kindness itself to me,' she said reproachfully. 'Now just listen for a change and stop interruptin'. It were the fish that ponged. Dana works in the Great Charlotte Street fish market Fridays and Saturdays and the old woman what runs the stall give her a couple of pieces of plaice and some brown shrimps. Dana said they were fine an' fresh, but a'course it were a warm day and . . . well, she give the fish to the moggies, anyway,' she ended sulkily. 'So

146

what can you make of that, eh? I suppose you wouldn't laugh or think it funny, Mr Clever?'

Ernie was beginning to reply when the waitress returned with their tea and toast and Polly put milk in the cups and added the strongly brewed tea. She compressed her lips when Ernie said rather less aggressively that he was sorry if he had upset her, but he could not help feeling that, had he been present, he would have been as much use as Dana, probably more. 'After all, she could have give you a job when them girls had the tea room, but she never,' he pointed out righteously. 'And if she's workin' at the fish market she can't do much for you now. In fact, if you'd come to me earlier . . .'

Polly stared at him, her eyes rounding with astonishment. 'If I'd come to you earlier what the divil d'you think you could have done?' she demanded. 'Oh, I suppose you'd have took me into your dorm in the hostel and let me sleep under your bunk! No one would have said a word when you brung me downstairs to share your breakfast, oh no, not they!'

'Well, I'd have punched old Griffin on the nose for a start,' Ernie said sulkily. 'And I'd have talked to that old bag what runs the lodging house, told her you'd paid in advance and was entitled to stay wi' her until you found somewhere else. Then I'd have gone to – to – the woman what runs the YWCA, and . . . and . . .'

It was now Polly's turn to give a derisive sniff. 'Oh yes, I can just see it! You'd be slung into jug by the nearest scuffer for grievous bodily harm, if that's what they call punchin' old women on the nose. Look, Ernie, I don't want to quarrel wi' anyone, particularly you, what's me bezzie, but I shall if you don't shurrup and let me finish me story.'

Ernie took a large bite of his toast and then picked up his cup and downed most of it in a large, and lamentably noisy, swallow. Then he wiped his mouth on his sleeve and grinned at his companion. 'Awright, awright, queen. I won't say another word until you give me the go-ahead.' He began to twiddle his thumbs and cast his eyes heavenward with such a comical look that Polly had hard work not to laugh. But she remembered how nasty he had been about Dana, and hardened her heart.

She told the story quickly, aware that for some reason Ernie was not prepared to give Dana credit for rescuing his little pal from what might have been a very difficult and unpleasant situation, and when she finished she looked almost defiantly at him. 'So she's goin' to help me look for a job, and until I get one we're goin' to share her rooms in Temperance Court,' she finished firmly. 'And so if you want to go on bein' me best pal you'd best not make cracks about gals wi' ginger hair. Because she saved me bacon, honest to God she did.'

Ernie seized the teapot and poured them both a second cup, then swivelled his chair so he could look at the clock above the long counter. 'Awright, I admit she got you out of a hole,' he said grudgingly. 'And time's gerrin' on, so we should put our best foot forward, else you won't be back at Badtemper Court by noon. But just you remember, if I'd been there . . .'

Polly grabbed her cup – the tea was nearly cold – and drained it, then turned a defiant look on Ernie. 'Shut up!' she yelled. 'You're stupid, you are! Dana won't charge me rent until I'm in work; she came wi' me to me lodgings and outfaced the landlady. She's got a 'lectric iron and said I can use it to smooth me decent dress so when we go job-hunting tomorrer I'll look me best. But all you can do is say horrible things about red hair and posh voices. You make me sick, Ernie Frost! And if you don't eat your bleedin' words right here and now you won't be me bezzie any longer. So there!'

'Well, I'm sorry if I offended you . . .' Ernie began, then changed tack. 'I reckon that Dana's lonely and wanted a flat-share, someone she knew and could trust. I reckon if someone real posh comes along you'll find you're out on your ear, and then I hope as you'll remember your old friend and come to me in – in your hour of need.'

Polly bounced to her feet, almost overturning the table and causing the waitress to come hurrying across the room towards them. Ernie also stood up, but Polly was so furious that she put a hand on each of his thin shoulders and pushed him back into his seat. 'Stay there!' she yelled, snatching up her ancient handbag and overturning her almost empty cup of tea. 'Don't think you're goin' to see me home because you ain't! Thanks for the tea and toast; when I'm earnin' again I'll pay you back for it!'

Ernie began to stand up again, muttering that he didn't mean – it was she who had started the scene – he had been joking – couldn't she take a joke? For the love of Mike, a feller couldn't always be serious . . .

But Polly was already slamming out of the door and, when Ernie would have followed her, the waitress, smiling but steely-eyed, reminded him that he had not yet paid the bill for a pot of tea for two and buttered toast.

Ernie, fishing in his pocket for change, snorted. 'That were margarine, not butter,' he said, but he said it under his breath. He had just noticed that beneath her little lace cap the waitress sported a mass of bright red hair.

149

Chapter Six

The coldness between Polly and Ernie lasted until the summer was over, and it was Ernie himself who ended it. He hung around the area waiting for Polly, and whenever she appeared unaccompanied by Dana he would reiterate how sorry he was for his behaviour and how he missed his little pal. He begged to be allowed to meet Dana, but on this point at least Polly was adamant at first. She had acknowledged to herself that ridiculous though it might seem, Ernie was actually jealous of her friendship with Dana. He would have liked to be able to help her in some way but whilst he remained out of work this was not possible, and Polly was mortally afraid that if she allowed him to meet her friend he would make some remark which might be interpreted by the quick-witted Dana as criticism. No, better to keep them apart until Ernie's resentment had begun to fade.

The girls' search for work, however, was not crowned with much success, and even Dana's job at the fish market was reduced from two days to one. However, they found employment eventually: tempory and part-time, but at least it meant that they could pay the rent. Dana came back from Fridays at the fish market not only tired but smelling strongly of her wares, and though she always wore a large overall, which she took home with her and washed thoroughly, nothing, she felt, could entirely rid her of the smell of fish.

'You want to wash your overall at work,' Polly advised her. 'Cripes, Dee, you can't explain to folk what hold their snitches when you walk past that it's the overall stinkin' of fish and not yourself.'

'Oh, I know, but there's only the one tap between the lot of us, and at the end of the day there's always a queue waiting to clean down the stalls and wash their hands,' Dana explained. 'I always make very sure that I don't smell of fish by Saturday, though.'

Polly giggled. 'Yes, it wouldn't do to turn up at Mulligan's Tea Rooms smelling of fish,' she agreed. 'The waitresses are almost as posh as the customers, from what you've told me.'

'They are,' Dana said gloomily. The girls were in the washhouse on Margaret Street, doing their weekly washing at two adjacent sinks. 'And fussy – well, if the staff at the Willows worked at Miss Mulligan's, they'd have a blue fit. Sandwiches must have the crusts cut off, tomatoes have to be skinned, sugar has to be lump and not loose, and if the dear little silver tongs have so much as a grain of sugar adhering to them the customer will send them back to the kitchen and demand a clean pair.'

'And to think Miss Mulligan employs you as a waitress, ginger hair and all,' Polly said. 'Has she asked you to dye it black yet?'

Dana, scrubbing vigorously at the neck of one of the white blouses she wore to work, lifted it from the suds, wrung it out and dropped it into the more or less clear water in Polly's sink. Then she pulled the wooden plug from her own sink and dried her hands on a scrap of towelling. 'Not yet,' she said cheerfully. 'But she wasn't worrying about my hair when she interviewed me – I got the job because . . .'

'Because you speak like a lady,' Polly ended for her. She swished Dana's white blouse through the rinsing water, then wrung it out and threw it into the laundry basket. She glanced outside and remarked that it was not yet raining, then helped Dana carry the washing basket and its now clean contents over to the line of mangles which stood near the door.

Polly began to shake the clothes out and feed them through whilst her friend turned the handle, though Dana gave a shriek of protest when Polly picked up her precious white blouse. 'Don't you *dare* mangle my blouse,' she said. 'The buttons will pop off like – like popcorn, and I won't have anything to wear at work. Not that I'll be working at Miss Mulligan's for long, alas. She says she can manage without me now and won't need me again until the Christmas rush starts.'

'Oh, charming,' Polly said sarcastically. 'It doesn't occur to her that you've got to eat in the weeks between now and Christmas, I suppose?'

'Oh well. Maybe I'll get another job; the corner shops will often take on someone part-time so the owner can go shopping at one of the markets,' Dana said tolerantly. 'How's Ernie's job-hunting going? I know he's been cleaning cars for a garage on the outskirts of the city, but you said a few days ago that the work seems to be drying up.'

'Dunno.' Polly paused, then came to a decision. 'But I thought, if you agree, Dana, that I might ask him back to tea this evening. Well, it'll be supper really, seeing as how we shan't be finished here for another thirty minutes or so, and then we've got our messages to get. But late Sat'day evening is a good time for picking up bargains, so I thought we might get a cheap meal together and share it wi' Ernie . . . if you're agreeable, that is.'

'Of course I am,' Dana said at once. 'I've not met him since you and I began to share the room but I've seen him hovering. Once or twice I nearly asked him why he didn't come to the door like a Christian and ask for you, but it seemed a bit cheeky somehow.' She looked narrowly at Polly. 'Has he suddenly become shy? I don't remember much about him at the Willows, but from what little I can recall he was pretty bouncy and self-confident.'

'Self-confidence goes down the drain when you're out of work for weeks and weeks,' Polly said gloomily. 'Don't I know it! But if it's all right with you I'll go round to the hostel when we finish here.'

'Suits me,' Dana said at once. 'Only haven't you noticed? He's been walking up and down the street outside for the last ten minutes and peering into the washhouse every now and then. I'm surprised you haven't spotted him.'

'I've better things to do,' Polly said loftily, but rather spoiled this high-handed remark by adding: 'Next time you see him, give me a nudge and I'll run and waylay him. He can come with us and carry our messages, if you don't mind, that is.'

'Oh, for goodness' sake, stop shilly-shallying; you know very well you've every intention of asking your friend to supper,' Dana said, smiling at her. 'As for carrying our shopping, he's more than welcome to do that.' She left the mangle and darted across to the open door. 'Hey, Ernie, don't rush off; there's a pal of yours in here wants a word.' She waited until the young man had turned and headed towards her, then popped back into the washhouse and gave Polly a push. 'Go on, invite him to supper,' she hissed, and watched with approval as the two young people began an animated conversation.

Then they parted, but before he left Ernie raised a hand and, staring straight at Dana, shouted: 'Thanks for the invite. See you later, queen!'

Half an hour later, when the girls emerged from the washhouse with the clean but damp linen in the laundry basket, Ernie was waiting. He insisted upon taking one end of the basket and scarcely sagged at all beneath its weight, though Dana, grinning to herself, thought that he would be glad to relinquish it when they reached Temperance Court. The three of them chatted idly, mostly about the difficulties of managing on the small amounts of money employers paid. But it soon became obvious to Dana, and had probably been obvious to Polly all along, that Ernie had some news which he was dying to impart.

Finally, when they had returned from their shopping trip and were unloading the provisions they had bought into a cupboard they used as a pantry, Polly put the kettle on the Primus stove, pushed Ernie into a chair and stood menacingly opposite him. 'What's up?' she demanded bluntly. 'You've been like a cat what's got into the dairy and found a pan of cream ever since we axed you to supper. You've gorra job, haven't you? Oh, Ernie, I hope it's a good 'un.' She turned to Dana, her face glowing. 'What do you think, Dee? We're all after work and I reckon he's beat the pair of us. C'mon, Ernie, cough up!'

Ernie looked bashfully from face to face. 'Well, you're right in one way,' he said. 'Only it's not straightforward exactly. I applied to join the army. I shan't mention the asthma, and though I'm small for me age I'm pretty strong. Other fellers from the hostel have signed on for one of the services, and though we're none of us built like Johnny Weissmuller they've all been accepted, so I reckon I'll be the same.'

The two girls stared at him, speechless. 'Oh, gosh,' Dana said at last when it seemed obvious that Polly had been struck dumb. 'I think that's awfully brave of you, Ernie. Everyone's talking about a war; one of my customers at the fish stall told me they've got to stop Herr Hitler from annexing any more countries in Europe otherwise we'll find ourselves entertaining storm troopers or being bombed like Madrid.'

Ernie looked gratified. 'My father were a soldier, a gunner,' he said eagerly. 'And it's all found; they gives you three square meals a day and all your uniform.' He turned to Polly. 'Of course, I might have to go abroad if this here war starts, like soldiers did in the last war, but France isn't that far away and I'll come home for me furloughs.'

Polly sniffed but Dana could see she was pleased. However, it seemed she did not mean to let on. 'Don't count your chickens,' she said gruffly. 'You ain't in yet. Then there's that there asthma of yours – but mebbe they'll overlook it.' She must have become aware of the disappointed look on her friend's face, Dana thought, for she suddenly put both arms round Ernie's neck and kissed him on his cheek. 'Oh, don't listen to me; I think you're brilliant, Ernie Frost. I'm sure they'll take you in the army, but if they don't, you just try the Navy, or even the air force. Everyone says there's going to be a war and Mr Rathbone – he's the grocer I deliver for once in a while – says that them as volunteer will be trained to do a proper job, whereas them as is conscripted won't have no choice.'

'But they'll only conscript fellers once they're certain sure that war is coming,' Dana felt impelled to point out. 'Still, I'm sure you've done the sensible thing, Ernie. You must tell us as soon as you've passed the medical and are given a posting.'

'Given a posting?' Polly said blankly. 'What does that mean when it's at home?'

'It means that once he's passed the medical he'll know where the army are going to send him for basic training,' Dana said patiently. 'Goodness, Ernie might go anywhere in Britain.' She smiled at Polly's shocked countenance. 'Oh, Poll, you didn't think he'd stay in Liverpool, did you? Well, he might be sent back here, I suppose, but I believe soldiers do basic training for the first six months of their service.'

'Cor!' Ernie exclaimed, making it all too clear that he, too, had not expected to be sent away from the city. 'Oh, but six months ain't long when you come to think of it, and once I'm trained then I dare say there's a fair chance I'll be sent somewhere near here . . .' he turned to Dana, clearly considering her a mine of useful information, 'wouldn't you say?'

Dana judged it best to agree, and she and Polly began the preparations for their meal, though Ernie insisted that he should scrub the potatoes and fetch in water from the big brass tap at the end of the court. 'Might as well make meself useful whilst I'm still around,' he said rather gloomily. 'I'm goin' to say I'm experienced wi' motor cars, which is true, after all, then mebbe I'll be a mechanic, or better still, a driver!'

'You're experienced in peeling spuds,' Polly said truthfully but cruelly. 'Better watch out, chuck, or you'll find yourself in the cookhouse, choppin' onions and weepin' into your stew.'

Fortunately, Ernie thought this a great joke, and presently the three of them sat down to meat pie, mashed potatoes and cabbage, with apple pie for afters. Then Dana suggested that they might listen to the wireless and catch up on the news, but Ernie shook his head. 'It's been grand, and you two must be the best cooks in Liverpool, but I thought I might take Poll to see a flick; then I want to get back to tell the fellers in me dormy that I'm to have a medical for to join the army.' He took his cap and jacket off the hook by the door and helped Polly into her coat, then turned to Dana. 'I know I've not said much but I'm real grateful for the way you've looked after our Polly,' he said gruffly. 'And I'll feel a whole lot happier joinin' the army knowin' you're goin' to keep an eye on her. If – if she gets in any trouble I guess you'd let me know.'

Dana laughed and said of course she would, then waved the pair off, tuned the wireless set and made herself comfortable, even brewing another pot of tea so that she could greet Polly on her return with a hot drink and a biscuit.

*　*　*

As soon as Polly and Ernie left Temperance Court, Ernie put his arm round Polly's waist and gave her a squeeze. 'I ain't gorra deal of money but I'm savin' up so's I can buy you a ring,' he said. 'I don't want some perishin' civilian stealin' you when I'm far away, fightin' for me country in foreign parts.' He turned and nuzzled his face into Polly's neck, giving her a rather wet kiss. 'Want to go to the flicks? It'll have to be the stalls, but I've got enough money for that, or for the Daulby Hall if you fancy a dance.'

Polly gave him an indignant shove and rubbed her neck vigorously where his kiss had landed. 'Stop it, Ernie. We're both too young to start getting serious,' she said severely. 'Besides, for all you know, the army may turn you down. What's on at the flicks anyway?'

'And you a film fan!' Ernie marvelled, grinning. 'I never met anyone who knew as much about the cinema as you do, Polly Smith, but if you'd rather we could go dancing. Then I could hold you in me arms . . .'

'Oh, Ernie, do shurrup, talkin' so soppy,' Polly said impatiently. 'As you've guessed, I'd much rather go to the flicks than go dancin'. How *could* I go dancin' in my workin' skirt and blouse, come to that? But if you've got it into your head that you can maul me about in one of them double seats at the back of the stalls, you can bleedin' well think again. You're right, I am a film fan, and that means I like to watch the screen without any silly distractions, so now you know the score.'

'I thought the score said that if you took a girl to the flicks – or a dance hall for that matter – you was entitled to a bit of a kiss and a cuddle,' Ernie said sulkily. 'I don't see why you're bein' so bleedin difficult.' Another thought struck him and he pulled Polly to a stop. 'And what do you mean, the army might not accept me? You've got a flamin' cheek! How can you suggest that they might turn down me manly charms? I tell you, you want to make the most of me whilst you've got the chance! Once I'm in uniform I'll have me pick of every girl what passes. So now, shall it be the Commodore? It's early, I know, but we can see the main feature round twice, if you like. It's *The Prince and the Pauper*, starrin' that Flynn feller.'

'Oh, then let's get a move on,' Polly said. She grinned at Ernie. 'Errol Flynn, eh? I've not seen him yet, apart from his photograph in the magazines, but they say he's even better than Douglas Fairbanks. Cor, I can't wait.'

By the time Polly and Ernie left the cinema fog had come drifting up from the river and it was definitely not a nice night to be abroad. The film, however, had lived up to Polly's expectations; all she wanted to do was to go over the story and discuss the charms of Errol Flynn, his magnificent physique and his brilliant acting, whilst what Ernie wanted was the kiss and cuddle that Polly had sternly forbidden him, even in the back row of the stalls. 'But no one can see,' he had objected, a hand sliding hopefully down from Polly's slender shoulder. 'The usherette's gone away . . .'

'Gerroff!' Polly had said sharply, her voice loud enough to cause Ernie's hand to fly from her arm as though of its own accord. 'I told you, Ernie Frost, I didn't want none of that. Keep your bleedin' hands to yourself, or I'll be forced to punch you on the snout.'

This remark, uttered far too loudly for Ernie's peace of mind, had caused a good deal of muffled giggling, whilst people in the row in front turned to stare. Naturally enough this annoyed both parties, but when Ernie began to expostulate Polly reminded him of her earlier strictures. 'We're pals; bezzies you could say,' she told him. 'And if you want it to stay that way, keep your hands to yourself.'

Ernie had mumbled a protest, but by the time they left the cinema all was forgotten and forgiven. Ernie had mugged them both to a choc ice, Polly's favourite food, and when he saw the mists swirling up from the river he offered to buy them two penn'orth of chips, for by this time the delicious stew and mashed potatoes was only a distant memory. So Ernie bought the chips and all might have been well had he not manoeuvred his pal into a convenient jigger, where he began once more to engage in the activity described by Polly as mauling her about and by Ernie as a kiss and a cuddle. In Polly's efforts to free herself her elbow met Ernie's left eye with a resounding and painful *clunk*. Ernie squawked with pain, his hand flying to his injured eye, whilst chips flew everywhere. Poor Ernie, his eye watering freely said crossly, 'Now look what you've done, you halfwit!'

But Polly did not mean to accept the blame. She gave him a shove which sent him staggering back against a brick wall and marched towards the nearest tram stop. 'I warned you what would happen if you kept on, but did you listen?' she demanded wrathfully. 'Oh, and I were lookin' forward to them chips; I'm that hungry me belly thinks me throat's been cut.'

'It weren't my fault, it were all your doin',' Ernie said, mopping his sore eye. 'I don't know as I want you for me girlfriend, Polly Smith. All I done was to give you a grand evenin' out and what's me reward? An eyeful of elbow and me chips scattered to the four winds and not a word of apology.'

Polly began to say, grudgingly, that though it was mostly his own fault she had not meant to elbow him in the eye, but at this inopportune moment a tram clattered to a halt beside them and Polly saw from its destination board that it was the one which would carry Ernie to his very door. She gave him a rather unkind shove. 'Oh, go and get aboard, you idiot,' she said crossly. 'It's foggy, and the trams will stop runnin' any minute.'

'I can't just buzz off . . .' Ernie began, but Polly cut across his words.

'Will you bleedin' well go? You can see I don't want you hangin' about,' she said crossly. 'Don't you know when you aren't wanted? Oh, here comes mine! Cheerio, Ernie. See you tomorrer.'

Still protesting, but less forcibly, Ernie climbed aboard his tram. As the vehicle pulled away he turned and mouthed something at his erstwhile companion, but Polly, as her tram drew up beside her, simply ignored him completely. She was still cross, knowing that the death of the chips had been her fault yet blaming Ernie nevertheless. Indeed, she never even waved as Ernie's conveyance disappeared into the mist. Instead, she leapt aboard her own almost empty tram and settled herself in one of the seats with a sigh of satisfaction. The film had been wonderful, but Ernie's behaviour had marred her enjoyment and she knew that the incident of the chips would be difficult for either of them to forget. It was all very well for her to blame Ernie, but if she were honest she knew that most boys expected certain favours in return for taking a girl dancing or to a cinema. To be sure, she had explained to Ernie over and over that she did not want a boyfriend, but he had been difficult to convince. Now, however, perhaps he would believe her, in which case they could remain good friends. Once he was in the army, of course, she supposed he would consider himself a man; at any rate their relationship would change. Either he would be a proper boyfriend or they would part company, and right now she realised she was too tired to consider which outcome she would prefer. It was at this point that the conductor, who had been chatting to his driver, came swaying down the aisle of the tram, yawning behind his hand. 'Fares please, chuck,' he said laconically. 'Filthy perishin' night, ain't it? This 'un's probably the last tram tonight.'

'I'm not surprised; fog's getting thicker,' Polly said, plunging her hand into the pocket of her trusty navy overcoat. 'Me and me boyfriend have been to the Commy to see this here new feller . . . Oh my Gawd!'

'Whazza matter?' the conductor said, though not as though he cared very much. He gave another enormous yawn. 'Tuppence please, miss.'

'Hang on a minute,' Polly said breathlessly. 'I can't find – I seem to have lost – oh I say, I'm awful sorry; me boyfriend got on the tram before this 'un not realising I didn't bring me purse out and I've not gorra penny to me name. But if you've got a pencil and a bit of paper I'll leave you me name and address and I'll pay you double fare tomorrow. Or you could give me your name and I'll drop it off at the depot, just as soon as I've got my purse.'

The conductor grinned, then shook his head sadly,

'Good try, miss, but you know full well I can't go doin' no deals with me passengers. You'll have to gerroff,' he told her. And then, as she got reluctantly to her feet and hesitated, clutching the pole and turning to try to persuade the man to let her remain aboard, he detached her clinging fingers and gave her a shove as the tram came to a halt. 'Goodnight, Miss Tuppence Short,' he said sarcastically and then rang the bell once more. 'Off we go, Reg!' he bawled at the driver. Polly, unable to think of a stinging retort, began to trudge in the vehicle's wake, shivering as the chilly fog swirled around her. But she told herself firmly that a walk would do her good and plodded determinedly on.

It had been late when they left the cinema, later still when she and Ernie had parted company, and now she guessed it could be getting on for midnight, not at all the sort of time a nice girl should be walking beside the docks. But she tucked her hands into her pockets, turned up her coat collar and trudged on, knowing that she had a long walk ahead of her. What a fool she had been! There had been bad feeling between her and Ernie, but she knew very well that he would not have dreamed of leaving her alone and penniless had he suspected even for an instant that she might not have her tram fare tucked away somewhere. As she walked Polly mused on the fickleness of fate. She always kept a few pennies, usually more, in the pocket of her working coat but tonight for some reason they had not been there. She plunged her hand into her pocket once more, then stopped short, her other hand flying to her mouth. There was a small hole in the lining of the pocket, and now that she had remembered the hole – which she had been meaning to mend for weeks – she also realised what must have happened. Usually she carried large copper pennies and halfpennies in that pocket, but she had decided that it was partly the weight of the coins which had worn the hole so only the previous day she had exchanged the coppers for a sixpenny piece, a coin just the right size to slip unnoticed through the hole and go tinkling off on its own affairs. Infuriatingly, her searching fingers might actually have pushed the tanner through the hole while she was still aboard the vehicle she had just left. But knowing this was no comfort whatsoever; even her anger with the unfriendly conductor was not enough to keep her warm, so she pulled her beret down over her ears and increased her pace. She wished she had been wearing her warm boots, had thought to bring her woolly gloves and a scarf, but she had not done so. Such clothing was a nuisance in the well-heated cinema and neither she nor Ernie had even considered having to walk further than the nearest tram stop. Sighing heavily and telling herself it would be a lesson to her, Polly slogged on.

By the time she reached the dock where the big liners were berthed she had begun to warm up a little, and she slowed down to peer through the swirling yellow fog at the dim shape of an enormous ship. There were a few people milling around below though it seemed a strange hour for passengers to be coming ashore. On the other hand, she knew that arrivals and departures were dependent upon the state of the tide, and anyway the figures that she could see, stumbling up to the roadside, might be crew and not passengers at all. Polly speeded

up again, then paused as someone called her name. 'Polly
. . . Over here, girl.'

Polly, who had begun to feel very vulnerable, felt a
great wave of relief flood over her. Ernie must have
guessed that she had no money, must have disembarked
from his own tram as soon as he realised, and was coming
to her rescue. Polly turned a big smile upon the
young man running towards her . . . then realised with
a sinking of the heart that it was not one man but three
and that none of them was Ernie. In fact they were all
total strangers . . . but how had they known her name?
She voiced the question as soon as they reached her.

'Who the hell are you and why did you shout me
name?' she asked belligerently. 'I thought you were me
pal.'

The three men took no notice. They had surrounded
her and were pulling her away from the bright street
lights towards the shadows of the piled-up boxes, barrels
and other impedimenta awaiting delivery. 'I'm your pal,
'cos I reached you first,' the tallest of them said. He was
also the fattest, and he had a great beefy hand with fingers
like sausages gripped tightly around Polly's skinny wrist.
'Got any friends, queen? Else you'll have to do between
the three of us.' He grabbed her chin in his hands and
turned her face up and Polly smelt the beer on his breath.
'You're nowt but a scrawny chick. I likes a woman wit'
some flesh on her bones,' he added discontentedly.

'She'll do me,' another voice chimed in. This one
belonged to a younger skinnier man with a weasel face
and a drooping mouth.

Polly stared defiantly from face to face. 'You've got it
all wrong. I just gorrof the tram too early and am on me

way home to bed,' she said, but was unable to stop her voice shaking a little. 'Me name's Polly. I thought that was what you were calling.'

'Nah, we was calling *Oy, you!*' the third man explained. He was older than the others, grey-haired and deeply tanned. He turned to his mates. 'I reckon we've made a mistake,' he began, but was immediately overruled.

'No matter; she'll do,' the weaselly one said. He reached out and grabbed Polly by the front of her coat. Buttons popped and Polly began to fight, horribly aware that if she did not do so at once she would speedily find herself in real trouble.

The weasel-faced one laughed hoarsely and grabbed for Polly's blouse. More buttons popped, but the man gave a grunt of pain as Polly's well-aimed knee caught him somewhere soft and yielding. The fat one was laughing, cheering his mate on, whilst the older man said uneasily that if this was no dockyard trollop they could easily be in for it. Polly had fallen to her knees and was trying to drag her clothes around her. On her way down she had bitten the fat man's hand to the bone and hacked weasel-face in the shins, but she was all too conscious of their superior strength as well as numbers and began to scream for help at the top of her voice. Weasel-face promptly threw himself on top of her, endeavouring to gag her with one long and filthy hand. Biting that hand was a pretty disgusting experience but Polly bit anyway and to some effect. Weasel-face screamed with pain, his voice mingling with Polly's cries for help as she kicked and fought, and to her unutterable relief she heard a man's voice say sharply: 'What's all this? You must be seamen from the SS *Georgia*. I'll see you reported to your officers.'

The weaselly one, struggling to his feet, began to whine that it were nothing to do with him; all he'd done was try to help the young lady to her feet after she'd fallen over a spar of wood, but the wild cat had misunderstood and bit him to the bone till he was likely to die from the poison . . . here the fat man gave a contemptuous snort. 'Don't you take no notice, sir. These dockside whores scream when us pleasures them,' he began, only to be told that dockside whore or not the girl had received pretty rough handling from three great brutes who no doubt intended to cheat the lass of her fee.

This was enough to jerk Polly to her feet. 'I got off my tram a stop too soon and these – these creatures got quite the wrong idea. I'm as – as respectable as you are your-self,' she said tearfully, speaking as Dana was trying to teach her to do, though she reverted to her Liverpool accent as a rule when not in Dana's company. 'I told them and told them that I wasn't the sort of girl they were looking for, but they wouldn't believe me.' She looked down at herself, at the buttonless blouse and coat, and burst into tears.

The three men who had attacked her saw that the newcomer's attention was all on their erstwhile victim and made off, though the grey-haired one shouted over his shoulder that he was sorry and had had no part in what had gone on. Then her rescuer ushered Polly gently out from behind the pile of crates and she saw that he was accompanied by another man, who had not yet spoken. The two of them stood gazing anxiously down at Polly. 'Do you want to call the police?' the man who had confronted her attackers asked. 'Are you much hurt?

Those brutes should be taken in charge and prosecuted for assault, but by now they'll be half a mile away, running like rabbits.' He chuckled. 'You were giving a pretty good account of yourself, from what we could hear as we ran across the quay looking for you.'

'Oh, thanks ever so much, but I'm all right now,' Polly said, her voice almost steady. 'They thought I was – I was a bad girl, though I really don't know why.' She took a couple of experimental steps, then groaned. 'Ooh, me legs are a mass of bruises and I don't have a penny piece on me. How'll I get home, sir?' She looked hopefully at her rescuers. She judged them to be thirty or forty and they were of medium height and both clad in raincoats, scarves and checked caps. Polly peered into their faces, forgetting her own problems for a moment. 'Are you twins?' she asked. 'I can't see much, what wi' the fog and them caps, but you're that alike . . .'

Both men laughed, showing excellent sets of white teeth, which reminded Polly of the film she had just seen. Errol Flynn had just such gleaming white fangs, she remembered. The man who had been first on the scene was answering her question. 'No, but we are brothers. I'm Jake Freeway; I'm older than Ralph here by several years and if we weren't all muffled up you'd not even suspect we were twins. I'm the handsome one, you see; Ralph's plain as a boot! But to answer your other question, if you can recommend a decent hotel we'll get a cab and drop you off at your home. I take it you live hereabouts?'

'That's right,' Polly said nervously. Nice though these men seemed she realised she did not much want to share a taxi with two strangers after her nasty experience with the men from the SS *Georgia*. On the other hand her legs were trembling, her arms ached and she was uneasily aware of the cold creeping in past her buttonless clothing.

The man who had introduced himself as Jake Freeway, however, seemed to divine her problem. 'You'd best sit in front with the cabby,' he told her. 'Then you can direct him to your house before he takes us to the hotel.' He smiled at her kindly and bent to pick up a large suitcase which he must have dropped before frightening off her attackers. 'How far do we have to walk to find a cab?'

'I don't know; the trams and buses don't run late at night when it's foggy and I've never caught a taxi – cab, I mean,' Polly said doubtfully. 'We'd best walk towards the Pier Head; that's where all the trams and buses turn round. As for hotels . . .' But the younger man had put two fingers in his mouth and produced one of the shrillest whistles Polly had ever heard, and before she could do more than give him a startled glance he was holding up an arm and a taxi was screeching to a halt beside them.

'Well done, feller,' his brother said approvingly. 'I guess cabs and their drivers are the same the whole world over.' He opened the front passenger door and bundled Polly inside, then both men hefted their suitcases into the vehicle and climbed in after them. 'Home, James, and don't spare the horses,' the one called Jake said cheerfully. He leaned forward to address the cabby, who had twisted in his seat and was staring enquiringly from one face to the other. 'We're taking this young lady home first and then we'd like you to take us . . .' He hesitated, and Polly cut in.

'It's awful late, and most of the little hotels, the cheap

ones, don't have a night porter,' she said. 'But the Adelphi stays open all night just about. It'll be pricey, but if you just sign in for the one night . . .'

Both men laughed. 'I guess we won't go broke for one night in a good hotel,' the younger of the two said, speaking for the first time; Ralph, wasn't it? 'Now give the cabby your address. Will your ma and pa still be up?'

Polly frowned; ma and pa? Clearly this young man thought her still a child. 'I haven't got neither; me and my friend Dana have a room-share. It's in Temperance Court, so if the cabby will drop me beside the arch I'll be home and dry in half a minute.'

Ralph said that they ought to drive her right to her door, but the cabby knew that this was impossible. 'S'all right,' he said resignedly. 'You ain't English, are you, lerralone you ain't Scousers else you'd know you can't drive into the courts. But we'll watch the young lady until she gets indoors if that'll satisfy you.'

'Oh, but I want you to meet Dana; I know she'll want to thank you,' Polly said. She had been puzzled, she now realised, by the men's accents but had assumed them to be Irish. Now she thought again. 'Me and my pal had just left the cinema. The film was the new Errol Flynn . . . are you Americans, sir?'

Both men laughed but it was Ralph who answered. 'Yeah, we're Yanks, as you Limeys call us. At least, we've lived in the States for the past ten years. Over there they say we've got English accents but I guess over here everyone will think we're genuine citizens of the good old US of A.'

'Gosh, Americans,' Polly breathed. 'Are you here on holiday? Or visiting long-lost relatives? Or are you touring Britain the way I've heard Americans do?' She sighed. 'It must be grand to travel. I say, are you anything to do with the cinema?' Her voice grew awed. 'I suppose you aren't film stars, are you?'

The men were laughing and denying it, though the elder of the two admitted that they did have cinematograph connections, as the taxi drew up beside the entrance to Temperance Court. Polly prepared to alight, profuse thanks on her lips, but Jake Freeway shook his head chidingly and got out of the cab. 'I'll see you to your door and explain what's happened to this friend of yours,' he said firmly. 'Here, take my arm – your legs are still shaky.' He chuckled suddenly. 'Don't worry, I'll see you safe indoors, have a quick word with this friend of yours and then book in at the Adelphi.'

As Polly had foreseen, Dana was not only still up but beginning to be very worried indeed. As Polly pushed open the door she erupted into the hallway, almost knocking Polly over with the strength of the hug she gave her.

'You're safe! Oh, thank God, Polly . . . I've been so worried . . .' Over her friend's shoulder she saw the looming shape of a tall, heavily built man muffled up against the cold. She gave an involuntary gasp and stepped back and Polly hastily broke into an explanation.

'Oh, Dana, this is Mr Freeway. He and his brother just about saved my bacon this evening.' She turned to the man behind her. 'Mr Freeway, you must be just as tired as I am, but I really would like to thank you properly and I know Dana will feel the same when I've explained the situation. Would it be possible for us to meet tomorrow – after work, I mean? We both have jobs of sorts . . .'

'That'll be just fine and dandy,' her companion said easily. 'I think we'll be at the Adelphi for two or three nights, so if we ask you to come to the hotel at six thirty would that be possible? You see, I think with your local knowledge you might be of great assistance to my brother and myself.'

'Yes, of course we will,' Polly said eagerly. 'But right now what I want most in the world is a cup of cocoa and my bed.' She turned as she spoke and Dana saw her torn and buttonless clothing for the first time. She gasped, pointing a quivering finger at the ruined garments, but the strange man reassured her.

'It's not as bad as it looks, Miss Dana,' he said earnestly. 'We reached your friend before any real harm had come to her. But I'm sure she'll explain far better than I could.' He had taken off his checked cap as soon as he and Polly had entered the hall and Dana saw that his hair was greying at the temples. She thought he was probably in his mid to late forties. He smiled at her, replaced his cap on thick, wavy dark hair and turned towards the still open door. 'Good night, ladies. See you tomorrow evening. Six thirty at the Adelphi, and ask for the Freeway brothers.'

As soon as their visitor had gone Polly plunged into the story of her evening, though she did not say much about the row with Ernie which had resulted in her getting on the tram unaccompanied and penniless. Instead she gave a graphic account of the attack by members of the crew of the SS *Georgia* and of her rescue by the American brothers.

'Oh, Polly, you poor kid, what a ghastly thing to happen,' Dana said remorsefully. 'But I'm surprised at Ernie letting you go home alone.'

'Oh, dear. I suppose I'll have to tell you the rest,' Polly said rather forlornly. 'The truth is, we had a bit of a barney.' Dana listened to the story, torn between amusement and pity for poor Ernie. She was pretty sure he would never overstep the mark, but realised that Polly was in the right of it. If she did not love the lad then it would be unfair to encourage him to hope by permitting kissing and cuddling. Ernie was two or three years older than Polly. She would have a word with him; try to explain that Polly was still too young for a warmer relationship than that which already existed between them and could be best described as friendship. But right now she was just in time to grab Polly's half-empty cocoa cup before its owner actually fell asleep sitting at the kitchen table on one of the hard wooden chairs.

'You're worn out. If there's anything more to tell you can do so tomorrow before we go off to work,' she said severely. 'It's very wrong of me to expect to get any sort of explanation out of you at this hour. Do you realise it's after midnight?' She pulled the younger girl to her feet and began to bustle her through the door.

'Oh, Dana, I wonder why they want to talk to us? What use can we possibly be to a couple of rich Americans? They must be rich since they're staying at the Adelphi . . .'

'Polly Smith, will you kindly shut up and start getting ready for bed,' Dana said firmly. 'You've got to be up early tomorrow because you'll have to mend your blouse

173

and your coat. Well, I suppose you can wear your other blouse, because the one you've got on won't ever be much good again, but your coat is the only one you've got. Did you pick up the buttons?'

Polly, already tearing off her clothes with wild abandon and struggling into her nightdress, gave a wail. 'Oh, Dana, as though I could've picked up the bleedin' buttons in the dark with the quayside covered in boxes and packets and such like. Anyway, I never even thought of it. Oh, what'll I do? Don't ask me to go back there and crawl around on all fours, for I doubt if I'd find even one, let alone six.'

Dana, pulling her own nightgown over her head, gave a muffled giggle. 'Honestly, Polly, you can buy a new set of buttons off Paddy's market for a tanner; maybe less. We'll do that first thing. I've got a long scarf you can borrow. If you leave it loose round your neck it'll hide the fact that you can't button up your coat. And now go to sleep for goodness' sake or we'll be a couple of nervous wrecks by morning.'

Despite the traumatic events of the previous evening both girls woke early, and when someone knocked at the front door Dana went to it at once with her mouth full of toast, expecting to see the postman with a package for some other tenant who hadn't answered his knock. However, it was not the postman but Ernie, looking flushed and worried. Dana had barely got the door open before he had pushed past it and grabbed her hand, his own so hot and sweaty that she detached her fingers from his as soon as she decently could and wiped her hand across the back of her skirt. She opened her mouth to tell him that all was well but had no chance to say a word before he broke into speech.

'Where's Polly? Is she home? Oh, Gawd, Dana just tell me she's safe . . . but I reckon she must be or you wouldn't be standin' here but round at the nearest police station, tellin' the scuffers she were lost.'

'She's here, don't worry.' Dana would have said more, but Ernie gave a huge sigh and closed his eyes for a moment, then opened them and fixed them on Dana's face.

'Oh, thank Gawd,' he breathed devoutly. 'I bin imaginin' her in all sorts o' trouble. The thing was, you see, that we'd had a bit of a disagreement in the picture house; nothin' to write home about, just what you might call a lovers' tiff . . .'

'It weren't nothin' of the sort,' an indignant voice said from the doorway of the girls' room. 'I'll thank you not to go tellin' Dana a load of lies, since I've already told her the truth and she knows just what happened.'

Ernie's shoulders sagged with relief. 'I never should've let you get on that tram wi'out me, though. I thought you mightn't have any money, but by the time it occurred to me the tram I were on was going full pelt along the Dock Road.' He turned to Dana, who was hustling them all into the living room and closing the door firmly behind them. She had no desire to make their doings public property, and Mrs Bowen who had the rooms on the first floor was notoriously nosy. Ernie began to gabble an apology, adding what a good thing it was that his Polly had a head on her shoulders and had thought to provide herself with a tram fare in case of emergencies such as the one that had arisen the previous evening. Polly interrupted him without ceremony.

175

'I did have me tram fare but it fell out through a hole in my pocket,' she began, and told Ernie the whole story. Dana watched as Ernie paled.

'Oh, Polly, will you ever forgive me?' he asked huskily. 'And them fellers what rescued you – them Yanks – are you sure it's wise to go to the hotel to meet them? Suppose they got the wrong idea, thought the fellers from the SS *Georgia* . . . or mebbe they's what they call white traders, pickin' up gals off the streets and shippin' 'em to South America . . .'

He got no further. Polly clapped a hand over his mouth and boxed his ears when he protested. He began to ask indignantly what he had done to deserve such treatment and she enlightened him at once. 'You're sayin' they think I'm a bad girl, what that horrible man called a dockside whore,' she said bluntly. 'Well, if that's what you think, Ernie Frost, you can just bugger off and never come near me again.'

Ernie began to protest that he had neither said nor meant such a thing; Polly insisted that his remark had mortally insulted her; and Dana, laughing helplessly, got between them. Then she made them both sit down whilst she poured cups of tea and started toasting bread. 'You are a pair of idiots, honest to God you are,' she said when both parties had ceased to shout and were merely sipping tea, crunching toast and glowering at one another. She turned reproachful eyes on Polly. 'Of course Ernie didn't mean to insult you; I'm sure he knows by now that your morals are strict enough for a bishop. Now calm down and see if Ernie can think of a way we might be able to help the Freeways.'

Ernie began to say rather sulkily that he could think

of nothing, then suddenly stopped and stared from one face to the other. 'Freeway, Freeway,' he said thoughtfully. 'Now where have I heard that name before?' He appeared to cogitate, a frown etched on his brow, then it cleared and he snapped his fingers. 'Got it!' he exclaimed. 'Remember that old cinema, Poll, the one out in the sticks where we went to see *Snow White* 'cos you'd not seen it when it first come out? I went past it a week or so ago when I were doin' messages on me bike for the greengrocer at the top of St Domingo's Road. It were pretty run down when we was there and I believe it closed only a couple of weeks later. But now someone's done it up real posh. The frontage was white marble, with gold edgings to each block. It used to be called the Harmonica – well, maybe not that, but something similar – but now it's got a new name what's writ in that stuff what lights up at night and it's called the Freeway Cinema. Well, if that ain't a coincidence it's pretty damn weird.'

'I don't know about that,' Polly said having thought the matter over. 'Perhaps it really is just one of those odd coincidences. Or might you have remembered the name of the cinema wrong? Might it be the Fairway? Or the Freedom? You never know.'

Ernie, however, shook his head, 'No, I'm sure I'm right,' he insisted, 'and what's more there's something else, something I never even thought of until just now. I've got a pal, a feller named Bruce Evans. I met him a couple of days ago and asked him where he's been, 'cos we've not met for years. He told me he's been workin' at a cinema in Manchester. He's a trained projectionist, but his cinema is closing and he'd had news on the grapevine that someone's reopening an old picture house on the outskirts of Liverpool. I reckon it's that one. No, don't you scoff, Polly Smith.' Ernie tapped his head. 'There's a lot more to me than meets the eye. What do you bet me, those two Yanks is a-goin' to reopen the old Harmonica? I'll give you odds of ten to one if you like.'

His tone was so convincing that Polly declined to bet, and even Dana said firmly that she would keep her money in her purse thank you very much but would be the first to congratulate him if he proved to be right.

Ernie crunched down the last piece of toast, swigged his tea in one long swallow and set off for the outside world. 'Can I come with you this evening to talk to these here Yanks?' he enquired hopefully, a hand already on the doorknob. 'If there's jobs going . . .'

Both girls cried out at this but agreed that he might come round to their place at about nine o' clock to be told what had transpired.

All that day both Dana and Polly dreamed wonderful dreams. Suppose Ernie was right and the Freeway brothers really were rich Americans, perhaps even film stars? Suppose they had taken a liking to Polly and Dana and meant to offer either one or both of them a part in a film being made at Pinewood Studios? But by the time work was over and the girls had enjoyed a strip down wash in front of the fire and dressed in their best, they were beginning to face the difference between their wild imaginings and what was likelier to be the truth.

They took a tram to the city centre and entered the Adelphi dead on half past six, to be greeted in the foyer by a smart young woman in a plain black skirt and frilly white blouse, who seemed to be expecting them. 'You'll be the two young ladies who've come to see Mr Freeway and his brother. Follow me and I'll take you to the inter-view room.' Obediently following, Polly hissed, 'Interview room? Does she have the right people? They never said . . .'

'I expect it's just that they want to talk to us quietly,' Dana reassured her. 'Or they may really have work for us and need to know if we're suitable for the sort of job they have in mind. I wonder if Ernie was right and there's some connection between them and that cinema?' At this point the young woman ahead of them stopped outside a white-painted door, knocked gently on the panel and then, upon hearing a voice bidding her to enter, pushed the door open and gestured the girls to go inside.

Here, a considerable surprise awaited them. They had expected to see the Freeway brothers and indeed they were there, smiling a welcome, but so were several other people. A plump, motherly-looking woman in her fifties, two neatly dressed girls, a young man with hornrimmed spectacles and another, younger, with a quiff of blond hair and a cheerful grin. 'Ernie!' Polly exclaimed. 'What on earth are you doing here?'

By the time everyone had been introduced and everyone's story told, it was getting on for ten o'clock and the Freeway brothers insisted on sending everyone home by taxi. Ernie and Bruce – the young man with the horn-rimmed spectacles had turned out to be Ernie's friend the projectionist – joined the girls in their taxi but very little was said until the four of them were in the girls' room, where Dana made everyone cocoa and they discussed the glorious news that the Freeway brothers had told them.

179

Apparently, Jake and Ralph – they had insisted that Christian names must be used – had been interested for some time in acquiring an old cinema, in order to emulate a young American who had done just that in what Jake described as small-town America. Seeing his success, both Jake and Ralph had thought they would like to do as he had done, but if possible in England, for though they had been absent from the country of their birth for a decade they both wanted to return to their roots.

'And it's not as though we have family in the States,' Jake had explained. 'Our parents are dead, but we owe a great deal to our father's younger sister. She gave us money for our fares to America when we decided to try our luck over there, and though we repaid her as soon as we got jobs, we felt we'd like to be near her.' He had grinned at the motherly-looking woman, sitting primly on a straight-backed chair. 'Meet Auntie Jane – Mrs Jane Mullins to you. We asked her to keep a lookout for any cinema likely to come up for sale over here, and a year ago she got word that the Harmonica was failing. Six months after that she told us that the place was on the market. We came over, bought it and arranged with someone Auntie knew to refurbish it completely. We were both working in the cinema industry and sent money home to our aunt every month to pay for the renovation. The workmen did a good job and Auntie thought it was about time we returned to start trading, so we booked our passage on the SS *Georgia*. We were lucky in that Bruce contacted us, sending excellent references, so naturally we hired him – by letter of course – and told him to keep his eyes open for other likely employees, because we knew we'd need a fair number of 'em. But we'd had a bad experience in the States – a front of house manager was systematically stealing from us, and when we began to suspect he took off with just about every cent we'd made. So you see, we didn't mean to employ folk we didn't know; and that, guys and gals, is why you find yourselves here today. Every one of you is known to either ourselves or our aunt, so no strangers will be involved, for now at any rate. We'll need a projectionist, that'll be Specs here, half a dozen usherettes, a fair number of cleaners, a cashier, and a clerk to do the books. Eventually, when we get going, we'll be opening a cafeteria on the third floor, though that's for the future.'

Polly's hand had shot up and when Jake raised his eyebrows at her she asked bluntly: 'What about Ernie? Oh, I don't deny he's honest as the day and a real hard worker, but I don't see him as an usherette, somehow, nor a cleaner neither.'

Everyone had laughed, except for Ernie, who flushed and looked defensive. 'I come wi' me old pal Bruce here, but truth to tell I come along to make sure our Polly was all right.' He looked Jake Freeway straight in the eye. 'You don't know about Cathy's Place, of course.'

When he had told the story, Jake had slapped him on the shoulder and turned to grin at Dana. 'Well I'm jiggered!' he exclaimed. 'Honey, you're the answer to a cinema owner's dream. I was going to ask you to act as usherette a couple of times a week, but with your experience in catering you'd be the ideal person to start up our cafeteria. Oh, not at once, but as soon as we see it's needed and will bring a decent profit. Are you on?'

Dana had replied that nothing would please her more

181

and she would let him have references from employers past and present just as soon as she could.

By now everyone was on the best of terms with everyone else, so when Jake had clapped his hands for silence an instant hush had fallen on the assembled company. 'Any more questions? Then I'll say goodnight, and you will all get letters confirming your jobs as soon as we've sorted things out,' he said briskly. 'And since I only hired this room for two hours, and it's already nearly ten o' clock . . .' Amidst much laughter the party had broken up, and the girls had invited Ernie and Bruce back to their room for cocoa and biscuits.

'Well, I reckon we've landed on our feet,' Bruce said when the cocoa had been drunk, the biscuits eaten, and the wonderful opportunity thoroughly discussed. 'And I liked it when he said that we'd all muck in and help with any job which needed doing. I know cleaning a cinema doesn't sound very glamorous . . .'

'But who cares about that when they say we can watch films free,' Polly said excitedly. 'I'd rather go to the cinema than to a theatre or a dance hall or even to a fun fair, so I'm on. Ralph said they'd be showing mainly U certificates at first, because on the whole they'll be cheaper to hire than A or H films. He doesn't mean to try to compete with what you might call the premier league – Gaumonts and Odeons and that – but who cares? He'll start off with black and whites, of course, mainly B pictures rather than main features, but I suppose they'll get round to affording Technicolor once they get going.'

'Yes, all right, but now all I need is me bed. Me head's swimming with all this talk of picture houses and films and who's going to do what,' Ernie said rather crossly, and Dana realised that he must be feeling left out. She turned and gave Polly a nudge.

'Ernie's quite right. We've spent the whole evening talking about the Freeway Cinema, but until they get their first films organised we'll have to go on working in the market,' she said. Both boys had risen to their feet and she went over to the door and held it open. 'Sorry, lads, but I guess you're as tired as we are. Goodnight!'

Bruce grinned. 'I reckon we've overstayed our welcome. Put it down to excitement,' he said cheerfully. 'Goodnight, girls. I reckon them two Yanks are what they call hustlers in the States, and we'll all be working together in no time.'

Chapter Seven

Despite the lateness of the hour the girls continued to conjecture as they got ready for bed. They had bought Polly a bed of her own as soon as they could afford it and Polly often said it was a good thing she was under-sized since the bed was both narrow and short. 'But it's a lot better'n the bed I had at the home,' she told Dana. 'One of these days, when you an' me's rich and runnin' our own tea room, I'll have a big, old-fashioned feather mattress, like what you talked about t'other night.'

Dana felt the hairs on the back of her neck stand upright. Oh God, she must have been talking in her sleep again! She thought she had completely forgotten the dream, but Polly's words brought it back and despite herself the very recollection of the incident made her smile. She and Deirdre, the girl from the village who came up to help Mrs McBride with the housework two or three times a week, had been making her parents' bed. The old brass bedstead was sturdy, but it was easy to snag the great striped feather mattress on a spring if one was not careful. Trying to hurry, Deirdre had pulled in one direction and Dana in another, and before they knew it the two girls had found themselves in a whirling snow-storm of feathers, made worse by the fact that they had opened the window and a spiteful wind had blown in, carrying some feathers outside and sending the remainder into a mad, whirling dance.

'Shut the window, Dana, or sure as me name's Capting Carruthers there'll be more of your mammy's feather mattress in County Cork than on this bed,' Deirdre shouted. 'Ah, 'tis a judgement on us for tryin' to hurry so it is!'

Dana, obeying the older girl's instruction, slammed the window shut and sank on to the bedstead, combing her hair with her fingers and coming up with a good haul of feathers. 'Gosh!' she exclaimed. 'More haste less speed, Mammy would say . . .' She eyed her companion curiously. 'But your name isn't Captain Carruthers, Deirdre; it isn't even Carruthers. You're a McCarthy.'

'Oh aye, but it were Capting Carruthers what I first heard say that,' Deirdre said, as though it settled the matter. 'Come on, alanna, let's start collectin' the feathers in a pillowcase, then when I've mended the tear we've made we can put 'em back – into the mattress I mean.'

'Right. But Deirdre, when you say you're Captain Carruthers and you aren't . . .'

Deirdre shrugged. ''Twill all be the same in a t'ousand years,' she said unarguably. She began carefully picking up the feathers one at a time.

Dana slid off the bed and was beginning to do likewise when another thought struck her. 'Deirdre, if you sew up the tear in the mattress before you tip back the pillow-case full of feathers, how will you get them in?'

Deirdre was a plump, rosy-cheeked country girl; Dana had known her all her life and loved her dearly, but was often puzzled by the way the older girl's mind worked.

Now, she waited with some amusement for Deirdre's reply.

Deirdre frowned, then a dimple appeared in her cheek and she gave Dana an admiring look. 'Haven't you a head on your shoulders, Dana McBride,' she said, her tone awestruck. 'Sure and I had it the wrong way round.' She ticked off the actions she should take on her fingers. 'First, we pick up the feathers and put 'em in the pillowcase. Next, we tip the feathers back into the mattress ticking, and, last of all, I get needle and t'read from your mammy's sewing box and mend the tear.' She beamed at Dana. 'Will we start right away? Only 'tis t'irsty I am and me stomach says it's time for mid-mornings, so if we go down to the kitchen we'll likely find tea and brack waitin' for us and I wouldn't like Cook to think we didn't 'preciate her food.'

Dana looked at the sea of feathers. Now that the window was shut they were drifting floorwards, but every time she or Deirdre moved the feathers moved too. She grinned at her companion. 'I reckon you've got the right idea this time. Whilst we're out of the room having our mid-mornings the feathers will settle and if we come in very, very carefully we'll likely get most of them back where they belong without too much trouble.'

Deirdre agreed eagerly and the two girls left the large and pleasant bedroom, closing the door carefully behind them. They ran down the wide, elegant staircase and went into the kitchen, entering just as Donovan McBride and Johnny Devlin came in through the back door. Mr McBride looked accusingly at his daughter. 'Have you been plucking a goose in our bedroom?' he asked aggrievedly. 'As Johnny and myself crossed the wild garden we thought it had begun to snow, but it was only—'

'Feathers,' Dana and Deirdre said in chorus, Dana adding: 'We had a bit of an accident with your feather bed; sorry, Daddy. We'll put it right as soon as we've had a cup of tea and a bite.' She reached up and took a feather out of her father's thick thatch of greying red hair. 'We snagged the mattress on one of those brass springs, but it won't take long to put things right.'

Mr Devlin grinned at her. 'And what about the ones that are now decorating the garden?' he said. 'Are you going to collect the feathers off every bush and flower? If you don't, your mammy and daddy will likely find themselves sleeping on bedsprings tonight.'

'Oh, ha ha, very funny,' Dana said sarcastically. 'Have some brack, Mr Devlin; it's good so it is. And where's Con?'

'He's long-reining the new colt,' Con's father said briefly. 'But he'll be in for his tay and brack, never fear.'

'Dana? Did you hear what I said? I'll have a feather mattress one of these days, like the one you and your pal split . . . Dana?'

Brought abruptly back to the present, Dana glanced across the darkened room to where Polly lay in her small bed. 'Have I been talking in my sleep again?' she asked. 'I suppose I must have been. Goodness, Deirdre and myself ended up feather-picking for hours and hours. Do I often talk in my sleep, Polly? I don't believe I ever did such a thing whilst Caitlin and I lived together.'

Polly, who had snuggled down, sat up again as though she needed to be upright in order to think things through. 'Is that so? Well, I reckon it'll be that bump on the head

187

which landed you in hospital. Odd, ain't it? But they say concussion can make you forget, so I suppose it can make you remember as well.'

'But I don't *want* to remember!' Dana had blurted the words out unthinkingly and clapped a hand to her mouth, wishing she could take them back. Hastily, she broke into speech. 'But you haven't answered my question. Do I often talk in my sleep?'

'I dunno; I sleep pretty sound meself. There's nights when you could quote the Holy Bible or Nuttall's dictionary for hours at a time, and I'd never hear a word. Never hear nothin' but me own snores, to tell you the truth. It's just occasionally, when something happens to keep me awake, that I hear you rabbiting on.' She laughed. 'Sometimes it's real interesting, a bit like listenin' to a play on the wireless. I feel I'm getting to know your parents and your pal Deirdre, and that feller Con what's your best mate . . .'

'Oh, but Polly, it's only dreams,' Dana protested. 'It's all nonsense really. Just you forget all about it, because I don't want to be reminded about my life in Ireland. Come to that, you never talk about your life in the children's home and I've never asked you what it was like.'

'I'll tell you some time, when you've a week to spare,' Polly said gruffly. 'And now let's go to sleep or we'll be fit for nothin' in the morning.'

Ernie was now a regular visitor at the house in Temperance Court. His medical had been deferred since the armed forces were having a rush of would-be recruits following the Japanese attacks on British and American shipping on the Yangtze river in December, but this did not worry him; indeed, he thought it was in his favour since he had applied before the incident. Meanwhile, he had managed to get another job cleaning cars, vans and even the great horse-drawn drays.

Christmas had passed pleasantly for the two girls because Ernie and Bruce agreed to spend the day with them on condition that they provided a good deal of the food. They exchanged small gifts, cooked and ate a traditional chicken dinner, and played silly games which had them all in fits of laughter.

When the day of Ernie's medical arrived, Polly saw him off on the overhead railway to Seaforth, where it was to be held, but could not meet him on his return since he had no idea which train he would be on. He visited them later that evening, however, and told them that nerves had made him wheeze, though he had done his best to fool the Medical Officer who had sounded his chest. 'He moved that stethoscope thing all round and then on to me back, which he didn't do with everyone,' he said. 'So what I did was, I breathed real shallow 'cos I knew if I took a big, deep breath, like he kept tellin' me, I'd start a-coughin' and that would never do.' He grinned at his audience, which included Bruce. 'I don't mean to tell you any of the other things what went on, but I don't mind admittin' I couldn't understand a reason for the half of it. It were done – the medical, I mean – in a huge old hall. They lined us up and the medics went up and down the lines, each one doing somethin' different. When it was over, the last man patted me on the shoulder and said he thought I'd done all right and not to worry if the results was a time coming through because the paperwork had to be done and it took longer'n one would believe possible.'

'Oh well, that just means we'll have you with us for a bit longer,' Polly said cheerfully. 'We're goin' to miss you somethin' awful, young Ernie. But there'll be your leaves to look forward to.'

The end of January arrived and one evening after he had finished work Ernie turned up at the room in Temperance Court. He must have been back to the hostel first for he was clean and spruce, but the look on his face when Dana answered the door caused her to pull him inside and push him into a chair. 'What's up, Ernie?' she asked. 'You look dreadful! Don't say you've had bad news?'

Ernie nodded dumbly, and when Dana opened her mouth to ask more questions he fished a letter out of his pocket and held it out. 'Them buggers have turned me down,' he said huskily. 'I'm gutted. Oh, Dana, what'll Polly say? It were me asthma. No use applying for the Navy or the air force 'cos they'll want to know whether I've been turned down by any of the other services.' He looked up at Dana and gave her a watery smile. 'Reckon I'll be collectin' white feathers any day now.'

Dana shook her head reprovingly, then went over and lit the Primus stove. 'I'll make us a cup of tea,' she said soothingly, 'and as for white feathers, don't be so bloody ridiculous! You can scarcely help it if they've rejected you on medical grounds, and it's to be hoped that women will have more sense this time round than to accuse their fellow countrymen of cowardice simply because they're not in uniform. As for what Polly will say, I think she'll be relieved. Oh, I know she started off thinking that it was all very romantic and liking the thought of her boyfriend in uniform, but lately she's begun to worry. She told me the other night that she had nightmares about trenches and mud and bombing raids, and you being killed or captured, so of course she'll be sympathetic because you're disappointed but underneath she'll be as pleased as anything. Have you told anyone else yet?'

Ernie shook his head. 'No point,' he mumbled. 'At least I've got me job cleaning cars an' that. So long as Poll don't mind I guess things ain't so bad. Only if there is goin' to be a war I'd ha' liked to be . . . oh, I'd ha' liked to be a part of it.'

The kettle began to boil and Dana started to make the tea, speaking over her shoulder to Ernie as she spooned the leaves into the warmed pot. 'I know how you feel; but look at me! I don't know whether you realise, but I ought to be working right now, only the corner shop doesn't need me and apart from the fish market all my other little jobs have dried up. Of course I've evening work at the Freeway, but the truth is there's no money about. If Polly hadn't got the job as Jake and Ralph's assistant, with usheretting whenever she has time, we'd be struggling to pay the rent, let alone feed ourselves. But when I was moaning in the queue for ice at the fish market last Friday someone said that I'd soon be in work again because the government are building new factories all over the place, including Liverpool. They aren't ordinary factories either; they're making uniforms, aeroplanes, wireless sets, guns and ammunition . . . stuff like that. I reckon you and I will be earning good money at one of those factories once they start recruiting staff.

So you see we'll be doing our bit just as though we had been accepted for the services.'

'Do you think so?' Ernie said, brightening visibly. 'Aeroplanes! I'd be a dab hand at that, very likely. Cor, that 'ud be one in the eye for some o' the lads at me lodgings what keep sayin' they're goin' to join up, but haven't got round to it yet.'

'Well, the fellow who mentioned it in the ice queue has a brother who's on the council so he ought to know what's going on, and he said if I didn't believe him I ought to go out on the tram to what they call the suburbs and I'd see all sorts being built,' Dana said. She poured two mugs of tea and carried one over to Ernie. 'Here you are, get that down you! Yes, and he said if I were to ask one of the construction workers what was going on, he'd just shrug and say it were government business and move away quick like, not wanting to be questioned, see? So I honestly think he was telling the truth. It's about time the country woke up and began to arm itself, because you've seen the pictures on the newsreels showing Hitler's Brownshirts and the thousands of German planes and tanks and so on which are all a part of the war machine he's building up. But our politicians simply tut-tut and say this can't go on and do nothing . . . look at those Japs, sinking our ships, threatening to do worse. Talking is all very well, but in war it's actions which count.'

Ernie sipped his tea, then nodded slowly. 'Aye, I reckon you're right. I didn't want to work at the Freeway because I was hoping the army would have me, which would have meant letting Jake and Ralph down. So I'll stay wi' me car an' lorry cleanin' until they begin to advertise for workers in the factories and then I'll be first in the perishin' queue.'

Dana grinned at him. 'No you won't, because *I'll* be the first; you can be second!'

Shortly after this Ernie left, clearly heartened by Dana's attitude towards his failure, though she pressed him to stay. He shook his head firmly, however. 'Thanks, but I'd best be on me way,' he said gruffly. 'I'd like to wait for Polly, but if I do she'll think I've got good news. Oh, I know you say she'll be glad in her heart that I'm not joining up, but if I'm honest I'm still dead scared to see her face fall.'

'You won't,' Dana said at once, but Ernie was firm.

'You tell her, there's a pal, Dee,' he said anxiously. 'It'll come better from you. Then, when she and meself meet up again, she can hide her disappointment, or wharrever.'

But when Polly did come in, not long before midnight, she was all of a glow, pink-cheeked, bright-eyed, and obviously hugging to herself some secret or piece of news which she was absolutely dying to impart. However, she took off her coat, hat and gloves and commented that it were a vile night, and cold enough to freeze wharrever it was that brass monkeys were said to possess. 'And there's one of them there lazy winds,' she said, shivering and holding out her hands to the Primus stove which was boiling a kettle for two cups of hot cocoa. 'You know, a wind that's—'

'Yes, I know; too lazy to go round you so it goes straight through instead,' Dana said, having heard the description several times both in Ireland and Liverpool. 'And now stop fooling around and tell me why you're feeling so pleased with yourself. You're late coming home, but I can't think that's the reason for your bright eyes and big grin.'

'It's not,' Polly admitted. 'Look, let's sit down and drink our cocoa and I'll tell you what happened tonight. Ready?'

'I've a good mind to tell you to keep your gossip to yourself,' Dana said severely, but she knew she was not fooling her friend. She sat down, cradled her mug of cocoa in both hands and raised her eyebrows. 'Well? Cat got your tongue?'

Polly giggled. 'The truth is I don't know where to start. So I'll begin at the beginning . . .'

'And continue until you get to the end,' Dana said. 'Oh, do come on, Poll! I'm dying for my bed!'

'Well, all right, here I goes then,' Polly said, putting down her own mug and beaming at Dana. 'You know that Jake said they'd think about a cafeteria some time, but not yet? Well, I think he's changing his mind. He says there's a war coming and once it arrives they'll put an embargo – I think he said embargo – on any sort of new business which isn't connected with winning the war. So if he means to start anything it ought to be done at once.'

'Oh, don't say he's decided against catering!' Dana said through a mouthful of biscuit. 'It's the one bright spot on my horizon. What does he want to do with the top floor now? Sell books or records or something?'

'Wouldn't you like to know . . . all right, all right, I'm goin' to tell you,' Polly said hastily as Dana leaned across the table and tried to slap her. 'He asked me to go up to the top floor with him and see what I thought we could use it for . . .'

'And I suppose you didn't like to remind him about a cafeteria,' Dana said. She took another biscuit. 'And if you don't get to the point in the next two minutes I'm going to switch you off, like a wireless set, and put myself to bed.'

'I'm telling you, aren't I? Well, he and Ralph think the room would be ideal for a place to eat. He'd partition it so's the kitchen bit couldn't be seen by the customers . . . and he said with war on everyone's lips we shouldn't ought to wait but should get going right away!'

Dana squeaked and beamed at her friend. 'And did you remind him that Caitlin and I had started Cathy's Place? And that it was a real success with me in charge? Did you say we had made it one of the most popular eating places in Liverpool? Did you . . .'

'Course I did,' Polly said scornfully. 'Only I sort of made it sound as though it were just you. I didn't *lie*, exactly,' she added virtuously. 'I just sort of made it sound as though . . . well, as though you was the brains behind it and Caitlin were just a pretty face and when she left . . . well, what I did I sort of concertinaed it, like, so's I didn't confuse him too much. And he liked the whole idea and Ralph said it would make the place more productive without a huge outlay, and I honestly think he means to go ahead.'

'Gosh! To actually get another chance . . . but of course it wouldn't be ours, like Cathy's Place was. It's a pity you had to lie, but . . .'

'Excuse *me*,' Polly said indignantly. 'First go off, Cathy's Place were never yours, nor Caitlin's either. Oh, you thought it were, but remember, if that 'orrible Jimmy Mortimer hadn't poked his nose in and bought the lease, you'd never have started the place; no, not in a million years. And second go off, I perishin' well did not lie! I just showed him what a wonderful manageress you'd been and would be again and the up and down of it is, he wants to discuss the idea with you around eleven thirty this Thursday, if you can make it, your supreme majesty,' she added sarcastically. Dana saw that Polly was hurt by her accusation of telling lies, and quickly put matters right by rushing round the table and giving the other girl a big hug.

'I'm sorry, I'm sorry, of *course* you didn't tell one single fib, and you're the best friend in the world so you are,' she said warmly. 'Thursday, you say? Good job I don't work at the corner shop on Thursdays. I'll be at the Freeway on the dot of eleven thirty, and I'll have a business plan mapped out. I'll tell him I know a dozen girls who would love to waitress again, and I'll explain about uniforms and shifts and so on . . .'

'That's right,' Polly said. She looked self-conscious all of a sudden, Dana realised. 'Wear your black skirt and white blouse and them flatties you bought off of your pal in Paddy's market. Oh, and there's one other thing.'

'What's that?' Dana asked, but she scarcely cared. The prospect of full-time work, and work which she would enjoy furthermore, was heady stuff. But Polly was looking sheepish.

'Nothin' much . . . I mean it's a sprat to catch a mackerel, like,' Polly mumbled. 'I . . . er . . . I told him you'd work for a very small wage – mebbe thirty bob, just for the first month, just so's he could see how things were goin'.'

'You told him I'd work for thirty bob? Oh dear God,

Polly Smith, whatever were you thinking of?' Dana gasped. 'Where will the rent money come from? And how will we eat? You've put your foot in it this time! I wouldn't be surprised if your boss refuses to take me on if I'm that desperate and sacks you for suggesting it and then where will we be? We'll still have to eat, you know.'

'Oh, don't be such a misery,' Polly said. 'As for food, we can eat bread an' scrape for a month, can't we? Besides, there's always leftovers in catering, you know there are. We'll live on stale cucumber sangwidges an' half-eaten sticky buns until the month's up.' Dana tried to hide her smile, but knew she had failed when Polly broke into a broad grin. 'You'll give it a go, won't you, Dee?' she said coaxingly. 'Come to the meeting and do your posh act and they'll fall over themselves to employ you.'

'Ha ha,' Dana said, but she was smiling too. 'And I dare say we'll manage to eat and pay the rent if you don't mind shouldering most of it until I'm earning properly again. I'll have to give up the market and the corner shop and so on, and I'm afraid I don't have a posh act, whatever that may mean, but I'll be over the moon if we get along – that's half the battle, you know – and he offers me the job of manageress! Even waiting on at a new place would be fun, but of course I do know what I'm talking about when a tea room is the subject of conversation so there's no reason why he shouldn't at least give me a trial.'

'Give it your best go, gal, and we'll be in clover, the pair of us,' Polly said triumphantly. 'Imagine, Dee, free cinema shows and free grub! We'll be made up so we will.'

* * *

True to her promise, Dana spent every spare minute over the next few days working out how to run a café in conjunction with a cinema. She talked it over with Polly, who talked it over with the Freeway brothers. Until the café project had been mentioned, Polly had been rather in awe of Ralph, who was a hard worker and expected his staff to follow his example, but now she asked questions about the proposed cafeteria and found him far more approachable than she had dreamed, which cheered Dana immensely, and made her think that she might get through the meeting without making a fool of herself.

'Both Jake and Ralph were talking about teas, coffees, scones and little sandwiches,' Polly told her importantly. 'But I guess they'll be guided by you; I should say by whoever gets the job of manageress, I mean,' she added hastily. It seemed that Ralph, whose baby it was, had made it clear that nothing was cut and dried.

'I've a thousand ideas,' Dana said enthusiastically as she and Polly walked to the tram stop on Thursday. 'But I mustn't crowd him, you said. Oh, I wish it were over and I'd got the job!'

Polly accompanied her to the cinema, pointed out the door of the manager's office, then wished her luck and went off to check that her circle seats were all respectably clean and ready for the rush of customers at around two o'clock. Dana knocked, and almost before her hand had fallen to her side once more the door was opened and Ralph Freeway ushered her into the room. 'So we meet again, Miss McBride,' he said, grinning. 'Sit yourself down.'

The meeting went well from the moment Ralph began

to outline his ideas. Dana listened, nodded, waited until he had finished and then asked him whether he had considered who his customers would probably be. 'Oh, elderly ladies, who want a drink – tea, almost certainly – and a nice squashed fly biscuit before tackling the homeward journey,' Ralph said, but there was the suggestion of a question in his tone and he smiled when Dana, after only a slight hesitation, shook her head.

'Forgive me, but that isn't quite how I see it, sir. I think your customers will be girls and young men who want to see the film but don't have much time to spare or a great deal of money either. I think they'll come into your café either before the show or after it, and they'll want a proper, filling meal, the sort Joe Lyons provides. Oh, nothing elaborate, just something on toast, poached eggs or baked beans or even a well-filled sandwich, you know the kind of thing. Nothing which needs much time to either cook or prepare. And then a stodgy sort of pudding. Apple pie and custard, spotted dick, plum cobbler . . .'

'Hey, hold on a moment,' Ralph said. Dana's hand shot to her mouth. Polly had warned her not to try to take over; had she been overdoing it? But when he spoke next he sounded more amused than angry. 'I'd not thought of it like that, but I'm pretty sure you're right.' He sighed dramatically. 'Bang goes my vision of a nice little old lady gasping for a cuppa and collapsing into a comfortable chair in our café in order to ask the waitress for a pot of tea and a Lincoln Cream!'

Dana grinned back. 'After a little old lady had climbed all those stairs to reach the top floor she'd probably need more than a cup of tea to revive her,' she observed, and saw once more his tight little grin. She had thought him pleasant enough when they had met at the Adelphi, thinking him not a bad sort at all, but now she changed her mind. She actually liked him, liked him very much. He had a lively sense of humour and might prove fun to work with, and what was more he reminded her a little of Con, though she did not kid herself that Con was as handsome. It was something in Ralph's lopsided smile, she concluded, and smiled more broadly than ever.

'Very well, Dana McBride; it's clear you know what you're talking about.' Ralph got to his feet and held out a hand. 'Goodbye for now; I'll be in touch some time in the next few weeks.'

Dana bit back a squeal of dismay; the next few weeks! She had thought she would leave the cinema as either a disappointed applicant or the future manageress of a thriving cinema cafeteria! But she hid her feelings, thanked Ralph politely for his time and made her way back to Temperance Court.

'Post, Dee!' Polly thumped a small bundle of mail down on the table, a smile on her face. She had seen that the envelope her friend was waiting for had arrived, and whilst she knew Dana had been in agonies of apprehension in case the letter was a polite one telling her that she had not got the job, she herself was pretty sure that the letter would appoint her friend as manageress of the new café. Both Ralph and Jake had made no secret of the fact that Ralph had been impressed by her interview, but Ralph had said that however slowly the mills of God might grind, their own mills ground even slower. 'In fact it might be a month before the bank gives me the go-ahead to start setting the place up,' he had said. 'I'm sure they'll agree in the end, but not until they've dotted all the i's and crossed all the t's, by which time I'll be half mad with impatience and beginning to think it wasn't such a bright idea after all.'

'Post!' Dana said now, stirring porridge over the Primus. She nearly overturned the pan, but managed to right it before a disaster could occur. 'Oh, you read it; I bet it's bad news.'

Polly glanced critically at her companion, then shook her head. 'I couldn't possibly read your letter,' she said righteously. 'Besides, I've always thought you a brave sort o' person, one to look wharrever comes in the eye, but now . . .'

'All right, all right,' Dana said. She carried the porridge pan over to the table, snatched up a tablespoon and served the contents into two bowls. Then she took the letter from Polly, handling it with the tips of her fingers as though she believed it to have been soaked in some noxious fluid. She glanced across at Polly, scowled, then ripped the envelope open. 'Oh, I suppose you're right. Only a coward would . . . oh, Polly me darlin', me little princess, you knew it, didn't you? You knew it was good news so you did, I can tell by your smirk! Oh, Poll, I've got the perishin' job and start on Monday next!'

Chapter Eight

Spring 1938

'You had another of them dreams last night.' Polly spoke abstractedly, as though her words meant nothing, but she shot a keen glance at Dana from under her lashes. Her friend seemed happy enough, though once the cafeteria was up and running she had confessed to Polly that much as she enjoyed the job and the challenge of creating something out of nothing, so to speak, it was not the same as it had been when she and Caitlin had started Cathy's Place.

'We were working for ourselves, truly believing that we were building a little empire, and would go on to greater things: a proper restaurant, perhaps management so we could start up other businesses,' she had said rather shyly, when she and Polly had discussed how she felt about her new job. 'Both Caitlin and I wanted to go home as successful business people . . . it sounds daft now, when I say it aloud, and I wouldn't say it to anyone but you, Poll, but we both wanted to prove ourselves and set our – our people back on their heels. Working for a wage, even quite a good one, isn't the same, somehow. Oh, I'm not grumbling. I'll be eternally grateful to you, Poll, for getting me that first crucial interview, and to Ralph for listening to me and then either adopting my ideas or saying that they wouldn't do, only saying it so nicely that only a fool would have taken offence.'

At the time, Polly had smiled to herself. Ralph had very soon got on the best of terms with his new employee and had asked her out at the end of her first month in order, he said, that they might discuss certain matters. Dana had agreed at once, and when other invitations followed had accepted them with pleasure; she liked her employer more and more, but did not have the slightest intention of allowing their relationship to go beyond a warm friendship.

Polly had said, straight-faced, that she had guessed as much, but this was not strictly true. She thought Dana and Ralph were already more than friends, and in fact believed that it was only this fellow she dreamed about so much, this Con, who stood between them. And dreams, no matter how realistic at the time, were only dreams. Once they get to the kissing stage everything will change, Polly thought, and metaphorically smacked her hand. She and Ernie were now at 'the kissing stage', and very nice she found it, but she knew she and Dana were very different. She admired her friend very much and worked hard to copy her unaccented voice and to read books Dana recommended. Because they were together so much she listened to the programmes Dana liked on the wireless and joined in discussions when the subject was one she understood.

'Oh?' Dana's voice brought Polly abruptly back to the present. Right now they were preparing a meal, Dana mashing potatoes and Polly making gravy with the juices from the small joint they had just roasted.

'Yes, you were dreaming again,' Polly said, heating

the fat from the joint in the pan and sprinkling in flour in tiny amounts as she stirred. 'But it were – was, I mean – quite a nice sort of dream. I think you were at the seaside, you, your mam and dad, that feller Con . . . it sounded fun, to tell the truth.'

'Oh, yes, you're probably right,' Dana said casually. 'But it's too bad of me to keep you awake when you need your sleep. I keep meaning to suggest that now we're both in regular employment perhaps I ought to sleep in here, in the living room. Then you wouldn't be disturbed even if I had the most horrible dreams . . . you've had to wake me more than once when I've had a nightmare.'

'Snap,' Polly said, grinning. 'Remember when I had the nightmare that there was a crocodile trying to knock down our door to get at me? Only it were just Ernie, come calling early, and fair frightening the life out o' the pair of us.'

Dana grinned too. 'And when I dreamed I was left in charge of the whole cinema and I was trying and trying to get the new spool into the projector, and couldn't, and Mr Chamberlain was shouting at me to get a move on or the Nazis would just march up the stairs and take over.'

Polly chuckled. 'And when I thought I was back at the children's home and old Miss Mona Jones was chasing me round and round the dining room because I'd dared to ask for a second helping,' she said. 'So go on, tell me about the seaside. I've never been, remember, but I've read books . . .'

'Right,' Dana said. 'Not that I can remember what I dreamed last night. I know; why don't I tell you about the first time I went to the seaside . . . the first time I can remember, at any rate. Will that do?'

'Sure,' Polly said. She stirred her mixture with a large wooden spoon, then began to add the vegetable water little by little. 'Fire ahead. Start with leavin' Castletara . . .'

'And go on until you stop,' Dana said. 'Well, it was a fine day, the sort of day you don't always get when you want it! The sky was brilliant blue and Mammy had packed a picnic lunch in a big basket. Mr Devlin and Con came too, all of us squashed into the pony cart except Daddy; he rode his chesnut mare, and got to the beach first, of course.'

'Of course,' echoed Polly. She was already aware that Dana's daddy meant more to her than anyone else on earth. 'Go on.'

'Mammy, Mammy, where's me little spade an' bucket? Con's got a much better one than me, so he says he'll dig out the sand whiles I find shells, then we'll make the most bootiful, most perfick castle in the whole world so we will!'

Feena McBride leaned across the breakfast table and pushed a lock of the child's bright hair back from her forehead. 'How do you know we're going to the seaside?' she asked teasingly. ''Tis a fine day sure enough and Mr Devlin says the weather's broke at last but that doesn't mean we can leave Castletara to its own devices while we go a-pleasuring.'

Across the table the small Dana frowned thoughtfully. How *did* she know? But of course though she was only five and had not even started school, could not read and had only recently learned to tell the clock, she had her own means of identifying the seasons. When the rambling, crumbling wall which surrounded the castle was suddenly covered in the pink, dark red and white of valerian blossom she knew it was summer. When the golden rod blazed forth in the wild garden it was autumn. Spring was primroses clustered thickly on the banks of the lane which led to the village, their faint scent even lovelier to Dana's mind than the little purple violets which bloomed at the same time. And winter of course spoke for itself: bare trees, icicles on the wall, snow biting one's face if one ventured outside during a storm.

'Well, alanna? Sure and I'm still waiting for an answer! What makes you think we're off to the seaside?'

Dana giggled. 'I know 'tis summer 'cos the village children has their holidays now, and I know 'tis summer as well when the valerian blooms; spring means primroses and that,' she explained. 'And I know we're going to the seaside because Con told me to dig out my old spade and bucket.'

Feena McBride laughed and got up from her chair. 'Sure and aren't you the clever one!' she said, pausing to help her daughter get down. 'Very well, run along and do as Con says. We're going in the pony trap . . .' she ticked the passengers off on her fingers, 'me, you, Con and Deirdre; Mr Devlin will drive. And Daddy will ride, of course.'

'Oh, it's not fair; if Daddy can ride why can't I? Oh, I know I can't go on me little pony, but couldn't I sit in front of Daddy? I'd be ever so careful, ever so good.'

Feena McBride sighed and shook her head. 'You know very well that having you aboard would spoil your daddy's day, since he means to get to the bay before the rest of us. He'll not ride Thunderer – he's taking Strawberry, because she won't mind saddle bags full of towels and bathing suits – but even so he'll enjoy a gallop, which he couldn't do with two up.'

Dana sighed; it was fair enough and she knew it. Vaguely, through the mists of time – for each year before one's five seems half a lifetime at least – she remembered other occasions, other pleas to be allowed to go with Daddy instead of sitting sedately in the pony trap. But what did it matter, after all? A day at the seaside with all the people she loved most would be wonderful enough.

They reached the bay, a tiny bite of golden sand between rugged rocks which ran down into the sea, making it a perfect spot for bathers who were not yet capable of withstanding the strong tidal surge on other parts of the coast. Here even Dana and Con could safely learn to swim and enjoy the water without fear. Mammy and Deirdre helped Daddy and Mr Devlin to carry all the paraphernalia of their day out down the steep little cliff path and on to the warm dry sand at the top of the beach. There was no breeze and the sun shone calmly from a blue sky on to blue water. Untroubled by wind or waves the little bay seemed to smile a welcome, and Dana thought that it really did welcome them, smiling at them to show it was glad of company after so long alone, for Daddy always said they were the only family to visit the tiny cove.

As soon as everything had been carried down on to the beach Dana and Con threw off their clothing to display the bathers they had put on at home and charged into the sea. Dana closed her eyes as Con began kicking water over her and tried rather feebly to splash him back, screaming and gasping as the cold water struck her warm flesh. Mr Devlin, however, soon put a stop to such horseplay. He too wore his swimming costume and presently both Mammy and Daddy joined them. Deirdre always shuddered at the mention of sea bathing – she could not swim – but the McBrides and Johnny Devlin swam strongly out of the encircling arms of rock to where the sea ran deep and strong and the waves were white-topped. Con, older and bolder than Dana, would have liked to accompany them but knew he was not strong enough and would be walloped by his father if he made the attempt. So he and Dana swam and played in the shallows and came ashore when they grew tired, scorning Deirdre's offer of a towel and beginning to explore the pools amongst the rocks on each side of the bay.

'Mind your toes,' Con said, giving her his wicked lopsided grin. 'If you lift that curtain of weeds there's bound to be crabs hiding away – they don't like the hot sun, you know, and search out a cool place – and if you disturb them they'll have your toes soon as look at you.'

'You're a liar you are, Con Devlin,' Dana said stoutly, but she lifted the curtain of weed with a good deal of caution. She shrieked as something grabbed her toes, but it was only Con, laughing fit to bust and calling her a weedy little twerp who was scared of her own shadow.

'I am *not*; you are trying to frighten me. If I tell your daddy you'll be for it so you will and serve you right,' Dana said indignantly.

She aimed a blow at her tormentor which he easily parried, but he rumpled her hair affectionately, saying remorsefully as he did so, 'Sorry I am to tease you and you the best and bravest kid I ever did meet. Tell you what, this small pool will be like our sea aquarium. We'll put everything we catch into it and see how many critters we can collect. Or we could have a contest; you put your finds in that pool . . .' he pointed, 'and I'll use this one.'

They agreed to do this though Dana pointed out that it could scarcely be fair since each pool would already contain a great many sea creatures, but Con said that didn't matter. ''Tis only a bit of fun; no prizes for the winner,' he pointed out. 'Tell you what: the winner will be the one who gets the weirdest, rarest thing in their pool. Shall we use shrimping nets or just hands?'

'Your hands are huge compared to mine; we'll use our shrimping nets,' Dana decided, and very soon she was finding crabs smaller than house spiders and stripy shells whose occupants clung firmly to their piece of weed and came out to peer indignantly at this interruption to their quiet lives. By the time Deirdre called them back for lunch they had found hermit crabs, translucent shrimps – difficult to see, let alone catch – little fishes and anemones: fat cushions of scarlet jelly with waving arms which they enticed you to touch and then withdrew indignantly into their bodies. The children decided that the most peculiar things they found were the small prickly porcupines which Mammy assured them were called sea urchins.

'The tinkers call hedgehogs urchins,' said Con, but Deirdre said smartly: 'And who are you to be talking to tinkers what everyone knows to be bad lots?' which shut Con up pretty fast.

Mammy had prepared a lovely lunch. Cold chicken, salad and new potatoes boiled in their skins the way the children loved them. Afterwards there was fruit: raspberries and Beauty of Bath apples. Then the grown-ups lay down on the rugs with their straw hats over their faces. Daddy said they would just have five minutes so they'd be obliged if the children could play quietly, but Dana and Con knew it would be a couple of hours before the three adults awoke. Deirdre announced her intention of climbing up to the top of the cliffs to see if Strawberry and the pony, Colette, needed moving, so Con said he would walk along the beach to where there was a cave which he longed to explore. Dana went with him which was brave of her because on some previous occasion he had told her it was inhabited by an evil enchanter called Prospero who ate small children for breakfast or turned them into crabs or lobsters, depending on his mood. However, once they left the sheltered bay behind it was possible to collect a fair quantity of driftwood, and although this task was usually performed by the men of the party today Con told Dana that they would surprise and delight their elders by returning to the little bay laden with the best and driest driftwood they could find. Mrs McBride liked the curly-twirly pieces for her flower arrangements, which won many prizes at village shows, but the men always made a huge driftwood bonfire with the rest and cooked supper over the flames.

So Dana and Con had explored the cave, which smelt excitingly of the sea and the great beds of rubbery seaweed which flourished in the deep ocean and only came ashore after a storm. They went right to the back, where the roof came down until only a tunnel was left;

Dana could perhaps have wriggled through the tunnel but Con suddenly became aware of his responsibilities and refused to let her try on the grounds that it would be his head that rolled if she got stuck – or met the magician and got magicked by him.

Then they collected driftwood, great armfuls, and returned to the bay to find their parents awaiting them. Deirdre had told them where the children had gone but even so they were greeted with relieved smiles, although Mr Devlin said apologetically that he had known Con would take good care of Dana. Deirdre reported that Strawberry and Colette had already eaten three quarters of their way around the sweet-smelling herbage, so she had moved their tethers to give them fresh grazing and thought both were very content. She herself, after the stiff climb up the cliff, had sat down with her back against the rock and snoozed for a good twenty minutes.

Now they piled up the driftwood, the men adding their own contribution, and as the sky darkened and the fire blazed they roasted sausages on sticks and ate Mammy's new potatoes cooked in an old blackened tin of sea water, which were regarded as a great delicacy by all concerned. This, Mammy declared, as they ate the exciting, smoke-flavoured food and watched the sparks fly into the darkening sky above, was the perfect end to a perfect day.

They lingered on the beach until the sun set, then slowly made their way home. The climb up the cliff path had been negotiated on Daddy's shoulders when she was very small, but now she was five Dana merely took her mammy's hand and together they pushed their way through the valerian, pink, deep red and purest white.

The climbing moon, of course, had robbed the flowers of colour, but nothing could steal their faint scent of summer.

Dana finished her recital in a dreamy voice like the buzzing of a contented bee and Polly stared at her, open-mouthed. 'Oh, Dana, you don't know how lucky you are! It ain't only that I've never been to the sea; I can't remember a time when I was really happy.'

'Well, I suppose orphans don't have the same fun that I had as a kid . . .' Dana began, but was quickly interrupted.

'I'm not an orphan. Didn't you realise that? I had a mother and a father – still have for all I know – and I wasn't sent to the children's home until I was three or four, maybe even five. But the years before . . .' She looked consideringly at her friend. 'I don't much like to talk about it, but maybe I ought to. It would show you how very lucky you are. Oh, I know your father's dead and I'm very sorry, of course, but if someone were to tell me tomorrer that mine had fallen off his perch I'd probably think it were a good thing 'cos he wouldn't be smacking kids or fighting his wife no more.' She looked solemnly across the kitchen at Dana's startled face. 'Yes, I mean to tell you what life was like for me when I had a home and a fambly. So pin back your lug'oles and don't you go interrupting.'

Polly sat on the dirty cobbles of the court, wearing a ragged man's shirt which was much too big for her. In order to stop it trailing on the ground and tripping her up a length of orange box rope had been tied round

212

her waist and the shirt pulled up so that it resembled a frock of sorts. She was watching half a dozen older girls skipping rope, and could hear the words they were chanting: 'salt, mustard, vinegar, pepper' followed by the triumphant cry of 'out you goes Sally-Anne big nose'. One of the girls twirling the rope was her sister Hannah, the other Hannah's friend Susie. Polly, sitting on the paving stones drawing pictures in the dust with one extremely dirty forefinger, wished that she were bigger so that she might join in the skipping, but you could only do that if you were old enough to go to school. Polly did not know her age and birthdays were not celebrated in the Smith family, but she rather thought she was probably nearly five or possibly nearly six; it was not important. What mattered was that you weren't allowed to go to school unless you had boots and so far as she could recall she had never owned a pair. This made her one of the barefoot brigade, of which there were plenty in this particular court. Hannah was nine or ten and went to school but she had found somewhere safe to hide her boots, otherwise Mam would've pawned or even sold them. Polly remembered the Salvation Army lady once giving her a real nice pair of plimsolls, but no sooner had her mam clapped eyes on them than she had whisked them away. 'I shall give 'em a good clean so's you can wear 'em when the weather gets cold,' she had said, but since the month was January at the time and the puddles iced over Polly knew that this was just an excuse, knew too that she would never see her lovely plimsolls again.

'Polly perishin' Smith – oh, where's the bleedin' kid got to this time?' Her mother's sharp voice caused Polly to flinch and scramble hurriedly to her feet. She looked around and there were the twins, Andrew and Alex, both sitting as she was on the paving stones but not watching the skipping; they had other fish to fry. Andy held a large red apple which the boys were sharing, bite and bite about, and Alex held – oh bliss – a banana, which was being shared too. There were two sets of twins in the Smith family and Alex and Andy were older than she; they came somewhere between herself and Hannah. Since they were the only boys in the family it stood to reason that they were her mam's favourites. Blessed with golden-brown skin, dusky black curls and sturdy bodies, they never lacked for food – or boots for that matter – so if anyone went short it would be Polly. Little skinny Polly, with her thin yellow hair and plain features, Polly who was always hungry, who never stood up to either parent though she dreaded her seaman father's occasional homecomings most, and clung to Hannah like a drowning man to a spar, knowing that Hannah would protect her if she could.

'Polly! Come here at once or I'll give you a clack you won't forget in a hurry!' Her mother's strident voice caused the skipping children to turn round eyes in Mrs Smith's direction, though the steady twirling of the rope did not falter. Polly, who had already jumped to her feet, ran to where her mother stood at the top of the three steps which led to their home. It did not do to delay when Mrs Smith had that nasty look on her really rather nasty face.

'I's here, Mammy,' Polly said breathlessly, though the breathlessness was not caused by the speed with which she had answered her mother's summons but by fear that she was in trouble of some sort. She gave a tentative smile. 'Does you want messages runnin', Mammy—'

Her mother cut across her. 'No, I don't want no messages.' The woman stared down at her daughter as though seeing her for the first time, an expression of distaste crossing her face. 'You're filthy,' she said accusingly. 'Best clean you up a bit or they won't take you.'

Polly knew she was filthy; only the previous day one of the Barlow children had said that Polly Smith was the dirtiest child in the court. At the time Polly had thought this a compliment, but Hannah had speedily disabused her. 'It's a perishin' insult but it ain't your fault, queen. Our mam gives you rags to wear and never so much as puts your head under the pump.' She sighed dramatically. 'I do me best but our mam expects me to look after the littl'uns and I'm tellin you they're a full-time job.'

The younger twins were six months old and very pretty with big blue eyes and soft sooty curls so it was natural that Mam favoured them as well as the boys. But now, as she was dragged indoors and into the big untidy kitchen, an optimistic thought struck Polly. As her mother seized a torn-off scrap of towelling, dipped it into the basin of none too clean water and began vigorously attacking Polly's face she asked the question uppermost in her mind. 'Is I going to school, Mammy?' she asked hopefully. 'Have you found me some boots? Though it's summer, so plimsolls would do fine and they's cheaper.'

Mrs Smith snorted. 'What does a kid like you want wi' school?' she asked scornfully. 'And it's the summer holidays, ain't it?' Polly was wondering whether she dared question her further when she saw a look of extreme cunning appear on her mother's face. 'Though in a way you ain't far out; you'll go to school all right when it starts up again.' She began to scrub Polly's small paws, tutting over her blackened nails, whilst apparently not noticing the state of her own. 'Now where did I see that bleedin' hairbrush?' She was rootling around on the dresser when a wail from upstairs announced that a baby was awake, and once one of them stirred the other would be swift to follow. Mrs Smith cursed, grabbed the brush and handed it to Polly, then left the kitchen. Polly heard the front door crash open, heard her mother shout for Hannah to come at once and began inexpertly to brush her hair. She supposed from her mother's words that there must be some sort of interview before one could enter school. Perhaps Mrs Smith just doubted that any school would want her daughter. Well, now was her chance to prove her wrong, Polly thought exultantly, wielding the brush. She could not read, despite her best efforts, but she knew her letters and understood the value of money, though little of it came her way. But when one had a short-tempered mam who sent one on messages and expected a rendering of every last penny on one's return, it became very important to know about money.

The wailing upstairs suddenly doubled and Polly knew that Milly and Maisie were now both awake and needed attention, so she gave one last despairing dab at her hair with the almost bristleless brush, then set off for the stairs. Mam worshipped the twins, and if they were allowed to cry unattended she would blame Polly and add another clack to the many her daughter had already received.

As soon as she entered the bedroom the babies stopped screaming and Milly – she thought it was Milly – gave her a watery grin, revealing the fact that she was the proud possessor of four teeth, two top and two bottom. This confirmed that she was in fact Milly, since Maisie had only managed to produce two teeth so far.

Polly bustled over to the ancient cot as the babies began to grizzle again, and was struggling to get Milly over the rail when Hannah entered the room. 'Leave 'em Poll; Mam wants you downstairs. I'll bring the twins.'

'Thanks, Hannah. They's a bit too heavy now for me to carry,' Polly admitted. 'I say, where's Mam taking me, do you know? I guess it's got something to do wi' school, 'cos she's washed me face and hands . . .'

Hannah heaved both babies out of their cot and headed for the stairs. She pushed Polly ahead of her, saying gruffly: 'I dunno, chuck. Did she tell you to find a clean frock?' Polly was saying that so far as she knew there was no such thing as a clean frock in the house when they reached the kitchen. Mrs Smith beamed at the twins and sat herself down in the creaking wicker chair drawn up before the stove, though because of the heat of the day the fire within was unlit. 'There's a couple of bottles of milk on the draining board; give 'em here!' she commanded. 'I've been to Paddy's market this morning, bought the kid a frock. It's in the top drawer of the dresser, and there's plimsolls there too. Make her respectable while I feed me little darlins. Then I mean to take her out – never you mind where – so you're to stay indoors with the babies until I comes back.'

Hannah fetched the two bottles of milk and watched whilst the twins attached themselves eagerly to the teats. Then she said in a small voice: 'Where's you takin' our Poll, Mam? Only it can't be school because it's the summer holidays . . .'

Despite being burdened by the twins, Mrs Smith began to surge to her feet and Polly, seeing retribution about to fall on her favourite sister – the only member of the family who had ever given her any affection – hastily intervened.

'It don't matter, Hannah; I'll go wherever Mammy takes me,' she said. And then, as her sister produced from the dresser drawer a blue gingham frock and a pair of ancient black plimsolls, she gave a squeak of delight. 'Oh, Mammy, is they really for me? Why, they's just like the frocks the girls what go to St Margaret's wear.'

This remark seemed to mollify her mother, and indeed when Hannah presented Polly, washed, brushed and dressed in the lovely new clothes, that harsh critic gave a slow smile and a grudging nod. Then, as the babies drained their bottles simultaneously, Mrs Smith handed them both to Hannah. 'Bring up their wind and put 'em in the old play pen,' she commanded. 'There's spuds and a block of margarine; cook the spuds, mash 'em wi' a spoonful of the marge and let 'em have it if they cries again. Otherwise we'll all eat together when I gets back.'

Polly saw the troubled look on her sister's face, saw her lips begin to frame 'Back from where?' and nudged her hastily. Hannah had enough on her plate looking after the twins and cooking the blind scouse which would go with the mashed potatoes; she did not need a clack across the head which would send her dizzy for quite ten minutes, in Polly's experience. She waited until Mrs Smith was struggling into her stained and shrunken coat, then whispered, 'Don't worry; I'll tell you where we've been when we gets back, or mebbe when we's in bed, if Mam don't want me to tell.'

But Mrs Smith was now slamming her black cloche hat down on her untidy thatch of greying hair and gesturing to Polly to accompany her out of the house. As they crossed the court and headed for the main road Polly spotted her friend Nat. If she was the dirtiest child in the court, she reflected, then Nat ran her a close second. He was about her own age, the middle child in a large family, and Polly knew his hair was yellow because when he'd been swimming in the Scaldy the dirt floated off and what had looked like a crop of brown curls became as yellow as a day-old chick. Despite being the fourth or fifth child in a family of eleven, Nat was cheerful, reasonably well nourished and well loved. Mr Harris was a seaman aboard a coaster and seldom home, but he was not a drinker, hardly ever struck his children and was unashamedly fond of his fat and feckless wife. The Harris family had very little money, but Mrs Harris cleaned at a couple of local pubs and frequently sent Nat out with a bit of bread and scrape or even a sugar bun for his pal Polly. Polly longed to be a Harris too, but being Nat's friend was the next best thing, so now despite her mother's tight grip on her thin little shoulder she broke free and ran across to where Nat was beckoning. The blue gingham frock was far too big and she had to gather the skirt up in one hand to avoid treading on it, but when she reached him Nat whistled admiringly. 'Cripes, queen, you're that smart I near on didn't reckernise you,' he said. 'Where's you off to, then?'

'Dunno, but I don't suppose we'll be long; I think it may be something to do wi' school,' Polly hissed. 'I'll tell you when I get back.'

She and her mother scarcely spoke a word as they

walked. Polly ventured several remarks and after twenty minutes of plodding along hard and crowded pavements suggested timidly that they might take a tram. This however only caused her mother to call her a lazy little tyke, which was unfair because Polly had not suggested catching a tram for her own sake but for her mother's. Mrs Smith was scarlet-faced and puffing like a steam train, for though it was four o'clock in the afternoon the day was still humid, and Mrs Smith was both overweight and unfit.

After they had passed well out of the area of the city which Polly knew, a most unpleasant thought suddenly occurred to her. If Hannah was in a good mood and had the time she told the children bedtime stories, and she had recently related the tale of the Babes in the Wood. She had told how the wicked stepmother had led the babes deeper and deeper into unknown country, following this trail and then that until the children were thoroughly lost. She told herself she was being fanciful and foolish but there was no doubt about it: Mrs Smith might be able to find her way back, but she, Polly, would not. If her mother were to jump aboard a tram as it passed, shouting to her daughter to make her own way home, Polly would not have the slightest idea even of the direction in which she lived. She comforted herself with the thought that Mrs Smith, scarlet-cheeked and with sweat pouring down her face, was about as capable of jumping aboard a moving tram as of flying to the moon; no need to worry about that then. And presently they reached a road lined with very smart houses indeed. They passed a number of these without pausing but then Mrs Smith stopped before a particularly large one, three storeys high, its entrance guarded by tall wrought iron gates. It looked like a school, and as they approached the front door up a flight of impressively whitened steps they could hear the sound of children's voices within.

Mrs Smith rang the bell and presently the door was opened by a severe looking woman in black. She wore a tiny pair of spectacles on a long black ribbon and her hair was pulled back into a tight bun on the nape of her neck. Her dress was very plain, long-sleeved and high-necked with a skirt reaching to her ankles, and she raised her eyebrows as she spoke. 'Yes?'

'Me name's Smith, Mrs Smith, and this here's me daughter Polly,' Mrs Smith said. 'I'm in desperate need, ma'am . . . I'd best see the principal.'

The woman nodded. 'Very well.' She turned to Polly. 'Do you see that little chair? You sit there while your mother explains herself to Miss Hebden. And don't move. I don't suppose you can read?'

Polly shook her head. 'No, but I knows all me letters and me numbers too.' She screwed her eyes up tight. 'Twelve pennies make a shilling, twenty shillings make a pound. A, B, C, D . . .'

'Yes, all right. Sit there and don't move a muscle while I take your mother into the principal's office, then I'll come back and give you a picture book to look at. Would you like that?'

Polly began to say that she would rather accompany her mother but saw the involuntary twitch of her mother's hand and changed her mind. No use asking for a clack round the ear in front of a total stranger, so instead she said humbly that a picture book would be very nice, especially if it contained letters as well as pictures. Truth to tell Polly had never handled a book in all her life, though she had seen such things in shop windows and had marvelled at the beautiful pictures on their covers.

The stern lady waited until Polly had settled herself in the small chair then beckoned to Mrs Smith and the pair of them disappeared down a long corridor. If Mrs Smith had been a fond parent, Polly thought she would have run after her begging not to be left alone in the dark and lofty hall, but this not being the case she gripped her hands into fists so tightly that the nails dug into her palms and began to say her letters; anything to take her mind off the babes in the wood.

She wondered how long she would have to wait, but the lady with the little gold spectacles came back quite quickly with a large and somewhat tattered picture book, which she placed upon Polly's skinny gingham-covered knees. 'There you are; that will keep you happy until your mother and Miss Hebden have settled things,' she said rather obscurely. 'I expect she's explained to you why you have come to Egremont House?'

Polly shook her head but the lady continued to talk as though she had not noticed the movement. 'My name is Miss Eleri Williams. There are two Miss Williams on the staff, myself and Miss Mildred Williams, so you must learn to use our Christian names – to avoid confusion, you know.'

She seemed to expect a reply so Polly, now completely at sea, muttered that she understood, ducked her head and began to turn over the pages of the picture book. At first she scarcely noticed what was before her eyes, but suddenly she came upon a picture of a nursery rhyme which Hannah often sang to the baby twins. Yes, there she was, Little Bo Peep searching for her sheep, plain as a pikestaff! It was a beautiful picture of a girl in a wonderful fairytale dress, a shepherd's crook in one hand and the other shading her eyes as she gazed at a distant hilltop upon which grazed a number of incredibly white and woolly sheep. And beneath the picture, words . . . words that she knew! She traced them with a finger, saying each one beneath her breath. *'Little Bo Peep has lost her sheep and doesn't know where to find them. Leave them alone and they'll come home, bringing their tails behind them.'*

I can read! And it's not difficult, it's easy, Polly told herself ecstatically. Wait till I tell Mam – well, no, she won't be interested, but Hannah will be so pleased. She said I needed proper books, old newspapers wasn't enough.

Excitedly she turned the page, first identifying from the picture which nursery rhyme would be found below, then reading it just to be sure. She found 'Jack and Jill', 'Oranges and Lemons', 'The Grand Old Duke of York' and 'Higgledy Piggledy My Black Hen' before Miss Williams returned, with Polly's mother beside her. 'Come and say goodbye to your mother, my dear,' Miss Williams said. 'You've come to stay with us for a few weeks at Egremont House, just until Mrs Smith has managed to sort out her problems. With eight other children, the birth of yet another pair of twins has made things very difficult, but I'm sure your family will rally round and help with the new babies. Then you will be able to return to your home.'

Polly began to say that the twins were six months old and could scarcely be counted as newborns, but before she could get the words out her mother bent over her, almost smothering her against her huge wobbling breasts, and hissed in her ear that if she so much as opened her mouth she would regret it. When Polly was released her mouth was already opening to demand an explanation, but her mother glared at her so threateningly that she said nothing, save to squeak 'When's I coming home?' in a small, desperate voice.

Mrs Smith, already standing beside the opening door, glanced over her shoulder and spoke as she was descending the steps. 'As soon as the twins is a bit older and your dad's gorra job. Goodbye Polly; be good or I'll skelp the hide off of you.' And with that she was gone.

Polly turned what must have been a white and bewildered face towards Miss Eleri Williams. 'Why's I here? I ain't done nothing wrong,' she whispered. 'Where's Mam gone? What is this place?'

Miss Eleri Williams hissed in her breath. 'Did your mother not explain? I understand that your father has recently lost his job and your mother, who already has a great many children, gave birth to twins two or three weeks back. Someone told her that Egremont House takes in girls for short or sometimes longer periods when times are hard. I'm sure your mother will return for you in a month or two.'

Polly's eyes dilated with horror. Her home in the court might be pretty horrible, the food scarce and parental love non-existent – though she was sure Hannah loved her – but that home was all she knew. This place was utterly alien. If her mother had appeared at that moment, ready to batter her for not complying with her wishes, she would have welcomed her with open arms. But Miss Eleri was talking.

'Come along, my dear, and I'll show you to your dormitory. Most of the children here are orphans, but we have a special bedroom for short-stay children whose parent or parents are temporarily unable to cope. You will soon make friends and grow accustomed to our ways. During term time the children attend school, but now as it's holiday time they work at various tasks, assist the staff and do a couple of hours of school work each day. You will soon—'

Desperate, Polly broke in without compunction. 'Please, Miss Eleri, a lot of what you've just said ain't true. The twins is past six months old, not new babbies at all, and me dad's a stoker aboard a transatlantic liner . . .'

Miss Eleri sighed. 'And now you're going to tell me there aren't ten children in the family, counting the twins,' she said resignedly.

'No, there's just Hannah, Alex and Andrew, me and the littl'uns,' Polly told her. 'I don't know why Mam said different.'

'Well, I'll have a word with the principal. Do you know your address?'

'Oh aye, it's four Spencer Court,' Polly said eagerly. 'Can I go now, miss? Only someone will have to show me which way to go 'cos I never been in this here street before.'

Miss Eleri Williams shook her head. 'We are responsible for you until one or other of your parents comes to claim you,' she said. 'Come along. I'll take you up to your room and tonight after you're in bed I'll alter that frock so that it fits you and doesn't drag on the ground.' She took Polly's hand, no doubt meaning it kindly, but to Polly it felt like the grip of a prison warder. 'Don't be afraid; Egremont House isn't a bad place and your mother may return sooner than you expect.' They reached the head of the stairs, crossed the landing and entered a bedroom with a large figure six on the door. It contained six beds, six lockers and a rail upon which hung a variety of garments. Miss Eleri pointed. 'That will be your bed, the one with the blue counterpane. Now I'll take you downstairs and introduce you to the other girls in dormitory six. I'm sure it won't be long before your mother returns for you.'

Dana had listened to Polly's story without once interrupting, but now she stared at her friend, and Polly saw the shock on her face. 'And did she come back?' she asked breathlessly. 'Or did you decide that you would rather stay at Egremont House? I guess it was a much nicer place than that court where you'd lived till your mam took you off. I mean, from what you've said, when you lived with your mam you were lucky to get one decent meal a day, let alone three. So go on, Poll; were you happier at Egremont House? It must've been quite exciting, because of course you'd go to school, which you'd always wanted to do. I read all the Angela Brazil books when I was a kid; life in a boarding school sounded great fun.'

Polly grimaced. 'It might be hard for you to understand, but at first I spent all my time waiting. Remember, I was only four or five and the only life I'd known had been in Spencer Court. I know what you're thinking: it

226

weren't a good life. Apart from Hannah and my friend Nat, no one took any notice of me; I were just one more dirty underfed kid folks saw playing out in the court or trailing to the shops with a great marketing bag, far too heavy for skinny little arms. But it was all I knew, and there was Hannah who did her best to look after me, and Nat who were me bezzie. Egremont House was huge, and though the girls in my dorm meant well, they couldn't understand when I woke in the night crying for my old life.'

'So your mam never came back for you?' Dana said sympathetically. 'Did you never see her again? But she sounds so horrible – sorry, Poll – that I should think you were glad of that. And I suppose as time passed . . .'

Polly nodded. 'You're right about one thing; as time passed I began to accept that my old life was lost to me. I ran away twice in the early days but the scuffers found me after a day or two and took me back to Egremont House. They were nice the first time – I think they'd been trying to find my family but hadn't been able to because they'd moved – but the second time I got a walloping, and only bread and water to eat for two whole days. Then I had a lecture from the principal saying that I must be a sensible girl, learn my lessons and make friends with others in my position. She explained that my family were no longer at Spencer Court so the sensible thing to do was to make the best of my time at Egremont House. I don't mind telling you, Dana, that it were hard. When I was in the infants we had three teachers who saw to it that food was evenly divided, but later on supervision weren't up to much so the best food and the biggest helpings went to the strongest girls. It weren't until I were working at the Willows that I realised I'd not been properly fed for years.' She grinned at her friend. 'So now you know why I gobbled up even boiled cabbage and spuds in stew so thin you were lucky to find one bit of scrag end, and apple pudding which were all crust and no fruit. Before, I always had a cold or a cough 'cos the doctor who come round the home when we was ill said I had no resistance to fight germs, but once I got to the Willows I never had any call to see the doctor, 'cos me resistance were built up by the grub I got, or so I reckon.'

'That explains a lot,' Dana said, eyeing Polly with respect. 'You look so frail, Poll, but you're as strong as me any day of the week. I used to wonder how a little thing like you could lift wire baskets full of cutlery in and out of the boiling water, when I always had to call for help.'

'So did I,' Polly pointed out. 'That's how me and Ern got to be pals.'

'Well, I'm glad you've told me how things were when you were a kid, though it's made me feel terribly ashamed,' Dana said. She pulled a face. 'I'd never have told you about my visit to the seaside if I'd realised how dreadful your life had been. Has it ever occurred to you, Poll, that the reason your mother never came back was because she died? I mean, she got angry very easily and even the walk across the city made her puff and pant. If she had died no one would've known where you were, so you can't blame Hannah for not coming to rescue you. I'm sure she would've done if she had known where to look.'

She looked enquiringly at Polly, but that young person

228

shook her head decisively. 'No, I'll lay my life my mam never told Hannah where I'd gone, but she didn't cock up her toes. I didn't say I never saw her again, because I did. She come round to Egremont House when I were fourteen or fifteen, just before I left for work at the Willows, begging to be allowed to see me. There were an interview room there for girls to be private with a visitor, so Miss Hebden showed me in there and the first thing I saw was me mam, red in the face and sitting squashed into one of the big leather chairs. When she saw me she squawked out, "Oh, Polly, me darlin' child, your mam's called for you at last! How we've missed you! But now our troubles are over and I've come to take you home."

'I said nothing, just stared at her, and after a few moments she tried to struggle out of her chair but she was so fat that when she stood up the chair tried to come with her. So she sank back again, which was as well, because my flesh crept at the idea of her touching me. The silence seemed to stretch and stretch and when she realised I was not going to speak she began to grumble that Hannah had gone off with some feller, that the twins were working but devils the pair of them, refusing to give their poor ole mam so much as a ha'penny for their keep, and that the younger twins and Sissy, Isobel and Mary, three little sisters I had never met, were limbs of Satan and in desperate need of an older sister to keep order.

'I guessed why she had come, of course. She wanted someone to look after the kids now that Hannah had gone, and she must've realised that I was old enough now to contribute to the family income as well. I still didn't say anything, and when the door opened behind me and Miss Hebden came into the room my sense of relief was so enormous that I could've cried. "Who is this woman?" I asked. "She says she's my mother but she is mistaken; I've never seen her before in my life."

'My mother wailed and swore I was her own little Polly, but when I persisted in refusing to know her she grew angry and abusive, and I slipped out of the room, leaving Miss Hebden to get rid of her, which she did. The teacher asked several questions, but I simply repeated that I did not know the woman and I think Miss Hebden realised that having abandoned me long ago she now had no claim on me. Within a week I had left Egremont House, first extracting a promise from Miss Hebden that they would never tell her where I had gone. They agreed without hesitation . . . and the rest you know.'

Dana heaved a deep, satisfied sigh. 'You did the right thing,' she said approvingly. 'After the way she treated you, your mother had no claim on you whatsoever.'

There was a longish pause before Polly spoke again. 'I kno-ow,' she said slowly. 'But I can't bear to hear that Bible story any more, you know, the one in the New Testament when Peter – was it Peter? – was asked if he knew Jesus, and denied him three times. I denied that the woman *was* my mother, though I knew perfectly well it wasn't true.'

'But I do think the cases are a little different,' Dana said apologetically. 'Your mother had done you great harm in the past, and had you gone with her would undoubtedly have done you great harm again. In a way, you could almost say that by denying her you were saving her from the sin of ill treating you all over again.

If you understand what I mean,' she ended, feeling rather confused herself.

Polly laughed. 'I never looked at it like that but I do believe you're right. She never liked me, you see. I was so different from the others in the family, being blonde and little, that I sometimes wonder now whether I was me dad's get or whether I come in by a side door. Once I were carryin' a paper of chips across the kitchen when I slipped on a patch of water, crashed on to me knees and scattered chips far and wide. It were an accident, and I couldn't have been more than four, but Mam battered me till I thought she'd kill me; if Hannah hadn't interfered I reckon she would've – killed me, I mean. I've heard tell there's always one child in a big family who's what they call the scapegoat – that's in the Bible too – and I reckon in the Smith family the scapegoat were me. So mebbe you're right, mebbe I saved her from the sin of murder.' She chuckled suddenly, seeing the look of horror on Dana's freckled face. 'Oh, don't look so worried, gairl; it were your suggestion in the first place. Only remember, Dana, you ran away from a good home, good friends and a loving family. You want to think hard before you cut yourself off from that Castletara you talk about in your dreams.'

Chapter Nine

January 1939

Dana had been running the cinema cafeteria for the best part of a year, very successfully, and her dreams continued; in fact, she knew that the most dreadful dream of all must be just round the corner and wished with all her heart and soul that she could elude it. However, she knew the dream would come, like it or not, so she went off to work one icy winter's day determined to do a big batch of cooking as well as all her usual tasks. Sometimes, when she was thoroughly worn out, she did not dream at all and she hoped that this might be one of those occasions.

When she arrived at the cinema Polly was already there, checking her area, for though the cleaners came in between every showing there was always the chance that a sweet paper or an ice cream wrapper might have become trapped in the tip-up seats, and nothing annoyed a cinemagoer more than standing up after the performance to find a toffee paper or a blob of melted ice cream adhering to skirt or trousers. Dana could hear the organist thumping out the music that followed the Pathé News, and grinned at Polly as her friend came through the swing doors. 'Reg having a practice run?' she asked. 'No more news from Mr Chamberlain, I suppose? Do you know, I've not met anyone who believes all that "peace for our time" nonsense he trotted out last year. If the government believed it, they'd scarcely issue gas masks or start digging trenches in Hyde Park, and they're doing both.'

'I dunno; I were checking my seats,' Polly said vaguely. 'I watch the news, of course I do, although it's pretty pointless really. I mean what can we do? And it's only depressing when you hear about folk being beaten senseless just because their noses are half an inch longer than Hitler reckons they ought to be. I don't understand the perishin' Germans. Can't they see that that feller Hitler's mad as a crab and oughter be put away? Why, when they first showed the German troops goose-stepping on the news there was roars of laughter from every soul in the cinema.'

'Yes, I know, but mad people are frightening,' Dana said. 'And I agree with you, there's nothing we can do. I keep hoping the ordinary German people will kick him out, but if they don't I suppose we'll have to; kick him out, I mean.'

'Oh, *if* there's a war,' Polly said. 'But I suppose there will be one, and sooner than later. When it comes I shall do my bit, like everyone else.'

'When it happens, I might join one of the services,' Dana said. 'I quite fancy the Wrens, because they have lovely black stockings and really smart uniforms, only their hats are just like those awful felt things the convent girls wear. Or I suppose I could work in one of the munitions factories, or make parts for planes, or uniforms. Yes, uniforms is a good idea because they teach you to use commercial sewing machines. I've never been any good with my needle but I might be brilliant on a sewing machine. What about you, Poll?'

'I'd like to stay here; I like Jake and Ralph and I love being an usherette,' Polly said wistfully. 'But ever since Ernie got the job in that hush-hush factory out in the country, he's been nagging me to go and work there. The money's awful good and he's saving up for a motor-bike, because unless you've got your own transport half your wages go on trams, buses and taxis. But I told him it's no use going on; Ralph says I'm one of the best of the usherettes, and when you count the overtime he pays I wouldn't be that much better off in a factory. But why are you in so early, Dana? You don't open till twelve.'

'I'm going to make a batch of scones and a couple of apple pies; they're our most popular dessert, served with custard, or Eldorado ice cream.'

'Ooh, I love apple pie, specially with ice cream,' Polly said. 'I'll come up in my afternoon break – unless I'm too busy, of course, but I shouldn't be, Monday's always a quiet day – and buy myself a slice.'

'You're welcome,' Dana said over her shoulder as she headed for the steep stairs which led to the cafeteria. Like Polly she knew herself to be a highly regarded member of staff, and of course the friendship which existed between herself and Ralph helped. But some-times, when they were discussing some problem which had arisen, something he said or did would remind her sharply of Con and force her to acknowledge that it was Ralph's likeness to her old friend which made him such an acceptable companion. The idea of taking him back to Castletara was laughable, however. He belonged in the new life she was painfully carving out for herself.

In her past Conan Devlin reigned supreme, or had done. But the Con who accompanied her in her dreams was the old Con, the one who had not yet transgressed.

Dana climbed the last few stairs, unlocked the door and entered her domain. She walked between the tables, clean and ready set for customers, and went into the kitchen. In moments she had her ingredients lined up next to the weighing machine, had lit the gas in the double oven and turned it to the heat she required. There was a big modern refrigerator in one corner, and as well as a large urn for the customers' tea or coffee there was an electric kettle so that the staff could make themselves a cup of tea without waiting for the urn to come to the boil. Within minutes Dana was inserting trays of scones into the oven and sipping her first cup of tea. If Ralph wanted her to stay late to discuss a change of suppliers – for one firm had proved unreliable – then she would raise no objection. She did not intend to dream tonight unless it was of Mr Chamberlain and his piece of paper or the digging of trenches in Hyde Park. Dana weighed, measured, stirred and rolled out, and tried not to think about war.

The weeks wore on. Dana was quieter than usual, answering everything Polly said but rarely instigating any topic of her own. Polly thought that her friend was mulling over the possibility of war and found herself hoping that war, if it came, would not change the life she had made for herself. Oh, I wish I was clever like Dana and pretty like Caitlin, but that's about all I'd change, she told herself. I've found a job I can do really well, I get to see the pictures without having to pay a penny, I share rooms with the best pal a girl could have, and then there's Ernie, wanting to take me out and spend his hard-earned cash on a boat trip in Prince's Park or a ticket to the dance hall, or even a voyage across to New Brighton when the weather's warmer.

A slit of light showed as a couple pushed open the swing doors and Polly hurried over to them, shining her torch first at her own feet, so that the customers could see she was approaching, and next at the young man's hands, holding out their tickets of admission. She checked the tickets and directed her beam towards two empty seats. 'Them do you?' she asked, for the cinema was by no means full and the tickets entitled customers to any seats in the circle. 'If you'd rather sit nearer the front . . .'

'Them's fine,' the young man said, shepherding his companion into the row indicated and settling himself whilst his girlfriend took off her coat and headscarf and produced a large bag containing some sort of sweets; toffees probably. The young man's hands were deeply grimed; not the sort of hands to buy a girl a large box of Black Magic, Polly told herself, before turning to face the screen once more. The titles were flickering up; presently the wonderful translucent golden drapes would be drawn across the screen and the fire curtain, far more mundane but far more useful, would descend. The young couple had timed it nicely, and sitting on the end of the row as they were they would not even have to leave their seats to purchase the ice cream, peanuts or chocolate bars with which Polly would presently parade up and down the aisles. Now folk would recognise friends, seats would be swapped, there would be much laughter and talk of the film to come, which was *Lost Horizon* starring Ronald

Colman, much admired by the females in the audience, though the men would have preferred Gary Cooper, or a glamorous female star.

Polly hurried to the office, filled her tray with goodies as the other usherettes were doing and arrived back just as the fire curtain descended. She began to parade along the end of the rows. 'Ice creams, peanuts, chocolate bars . . .' she intoned, thinking that upstairs, in the cafeteria, Dana would be removing her large cooking apron to reveal a smart black dress and a frilly white pinny just about now. Until the main meal in the evening customers mostly wanted sandwiches, scones and fancy cakes, none of which needed cooking, so Dana would assist the waitresses until requests for hot food began to come in and then she would revert to her overall once more. 'You get two workers for the price of one,' she teased Ralph from time to time, but Polly knew and assumed that their bosses knew also that Dana liked to be busy.

'Choc ice, sir? One choc ice and one tub, that'll be eightpence. I'm afraid we're out of ice lollies . . .' they never sold them, 'but I can let you have an orange squash and a straw . . .'

Polly made her way swiftly but cautiously along the ends of the rows, greeting old friends and regular customers, smiling at old jokes and assuring everyone that the film they were about to see was 'perishin' brilliant, one of the best'. When the show ended with the audience rising and standing stiffly to attention whilst Reg played the national anthem, Polly went up to the cafeteria. Her friend saw her as soon as she appeared, and gave her a large slice of apple pie. 'It's a cold night,

237

so you'd best have custard and not ice cream,' she said, accepting the money – staff rates – that Polly pushed into her hand. She glanced round at the tables, mostly empty, and sighed. 'Another twenty minutes and I can start cleaning down,' she said. 'Enid has already done all the middle tables so don't you dare sit at one of them or she'll curse you, but if you're willing to give a hand we could be out of here in under the half hour.'

Enid was head waitress, a skinny capable forty-year-old with a raucous laugh which Dana always said could be heard a mile out to sea. She had a short way with drunks, who sometimes reeled up to the unlicensed cafeteria demanding beer and becoming abusive when told they could not be served. Enid was skinny, but she was strong and ruthless. She had once thrown a drunk down the steep stairs; it was only by the grace of the gods who look after drunken men that he hadn't broken his neck, Dana had said, but Enid was unrepentant. 'Teach the buggers not to come worritin' us,' she had said, dusting her hands. 'He won't bother us again, not he!'

So now Enid and Dana dealt with the customers and cleaned down, whilst Polly gobbled apple pie and custard and admired the way the two women worked as a team. And presently they locked up and left, Dana and Polly saying cheerio to Enid as she boarded a tram but deciding to walk themselves, for the crisp cold air was inviting after the stuffiness of the cinema and Dana said hopefully that they would sleep all the better for some exercise.

Polly sometimes grumbled that in winter she scarcely saw daylight; she came to work in the dark and went home in the dark. Both girls longed for summer and the lighter evenings, though at present they were so involved

238

with the Freeway that even on a Sunday their talk was mainly of how to attract more customers, which food was most popular in the cafeteria, and whether the films coming up would attract large or small audiences.

'I wonder what 1939 will really bring?' Dana said idly as they stepped out, their footsteps ringing on the icy pavement. 'Will it be more rumours of war, or rumours of peace? Your Ernie keeps saying we'll be at war by March, but no one else seems to think so. Why does he say that, do you know?'

Polly sniffed. 'It's because they're actually being paid overtime to do one double shift each week,' she said disdainfully. 'As if that meant anything! But I tell you what, Dana, I think you ought to go back to Castletara and your mam whilst we're still at peace. I never think of Ireland as being a foreign country, but of course it is really and there's been no talk of Ireland going to war with Germany. I'm not saying Mr de Valera would join Germany against us, but . . .'

'Polly, how could you? Oh, I know in the past the Irish were wickedly treated by the English, but even so I'm sure we'd never dream of joining the Nazis,' Dana said reproachfully. 'And as for going home, I couldn't think of it. You simply don't understand what happened after my father died; if you did you wouldn't dream of suggesting I should go back to Castletara.'

'Then why don't you tell me? It's too bad of you, Dana, not to give any reason for the rift between you and your mother,' Polly said reproachfully. 'I told you how my mother treated me, and why I could never go home, so why shouldn't you pay me the same compliment? Is it such a dark secret that you can't even tell your best pal?'

Dana sighed deeply. 'Yes it is; a dark secret, I mean. It makes me sad and miserable whenever I think about it, so let's change the subject, if you please. What did you think of that apple pie?'

Polly laughed. 'It were prime,' she said gaily. 'Now tell me, Dana; we've all worked very hard in all sorts of different ways to repay Jake and Ralph for the trust they've placed in us and for the nice way they've treated us. So are you really happy? You're a part-time usherette, same as me, and in the cafeteria you're a part-time cleaner, cashier, cook, bookkeeper . . .'

'Oh, stop! Yes of course I'm happy, but if I'm absolutely honest I've discovered an important truth. Being the manageress of someone else's cafeteria is not quite the same as running your own, though I'm really glad the place is popular and doing so well. Ralph told me a few days ago that even when the main feature isn't particularly riveting people still climb the last flight of stairs and have a meal. That means that we're bringing in a steady income to swell the profits from the actual cinema itself. That's good, of course; Jake and Ralph think by the end of the year we'll be in a position to buy in better films, which should increase the size of the audience, and that means—'

'I know, it means that the cafeteria will take more money,' Polly said impatiently. 'Tell me, Dee, how are you getting on with Ralph? The two of you have been going around together for a while now.'

'We're like you and Ernie; just good friends,' Dana said, smiling. 'He's awfully nice, but we're both too busy to start getting all lovey-dovey. Which is a good thing, since I'm – oh, I'm not in the market for marrying. And

I suspect I'm not the only girl Ralph takes out now and then.'

'Oh, he's two-timing you, is he? He's full of courage, then, because that red hair of yours probably means you're jealous as any cat and keep a knife in your garter for unfaithful fellers,' Polly said, smiling too. As she spoke she heard a tram rumbling up behind them and jerked her friend's arm. 'Had enough fresh air? I have, because it's not only fresh, it's perishin' freezin', and I'm beginning to think lovingly of me bed,' she added frankly.

Dana agreed and they waved the tram down, but once settled on the leather seat – this one was a green goddess – Polly turned to her friend once more. 'Dana, you once said Ralph reminded you of someone. Was it Con, the feller you talk about in your dreams?'

Dana turned to stare thoughtfully at her companion. 'Do you know, I'm not sure,' she said honestly. 'Ralph's extremely good-looking, as I'm sure you'll agree, and I don't think Con's good-looking at all. Just – just familiar, I suppose. They're both dark, but which is the taller, or the sturdier for that matter, I really couldn't tell you. I suppose it's partly because the dreams started with me when I was five or six and have gone on more or less in sequence until I was fourteen or fifteen. Con's a year older than me, which means the last time I dreamed of him he would've been, oh, fifteen or sixteen I suppose. But what does it matter? As I keep telling you, dreams are only that, and Con is a part of my past, a past I'm trying very hard to forget. So if you don't mind – or even if you do – I should like to regard the subject as closed.'

'Oh would you?' Polly said indignantly. 'Well I think

you're being a real idiot. You had a marvellous home and loving parents . . .'

Dana shoved both fingers in her ears, wagged her head and began to shout 'Can't hear you, can't hear you' just as the conductor arrived beside her. She promptly unplugged her ears, feeling her face grow hot with embarrassment as she handed over her fare. When he had gone, whistling beneath his breath, she turned on Polly. 'Now we've talked about it I bet I dream tonight, and it's all your wretched fault, Polly Smith,' she said severely. 'So I'll thank you to stuff your ears with cotton wool and not listen to a word I say. It's awfully sneaky to eavesdrop on someone else's dream, you should know that.'

Polly was still arguing the point when the tram reached their stop and the two girls climbed down, made their way under the arch into Temperance Court, and presently were back in their rooms and setting about the tasks they did every night before bed. They had gone up in the world since working at the cinema and now had the whole of the ground floor – kitchen and parlour as well as their living room and bedroom – to themselves. The kitchen range was never allowed to go out, though it sometimes seemed a terrible waste to warm the room when no one would be in it. However, it was good to walk in and find it beautifully warm, so that it was the work of a moment to put the kettle on to boil for the mug of cocoa which Polly always swore helped her to sleep, and then refill it to make themselves a hot bottle each. Because the kitchen was so warm, they always changed into their night things there, then shot through the cold hall, into their bedroom and straight beneath the covers.

Once safely in bed Dana tried not to think about

Castletara. She had not dreamed of it lately and she was beginning to hope that her determination to tire herself out might have made such dreams a thing of the past. After all, most of them were about her early years; the incident which she most dreaded becoming a part of her dream life had taken place when she was just seventeen and could be counted as an adult. Besides, it was not a happy incident, it was downright hateful, and all her other dreams had been delightful, of times to be remembered with nostalgic pleasure. Surely now the dreams would end and she would be able to forget Castletara, her mother, Con and Johnny Devlin and everything connected with the family of McBride?

Hopefully, Dana pulled the covers up round her ears, and presently slept.

She was standing in the courtyard, holding Warrior's bridle near the bit and sipping the glass of mulled wine which Deirdre had just put into her hand. The courtyard was busy with riders and their mounts, the horses' breath emerging as clouds of steam whilst the riders stamped their booted feet, talked at the tops of their voices, and joked and laughed with Deirdre and the other girls from the village, who had come to help prepare a large and sustaining meal for the riders' return. Even Enda, who many thought was what Feena called 'tenpence in the shilling', was chattering away nineteen to the dozen as she watched the horses and their riders assemble. She was a pretty girl who came up to the house several times a week, always eager to help with any indoor or outdoor work in order to earn herself a shilling or two.

Dana chatted with the rest. This was not her first hunt;

she and Con had ridden out with the pack two or three times this winter already, but today was a special one. The Boxing Day hunt always set off from and returned to Castletara and was always well attended. Even Feena McBride, who often said she had mixed feelings about blood sports, rode with her husband's pack at the Boxing Day meet. She, her daughter, Deirdre and the other servants spent a great deal of time and effort preparing the meal and Dana's mouth watered as she remembered the last glance she had taken at the Castletara kitchen. The room was decorated for Christmas with holly and mistletoe, paper lanterns, glittering baubles and a Christmas tree on whose branches a hundred tiny scarlet candles would glitter when the hunt returned. On the long table, which stretched the length of the room, there were great dishes of every sort of meat pie imaginable waiting to be popped into the Aga, as well as tureens which would presently hold vegetables. Deirdre would produce potatoes in their jackets, crisp without and floury within; the great pats of yellow homemade butter were already in place, to be joined later by a baron of beef, two enormous joints of pork and half a dozen chickens, roasted to a turn.

On the dresser were ranged what Deirdre called 'desserts': golden-crusted fruit pies, trifles rich with cream, jellies and blancmanges. Everything and more you could desire, Dana thought fondly, for though she was frequently condemned by her parents for being 'skinny as a rake' she was a grand little eater so she was, and could pack away nearly as much food as Con could, though he was four inches taller and a good deal sturdier as well.

'Are we all ready?' That was the Master's voice, gathering his pack of slavering bright-eyed hounds, ready to give them the off. One hound – Dana knew it was Bella – was still snuffling up the crumbs from the Cornish pasties which had preceded the mulled wine and she lingered until the Master's whip cracked too near her tail for comfort. Then she joined her companions, first giving the Master a reproachful look from her liquid dark eyes. She was his favourite and knew it, would be the first to pick up the scent . . .

'Come along wit' you, alanna; what's keeping you? Don't say you need a leg up!' That was Con, already in the saddle. He, his father and Donovan McBride were all riding horses which they hoped to sell as hunters, either to one of the men present today or at the big horse sale when it took place in the nearby market town. Warrior, however, was Dana's own. A neat little gelding, he was just on fifteen hands high, steel grey with a white mane and tail and the first horse Dana had ever owned, for previously she had ridden ponies.

Dana snorted. Con rode a beautiful chestnut, something over sixteen hands high. The gelding's mane and tail were creamy white, and he had four white socks and a white star – only Dana thought it more like a diamond – on his broad, intelligent brow. 'A leg-up? Ha!' She swung herself neatly into the saddle and pulled a face at Con. 'Bet you had to use the mounting block!'

'Bet I didn't!'

'Did!'

'Didn't!'

'Wish I'd seen you then; I bet you clambered into the saddle like a monkey up a stick,' Dana said mockingly.

245

'Bet you won't jump the big hedge into the downs, but will go through the gate, like all beginners do.'

'How dare you!' Con said in pretended wrath. 'I've been riding with the hunt for two years, and I've never used a gate when my mount could jump the hedge. And when you aren't riding I've always been in at the kill, but of course when you're out I have to take you home so you don't see anything horrid.'

Dana considered that this remark was below the belt. It was true that she always turned for home whenever it seemed likely that a kill was imminent, and it was also true that Con always accompanied her, though they both told anyone who questioned them that they had returned to the house to help the servants prepare and serve the meal.

Now, however, it seemed that Con was using her squeamishness against her, and Dana was opening her mouth to tell him so when her mother joined them. She was riding her own mare, a bay, rather boringly called Darkie, and tutted, wagging a reproving finger at them. 'Really, you two, anyone listening to your conversation would assume you were both about five years old! You are supposed to be showing off that chestnut's paces, young man, so you'd better leave Warrior and Darkie here to take the fences in their own time. Ah, off we go!'

It was a good run, for though it was a very cold morning the ground was not too hard, and as the sun came up, a great red ball inching its way slowly above the distant hills, Dana knew that this ride would be unforgettable, would be remembered for many years as one of the most enjoyable moments of her life. Warrior and Darkie were good stable companions, knowing each other's paces and never trying to push ahead or cram at fences. Because it was so early, a low mist hung over the meadows, and where the sun had not yet touched the frost still dusted the grass, giving the scenery a magical beauty through which the hunt thundered, seemingly indifferent.

Now and then, when the horses bunched to take a fence at the lowest point, Dana could see, well ahead of them, Con's bright chestnut and the gleaming quarters of Beauty, the big black gelding which her father hoped to sell as a result of this morning's hunt. The horse certainly showed to advantage, Dana told her mother as, practically knee to knee, they cleared the last straggling hedge which separated the McBrides' cultivated acres from the beautiful wild downs, with their copses, streams and gentle hills. Here large areas of crisp brown bracken glowed gold in the light of the rising sun, and little rills reflected the blue of the sky. Warrior tossed his head and snorted, eager to lengthen his stride and overtake the horses ahead, but Darkie, who was twelve years old, kept a steady pace and Dana reined Warrior back so that she and Feena could continue to ride together. They had not yet found, for foxes would not have been popular on the McBrides' well-tended acres, but here on the downs they stood a good chance of rousing a big dog fox, who would give them a good run for their money and, Dana hoped, go to earth as the hounds began to tire. The McBrides had never approved of blocking a fox's earth, Donovan remarking that the sport was in the chase and not in seeing an innocent creature torn apart by hounds. 'After all, if you kill a fox in country such as this, where they do no harm to our livestock, then what'll you hunt next time round?' he was wont to remark; and since he was the largest landowner for many a mile his neighbours tolerated his views, though some, who kept poultry, must have silently disagreed.

The hunt reached a river and streamed over, knowing the water here to be shallow, the bed sanded. By now the sun was well up, gilding the water, the reeds and even the riders and their mounts. Warrior and Darkie slid down the bank and began to splash towards the opposite side and Dana, looking down into the water, watched its crystal clarity disappear as Warrior's hooves sent up cloudbursts of sand.

Feena, following her daughter's gaze, laughed. 'I'll be bound we've given the little fishes something to tell their mammies and daddies,' she said gaily. 'For weeks they've growed from little tiddlers to bigger ones wit' nothin' to disturb the clear water, and now there's horses, sand and noise. Poor little t'ings . . . oh, look, there's a water vole.' She chuckled. 'See him, Dee? He's swimming for his life, headin' for the reeds by the bank; do you think he believes we're hunting him?'

Their horses scrambled up the slippery bank and needed no encouragement from their riders to quicken their pace as soon as they were on firm ground again. They were both experienced hunters and Dana knew that when Darkie – or Warrior for that matter – had had enough they would let their riders know by subtle means. A slowing of the pace, a drooping of the head, even an alteration in their length of stride, would tell Feena and herself that the time had come to ease off a little, perhaps even to turn for home. But now they were approaching woodland, beautiful even at this time of year, for this was a broad-leaved copse whose foliage overhead had long gone, and a wind frost had delicately dusted every branch with white, making the scene before them so lovely that even hardened members of the hunt paused to stare before riding into the trees.

Shortly after this, hounds put up a feral cat. Black as pitch with big green eyes and long white claws, the cat fled through the trees, hounds close on his tail, until, realising his peril, he shot twenty foot up a beech tree, glaring defiance at the animals baying beneath him and causing Dana and Feena to laugh as the Master's long whip cracked and the hounds, who had been barely six feet from the cat's bushed out tail, yelped and whimpered, but did not seem unhappy to move away from the trunk of the tree. They probably knew that a feral cat could give a good and painful account of itself, even if they managed to kill it in the end, through sheer weight of numbers.

The hunt rode on. As they emerged from the trees the horses bunched whilst the hounds spread out, searching for a scent, and Con came over to them, grinning broadly. 'So you're still with us?' he said, absently patting the neck of the big chestnut. 'I thought you might fall by the wayside when we reached the river, 'cos I know how you hate getting your feet wet.'

'Don't be silly,' Dana said coldly. 'You know very well I love the water. I supposed you're referring to the time Warrior caught his foot on a stone in the river bed and pecked and I went in over his head.' She glared at her old friend. 'I was eight years old, and it's a rotten thing to throw something I did as a little kid in my face.'

Con pulled off his hat and gave Dana and Feena a

mocking bow. 'Sorry, ladies, that was ungentlemanly,' he said. 'You're keeping up grand so you are. Did you see that wild cat? The size of him! I reckon he was as glad as I was when he shot up that tree. A cat like that goes for the eyes and nose; we'd have had Bella and Roy blinded if he'd not took off – the wild cat, I mean.'

Both women agreed that they too had been relieved when the cat took to the trees, but then there was a shout from the Master and hounds which had been desultorily sniffing in patches of bracken and around the roots of trees began to stream after Bella, who had once again proved her ability to find.

The run over the downs was always good and today was no exception. Fast and furious the hounds and the hunt streamed across the countryside, led by the little red feller, as Donovan McBride always called the fox. Through bogs, copses and rocky uplands sown with straggling birch trees, through patches of bramble and great clumps of gorse they streamed, and the two McBride women were not the first to give up the chase by a long chalk. Older neighbours who enjoyed the ride until their elderly mounts grew tired, or they themselves could no longer keep up, had gone before the river crossing; others had turned back before the incident with the feral cat. Now Dana and Feena, though with some reluctance, did not even try to skirt the bog through which several experienced members of the hunt were struggling. Both were bright-eyed and exhilarated from the excitement and the exercise, and as they made for a nearby lane which would take them more or less straight to Castletara, Feena leaned over and patted her daughter's hot cheek. 'We've done really well, so we have, to keep up until now,' she said gaily. 'Daddy will be proud of us, for he knows where we left him. Con must have seen us moving towards the lane, for he said something to your daddy who turned and gave me a thumbs up sign. Now we'll take it gently for Darkie's sake, but even so I reckon we'll be home in time to get everything ready for when the rest arrive.'

'That suits me,' Dana said thankfully. 'I don't think I've given Con any reason to gloat, do you? After all he's a whole year older than me, and he's hunted for at least two seasons more than I.' She glanced sideways at her mother under her lashes. 'You know the McCulloch girl? Was she still keeping up when we left?' She tried to make it sound as though her mother's answer did not matter, but guessed by Feena's twinkling glance that she was well aware of the rivalry which existed between the two girls. They both attended the nearby Catholic girls' school, first one leading the class, then the other, but recently Con had started to show an interest in Sinead McCulloch and more recently still the other girl had begun to show a reciprocal interest in him.

'Sinead? But she doesn't hunt; doesn't even ride so far as I know,' Feena said. 'Oh, was she following? But the folk on foot turned back ages ago; didn't you notice?'

'Not really; we've been too busy keeping up ourselves to worry about anyone else,' Dana said airily, though in truth she felt a surge of relief. Foot followers were welcome to join the members of the hunt at Castletara when the excitement was over but rarely did so, and Dana found herself hoping that her schoolfellow would have gone home long since. Hunting foxes was bad enough but hunting fellows even worse. She said as

251

much to her mother, causing Feena to gurgle with amusement.

'You're daft you are,' she said affectionately. 'If you don't know that Con's been fond of you ever since he came to live at Castletara then you're not as clever as I thought you were. But darlin', you and Sinead were good pals; Daddy used to say you lived in one another's pockets during term time. A girl needs . . .' She hesitated as though considering how best to put her thoughts into words. 'A girl needs girlfriends; quite a different thing from boyfriends,' she said at last. 'I know you and Con are close, but you mustn't miss out on girl talk because it's important, a part of growing up. You and Sinead are both seventeen and very soon now you'll begin to be interested in things like clothes and makeup. You'll want to experiment with your hair – different styles, I mean – and with boyfriends too. I do beg of you not to let your friendly rivalry turn into something less pleasant, just because you both like Con.'

Dana turned to her mother, her eyes widening with surprise. 'But Mam, just now you said Con had always been fond of me. If that's so then surely he shouldn't start being fond of Sinead as well?'

Feena laughed. 'Con's growing up just as you and Sinead are. I should like to think that you'll make other friends – friends who are boys – because otherwise you have no comparisons and might make bad choices. The same goes for Con, of course. I know he's taken you to the cinema and once or twice to local hops at the village hall, but if he kisses you they'll be puppy kisses, because he's experimenting just as you and Sinead are . . .'

Dana interrupted, feeling her cheeks flame. 'Honestly,

252

Mother, what a thing to say! So far as I'm aware, nobody kisses anybody else; as if we would!' And then, coming rapidly off her high horse, she added, 'And if Con starts kissing Sinead, 'tis a punch on the snout he'll get off me!'

Feena began to chuckle, then to laugh so heartily that she had to fish a handkerchief out of her jacket pocket. 'What a wildcat I've given birth to!' she said, mopping at her streaming eyes. 'But have a think about what I've said, darling Dee. You and Sinead will only be at the high school for one more year, then you'll have to think about what you want to do next. Oh, I know you say you want to come into partnership with Daddy, Johnny and myself – and Con, of course, if that's what he wants – but in a year's time, with a bit more experience under your belt, you may want to become a beautician, or a hairdresser, or – or . . .'

Dana giggled. 'I don't think I'd be very good at either of those, Mammy. No, there's nothing I want to do more than continuing to help you and Daddy on the stud farm. You've made your name famous throughout Ireland; I intend to spread our fame to England as well. If you honestly think I'd swap that even for being Queen of England, you're wrong.'

Feena flung up a hand in a gesture of defeat. 'All right, all right, you know which path you want to tread and by the way you've reacted over Sinead, you'll want to tread it with Con and nobody else.' She looked quizzically across at her daughter, and then ahead to where the little lane they were following became flanked by steep banks. In the spring, Dana thought, this was where she would pick great bunches of primroses; in summer the tiny scarlet strawberries and in autumn the nuts from the hazel trees whose branches almost met above the lane.

'The horses have had it easy for the past twenty minutes or so, Mammy. Shall we trot?'

As Feena had foretold, they arrived at Castletara in good time to help with the making and serving of the enormous meal. The Aga was full of pies and pasties, baking potatoes and the big sausage rolls for which Feena was famous, but the hunt must have gone further than usual for time passed and no one returned until Con careered into the stable yard, almost colliding with Enda, who had started forward with the obvious intention of taking his horse. But Con did not seem to notice the girl; he slid down from his mount and shouted urgently for Declan, the McBrides' head groom. Then he came running across to the back door, flinging it open and letting in a blast of icy air. He glanced quickly round the room, his eyes wide, then held out a hand to Feena, grasping her own tightly in his. 'Auntie Fee, there's been – there's been a bit of an accident,' he said. 'Can you come? Bring a blanket.' He whipped round on Dana. 'Stay here!' he commanded brusquely. 'There's nothing you can do; keep your nose out for once and don't ask questions.'

Dana, who had begun to move towards him, fell back as though she had been slapped. But as the buzz of talk and conjecture rose from the helpers she caught hold of her mother's arm. 'What's up, Mammy?' she demanded anxiously. 'Con said a blanket, not water or bandages . . . does that mean someone's hurt real bad?'

'I don't know, but I do know Con wouldn't have told you to stay in here if it wasn't important,' Feena said, and Dana saw that her mother's face was white as a sheet. 'I'll come back as soon as maybe; if someone's hurt bad the men will be taking one of the stable doors off its hinges. Be a good girl now and do as you're told.'

She hurried out of the room as she spoke, snatching up a blanket and running across the stable yard towards the arch which led out to the lane, and Dana followed her. Afterwards, long afterwards, she wished she had not done so, but wishing came too late. Four men were carrying a gate upon which lay her father, ominously still. Dana stared. There were his highly polished leather boots, now mud-splashed from the day's adventure, there were his grey riding breeches, as familiar to her as the backs of her own hands, there his tweed jacket and beneath it his stiff white shirt, but all these things were splashed and mottled with blood and when she looked into his face, though she knew it must be he, there was not one feature remaining. It was just a mask of blood and other indescribable things, beneath which she could just see the terrible disfigurement which made her hope for one desperate agonising second that this was not her father, not the man who had ridden out so gaily that morning, eager to show off the black hunter. It must be another rider, another horse whose great iron-clad hooves had wreaked the terrible damage which she saw before her.

Even as she stared, doubting the evidence of her own eyes, Enda, who had run out of the courtyard, swerving to avoid the four members of the hunt and their dreadful burden, came back and stopped by them. Very gently she placed a bouquet of Christmas roses, pink, purple and white, to hide that terrible face.

255

Then someone screamed. She started forward, wanting her mother's reassurance that this nightmare was just that, a nightmare, but someone was shaking her, slapping her face, telling her to pull herself together, asking why she had not done as she was told and stayed away. 'I didn't want you to see . . .' It was Con's voice, and then she felt his arms lift her from the ground and knew she must have fainted. 'Oh, my love, my love, we wanted to spare you . . .'

She knew, then, that it was she who had screamed, who whimpered still, she who had ignored Con's express wish that she should remain indoors. He had laid her gently in one of the old cane chairs and she opened her eyes and began to tell him how sorry she was that she had disobeyed, but her voice came out as a tiny thread, no more than a whisper, and Con had moved away; he and Johnny Devlin were comforting Feena, making arrangements. Without realising it she had heard those arrangements, knew that the blanket should have hidden the appalling sight, knew too that they were carrying her father around from the stable yard to the front door, so that what was left of him might lie in the parlour, a room which was seldom used, until it was ready for burial.

Presently, Dana struggled to her feet. Neither her mother nor Con was in sight, but the servants and some members of the hunt were milling around, talking in hushed voices, though even Mr Devlin and Declan had disappeared. Dana straightened her shoulders and banged on the table for silence. She knew that a good few members of the hunt, probably even the Master, would not know that Donovan McBride was dead, or, if they knew something had occurred, might still think him only badly injured. It was only those who had seen him before Con had covered him with the blanket who would realise the enormity of what had happened. But I am a McBride, Dana told herself. I may be only seventeen, just a kid with ginger hair and a million freckles, but I'm still a McBride and these people are my guests. So she rapped on the table again, louder this time, and when all the faces in the room had turned towards her, and when the little groups still standing outside in the stable yard had done likewise, she spoke as her parents would have done.

'There's been an accident. My – my parents are dealing with it, but I am their deputy and ask you all to fill your glasses and drink a toast to the success of the hunt. When you have done so, please eat heartily of the meal which has been prepared.'

She smiled as brightly as she could, then beckoned Deirdre to begin filling the long lines of glasses from the jugs of punch and, to set good example, cut herself a wedge of steak pie. Then she began to help others to the food upon the long kitchen table, and even as she bit or pretended to bite into her slice of pie, knowing that it would choke her if she tried to swallow, with the image of her father's ruined face still in her mind's eye, she heard a soft voice behind her. 'Well done!'

It was Con, of course, ready to help, to take command, to do anything she asked of him. It would have been nice to turn into his arms and let loose a great wail of sorrow and anguish but she told herself that she was a McBride, someone of importance in the community. She and her mother must somehow weather this storm and they would begin by hosting the party which the head of their house had planned and would want to see held. So she turned and smiled brightly at Con before asking, 'Where's my mother?'

'In the parlour with Deirdre and old Mrs Murdoch and one or two of the other ladies,' Con said. 'I know I needn't tell you that you mustn't go in there; it was only shock and fear that sent you flying into the stable yard, but oh, Christ, acushla, I wish to God you'd not had to see . . .'

'It was my own fault,' Dana said through rigidly smiling lips. She would not think of the sight she had seen in the stable yard, though she was sure it would haunt her for the rest of her life. 'Come on, Con. Daddy would say . . .' her voice trembled and she had to pause before completing the sentence, 'Daddy would say that guests must be fed and watered after such a day. Mammy's too busy and so are the older women, but this is something we can do: feed and water 'em, like Declan and your daddy are doing to the horses out in the stables right now.'

An hour later, the servants were clearing away the remains of the food and drink; there was not much left, for no matter how tragically the day had ended it had been a grand hunt much enjoyed by everyone. Even the little red feller had made it to his earth before the hounds had caught up with him, so the day had been a success for him too. And now alone at last, with Donovan McBride's body decently prepared for what must follow, Feena and Dana, Con and his father slumped on to straight-backed wooden chairs in the kitchen, ate food which might have been sawdust, drank wine that tasted like water and tried to come to terms with the realisation that their lives had depended almost totally upon one man and now he had gone.

'My husband would have wanted everything to continue as though he were still alive,' Feena said stiffly, reaching a hand round to rub the small of her back. 'Ah God, but it's weary I am. However, the bailiff from the Creech place says his master wants the chestnut Con was riding; fortunately he and my husband reached an agreement on the price before . . .' She hesitated, her voice breaking. Then she shook her head and spoke firmly once more. 'Earlier in the day, I should say.'

'That's good, so it is,' Johnny Devlin said approvingly. 'He's a generous man and will pay up before quarter day when he hears how you're circumstanced, Feena.'

He seemed about to say something else, but Con cut across him. 'The Englishman wants Beauty. The price is poor for such a grand chaser, but I thought since it'll be a cash sale . . .'

Feena and Dana spoke in chorus. 'Yes, let him go,' they said, Dana adding: 'We'll be better off with him gone, though I dare say it was none of his fault.'

'That's true,' Con said. 'He caught his hoof in a rabbit hole, and when Mr Donovan shot over his head the poor feller couldn't stop himself . . .' He finished in midsentence as Feena gave a little moan. 'Sorry. But Beauty's a grand horse. The Englishman's got a real bargain.'

Real bargain . . . real bargain . . . bargain . . . gain . . .

And Dana was lying in her bed at Temperance Court, her pillow wet with tears and Polly's small hand on her shaking shoulder.

'It's all right, you're safe, Polly's got you,' her friend was repeating. 'Whatever was all that about? Oh, Dana,

259

you've been having the most awful nightmare. It took me almost five minutes to wake you.'

Polly had been having a good day. She loved her work at the cinema but particularly enjoyed those days that she worked as an usherette, because she got to see the films through twice. Today the B feature was in black and white, and starred the Marx Brothers in *A Day at the Races*. Polly laughed so hard that she had to nip out of her seat and rush along to the ladies' cloakroom before going to the stock room to fill her tray before the main feature, which starred Bette Davis. She was looking forward to her supper, for today was Friday. Ernie would be meeting her outside the cinema and had promised her fish and chips. She had not seen him for a couple of weeks and thought when they spoke that he had seemed distracted, as though his work and his friends there were more important than she. Piqued by his attitude, Polly had exerted all her efforts to persuade him to meet her outside the cinema when her shift ended on Friday, telling him that she wanted a serious talk.

'Right; I'll pay for the fish and chips, our Polly,' he had said grandly. 'You can buy a bottle of cherryade if you like. Pity the cafeteria don't do fish and chips, but Dana says . . .'

'. . . Dana says the smell of the fish and chips would put folk off, especially the next day, 'cos it's real difficult to get rid of the smell,' Polly finished for him. 'Of course you could take me to the cafeteria anyway, 'cos it stays open after work so's the customers can have a meal before going home.'

'Oh aye, poached eggs on toast and that,' Ernie said

disdainfully. 'But after a long day at me factory I need summat real sustaining . . .' he had paused, and she could picture him grinning at her, his eyes alight with mischief, 'summat like smelly old fish and chips,' he concluded.

Polly often had her supper up in the cafeteria but now, thinking it over, she decided she was glad Ernie had suggested that they should have fish and chips. The fact was she was very anxious to have a serious talk with him and she had no wish for Dana to hear even scraps of their conversation, since a good deal of it would revolve around Dana herself.

So when the performance ended Polly fetched her light jacket, said goodnight to various friends and members of staff and made her way out of the cinema by the side door, grinning widely at Ernie, who was waiting outside, for though it was ten thirty in the evening the June days were long and light and a jacket was all that was necessary, even if they walked all the way home and did not bother with the tram. As she joined Ernie he caught her hand and tucked it into the crook of his elbow, remarking that he could just murder a plate of cod and chips. 'We'll walk to the fried fish shop, then we'll catch a tram to Temperance Court and eat in your kitchen, so we'd best buy enough for Dana as well,' he said, but Polly pulled him to a halt, shaking her head.

'Ernie Frost, you've got a head like a sieve,' she said severely. 'Don't you remember me saying that I wanted to have a talk about something which has been worrying me? I don't want Dana overhearing, so let's buy the fish and chips and take 'em down to that little garden on the corner. There's a seat among the bushes and unless a tramp has taken up residence we should be able to talk without interruption.'

Ernie was agreeable so the two of them joined the queue at the fried fish shop, were lavish with salt and vinegar and then made their way to the small square of garden, Polly giving a crow of triumph as she saw that the bench was unoccupied. They settled themselves comfortably, unwrapped the newspaper and began to eat, Ernie courteously slowing down when he realised that his share of the food was almost finished whilst Polly, though she had eaten all her fish, still had quite a pile of chips to go. Finally they both produced handkerchiefs and tidied themselves up and Ernie turned expectantly towards his companion.

'Well, what's up?' he enquired curiously. 'I hope you and Dana haven't fallen out, though I doubt that. In all the time I've known the pair of you I don't believe you've ever had a cross word; ain't that so?'

Polly nodded vigorously and shoved her now greasy handkerchief into her pocket. 'And we've not had a cross word now,' she confirmed. 'The truth is, Ern, I'm real worried about Dana. Way back, I think it must've been around February sometime, Dana had one of those dreams I've told you about, about her old home. You know that she talks like anything in her sleep and to tell you the truth I've been woken more than once by her laughing and teasing one of her parents or her friend Con or someone called Deirdre.'

'Well? What's wrong wi' that?' Ernie said as his companion fell silent. He laughed. 'Sounds like fun, if you asks me.'

'Ye-es. And so it was at first,' Polly acknowledged.

'Only then she had this awful nightmare. I couldn't wake her at first, and I got worried – she was screaming, shouting that something was horrible – then she just sobbed and sobbed. I kept shaking her, telling her she was safe, that it was only a dream – only it was more like a nightmare – and she must wake up. She did, of course, but she didn't want to tell me what it was all about, and I just thought she'd forget it, like I forget it when I have a nightmare. Only . . .'

'Only what?' Ernie prompted when Polly stopped speaking and simply stared straight in front of her. 'Only what, Poll?' he repeated. 'Dammit, that was months ago! What exactly are you trying to tell me?'

Polly thought for a moment, then gave a loud sigh. 'I know it was ages ago, but ever since that night she's been . . . well, I suppose you could say she's been different. She's been going out quite a lot with Ralph and obviously enjoys his company. Well, you know that since we've been out in a foursome with them; I suppose you haven't noticed that she's been much quieter lately, though. It used to be she who joked, suggested outings, made beautiful picnic lunches, but she hardly ever does so now. In fact it's you and me who do most of the talking, because Ralph is quite a quiet bloke, wouldn't you say? She talks about joining one of the services but she hasn't done anything about it. I don't s'pose anyone else would notice there was anything wrong . . .'

'Nor there is; anything wrong, I mean,' Ernie said firmly. 'For goodness' sake, girl, she works hard and plays hard; what's wrong with that? It sounds to me as though you're making a mountain out of a molehill. We all had a good laugh that Sunday when we took a bus into the country and went strawberry picking. She was in fine form then. She and Ralph picked twice as much as you and me; and ate twice as much as well.' He chortled, digging Polly in the ribs. 'I often wonder how them farmers who let you pick your own punnets o' fruit manage to make a living since everyone gobbles strawberries before they start.'

'Dana says they charge twice as much to cover what we eat,' Polly said wisely. 'Oh dear, Ernie, you're making me wonder whether I've imagined the whole thing, but honest to God I *know* I'm right. She's terribly unhappy underneath. She hides it most of the time and I bet not even Ralph has noticed, though he thinks of himself as a pretty close friend, if not actually her boyfriend. But I'm sure as I can be that what she really wants is to go home. I think she's worried about the McBrides, wants to know how they're getting on. She told me ages ago, quite soon after Caitlin left, that she had to leave home to earn some money because her family had fallen on hard times. She must wonder how they're getting on without her; it's been ages!'

'Well, what's wrong with that?' Ernie demanded. 'It's what's happening in no end of families, especially in Ireland, they tell me. My friend Euan has left his family in Dublin and come over to work for the railways because he couldn't get work over there. So you see it'll be the same for Dana; I bet she sends most of her wages off to this Castletara you've mentioned.'

Polly gave a crow of triumph. 'Now that's where you're bleedin' well wrong! She doesn't send so much as a penny piece home. She doesn't write to her mam and her mam doesn't write to her and if that isn't odd I don't know what is! Besides, the McBrides don't live in a big city like Dublin. I'm sure I've told you over and over that they live in a place called Castletara; their home is called that and so is the village which means they must be quite rich, or if not rich at least well-to-do. But if they don't need financial help then why on earth did Dana ever leave home? Until the last dream I would've said she was really happy, because after the earlier dreams she sang around the house and told me little bits about her life at Castletara. Well,' she amended, 'I asked questions and she answered them. She won't do that any more, though; she just changes the subject or bolts into another room. Honestly, Ern, she won't tell me what's wrong and she won't go home, not even for a week. I told her she was working too hard and needed a little holiday. I said a week at Castletara would set her up for whatever is to come – because of course we're all convinced it's going to be war, aren't we? But she just tightens her lips and shakes her head and when I said she wasn't herself and needed a break she told me to mind my own business, speaking so sharply that I could only stare. Honestly, Ern, it's not a bit like the old Dana. So now you've heard what's worrying me, what do you think?'

Ernie scowled down at the backs of his hands resting on his knees. 'You can't force someone to confide in you,' he said thoughtfully. 'Still, it's no use pretending I can tell you what's up because I just don't know Dana well enough. But I do know you, Polly Smith! You've got an idea, haven't you?'

Polly beamed at him. 'Yes I have. I've got a week's holiday due to me . . . well, it isn't exactly due, it's just that what with conscription coming in last month and

Bruce waiting for his call-up papers for the air force the Freeways would rather we got a bit of holiday before all sorts of new restrictions are put in force.' She put a small hand over Ernie's fingers and squeezed gently. 'If she won't go to Ireland then I mean to do so. I shall tell her I'm going to the Peak District because she knows I've always wanted to see the limestone caverns and underground rivers, but really I shall get on the ferry and go to this Castletara place and find out just what's going on. After all Dana has been away now for three years or more; things must have changed in ways she can't possibly know about. Only, darling Ernie, I can't go alone. Please, please, please will you come with me?'

Slowly a big smile spread across Ernie's face, but then it faded and he shook his head regretfully. 'Sorry, queen. I'd give a lot to be able to say yes, but I reckon me boss would have me guts for garters if I did. You know how hard we've been working . . .'

'I do, and that's a good reason to press for a few days off,' Polly said eagerly. She put her head on one side and gave Ernie her sweetest smile. 'Please, Ernie; you've told me many times how useful you are, because you understand engines in a way the other blokes don't,' she said coaxingly. 'You could promise to do double shifts to make up the time you'd be off. I suppose you could say you would take a week without pay, because you've done so much overtime lately that you must be rolling in gelt. Oh, Ernie, I'm sure if Jake will let me go off for a week then your boss would do as much for you.'

'He might, but then again he mightn't and I don't want him to think I'm the kind of fellow to take time off just because the weather's so good,' Ernie said. 'But look, chuck, you'll be perfectly all right on your own. I'll see you safe aboard the Irish ferry and once you get off on the other side all you have to do is ask someone the way to Castletara. You'll mebbe have to catch a bus or a train but you're a sensible kid, you'll find out which stop you need and gerroff at the right place. Then you'll be home and dry in no time at all, just see if you ain't.'

Polly sighed, conquering an almost irresistible desire to snarl at Ernie that from what she had gleaned from her friend, Castletara was a good journey from Dublin. Lacking any information other than that her friend's home was on the outskirts of a tiny village and not too far from the sea, she realised that it might take her several days just to reach the place. Once there, of course, she supposed doubtfully, she might be able to discover just why Dana had left home. Once she knew that, she hoped to be able to persuade her friend to go back to Ireland herself, but if not at least to write home and tell them she was well, had a good job and would go back one day. But when she voiced these thoughts to Ernie he shook his head.

'It's none of my business, chuck; none of yours either,' he assured her. 'I don't think you ought to interfere, and that's God's truth. You already know what Dana's like over these here dreams of hers: she don't like the feeling that you're spying on her . . .'

'Hey up! I've never spied on anyone in me life,' Polly said indignantly. 'Just you take that back, Ernie Frost, or I'll box your ears till they ring! If you share a bedroom with someone who talks in their sleep you ain't got no choice but to hear what they say. Oh, Ernie, please say you'll come with me. I dussen't go alone.'

'Well, I suppose I could ask . . .' Ernie began, whereupon Polly put both arms round his neck, kissed him violently, and hugged him, nearly strangling him at the same time.

'Oh, thank you, thank you, Ernie. You see, I've lived all me life in Liverpool. The furthest away I've ever got is when you and Ralph took me and Dana off to New Brighton for the day. Oh, and we went to that farm on the Wirral, fruit picking. But Ireland's a foreign country; they don't even talk like us, and I've never been on a great big boat . . .'

'Ship, you mean,' Ernie said absently. 'I know the Irish have their own language, but I believe they only use it in the country districts and they all speak English as well. Now listen, Poll, I'll see what the boss says and let you know as soon as I know meself, which will be on Monday. What shift are you on?'

'I'm cleaning on Monday; the whole circle all to myself,' Polly said rather gloomily. 'Then I'm giving a hand in the cafeteria because Brenda's been and gone and signed up for the ATS. I thought it'd be dead easy to replace her – she's one of the waitresses, you know – but Jake told me it's not so. The factories pay awful well and there's a lot of glamour attached to a uniform so he's finding it quite difficult to get staff.'

'Then it's real good of him to let you take a week off. Just when is that week, anyway?' Ernie asked, suddenly suspicious. He pointed an accusing finger at Polly. 'It would be just like you to tease me and bribe me into taking a week's holiday only to find out that Jake couldn't spare you after all.'

Polly felt her cheeks grow warm. Ernie had described something which was far too near the truth for her liking, and she saw that she would have to come clean. 'Now that's not fair, Ernie,' she said reproachfully. 'When have I ever let you down?'

'At least half a dozen times. Once when we'd planned to go to Prince's Park to watch a cricket match, then when you said you'd take me to Seaforth Sands to see where you thought your great-grandpa had once had an allotment. Then there was the time . . .'

'Shut up, Ernie! That was all ages ago, when we were both working at the Willows, and none of them were my fault. It were all Ma Haggerty sayin' she didn't need me one minute and loading me up with work the next. Now come on, be honest! When have I let you down myself, not through no fault of my own?'

'Poll, you're avoiding the question,' Ernie said severely. 'Have you or have you not been given leave to go off on this wild goose chase? And if you have, when does your time off start and finish? It may not matter to you but it'll matter to my boss, I'm tellin' you.'

Polly sighed deeply; she could feel the hot colour rushing up her neck and into her cheeks and guessed that Ernie would notice it too. 'The thing is, Ernie, I couldn't ask Jake or Ralph for definite dates until I knew what time your boss would let you have off. But Jake said almost any time until the school holidays started, so that means sometime in the next month, 'cos I think the kids break up around the middle of July.' She leaned across and gave his hand a squeeze. 'If you'll ask your boss when you get into work on Monday morning and come round to the Freeway as soon as you can on Monday evening to let me know, then I'll confirm the dates you've been given with Jake and we can start looking up sailings and train times and things.' Highly daring, she flung her arm round his neck once more and kissed his cheek. 'You will come with me, won't you?' she pleaded. 'And you'll tell everyone we're off to the Peak District? Because you know how it is – if you tell one person the truth it will get back to Dana sure as eggs is eggs.'

'I'll do my best,' Ernie said, and was rewarded with another ecstatic hug, 'But I don't think we ought to tell folk we're going to the Peak District, because when we come back someone is bound to ask about our holiday and trip us up. Better say Wales; we used to go to Rhyl on school trips when I were a lad and before you came to the Willows a group of us went on a climbing holiday in Snowdonia. We had a great time. Wish we could really go there,' he ended wistfully.

But for Polly it was quite sufficient that he appeared to have accepted her request for his company. She gave him one last hug and jumped up. 'You're the best pal a girl could have,' she said, taking his hands and pulling him to his feet. 'If you'll walk me home I'll make you a nice cup of cocoa so you'll sleep like a top, and we'll tell Dana the holiday is on.'

Ernie sighed, but slipped an arm round her waist. 'I'll walk you home and tell Dana and anyone else a load of lies since it's what you want,' he said. 'But don't forget, my little deceiver, that we shan't know for certain whether I can get the time off until I've spoke to Mr Reynold.'

They went back to Temperance Court together but when Dana seconded Polly's invitation to have cocoa and biscuits with them Ernie shook his head. 'Polly always swears cocoa makes her sleep and I don't mean to nod off on the way back to my digs,' he explained. 'I shall need all my wits about me when I face Mr Reynold on Monday morning to ask for time off.'

Dana nodded. 'I told Polly it wouldn't be easy for you because the work you do is important,' she said. 'But as Jake keeps telling us, it's only a matter of time before we're at war and once that happens holidays will be a thing of the past. Oh, once they get themselves organised it'll be different, but at first it'll be chaotic. So if you can go off and enjoy yourselves, you do it. I've told Jake I'll stand in for Polly whenever the cafeteria is quiet, which is mostly when the films are actually showing, and that's when Polly is busiest, of course.' She grinned at him. 'Good luck! Come and tell us when Mr Reynold has given you dates, then Polly will be able to put in for time off officially, and I'm sure she'll get it. Ralph is talking about joining the RAF and Jake is looking for a really responsible manager so that he can join the forces as well. They're only conscripting men in their early twenties so far and he thinks it will be a while before they get round to older blokes, but he says he means to be prepared.'

'Right. Then as soon as I know for certain, which should be when I leave work on Monday, I'll come straight to the Freeway and we can begin to make our plans,' Ernie said. He gave the girls a mock salute. 'Goodnight, ladies!'

All the way back to his lodgings Ernie hugged himself with glee. It had worked out just as he had hoped. Two or three weeks ago he had been complaining at work that his darling Polly did not seem to take him seriously. True, she was very young, but he was not a lot older himself, so if he knew that Polly Smith was the only girl for him why could she not see that he, Ernie, was her only possible mate? This had made some of the younger apprentices jeer and tell him that he might as well play the field, enjoy himself whilst Polly did not feel she had any claim on him. Others suggested that some of the girls working in the offices or the big canteen at the aircraft factory might be glad to walk out with him. "Cos once there's blokes in uniform milling around, taking over the dance halls and cinemas, splashing money about and impressing every little floozie in the city, you'll be hard pressed to get any girl,' one of the lads said. 'Jimmy's right: play the field, feller, while you've got the chance.'

But one of the older men gave him different advice. 'Play hard to get; act cool towards her. Don't be fighting for kisses and hugs, hold back a bit. Don't you listen to those youngsters, because they don't understand that there are some fellers who truly only want one girl and no other, and the way to get that one girl is to pretend you aren't that bothered, because girls is contrary critters. What they can have without effort they don't want, but what won't fall in their hands like a ripe plum they'll move heaven and earth to get. I'm experienced; it was how I got my old woman, by playing hard to get, and though we've been wed twenty years I'd not change her for Bette Davis, Jean Harlow and DD rolled into one.'

Ernie, who rather liked Danielle Darrieux – she reminded him of Polly – agreed rather doubtfully to give it a try and now he realised his friend had spoken wisely. Polly had never been so loving, so eager for his company. Oh, he understood that she had been sweet because she wanted him to go to Ireland with her, but she had hugged

272

and kissed him without his so much as stretching out a hand to her, and though the kisses had fallen on his neck and the side of his face they had been delicious to one previously starved of any display of affection. And she actually wanted him to accompany her on this ridiculous quest to learn about Dana's past! She had realised that this would take considerably more time than she had at first envisaged and Ernie thought that the week in Ireland would be sheer heaven – and what about the nights! Polly had assured him she had money saved up for rail fares and such and Ernie himself meant to withdraw his savings, which were not inconsiderable, and purchase a money belt from Paddy's market. But there were the nights. He and Polly simply could not afford to take a room each in a lodging house; would she consent to sharing? Ernie felt a delicious anticipatory shiver at the thought and was immediately ashamed. He reminded himself that he would not dream of taking advantage; he would carry a bedroll for himself and tell Polly to bring one too, and if the weather remained as good as it was at present they would sleep under hedges, or in haystacks or barns, wash themselves in streams or ponds and eat as frugally as possible. Satisfied on this score, Ernie jumped on the bus which took the workers to the pleasantly wooded countryside where the factory had been built. To be as near his job as possible, he and a couple of pals had a room-share in the suburbs, and once in his own bedroom he undressed and got into bed, still glowing with happiness. He would show Polly how much he loved her, would comfort her if they failed to find Castletara and would, he was certain, bring her home more aware of his good points than she had ever been before.

Chapter Ten

On the morning their great adventure was due to start Ernie went round to Temperance Court at what seemed like the crack of dawn to find Polly packed, ready and alight with a mixture of excitement and fear, which latter immediately dissipated when she saw his smiling face. He had not had to knock on the door since she must have been hovering at the front window, possibly for hours, watching for his approach. At any rate, before he could so much as climb the three steps to the front door it shot silently open and Polly, her bedroll beneath her arm, erupted into the court. To Ernie's surprise she dropped the bedroll, flung her arms round his neck and gave him a kiss which set every nerve end he possessed tingling. 'I thought you wasn't coming,' she said breathlessly. 'Oh, I know you said six o'clock and it's not yet ten to but I was so afraid you might change your mind, or Mr Reynold might change his . . .'

'Well, as you can see, nobody changed their minds so here I am,' Ernie said bracingly as they set off, his cheek warm and it must be admitted slightly damp from her kiss. 'Are you all set?' He tapped the haversack across her shoulders. 'No point in taking a load of clothes, but any food we can carry with us will save us buying.' He turned towards her as they went under the arch and out into the main road. 'I got a load of oatcakes, a big chunk of cheese and two ounces of strong peppermints. Water's free and bread's cheap so I reckon we won't starve.'

Polly tucked a small confiding hand into the crook of his elbow. 'I got a whole half pound of Everton Mints,' she said proudly. 'I reckon we can suck 'em if we can't afford a proper meal. And Dana gave me a big chunk of stuff – she called it Gur-cake – which she says keeps fresh for ever and is very sustaining. I've brought an old jumper in case the weather changes, but that's about all.'

Ernie nodded his approval. 'Good girl. Got your money tucked away safely somewhere? That's the ticket! Ah, here's the tram to the Pier Head. Wave him down, queen; there's always crowds queuing up to get over to Lairds at this hour of the day, which is why the trams are crammed. Hang on to me and push and shove, 'cos I want to get aboard the ferry in time to bag a nice sheltered spot for the voyage over.'

They stood in the prow of the Irish ferry gazing at the low line of hills which Polly had at first taken to be clouds. As they neared them, however, it became clear that these were hills, and hills of Ireland what was more. They were joined at the rail by several Irishmen, one or two of whom had tears in their eyes, and Polly heard murmurs about 'de ole country' which rather amused her, though when she began to giggle Ernie dug her firmly in the ribs. 'Some of 'em's been workin' in England without goin' home to Ireland for years, and they's the ones what'll join our forces if war comes, even though they don't have to,' he reprimanded her. 'The Irish aren't like the English; they show their emotions freely. And if we're honest we feel the same about our country as they do about theirs, only we've been brought up to believe in keepin' a stiff upper lip.'

'And isn't it . . .' Polly was beginning when she realised that they were near enough now to see details of the land they were approaching. Hastily, she picked up her bedroll, adjusted her haversack and turned a glowing face to her companion. 'We're nearly there!' she whispered. 'Oh, Ernie, I don't know whether I'm more excited or more frightened. If Dana could see us now she'd have a fit!'

'Yes, well . . .' Ernie began, but the ship was making her way carefully through a crowd of smaller craft and he stopped speaking to watch. Indeed, there was so much to see that neither he nor Polly spoke again until the ship had tied up alongside the quays and the gangway was lowered. As their feet touched the cobbles Polly broke the silence.

'We've done it! We're actually in Ireland. And now you could say our adventure has really begun.'

'You could,' Ernie admitted as they stood on Irish soil at last, staring around them. 'But what you just said has made me think. You say Dana would have a fit if she knew where we were, but has it occurred to you that we're going to have to tell her, otherwise what's the point of this adventure? Do you imagine she *won't* have a fit when she finds out we've been to Castletara, after lying to her by pretending we were going to spend a week in Wales?'

For a moment Polly looked both anxious and puzzled, but then her brow cleared. 'We don't have to tell her anything of the sort,' she assured him. 'I think we should say we went on a day trip and when we got to Dublin we got on that train which takes you all along the coast ... or – or perhaps we caught a bus, and we just happened to see Castletara on the signpost . . .'

'More lies. Lies always lead to trouble, but I dare say we'll discover a way round it,' Ernie said resignedly. 'And now let's find ourselves a friendly scuffer – only they call them gardai over here – so that we can ask the way to Dana's village.' He turned to his companion as they headed up the nearest street. 'Well, Polly, what do you think of Dublin?'

Polly turned and stared at him. 'Dublin? Is this really Dublin? Oh, Ernie, you must be mistaken! Dublin's got to be even bigger than Liverpool because it's the capital city, like London's the capital city of England. This is quite a small town; there aren't any huge warehouses or big offices like the Liver Buildings, or great wide streets with masses of traffic hurtling along. I know I haven't travelled much but I see lots of places on the Pathé news – Shrewsbury, Chester, Plymouth, Norwich – oh, lots. And they're all bigger than this 'un.' She waved an explanatory hand at the quiet streets and low buildings.

Ernie laughed. 'I know what you mean; it don't have an imposin' waterfront, does it? But there's a university, and lots of churches, and I've read about a huge park, Phoenix Park it's called, so don't be too quick to judge.' He looked down at Polly's small face and read disappointment there. 'Cheer up, chuck! We aren't bound for Dublin but for a village in the real deep countryside. The Irish countryside is something you and I know nothin' about, and this is our chance to learn. Come on, Polly, best foot forward! And keep your eyes open for fellers in uniform what can direct us better'n ordinary citizens could.'

Polly, who liked people, was soon amending her first feeling that Dublin was too small to be a capital city, and a strange place where she could never feel at home. Dana had told her more than once how badly the English government and even the landed gentry of Ireland had treated the ordinary people. She had made Polly's flesh creep with stories of the potato famine the previous century and of how, in the newspaper reports, they had not said that twenty people died of the famine but had merely written that twenty people were *destroyed*, as though the poor were mad dogs and deserved no better epitaph. Worse things had happened, of course; British ex-soldiers, recruited by the Royal Irish Constabulary had rampaged across the country when the Irish had been fighting for independence. These 'black and tans', as they were known because of the colour of their uniforms, neither knew nor cared whom they shot down. They were like hounds in full cry, and hounds in full cry will kill anything that crosses their path. Foxes, cats, wild pigs, all are torn apart indiscriminately as the pack surges on with the bloodlust upon them. So it had been with the black and tans, Dana had told Polly. Men, women and children had been killed and no reparation, no placing of blame, had followed these terrible acts. So Polly, keenly aware that every word Dana had told her had been the truth, expected dislike to be writ large on every Irish face as soon as they heard her English accent.

But this did not prove to be the case, for both she and Ernie were greeted everywhere with the utmost friendliness. The garda they approached for help took them to a bookshop and told them which of the large-scale maps they should buy in order to find Castletara, which as they had expected was so tiny that it only merited a little dot – unnamed – on the biggest map. They explained to passers-by that they needed to find a cheap market where they might buy provisions for their journey and everyone, from ragged paperboys to comfortable farmer's wives up from the country, directed them to the various large markets specialising in vegetables, meat or dairy produce.

When Polly, in an excess of goodwill, admitted that they meant to sleep rough, they met not with disapproval but with helpfulness. 'Ah yes, sure and 'tis grand to be sleepin' under the sky so long as you're tucked away 'neath good thick undergrowth if the rain comes, which it does awful often in Ireland,' one farmer's wife told them. 'But dere's always barns or a nice little niche in a haystack where youse can wriggle in to keep out of de wet. Most farm folk, when you tell 'em youse is on holiday, will sell you their produce cheap, maybe cook up a batch of soda bread if you give 'em a bag of flour and a knob or two of fat and asks nicely if they'll do a bake for you.'

In due course the two young adventurers took the garda's advice and caught a bus which carried them a good way out of the city. The day was fine and the sun had not yet sunk below the horizon, so they walked until they found a convenient little copse just off the narrow winding road they had been following. Ernie decreed that they should stop here for their first night and they settled down to a feast of bread and cheese, eked out with a handful of carrots which they had filched from a field. Polly had thought this rather a mean thing to do, especially after everyone had shown them such kindness, but Ernie, who assured Polly he had meant to ask if he might pay for them, said he saw no reason to consider it stealing. After all, they had walked up to the very gate of the farm, which was surrounded by a positive sea of grand food, and had been discouraged from entering – and therefore from buying – by three unkempt and ragged dogs which had charged at the gate, eyes bright with malevolence and jaws snapping.

'If that perishin' mean old farmer hadn't set his bleedin' dawgs on us we'd have paid for the carrots all right and tight,' Ernie had explained. He had been the one the smallest dog had managed to bite by pushing its sharp little nose through the bars of the gate and seizing his leg in its tiny but surprisingly powerful teeth. Polly, seeing her outraged pal under attack, had swung her haversack viciously at the biter and had had the satisfaction of seeing it returning, howling, to the farmhouse.

So now the two of them crossed a small bridge and washed the carrots in the stream, filled the water bottles the garda had advised them to obtain and then settled down and ate their feast beneath a canopy of oak and beech.

'We're like the babes in the wood,' Ernie said dreamily. He chuckled. 'Remind me to blaze a trail by chippin' a bit off each tree tomorrow so we don't turn in the wrong direction when we wake up in the morning.'

Polly giggled. 'Some chance,' she said dreamily. 'G'night, Ernie. Sweet dreams.'

Ernie struggled for a moment with a desperate urge to lean over and give her a goodnight kiss, which would lead to a cuddle, which might lead to . . .

But this would not do. Polly was in his care; she was younger than him and very innocent, and what was more she trusted him.

'Good night, Poll; sweet dreams to you too,' he said firmly, and lay imagining the wonderful moments he might have enjoyed had he been less honourable until he fell asleep.

'Poll, will you stop mooning over the beauties of the countryside and start remembering that we're here for a reason.' Ernie gave Polly's arm an admonitory shake. 'I know it's beautiful, but what we're supposed to be looking for is a bus which will take us on the next leg of our journey. We've still got a fair bit of money between us, but the sooner we get to Castletara the sooner we can turn for home.'

Polly sighed. The two travellers were leaning against the trunk of a large tree, eating the only food they had managed to acquire that morning, which was some not very fresh curd cheese, a large slice of bread apiece, and some small apples they had picked from the hedgerow which had proved to be so sour that they had cast them aside after one bite. It was raining gently and the grass was a little damp, but so far as Polly was concerned, at least, the view that stretched before them made up for any amount of discomfort. Below them was a lake and surrounding it woodland and gentle hills, with an occasional whitewashed cottage beside the winding lanes which led ever onward towards their goal. They had been journeying now for over two days and knew they must be nearing their destination, but Polly, who had spent her entire life in the city, was overcome by the beauty of the countryside and kept pausing to admire a particular view, or to draw Ernie's attention to a meadow thick with wild flowers, a stream tinkling over its rocky bed, or the wild beauty of a sunset which turned the sky to flame and rose. Now, however, she gave Ernie's fingers a squeeze.

'I'm real sorry, Ern, honest to God I am. Only it's all strange to me and I can't stop me mouth from saying over and over that Ireland's beautiful. In fact I guess if we were in Liverpool I'd be grumbling like anything, saying I was cold and hungry too and demanding to be taken home.' She grinned at her companion. 'So you see, a beautiful view does have its uses.'

Ernie grunted. 'Yeah, I know what you mean,' he said grudgingly. 'I don't mind the rain all that much, but I'm tellin' you, queen, I don't mean to sleep out for another night. We'll find some small farmhouse and get them to let us spend the night under a proper roof, even if it does cost a bob or two.'

'But we was in a barn with a roof last night,' Polly reminded him. 'I know it leaked and we got a bit wet, but we got even wetter when we had to leave because the farmer unchained his dogs, and we reckoned they'd come after us if they found us couched down in the straw.'

'But the thing is, queen,' Ernie said, scratching his chest, 'I'm covered in spots this morning, horrible little red itchy things. I've been bit by bedbugs before, but it weren't them; I reckon it was something what lived in the straw and took a liking to me lilywhite body. Were you bitten?'

'No, I've not got a single bite. They must've liked your taste so much that they didn't bother to try eating me,' Polly said complacently. She looked at the arm which Ernie flourished and her eyes widened. 'Goodness gracious me! There's scarce room to put a pin between the spots. Are you sure you've been bitten, Ern? It looks like measles to me.'

'Well it ain't; I had measles when I was ten and I don't recall the spots itching, or not like these does anyway. And besides, they haven't come all over exactly. I lay on my left side last night and the spots is all over my left arm, left leg and left side.' He glared at Polly, who was giggling. 'If you've ever heard of a case of measles which just affects someone's left side, then it's more'n I have. Why are you laughing?'

'Because I've just noticed your left cheek and neck,' Polly said. 'Oh, poor old Ernie, I'm really sorry because it's not a bit funny for you, and you're right, of course, we should get a proper lodging. We'll do as you say; catch a bus heading in the right direction, then maybe walk a bit until the sun goes down, and after that find somewhere to stay.' She got to her feet as she spoke and held out her hands to pull Ernie to his, then the two of them packed up their belongings and set off for the main road they had left the evening before.

When they reached a stream they parted by common consent to have a strip-down wash and Polly judged, by the cries of dismay reaching her ears, that as soon as he began to remove his clothing Ernie discovered that his little companions of the previous night were with him still. Sure enough when he reappeared he was clad in his only change of garments, whilst the shirt and trousers he had worn the night before were still dripping from vigorous washing. 'I've drowned the little buggers,' he said triumphantly as he re-joined his companion. 'And now let's get back to the main road and flag down the first bus we see going in the right direction.'

'Or any car or lorry which looks like the driver might give us a lift. We've done pretty well out of lifts one way and another,' Polly reminded him. 'Besides, Ireland isn't a huge country; we don't want to fall off the other end!'

They spent that night in a cottage where an elderly man and his wife welcomed them and asked two shillings for the room and a breakfast of porridge. 'And as much soda bread as you can eat,' their hostess promised them. The couple showed them the room which their own children had occupied before they left home, and accepted without question Ernie's assurance that he and Polly were brother and sister.

The woman took Ernie's wet clothes and draped them on the clothes horse before the fire, since the rain which had held off during most of the day came on again as evening approached. As the young adventurers got into wilder and less inhabited country they found it more and more difficult to understand local speech, but they were lucky with their host and hostess on this particular night. Both had come from Dublin and their brogue was easy to understand. As Polly had remarked to Ernie on more than one occasion, the locals who stopped speaking as soon as the English couple came within earshot might just as well have saved themselves the trouble, since neither she nor Ernie could understand a word they said.

As soon as Ernie had agreed with their landlady that they would take the room, he asked whether she might provide an evening meal. 'We meant to buy provisions in villages as we passed through, or even at farmhouses when the owners were willing to sell, but this is a very lonely part of the country and we've had no opportunity to buy anything,' he explained. Mrs O'Brien said at once that for another two shillings she could do them mashed potatoes, eggs from their own hens and sausages from the pig they had killed the previous autumn, a suggestion which made Polly's mouth water. Whilst they were spreading out their bedrolls on the big double mattress and Polly was urging Ernie to ignore his spots and stop scratching, however, something rather more important occurred to her.

'Ernie, you told Mrs O'Brien a whopper! Is it – is it very wrong for two people who aren't related to sleep in the same bed? Only why else did you tell Mrs O'Brien that we were brother and sister?'

'I ain't too sure, Polly,' Ernie admitted, and saw Polly's brow clear. Incurably honest, however, he added: 'Some folk might say it weren't right, of course, but who's to know? Only you and me, and we ain't likely to spill the beans.'

Polly stared at him for a long unnerving moment. 'I'll sleep on the floor,' she said decidedly. 'I've slept in worse places and at least Mrs O'Brien's house is beautifully clean. I don't believe either of us will get bit here.'

'I don't see why we can't share the bed if we put a pillow between us; that's what they did in the hostel when two of us had to share,' Ernie said. 'It'd be all right, honest to God it would.'

Polly heaved a sigh but stood firm, and though Ernie tried to persuade her that he would actually prefer to sleep on the floor she would not hear of it. It was probably a good job, since poor Ernie's flea bites kept him awake during the early part of the night and when Mrs O'Brien popped in to say breakfast would be on the table in five minutes he was deeply asleep whilst Polly, fully dressed, had rolled up her bedroll and was repacking her haversack.

The previous evening, upon their asking how far away Castletara might be, their hostess had cast an imploring glance at her husband. 'Sure and 'tis foolish I am over t'ings like distances,' she admitted. 'And I scarce ever go into the village unless Mr O'Brien here drives the donkey cart in to collect animal feed, and takes me along for a day out. Mr O'Brien, you know about distances . . .'

Mr O'Brien smiled in a superior fashion and patted his wife's hand. ''Tis twenty minutes by donkey cart and forty on foot,' he told them. 'That's to the village, of course. To visit the Tara house – only you're not likely to do that – you'd have to double the time, for 'tis furder from here.'

Both his guests assured him mendaciously that they only wanted to visit the village and ate their breakfast with real enjoyment, for it looked as though their quest was almost over and they would soon be at the McBrides' ancestral home and able, they hoped, to ascertain that all was well there. Presently they bade goodbye to the O'Briens, and shouldered their haversacks, and were about to depart when Polly had a bright idea. She turned to Mrs O'Brien, standing in the doorway to wave them off whilst a flock of fat and happy poultry clucked at her feet, obviously convinced that they were about to be fed again. 'Mrs O'Brien, our business in Castletara will probably take most of the day, and we shan't much fancy setting off to return to Dublin as dusk deepens,' she said. 'If we could leave our bedrolls with you, might we ask for another night's lodging?'

Before her speech was half over Mrs O'Brien was nodding vigorously. 'Two shillings for the room and breakfast and two shillings for supper,' she said happily. She waded through the sea of poultry, took both bedrolls, tucked them under her arm and disappeared into the cottage, leaving a flock of puzzled hens behind her.

'Are you sure you've done the right thing, Poll?' Ernie asked as they set off along the narrow lane which they now knew led to Castletara. 'Oh, I know the O'Briens were ever so nice, but we've never met their children, and if one of them pops in and fancies our bedrolls . . .'

'Ernie Frost, sometimes I despair of you,' Polly said reprovingly. 'The O'Briens won't allow anyone apart from ourselves to so much as enter that room until we leave it tomorrow morning. Now, let's go and take a look at Dana's home. We'll see what sort of state it's in and then try to get to know somebody who likes a gossip, either someone from the village or someone from the house itself.'

Despite Ireland's reputation for being a land where the rain fell more frequently than the sun shone, it was a lovely day. A gentle breeze stirred the branches overhead and despite the seriousness of their quest both Polly and Ernie felt a lifting of the heart as they made their way along the high-banked, twisty little lanes which led first to Castletara village and then, they were told, to the house itself.

'If I lived here I'd never have left, not if it were ever so,' Polly said wistfully as they walked. She paused to pluck a handful of little wild strawberries and shared them with Ernie, though he did not show the gratitude she expected.

'What a lot of pips,' he grumbled. 'Don't bother to give me no more; you can have the rest.'

Presently they found themselves entering the village, which, rather to their surprise, was a good deal bigger than they had imagined, certainly bigger than most of the villages through which they had passed. It had a blacksmith's forge, and a wheelwright, though that appeared to be part of the blacksmith's premises, as well as a feed merchant, a bakery, and a general store. Ireland did not seem to have public houses, but as in other villages Castletara's general store doubled as a purveyor of alcoholic beverages. The shop itself was of a reasonable size, the floor covered with sawdust and the walls lined with forms upon which customers could sit to enjoy their drinks. It was still early in the morning, but because it was such a warm day the two outside benches alongside the shop were occupied by several old men, two of them smoking pipes whilst the other three must have done their shopping, for they had large bags by their sides from which protruded loaves of bread still steaming gently. Everyone bade everyone else good morning, and then Ernie nudged Polly. 'No use asking them questions until we know what questions to ask,' he said. 'And I bet they only speak Irish. It'll be different up at the house; we know they speak English, because Dana does. Come on, will you; them old fellers is staring at us as though we were critters out of the zoo. Just bid 'em good morning again and leave 'em wondering.'

Polly obeyed, seeing the sense of Ernie's remark, and once again they threaded their way through incredibly beautiful countryside until at last their progress was halted by a high stone wall and two wrought iron gates, though these were flung open to show a neatly gravelled drive with a small but very pretty cottage to one side. 'That's a lodge; all big houses have a lodge at their gates,' Ernie whispered. 'The lodge keeper is supposed to see that no unwanted people get into the grounds of the castle, or manor, or whatever. Then at night – as soon as it grows dusk really – he'll close the gates and anyone wanting admission will have to holler out, or toot a horn, I guess, if they are in a car or a lorry. Folk on foot might get by – burglars and that – but a pal of mine told me once that's why rich folk gravel their drives. Even the lightest footfall on gravel makes a crunching noise and most lodge keepers have a dog what'll give the alarm if it hears the crunch.'

'Gosh,' Polly said, sinking her voice to a whisper. 'What'll we do, Ern? I thought Dana's folk had fallen on hard times. I remember Dana saying that the garden was a wilderness and the roof of her tower bedroom leaked. She said the big lawn was a hayfield and some of the windows needed panes replacing. This place looks like Buckingham Palace!'

Ernie laughed. 'You've only seen the lodge, the gates and a bit of the drive,' he said. 'Let's go take a look at the house itself. There's no one about as far as I can see.'

'Well, all right. Since we've come so far I suppose we've got to take a look,' Polly agreed. 'If we could just find Deirdre, or that boy Con even, we might be able to ask questions without being thought nosy. Only let's not walk on the gravel. The trees on either side are thick enough to hide an army in, so we should be safe from observation, unless we want to be seen.'

They set off, wending their way through beech, oak, pines and elders until they saw ahead of them a lightening of the shade, and presently they emerged from the trees to see Castletara ahead of them. 'This must be the great lawn Dana talked about,' Polly said in a hushed whisper. 'But it's not a hayfield, the grass is green and short. And look, the flowerbeds under the windows are full of what look like roses – wonderful roses of every colour you can imagine. Oh, Ernie, have we come to the right place? Or was Dana talking about her dreams and not reality? Oh, I just don't understand!'

Much later that day Polly and Ernie found themselves a comfortable bank upon which to sit and unwrapped the soda bread, the pat of butter and the small jar of strawberry jam they had purchased in the village. Ernie took out his clasp knife, divided the bread, spread butter and jam and handed her half to Polly. Then for a moment they simply stared at one another before Ernie broke the silence. 'Well, that's given us something to think about!' he observed wryly. 'You got a picture of vanished splendour which you passed on to me, and certainly whenever Dana mentioned her old home, which wasn't often, it was to say how run down it had become, how her father was the only man who could bring it back into good heart and how he was only interested in the stud farm.'

Polly nodded violently and licked a dribble of jam from the edge of her soda bread. 'That's right. But the Castletara we saw this morning was just about perfect. It must take an army of gardeners to keep the place up to the mark and that girl, Enda, the one who walked back to the village with us, says the McBrides employ a dozen men outside and a dozen women inside. She says Americans pay good money to stay in a castle, so it sounds as though the McBrides have another source of income beside the horses.'

'I agree, but if you ask me there's something very odd going on. When we asked that girl about the accident, she didn't seem to know what we were talking about, not at first . . .'

'Ah, but remember Dana's been in England for at least three years,' Polly interrupted. 'Three years is a long time. But what gets me is the fact that the girl talked about "the master", said the McBrides were a wonderful family so they were, everybody thought so. So do you think Dana can have made a terrible mistake? Seen her father's face all covered in blood and run away before they knew he was going to live? I think we ought to ask a few more questions – in the village this time – before we get hold of the wrong end of the stick.'

Ernie agreed. The pair settled down to eat the food they had bought, and then returned to the village. They saw Enda, who waved to them as they approached the blacksmith's forge and came over for a few words, but as soon as she had taken herself off the blacksmith tapped his head significantly. 'She's a grand gorl, so she is,' he said in his heavily accented brogue. 'But not one of de brightest, you understand. She told me you'd been up to the big house, talkin' about the dreadful accident. It's not somethin' we talk about, nor do the McBrides. It were turble, turble, but it happened six years ago and it's over. So if I were you, young master and missie, I'd leave the past to take care of itself.'

He grinned at them but would say no more, save that Mr McBride's horses were famous throughout the land so they were, and that the guests who came to the big house were generous and appreciative.

Polly and Ernie hung about the forge for a while, but the blacksmith had a horse waiting to be shod and did not address them again, so they began to walk back towards the O'Briens' cottage, chatting over the information they had gleaned as they went.

'If you ask me, Dana's father must have been badly injured, but is now able to run his home and his business once again,' Ernie said. 'It's odd that the blacksmith didn't want to talk about it, though. And did he say the accident was six years ago? He spoke so broad and so fast that I couldn't always understand him. I think, Poll, that all we can do when we're back in Liverpool again is to advise Dana very strongly to come home.'

'Right,' Polly said. 'And we can tell her that we've visited Castletara and everywhere was just lovely. The gardens were perfect, and the walled one, where Enda said they grow all their own vegetables and fruit, was even better than Dana had described. But the oddest thing was when she told us that Mr and Mrs McBride took in visitors. If I understood her correctly – and it was jolly difficult because her brogue was even broader than the blacksmith's – then most of their money comes from these parties of Americans who come over to see the country of their ancestors and pay large sums for the privilege of staying in an ancient castle. But as for the accident, and Dana running away, they just won't talk about it and that's final.'

As they had promised, they spent that night in the O'Briens' cottage, but the next day when Polly wanted to return to Castletara, in the hope of seeing for herself that Mr McBride was alive and carrying on his business, Ernie was against it. 'What do you think you'll achieve apart from getting slung out and told never to return?' he asked. 'Don't be a fool, Poll. I hope to God our poking around hasn't already come to the wrong ears. Leave it now, will you?'

But Polly shook her head until her little blonde ponytail wagged. 'I forgot to mention that Con feller and I mean to find out how he feels about Dana before I leave,' she said obstinately. 'Ralph is really fond of her, you know; it wouldn't surprise me if he asks her to marry him before he goes into the air force; or at least to get engaged,' she amended, seeing the sceptical look on her friend's face. 'However, it's my belief that Dana is only going around with Ralph because he reminds her of this Con. So if I can see him – I'll know him because he looks like Ralph – then I mean to give him Dana's address and tell him if he don't get in touch, she's going to make the mistake of a lifetime and marry the wrong feller.'

'And how are you going to do that? You can't just walk up to a castle and start quizzing folk,' Ernie pointed out. 'Have some sense, Poll. Let's turn for home. We've still got three whole days of our week left and we know which buses to catch . . .'

But Polly was shaking her head again, her eyes

sparkling with mischief. 'I mean to go up to the castle saying that a party of Liverpudlians are going to do a tour of Ireland next spring. I shall say I'm looking for houses which can accommodate a dozen couples at least, and I shall insist on a tour of the premises.' Her grin widening, she produced a businesslike shorthand note-book and pencil. 'I shall take notes on the number and size of bedrooms, the capacity of the dining room, the cleanliness of the kitchens, and so on, and that should be enough to get me admitted. No one can turn business away and the Depression ain't over yet.'

Ernie could not help smiling, though when he agreed to wait outside the castle walls for her he did so grudg-ingly. 'I've a darned good mind to turn for home myself and leave you,' he told her. 'I really don't approve of you actually snooping into Dana's old home, honest to God I don't.'

This threat, however, did not worry Polly at all. 'You won't let me down. I know you, Ernie Frost, and you aren't the sort to rat on a friend,' she said cheerfully. 'See you later, pal!'

But when they met up again, Polly had only failure to report. 'Dana's mam was very polite and showed me round, but I don't think she believed my story,' she told Ernie as they began the walk back to the village. 'At one point she said, very kindly mind, "Are you lookin' for work, alanna? Because if so, we don't tek on live-in staff and digs in the village would cost half of any wage we might manage to pay."'

Ernie chuckled. 'So she saw through you,' he said approvingly. 'Told you so!' And I bet you didn't see a twin to our boss, either.'

'If you mean did I see Con, then I didn't,' Polly admitted. 'But I'm sure he was there. I saw Mr McBride, though. He's tall with black curly hair and a thin, strong sort of face. Now he did look a bit like Ralph, come to think, though an awful lot older, naturally.'

'Right. And did Mrs McBride look like Dana?' Ernie asked idly as they turned into the lane which would lead them to the main road. 'I suppose you're satisfied with our adventure, queen? Do you mean to break it to Dana that her father's still alive? Because if you're wrong you could break Dana's heart all over again and from what you heard it's been broke pretty badly already.'

Polly considered the question, then sighed and shook her head. 'No, because you're quite right. But there is a mystery surrounding the accident and Dana running away, don't you think? What do you suppose it can be? Answer me that, Mr Know-it-all!'

'Can't; don't pretend to have second sight, nor I don't want it,' Ernie said at once. 'Then if you aren't going to tell Dana that you think her father may still be alive, what are you going to do?'

He had quickened his pace as they walked so that now Polly was almost running to keep up and when she spoke it was breathlessly. 'I'm going to tell her that we saw her home and it's in good heart. Then I shall say she simply must go back because her family needs her. You see, I think there could be another relative by the name of McBride who stepped into the breach when Dana wouldn't. Perhaps this other McBride had the money to start putting the castle to rights, which may make Dana feel that she's not needed. But I think she won't be happy again until she's seen that she really is necessary to

Castletara. Oh, not as a worker, it's in excellent heart, but as the rightful daughter of the house.'

Ernie slowed his pace and slipped his arm round her waist. 'You're a kind girl and a darned good friend,' he said approvingly. 'Dana's lucky to have you. Now as I remember we got off the bus quite near that big old oak tree so we're on the right road, and I'm telling you I don't mean to sleep rough for the next three nights. We'll get ourselves lodgings like respectable people do. Agreed?'

'Okay, agreed,' Polly said rather doubtfully, just as she heard the rumble of a bus's engine coming up behind them. She waved anxiously, for in Liverpool it was not unknown for a driver whose vehicle was already well laden to ignore would-be passengers in between stops, but this was Ireland. The bus drew up beside them with a screech of brakes and the conductor took their haversacks and ushered them into his vehicle.

'Next stop paradise,' he said cheerfully. 'Where's you going, young lady and gent?'

Chapter Eleven

3 September 1939

On a Sunday, Polly and Dana usually had a bit of a lie-in and Dana always relished the chance to get up slowly, discussing with Polly what they should do with their free day. If the weather was fine they usually either picnicked in one of the parks or caught a bus out into the real country. If it was wet they employed themselves indoors, darning stockings, ironing, and cooking for the week ahead. Today, however, was different. Today Mr Chamberlain, who had a year earlier promised 'peace for our time', would be telling the nation either that Mr Hitler had agreed to pull his troops out of Poland, or that he had ignored the British demand for him to do so, which would mean that the country was at war with Germany for the second time in twenty years. So Dana had got up at her usual time and roused Polly, who had apparently forgotten the importance of the day and had sworn at her friend and tried to heave the covers back over her head. Dana, however, would have none of it. 'Chamberlain's making his announcement at quarter past eleven,' she said brusquely, heaving the covers off Polly's curled up and reluctant form. 'Do get up, Poll. You invited Ernie round for Sunday dinner, remember, so you can jolly well give me a hand with the vegetables. I got a really nice piece of New Zealand lamb which was going cheap late last night, and Mrs Bicknell gave me a bunch of mint which she said wouldn't last till Monday, so we can have a really good meal.'

Polly opened one reluctant eye. 'You say I invited Ernie but I'm sure you asked Jake if he'd like to come too, so you'll have a guest as well,' she mumbled. 'You said he'd be lonely because Ralph's off at some training camp or other and won't get any leave for six months. What's the time, anyway?'

'It's half past ten,' Dana said glibly and also untruthfully, for it was only ten o'clock. 'And Jake refused our kind invitation. I'm going to leave you now, Poll, but if you dare go back to sleep you shan't have so much as a mouthful of the apple crumble I mean to make. Well, no one will, because I've not got time to peel, core, and slice all the apples as well as preparing the vegetables.'

'Oh, all right; fair's fair I suppose,' Polly said swinging her legs out of bed and standing up. 'Sorry, Dana; the fact is me and Ern didn't come straight home when the last house was over last night. We had a bit of a walk around and a chat and then I asked Ern in for a cup of cocoa; you know how it is.'

'Yes, I know how it is,' Dana confirmed, turning her head so that Polly should not see she was smiling. When the young couple had returned from their trip and airily confessed that they had actually gone to the Emerald Isle, had even visited Castletara, she had pretended indifference, shrugging when Polly had told her that her old home was immaculate, a far cry from the run-down and neglected place of her dreams.

'I know,' she had said unguardedly, and had had to

lie and say that in her more recent dreams Castletara had regained its old splendour. By the look of her, Polly had intended to carry her questioning further, but Dana had noticed that Polly had been uneasy ever since her return from her holiday, and it had seemed like a good time to find out why.

Accordingly, she had changed the subject adroitly from her old home to why Polly seemed worried by something which had occurred during her holiday. 'One minute you're being very sweet to Ern, kissing and cuddling when I'm not supposed to be looking, and the next you're pushing him back, acting outraged if he so much as tries to hold your hand,' she had said. 'What's up, Poll? Surely you can tell me. I won't say we're like sisters 'cos quite often sisters fight like cat and cat, but we're really good pals, wouldn't you say?'

The two girls had been getting their breakfast before going off to a nearby fair with Ernie and a couple of other friends and Polly had begun to deny that there was anything wrong, before suddenly bursting into floods of tears. 'Oh, Dana, I've been such a fool,' she hiccuped. 'And now I suppose I've got to marry Ern and I'm too young! But I've been a bad girl and now I've got to go through with it!'

'Go through with what?' Dana had been about to ask Polly just what she meant when Polly said something about sharing a bed which had Dana's eyebrows climbing rapidly towards her hairline. Scarcely had she framed a tactful question, however, before someone had knocked at the door and it opened to reveal Ernie's pink and cheerful face. He had let himself in, then raised his brows as Polly's noisy sobs turned into wails. 'Now what's the matter wi' you, our Poll?' he had asked, coming into the room and trying to put his arm round her shoulders, though she shrank away from him as though he had been about to strangle her. 'We're off on a grand day out, ain't we? So why the tears?'

'Because – because I were a bad girl and now . . . and now . . . Oh, I can't say it,' Polly had wailed as she rushed out of the room.

Dana's eyebrows could not climb any higher; she had stared at Ernie for a long moment before speaking and then she did so with some care. 'Ernie, did – did anything happen between you and Polly while you were in Ireland? She's been a bit weepy several times over the past couple of weeks, but I thought it was just because she loved the Irish countryside and knew it would be a long while before she could afford such a holiday again. Now it appears I was mistaken.' She had put both her hands up to her hot cheeks. 'Oh, Ernie, she thinks you'll have to get married. And I trusted you to take care of her!'

'And so I did,' Ernie had said indignantly. 'We had a few kisses and cuddles, of course we did; does she think that could give her a baby?'

Dana had decided that frankness was her best approach. 'No, she thinks sharing a bed might do it, and so it might,' she had said baldly. 'Did you share a bed, Ernie? Did you—'

'Course we shared a bed. Couldn't afford a bed each, lerralone a room,' Ernie had said at once. His worried look had faded to be replaced by a grin. 'Honest to God, Dana, we telled the landladies we was brother and sister and they give us a bolster to put down the middle of the

300

mattress. We each kept to our own side, I swear it on me mother's life . . .' He must have seen the sceptical look on Dana's face for he amended that to 'Polly's life then'. He had turned as Polly, red-eyed and miserable, came back into the room and put a brotherly arm about her shoulders. 'Whatever's the matter with you, me little sugar plum?' he had enquired gently. 'I told you there were no harm in sharing provided neither of us jumped over the bolster. Dana will tell you the same if you still won't believe me.'

Polly had turned swollen, tear-drenched eyes from one face to the other, and then a little smile had dawned. 'Oh, good,' she had said faintly. 'It ain't that I don't want to marry you, Ernie, 'cos I think that might be quite fun, but havin' babies hurts. The girls at the YW said your tummy splits . . .'

'All right, all right, that's quite enough of old wives' tales,' Dana had said hurriedly, seeing poor Ernie's pink cheeks becoming white as a sheet. 'And now we've cleared that little mystery up let's get on with our breakfast. Oh lordy, lordy, the porridge has caught and if there's one thing I hate it's burnt porridge. Polly, dry your eyes for goodness' sake and start toasting some bread!'

But that had been a month ago, and Polly had been her cheerful self ever since, singing around the house, joking with the staff at work and telling anyone who would listen that if war came she would do her bit. Now she joined Dana in the kitchen and began to peel a mound of potatoes, left ready for her on the draining board.

'You told me it were half past ten ages ago, and it's not even quarter past,' she said reproachfully. 'Still an' all, I guess it were fair enough. When he arrives, old Ern will give a hand wi' the spuds.' She giggled. 'If there's one thing he's good at, it's spud bashing.'

'And looking after his pals,' Dana observed. Ernie had brought Polly home the previous evening and had left a large bag of cooking apples on the kitchen table, saying that they'd been 'give me by a pal', and suggesting that she, Dana, might like to make the apple crumble for which she was famous. 'So if you and Ernie get going on the vegetables I'll start preparing the apples. Oh, and I'll need a packet of custard powder. Have a rummage in the cupboard, Polly my love, because Mrs Barker at the corner shop hates being disturbed on a Sunday, especially for a sixpenny packet of Bird's best.'

Both girls were engaged on preparation when Dana glanced at the clock and hurried across the kitchen to turn on their wireless set. 'It takes a while to warm up,' she reminded Polly. 'Hope Ern doesn't come bursting in just as Mr Chamberlain gets to the crux of the matter,' she added, for Ernie was an erratic timekeeper to say the least. And sure enough just as the solemn introductory music drew to a close he burst into the kitchen. 'Has he started? Whass he said?' he demanded breathlessly. 'The bloody tram were late; I've had to run like a perishin' rabbit all the way from the Pier Head . . .'

'Shut up!' both girls screamed in unison and were thus in time to hear the most important part of the prime minister's speech. The British ambassador had given the German government an ultimatum, he said: if Germany did not confirm by eleven o'clock that they were prepared to withdraw from Poland immediately, their two nations would be at war. 'I have to tell you now, that no such undertaking has been received, and that consequently this country is at war with Germany.'

For a full minute Dana, Polly and Ernie just stared at one another, even Polly speechless for once, and typically it was she who broke the silence. 'Well, I guess we all knew it was coming, it was just that we didn't know when or how,' she remarked. She glanced sideways at Ernie and saw, with a mixture of relief and dread, his little nod. Ever since they had returned from Ireland they had been waiting for the right moment to tell Dana that they believed her father had not died as a result of the hunting accident but had actually got better, and was now in full command at Castletara again. They had tried to persuade Dana to go back, believing that if she did so she would discover far more naturally that her father lived, but Dana had foiled every attempt to persuade her to return to her ancestral home. Every time either Polly or Ernie had so much as mentioned Ireland she had either walked out of the room or positively snarled at them to shut up.

'What I do and where I go is of no concern to anyone but myself,' she had told them. 'I shall go back one day, of course, but as yet, I'm just not ready. When I am you may be sure I'll return, but no amount of nagging will make me go one day sooner.' She had seen Polly's dismay and had laughed and given her friend a warm hug. 'I know you mean well, Poll, but it's as I say: when the moment comes you won't have to persuade me because I'll be on that ferry and heading for Castletara before you can say knife. And now let's change the subject please.'

Right now it seemed that Ernie thought the time had

come to share the knowledge they had gleaned from Enda and the blacksmith: that Mr McBride was alive and still breeding wonderful horses, and was well respected as a leader in the small community.

But Dana was bustling around the kitchen, still preparing their Sunday lunch, saying that though the war would affect everyone nothing much would happen for several weeks. 'Knowing the British, Hitler's storm troopers will have to be on our doorstep before the armed forces swing into action . . .' she was saying as she dropped into a chair and began to peel a cooking apple. Polly heaved a sigh and interrupted.

'Dana McBride, stop blathering on and listen to me for once! Every time Ern and I have tried to tell you about our visit to Castletara you've cut us off short. But now you're going to listen if I have to sit on your chest and gag you with that there tea towel you've been flapping around. We don't think your father's dead at all. We saw him – though not close, I admit. We've tried and tried to tell you that he must of recovered from his awful injuries, but—' Polly stopped, not because she wasn't determined to have her say but because Dana had jumped to her feet and actually hurled the apple she was holding at Polly's head.

'You stupid, stupid, stupid little halfwit!' she shouted. 'As if I wouldn't know that my own father was dead! Why, I went to his funeral – the committal, the wake, everything. Where the *devil* has your so-called brain gone? I slaved with my mother and the others to see that the stud didn't go downhill. For three long years I worked as hard or harder than anyone on the estate to keep the name of McBride at the top of the list of breeders in

Ireland. It was only when – when – oh, but why should I tell you? Where on earth did you get the idea that I was the sort of person who would leave my family in the lurch? I left because – because . . .' And Dana, who never cried, burst into tears and rushed out of the room slamming the door resoundingly behind her.

There was total silence in the kitchen. Polly and Ernie stared at one another, appalled. Dana had always made it clear that she did not wish to talk about her home or what had happened to send her flying over to England, but this was something entirely different. Polly ran across the kitchen and cast herself into Ernie's arms, fighting back tears. 'What'll we do?' she wailed. 'If that good-lookin' bloke weren't Mr McBride then who was he? Everyone we spoke to talked about the McBrides as though there were more than one of them. Oh, Ern, what'll I do?'

Ernie gave her a quick hug then turned her round to face the kitchen door and gave her a small shove. 'Go to her,' he urged, 'tell her we're both very sorry and ask her very humbly if she'll explain what really happened. Dana's your best pal, as I'm sure you are hers, and best pals shouldn't have secrets from one another.'

'But I'm scared she'll turn on me, stop being me best pal and tell me to gerrout,' Polly snuffled. 'Won't you come with me, Ern?'

Ernie shook his head. 'No, queen, this must be betwixt the pair of you,' he said gently. 'I'll get on wi' cookin' the dinner. And don't worry; Dana's far too generous to blame you for trying to help her, which is what you're doing.' He gave her another shove, a slightly harder one this time. 'Off with you, my brave girl.'

In the bedroom, Dana lay on her bed, dry-eyed now and no longer angry. She knew that Polly had only been trying to help her, understood how the misunderstanding had come about. And she knew, too, why her friends had decided to break what they thought was the good news at last. When Polly entered the room looking scared half to death she got off the bed, and held out her arms, and Polly flew into them. 'I think we'll leave Ernie to prepare dinner, Poll, because he's just as capable as we are,' she said. 'I've never told you why I left Castletara because it hurt too much, but one thing I will tell you right now: I inherited my temper and my bright red hair from my father. I would take a bet that the man you thought was Mr McBride was dark-haired. Am I right?'

Polly nodded dumbly, and Dana sat down on the bed and indicated that her friend should sit beside her. 'Right!' she said. 'Now I shall tell you everything, just as it happened.' She grinned rather lopsidedly at her friend. 'So pin back your ear'oles and listen hard and for goodness' sake don't interrupt.'

Dana slid off the back of the bay hunter, landing alongside the would-be customer, and pushed her hair off her wet forehead, for it was a hot day and she and Elvira, the mare, had spent most of the morning together. The customer was an American eager to buy horses of Irish stock to build up his stable, for though everyone kept telling everyone else that the Depression was as bad in America as it was in England there were clearly still people about with plenty of money. Dana raised her eyebrows at the customer but before he could reply to her unspoken question Johnny Devlin came up, a big smile on his face. 'Well, Mr Fitzgerald, what do you think? She's a grand little mare so she is, though perhaps a trifle light. You've taken two of our best stallions, however, so why am I encouraging you to take our best mare as well?' He struck his forehead, grinning as he did so. 'It's mad I must be!'

'Oh, come on, Mr McBride. You've many better critters than this 'un, though she's a grand little mover and your daughter makes her look an easy ride, though I doubt a beginner would find her so . . .'

The two men moved off, leaving Dana to rub the mare's velvety nose and lead her towards the stables. Ever since Donovan McBride's death Johnny Devlin, at Feena's request, had taken the name McBride, for they all knew well that it was the name which brought customers flocking to Castletara to see the McBride horses for themselves, and men, they knew, liked to deal with other men and not with women, however efficient and knowledgeable.

Dana had not liked it at first and even now preferred to refer to him as Johnny, but so far as the business went Johnny and Feena, working like dogs, had more than equalled Donovan McBride's attainments. Dana knew her father had been over generous, over easy in fact. If he liked someone he would sell them a horse for perhaps a third of its worth, laughing at Feena when she tried to explain that he was being a fool to himself. 'You never take into account the money we spend on feeding, grooming, shoeing and vet's bills for that same horse,' she had told him. 'And 'tis the same with all sorts. When a man comes to mend the roof and goes wit' the work only half done you pay him the full amount for the sake of his wife and children, not reckoning that he'll spend the money on porter and never complete the job.'

But Johnny Devlin had been brought up in a hard school and workers and customers alike soon realised that he was a very different proposition from the easy-going Donovan, and by and large they appreciated this and acted accordingly. At first they thought that pretty, gentle Feena would be a soft touch, until she proved them wrong by being, if anything, keener to get value for money than her husband had ever been.

And gradually, so gradually at first that Dana was unaware of it, everything began to improve. The castle itself, though always structurally sound, had needed many repairs and these were done whenever money was available, but now Feena had begun to clean up and refurbish the interior, long neglected, in order that they might let rooms to parties of tourists, many of whom came from the United States. Meanwhile the stables had doubled in size, so that sometimes it hurt Dana to see how her father's death had improved his property, but she comforted herself with the thought, often repeated by Feena, that Donovan McBride had been a wonderful, charismatic person, but no businessman. He had left Feena and herself – and the Devlins, to an extent – a wonderful inheritance. The fact that they could now improve it was not a criticism of her father but merely an acknowledgement that he had been above anything so petty as making money.

So Dana, who still loved her father dearly and adored her friend Con, had no intention of changing her way of life. She meant to live at Castletara, ride the wonderful horses they were producing, help her mother in the house when the tourists came – but only if no one else was available – and generally carry on in the same way, which was very little changed by her loss.

Then into the even tenor of her days had come an event so shocking that at first she had not believed the evidence of her own eyes. She had got up early one bright autumn morning to long-rein a colt, not to tire him out exactly, for he was a bright and energetic two-year-old, but to calm him a little so that when she rode him later in the school, where they showed off the youngsters to customers, he would not start bucking and showing off. Right now he was too full of energy for the gentler paces most customers wished to see. She had gone down to the kitchen by her usual route, expecting to find it deserted. The door at the foot of the spiral stair had opened quietly – under the new regime the hinges did not squeak – and she had padded barefoot on to the kitchen tiles, to stop short, frozen with horror. A man and a woman tightly clasped in each other's arms were leaning in the corner by the back door. The woman was murmuring softly but Dana could hear they were love words, and the man was kissing the woman with a restrained violence which made Dana's stomach clench. Even as she recognised Feena and Johnny Devlin she also understood that this was something they had done often; that they were lovers.

As though the little gasp she gave was enough to alert them to the fact that they were not alone, the couple broke apart. Feena gave Johnny a little push in the chest and turned to face her daughter. To Dana's disgust her lips were swollen from his kisses and her eyes were shiny. She came swiftly across the kitchen and caught hold of

Dana's hands. 'It's all right, alanna, we're doing nothing wrong,' she said breathlessly. 'Johnny and I are going to get married. Oh, I wanted to tell you weeks back, when we first realised we were in love, but Johnny said it was too soon. He's not told Con yet, though I think your pal has guessed something of the sort is on the cards. I'm sorry you had to find out like this, but we meant to tell you in a few days anyway. You see—'

Dana had interrupted, her voice cold yet shaking. 'How – how long has this been going on? Did Daddy know? First you steal his name, and now you plan to steal his wife. Well, I won't have it, do you hear?' She glared at Johnny Devlin, hovering uncertainly behind her mother's shoulder. 'And you needn't bother to tell Con, because I shall do so. We won't let you do this. Castletara is half mine . . .'

Johnny Devlin began to say that he had stolen nothing, whilst at the same moment Feena was saying that of course her dearest Donovan could not possibly have known, for until a long time after his death there was nothing to know. She explained, or tried to, that she had been leaning on Johnny ever since her husband's death, but that dependence had only turned to love nine or ten months ago. 'Your Daddy would understand, acushla; a woman needs a man she can rely on,' she explained, whilst tears ran down her cheeks. 'Please, me darlin', try to understand.'

But Dana had not done so. She had wrenched her hands out of her mother's grasp and headed for the back door, saying over her shoulder as she went, 'I take it Con now sleeps in the stable flat alone? If you two have been sharing a bed—'

Johnny had been comforting Feena, who was now

weeping unrestrainedly, but at these words he took a tiger's leap across the kitchen and grabbed Dana by her long ponytail of bright hair, jerking her to a halt. 'You nasty-minded little bitch,' he said violently. 'Take that back! There's not a word of truth in it, so I'm tellin' you. She's me promised wife and don't you forget it.'

But Dana had wrenched herself out of his grip and was off, charging across the courtyard and up the steep wooden flight of stairs to enter what they had always called the 'coachman's flat' at a dead run. In the doorway she collided with Con, who had obviously been about to descend to the kitchen. He and his father almost always ate with the McBrides, it being easier from both a marketing and a cooking point of view.

Con's strong hands grabbed Dana, abruptly stopping her onward flight. 'What's up? Oh, Dana, you've been crying, but I can tell it's tears of rage. Who's in the black books of Miss McBride of Castletara, eh?' His tone was teasing, but when Dana looked into his face she saw genuine concern there.

Hastily, without giving a thought to the fact that Feena had said Con's father had not yet confided his future plans to his son, Dana poured out the whole story. How she had gone into the kitchen to find Feena and Johnny wrapped in a close embrace and how they had explained that they meant to get married. Con's eyebrows began to climb, and when she reached the end of her tale, repeating the very words Johnny had shouted at her, he actually laughed! 'Well, what a mountain you're making out of a molehill, alanna,' he said, his tone light. 'Sure and haven't I known this age that me daddy couldn't take his eyes off your mammy and his every glance a caress! It's time and more that they got wed if you ask me. Oh, I know what you're going to say; but your daddy's been dead almost three years . . .'

'But Mammy loved him; when he died she said she loved him more than life itself, and but for me and Castletara she'd have prayed for an early death. Now, not even three years later, she's talking of jumping into bed wit' her husband's best friend and business partner! It's – it's obscene, Con! Daddy would have—'

'Your daddy would have cheered them on,' Con said firmly. 'Act your age, Dana! You are nearly twenty years old, quite old enough to know the facts of life, and one of those is writ large in biblical texts . . .' He put his head on one side, thinking, then quoted the phrase he had thought appropriate. ''Tis *better to marry than to burn*.'

Dana stared at him, her brows drawing together into a frown. 'It says that in the Bible? Well, I suppose in certain cases it's true, but my mammy and your dad have been working together for years and no one's mentioned marriage. Why now?'

Con began to speak, then he looked hard at Dana and to her considerable amazement he took her in his arms and began to kiss her. First they were little gentle kisses but then they grew harder, more demanding, and when the pair of them collapsed on to the bed it was all Dana could do to free herself from his embrace and leap to her feet, turning towards the stairs.

'You disgust me, Con Devlin,' she said thickly. 'So you won't help me to stop this marriage going ahead? Well, so far as I'm concerned, then, they can do as they like and burn in hell for it along with yourself, 'cos I'm off.'

* * *

Dana had been telling Polly the story as it had happened, with the pair of them sitting side by side on the bed so that neither had to see the other's expression as the tale was told. Now, however, they turned simultaneously to face one another.

'Well?' Dana asked harshly. 'Do you think I did wrong? Now I suppose Con was right and I should have understood why my mother needed Johnny. I was – oh, I was rather young for my age. And Con jumping on me like that . . . well, it didn't help. I felt completely alone for the very first time in my life. Daddy had gone, Mammy was about to go, because I was sure that once she was married to Johnny they wouldn't want me about the place, and Con . . . oh, Con was going to support them. He'd made it plain that he thought their marrying was a good thing. So I steered well clear of everyone that day, and stayed out of doors until I thought they'd all gone to bed. Then I went up to my room, packed a few clothes into a haversack, took a couple of my favourite books and lit out. I walked for miles and miles, burning with indignation, hoping they'd think I'd drowned myself in the river and blame themselves for my death. I must have walked thirty or forty miles, sleeping rough, until I reached a small town where I got casual work from a farmer whose son had put a pitchfork through his foot and so was out of commission. After that I made my way to Dublin and caught the ferry for Liverpool, reasoning that such a busy port would be sure to have some employment for me.' She grinned suddenly at Polly, looking both amused and ashamed. 'I actually intended to cut my hair off and buy some boy's clothing so I could get work aboard ship; wasn't that daft? Only before we docked I met Caitlin; she was a bit older than me and had visited Liverpool before. She said we'd be sure to get jobs of some description and suggested we pal up and get ourselves a bed at the YWCA until we could afford a room-share. She couldn't wait to tell me how she had been jilted and all about her family, but being Caitlin, and pretty self-centred, she never asked me one question about my home or why I had left it. And that, dear Polly, is where you come in. What is it they say? Oh yes, the rest is history. And you needn't tell me I've been every sort of idiot because I know it, but if I had to relive the whole awful business again I still don't believe I could meekly accept my mother's marrying Johnny Devlin. I suppose the me that sits beside you now would make the best of it, perhaps get a job somewhere else – something to do with horses, of course. But I don't believe I could've stayed at Castletara once they were wed.'

Polly stared at Dana, wide-eyed. 'I can't understand why you did what you did,' she said slowly. 'It's difficult for me, never having had loving parents, or a good home, to imagine walking away from happiness, security, even love. From what I can remember, whenever my father came home there were fearful rows. The only notice he ever took of me was to give me a clack round the head if I crossed his path; he were a nasty piece of work, I'm tellin' you. But as I've said to you before, Dee, if I'd had a mother or father like yours I'd have clung on to 'em no matter what. Did you hate Johnny Devlin so much, then? I guess he must be the feller Ernie and meself took to be your dad. Is Mr Devlin tall, with black curly hair, rather a thin face?'

'Yes, that would've been Johnny, and no I didn't hate him; I liked him a lot,' Dana said miserably. 'But when I saw my mother in his arms . . . oh I suppose it was sheer jealousy raising its ugly head. Just for that moment I hated him and I hated Mammy too, with all my heart and soul, though now I'm ashamed of myself.'

There was a short silence whilst Polly struggled to express her feelings without hurting Dana; she realised it would not help anyone to antagonise her friend, particularly as Dana had already admitted that she had been – was – at fault. Finally Polly decided that she could do with some help; this was indeed a tricky situation. She stood up, took Dana's hands and pulled her to her feet. 'We'd best go into the kitchen, because it's not fair to invite a chap for dinner and then leave him to do all the work,' she said. 'And as you must realise, Ernie knows as much as I do now about the situation, so all three of us should talk it over.'

She began to pull her friend towards the door, but Dana resisted. 'Hang on a minute, Poll,' she said urgently. 'What do you mean, "talk it over"? Talking isn't going to do much good. All this happened years ago and no one can undo it. Oh, I suppose I might write to my mother and Johnny and admit I was stupid, but I can't possibly go back to Castletara and claim anything from them. Don't you see? That was why I wanted to make a success of my own business – so that I could return as an independent person, having made my own way in the world . . .'

Polly snorted. 'You're talking rubbish and you know it,' she said. 'Your mother will want you back on any terms. Good mothers are like that, or so I've been told.

But it's not just that.' Here she opened the kitchen door and literally dragged Dana inside, pushing her into one of the chairs and beckoning Ernie to sit down as well. 'Look, Dana, you just heard old Chamberlain saying we're at war. No matter how you look at it, being at war will change things, or at least I imagine it will.' She looked across at Ernie. 'Go on, Ern, tell Dana what you think may happen.'

Ernie cleared his throat. He looked uncomfortable – who would not? – but determined, and when he spoke it was calmly, almost as though he had rehearsed what he was about to say. 'I've been thinkin' it out, Dana, and ever since Independence Ireland has been a foreign country. In time of war borders between countries close. It's quite possible that in a few weeks, travel to Ireland may be not just restricted but impossible. I suppose if that does happen you could go up to Scotland, take the ferry to Northern Ireland at Stranraer and then cross the border into Eire, unless that border gets closed as well. Polly and I talked it over before we knew for certain that war was coming and we both think you ought to go back to Castletara now without wasting time wondering if you're doing the right thing. Once you get there I'm sure your mother and this Devlin fellow will beg you to stay. Dana, they probably need you. I know you'll say they've managed without you for three years, but that was because they had no choice. And anyway, if you decide to come back to Temperance Court and the Freeway Cinema at least it'll be your decision. So will you go home tomorrow?'

Dana stared from face to face. Polly saw her friend's lower lip quiver and her eyes blink rapidly, but when at last Dana spoke it was calmly. 'What, and let the Freeway brothers down after all they've done for me? I don't want to sound conceited, Ern, but with almost all the truly trustable staff at the cafeteria having left to take jobs in the factories, which are paying so much better than we can, how can I turn round and tell Jake that I'm off to Ireland and there's nobody I can trust to run the place in my absence? Ralph joined the air force weeks ago and Jake's hoping that the air force accept him too, which he seems to think they will. So you see, going off tomorrow is out of the question and I wouldn't dream of it, but you can both stop nagging because the truth is I know you're right. If I can get someone elderly but reliable to run the place I'll think about going off in a couple of weeks. And now let's get on with cooking our Sunday dinner.'

But when on Monday morning the girls switched the wireless on it was to hear some news which caused Dana's plans to be brought forward. The government announced that all places of entertainment, such as cinemas, theatres, dance halls and fairgrounds, were to cease trading and close immediately, remaining closed until further announcements. Dana and Polly, sitting opposite one another at the kitchen table and spooning porridge, stared, round-eyed. 'Well of all the daft things . . .' Polly began, then stopped short, waving her porridge spoon. 'It's perishin' well a sign from above,' she said solemnly. 'If the cinema closes the cafeteria will close and that means you can start packing right now. I'll come and see you aboard the Irish ferry, because I'm sure they'll keep on sailing. Do you realise, queen, that we're both out of work?'

Dana scraped her porridge bowl clean and nodded. 'Yes, I suppose we are,' she acknowledged. 'Oh, all right, Polly, you needn't labour the point. I'll go back to Castletara, if only for a few days.' She sounded far from delighted, but as another thought occurred to her she brightened. 'Oh, Polly, me darlin' Polly, why don't you come with me? It would be so much easier if I wasn't alone. I'd pay your passage all the way to Castletara and back; do say you'll come!'

Polly, however, shook her head firmly. 'It's no good, chuck, this is one problem you're going to have to face alone,' she said. 'When the Prodigal Son – or in your case Daughter – returns, she don't go bringin' her best mate with her. And besides, I've plans of me own,' she added mysteriously. She leaned forward and peered into her friend's cup. 'Ah, you've drunk your tea. How about another cup before you start your packing?'

It did not take Dana long to pack; she simply thrust a change of underwear, a thick jersey and a tweed skirt into a paper carrier bag, only adding her comb and toothbrush when Polly, scandalised, reminded her that she really needed such mundane objects. All the way to the Pier Head the two girls discussed what would happen now that war was a fact, and not unnaturally Dana questioned Polly closely about the mysterious plans which apparently meant that Polly could not leave the shores of Britain. 'I bet you mean to get work in one of the factories,' she guessed. 'I know you, Polly; you'll want to be a part of the war effort. I say, where are all those kids going? It seems an odd time for a school outing!'

Polly tutted. 'Do you go around with your eyes shut

and your fingers stuffed in your perishin' ears?' she asked derisively. 'They're being what they call evacuated from all the big cities. Can't you see the labels tied on their coats? Poor little buggers, they must feel that yesterday they were kids and today they're just parcels. Some of 'em left even before war was declared, but most of 'em were told to go to their schools this morning with their stuff in bags or paper carriers and the teachers would take responsibility for them once they reached the station.'

'Aren't you knowing, Polly,' Dana said admiringly. 'I knew children were being evacuated to what the government called "places of safety", but I don't think I'd realised the numbers involved.' A sudden thought struck her. 'Will any of 'em be going to Ireland, do you suppose? If so, there may be no room for me aboard the Irish ferry!'

'Ha ha,' Polly said sarcastically. 'That would be a grand get-out, wouldn't it? Well, you're out of luck, Dana McBride, because the kids aren't likely to go to a foreign country, are they? No, they'll be off to North Wales, or the Wirral, or maybe somewhere even further off. But not, I repeat, *not*, to Eire!'

'All right, all right, no need to gloat so obviously,' Dana said, but she gave Polly her sweetest smile as she spoke. 'I've said I'll go back to Castletara so back to Castletara I will go. And you can keep your silly old secret, Polly Smith.'

'I intend to do so,' Polly said composedly. 'There's the ticket queue, Dana, so you'd better get in it. And don't forget if you mean to stay with your people just drop me a line, otherwise I'll worry myself silly, imagining you being torpedoed or shot or bombed or something.'

'You're daft,' Dana said, but she said it affectionately, and when she had purchased her ticket she and Polly hugged and Dana saw her friend's round blue eyes fill with tears. Polly began to say something to the effect that she had never loved anyone like she loved Dana but Dana had no wish to end up crying herself and gave Polly a shove. 'Shut up. This isn't goodbye, it's au revoir, and it's only that for a few days, because I mean to come back just as soon as I've sorted things out with Mammy and Johnny,' she said. 'Be good while I'm gone, Polly!'

Just as she was about to ascend the gangway, someone tugged her elbow. A fat and jolly Irish woman gestured behind her to the crowd on the quay. 'Your pal's shoutin' you,' she said reprovingly. 'Give her a wave.' Dana obediently turned and waved in Polly's direction, picking out her friend's little blonde head, though not without difficulty. Polly was shouting something, but though the words were drowned in the general hubbub Dana suddenly realised what her friend was saying.

'Give my love to Con,' Polly was shouting. 'He's the reason you wouldn't go home!'

Dana hastily turned back towards the ferry and continued to climb the gangway. Trust Polly to know her so well, she thought ruefully. It was true that the quarrel with Con had been as strong a reason for her leaving home as her mother's marriage to Johnny Devlin. Con had scorned her attempts to get him to agree that the marriage must be stopped. When the argument got really vicious both parties had said things they had never meant. Con had told her to get out of his life, because she had told him to get out of Castletara. Now, three years older and a great deal more sensible, she acknowledged that she had been wrong all along the line. Marriage is between the two people involved and nobody else. Both Johnny and Feena had a right to happiness, which was one of the many things Con had tried to tell her. But I was impetuous, self-willed and pretty damned stupid, she thought now. If only I'd written to Con at the start, admitting I was wrong and asking him to forget the horrible things I'd said. Oh, I did write, but it was a stiff and starchy letter because I was still clinging to my belief that, had he known, Donovan McBride would have forbidden the banns. And Con had never replied though she had given him – and only him – the name of the restaurant in which she worked. At the time she had expected him both to reply and to pass the address of the Willows restaurant on to her mother, but this had not happened; or at any rate, if he had done so, Feena had simply chucked the address into the fire, or so Dana had told herself at the time. Now, however, she was sure she had misjudged both Con and her mother. Letters do go astray, she told herself, leaning on the rail and watching the bustling departure on the quayside below. Yes, post gets lost all the time, so why didn't I try to contact my family again? But she knew the real reason, of course. Pride. After that one attempt to get in touch she had been too hurt to think straight and had decided only to return to Castletara as a successful business person. At one time she had thought she might marry Ralph simply in order to show Con that someone wanted her even if he did not, but she had soon realised that such a move would be madness. She and Ralph were pals but could never be lovers since neither felt strongly enough about the other, so now here she was on the ferry back to Ireland and for the first time she would be completely honest with herself. She loved her mother and she liked Johnny and hoped that their marriage was a success, but the way she felt about Con was quite different. She adored him still as she had done ever since they had played together as children. She could never contemplate marriage with anyone else, and if when she returned to Castletara he asked her to marry him she would immediately accept. The fact that by now he might have married someone else she considered totally unthinkable. Love such as theirs was not transferable; he would wait a lifetime for her as she would for him.

Dana dreamed happily as the ferry began to breast the waves of the Irish Sea.

Chapter Twelve

Dana spent the voyage watching the other passengers and trying to guess their reasons for quitting England and returning to Eire. Almost without exception they spoke with a degree of brogue and almost without exception their main subject of conversation was the war. Some, including the elderly Irish woman who had drawn her attention to Polly's shouts, were returning because they had no wish to be embroiled in a war not of their making. They had no time for Hitler, were disgusted by the behaviour of the German people, but wanted no part in the bloodshed they could plainly see was to come. It was less than twenty years since Eire had gained her own independence from Britain, and at what cost? But they would miss the money they had earned from the British. Who knew, if their search for work was not successful they might return, professing themselves eager to help in any way possible.

By the time the ship docked Dana felt that the majority of the people on board were like herself: testing the water. If England was invaded and crushed beneath the Nazi jackboot they would tighten their belts, keep themselves to themselves and wait for better times. If on the other hand the British took a more warlike stance and fought back then most of the Irish – or those aboard the ferry, at any rate – would return to help in the fight.

At first Dana thought this was too like running with the hare and hunting with the hounds, but she very soon realised her mistake. In no circumstances would the ordinary people throw in their lot with the huns – Irish memories are long and they had suffered alongside the English, many Europeans and eventually even the Yanks in the terrible trenches of the previous war. Germany had been the enemy last time, and would be so again.

But the murmuring to which Dana had only given half her attention was becoming louder as the misty outline of Ireland drew nearer, and presently she could make out trees and soon even leaves, russet, gold and palest fawn, ready to fall when the autumn winds blew but hanging grimly on now as the September sun gilded them into fiery beauty.

The voyage across the Irish Sea had been a long one, almost eight hours, and when she had arrived in Dublin Dana had been too tired to even consider travelling on that day. Instead she had found a cheap lodging on a small side street where the landlady had supplied a plain but delicious supper and a breakfast of soda bread and bacon, filling Dana's water bottle and giving her half a loaf of brack which, she said, would last for days so it would, especially if eaten with good farm-made butter. Dana had thanked her profusely and answered her many questions about Great Britain now they were at war, all of which seemed to imply that she believed Dana to be in personal contact with the prime minister.

So it was after a good breakfast that Dana set off once

more, heading for the railway station and the train which would take her some of the way. After that she would board a local bus and with luck would arrive at her destination halfway through the afternoon. By the time she arrived in Castletara village, she was weary, hungry and thirsty, though she had purchased both food and drink when the train stopped at small stations along the way. Now, looking around her, she was suddenly filled with a wild exhilaration. Though it was raining the air was fresh and sweet with the scent of leaves, salt water and trodden grass, and she was achingly aware for the first time since she had left it how she missed her home and its people. Here, even the accents were different from those of the Dubliners who were the most frequent Irish visitors to Liverpool. Softer and gentler, they reminded Dana of the sweet summer rain which falls so frequently and is so often cursed by the inhabitants of the Emerald Isle. But today Dana lifted her face to it, for it was like a mother's loving caress and as such she welcomed it, for even though she had a further five miles to walk she knew she was home at last. She began to walk, with a piece of poetry running through her head: *Home is the sailor, home from the sea, and the hunter home from the hill.* Well, she might not be a sailor, though she had spent some time on a ship lately, and she might not be a hunter though now she was hunting for forgiveness and a place in her old home. She could not remember the rest of the poem – if it was a poem – but it sang to itself in her head and she welcomed it as she had welcomed the soft Irish rain whose touch was so gentle that it could scarcely be felt, though it had already penetrated to her skin.

She reached the lane; only another mile to go and she would be able to see the towers of Castletara to her right across gently rolling meadows dotted with horses. She had already seen sheep, their woolly coats shorn, and on a downward-sloping meadow, at the foot of which ran the river in which she had learned to swim, cattle grazed and wandered down to paddle in the clear water, making Dana remember how the passage of the hunt had caused the sand to rise in clouds, stealing the river's clarity, though it could not steal its chuckling, bubbling song.

She reached the point at which a glance to her right should have revealed Castletara and for a moment she stood, hand flying to her mouth, shocked and horrified; there was no castle! No great high stone wall, no towers, no long gravelled drive thickly edged with evergreens. But before a great wail could break from her lips she realised that memory had played her false. Heart thumping with recent terror she walked on, probably less than a hundred yards, and then stopped by a gap in the ragged hedge, almost afraid at first to turn her head. Was it here? Had she made some terrible mistake, and was she perhaps walking along the wrong lane? But then she forced herself to look to the right again and her tumultuous heart ceased its frantic beating and became regular once more. It was there! Castletara reared before her, the wall with its tiny growths of hart's tongue fern, house leek and fat cushions of moss as solid as the day she had left, though from here she could not have identified the tiny plants which grew in the crevices between the great stones. She could see the gravel drive, still partly obscured by the straggly rhododendrons which her father had always intended to root up since he said they made the approach to the house too dark and depressing. She could see the towers, one of which was – had been – her bedroom. She could see her parents' bedroom windows on the floor below her own and for a moment her heart sank at the thought that the room would doubtless now belong to Feena and Johnny. Then she chided herself; life went on whether you liked it or not so she must accept the inevitable, make the best of it.

She lifted her chin and licked the delicate raindrops from her lips, resettled her haversack on her shoulders and set off towards the tall wrought iron gates which led to her home. She reached them, glancing sideways as she did so at the lodge keeper's cottage, half expecting to be challenged, for Mrs O'Leary and her husband had lived in the lodge in her time and surely lived there still; three years was, after all, not a long time in the life of an Irish estate. That glance at the lodge, however, showed her that one thing had definitely changed. The windows shone as brightly as mirrors, the curtains were fresh and clean and someone had painted the front door and polished the knocker, an object the young Dana had always envied the O'Learys. It was in the form of a lion's head and though the O'Learys, a rather slatternly couple, had always left their door open except when the weather was extremely bad, Dana had always announced her arrival with a gentle knock with the brass head. Even in those days the heedless child that had been Dana had thought vaguely that it was a shame to see the knocker gradually greening, and would surreptitiously rub at the brass with her sleeve. New brooms sweep clean, Dana thought rather sadly now as she bypassed the lodge. Either the O'Learys had changed out of all recognition or someone else lived in their old home. She was tempted to linger, perhaps even to knock, for that would delay her arrival at Castletara, but then she shook her head at her own foolishness and hurried on. With every step she was getting nearer the moment she most longed for and most dreaded; the moment of truth, she supposed. She had heard the expression many times on lips other than her own, but had never truly understood it. Now she did.

The gravelled drive led to a sweep so that carriages – only cars were more likely in this day and age – could approach the front door. Dana skirted the house and headed for the stable yard. She walked under the arch, and was immediately transported back in time. The yard, the stables – all the outbuildings, in fact – were miraculously unchanged, though they had been joined by a new wing, she saw. But other than that it was as though she had truly stepped back in time and was once more the Dana of long ago. She stood still for a moment, savouring the feeling. Her past was here, every moment of it; she could almost believe that Donovan McBride had never died, that Feena and Johnny Devlin had never loved, even that the O'Learys still lived in the lodge, trundling up to the castle whenever they were needed, Mrs O'Leary to scrub floors, wash paintwork and generally help round the house, though she never bothered about such things in her own domain, and Mr O'Leary to mow the lawns or dig and harvest in the kitchen garden.

She was standing there, stock still, when the back door opened and Johnny Devlin came out, accompanied by a tall rangy man unknown to Dana. A customer? Neither man saw her, so intent were they on their conversation, and Johnny led the stranger out through the white-painted wooden gate which led to the school. Yes, undoubtedly a customer. Johnny would be choosing his stock and showing their paces. The moment they were out of sight, Dana headed for the back door; it would be the ideal moment to catch her mother alone, she thought. Better to march in boldly, which she could not have done had Johnny been present. She reached the back door and realised that Johnny had not closed it behind him. It swung on the latch and she gave it a gentle push, then peered through the widening gap. Her mother was standing in the kitchen in front of the square of mirror, tying back her hair. She wore a scarlet roll-necked sweater, white jodhpurs and very shiny black boots, the costume she had always favoured when showing off a horse's paces to an interested buyer. Naturally she did not see the door swing open behind her, but as Dana stepped into the room Feena gasped and spun round and her daughter realised that her mother had seen her reflection in the mirror, perhaps had not even recognised her, thinking her merely an intruder. But then their eyes met and Feena gave a shriek a steam train might have envied and Dana hurled herself into her mother's outstretched arms.

'Oh, my lovely girl, my little darling! Oh, how wicked you are to frighten me so.' Feena almost sobbed the words. 'Oh, alanna, we've missed you sore! Why didn't you give us an address, so that we could write? Oh, Dana, one miserable little letter in t'ree long lonely years and all t'ree of us replied, begging you to come home, but the letters were returned *not known at this address*. Oh, you bad, bad, girl, but *how* I love you! You've not changed a bit. No, perhaps you're a little taller – but otherwise you're still my little girl. D'you know what I t'ought when I saw your reflection? I t'ought my darlin' Donovan had come back . . . me heart nearly stopped for joy, but when I saw it was you it was as though you'd never left. Now come and sit down and tell me what's been happening to you, why you stayed away so long . . . why you're here now, come to that!'

'Your letters must've been returned by that wicked old woman who employed the kitchen staff and hated the Irish,' Dana said miserably. 'Why didn't I think of that? Oh, if only I had! But all I could think was that you'd cast me off because I'd said such dreadful things. Oh, Mammy, will you ever forgive me?'

Feena tried to interrupt, to say there was nothing to forgive, but Dana overrode her. 'Mammy – oh, Mammy, I'm so sorry, so very sorry. I'm a wicked girl, so I am, to give you such grief.' Now she obeyed her mother's pointing finger and sank into one of the old cane chairs which flanked the enormous range upon which they did most of their cooking. Feena sat down beside her, still clutching Dana's hand as though she would never let it go, and Dana, looking at her mother's face properly for the first time, saw that though Feena was still beautiful there were little worry lines around her eyes. I put them there, she told herself. My mean selfishness has marked my mother's face. She felt deep guilt for what she had done.

'Go on, alanna; start from the moment you left Castletara all those years ago . . .' Feena began, then jumped to her feet. 'Whatever am I thinking of? What a poor welcome, and me waiting for the kettle to boil so I could brew tea when Johnny brings Mr Mason back to talk business.'

She moved over to where the kettle was just beginning to hiss, but Dana got to her feet and put a restraining hand on her mother's arm. 'Mammy, Johnny will be waiting in the school for you to go out and ride the horses. Had you forgotten?'

Feena struck her head with the back of her hand and then smiled rather self-consciously at her daughter. 'And wouldn't the good Lord himself forgive me for forgetfulness when the cause is me daughter's return after three long years? But you're right, of course, alanna. Johnny's been good to me.' She gave Dana a strange look, half ashamed and half defiant. 'We've been good to one another, you might say. Oh, my darling, perhaps now you're older you'll understand. Your father meant all the world to me, but I'm a woman who needs a man. I couldn't carry the burden of Castletara without help, and though Johnny was grand so he was, you might say he was neither fish, fowl, nor good red herring; neither the boss nor an employee, if you understand me. Besides, though no one could replace Don, I loved Johnny and knew he loved me.' She leaned closer to Dana, looking straight into her daughter's eyes whilst her own filled with tears. 'Have you come back to say you understand and have forgiven me? Oh, Dee, darling Dee, say you have!'

Dana laughed. 'Oh, Mammy, of course I understand, and there's nothing for *me* to forgive. When war was declared it seemed the ideal opportunity to come home, though I can't possibly stay. To be sure I've no job just now – I've been working in a cinema, running the cafeteria at the top of the building, but since the government closed all places of entertainment I'm out of a job – but there's plenty of work in Liverpool . . .'

'Oh, Dee, there are a million jobs here,' Feena said eagerly. 'Riding isn't something you forget and there's only me to show off our horses most of the time. We could find you work, indeed we could, and nothing would give Johnny and myself more pleasure than to have you back.'

'Oh, Mammy, I'd love to come back so I would,' Dana said, suddenly aware that she sounded like a wistful five-year-old; she, who had meant to return as a success! 'But it would be desertion, don't you see? It would seem like running away, going to a place of safety and leaving my pals, my work colleagues, even my boss, to face it alone. And be honest: you've managed without me for three years. This war may last three or thirty, but which-ever, I'm committed to fighting for the British. But of course I don't intend to turn round and leave immedi-ately. I'll sleep in my old room tonight and we can have a really good catch up, with all my old friends . . .'

To Dana's surprise a look of deep guilt crossed her mother's face, and she broke into hurried speech. 'Your old room . . . oh, yes, the tower room above where your daddy and meself used to sleep. But you're not a child, alanna! You must have the big room on the first floor; it's more fitting for the girl who will inherit all this one day. And now let's go outside. You can chat to Johnny and Mr Mason while I show off two or three of the hunter-chasers.'

She turned towards the back door as she spoke but Dana clutched her arm, pulling her back. 'Hang on a moment, Mammy. I want my old room! No point in making up the bed in the other room when all my things are in the tower. Don't tell me you've stripped my room and put someone else in it! They told me in the village that you take in parties of tourists now, but you'd not put a tourist into the tower room with all my books and paintings and clothes and other rubbish all over the place. So why can't I have it? Has Con taken it over?'

'Con? No, no, it's not Con,' Feena said vaguely. She heaved a sigh and looked up at the clock above the mantel. 'Johnny won't be expecting me down there for another ten minutes. Best get it over, I suppose. Come with me.'

Totally puzzled and more than a little annoyed, Dana followed her mother across the kitchen and up the steeply winding stone staircase which led straight into the tower room. At the top Feena signalled Dana to stay quiet, and pushed open the little wooden door. A plump young woman was bending over a cot and lifting from it a child whose age Dana was not qualified to judge, but it was dressed in a blue romper suit and gave an excited squawk when the two women entered the room. 'Mammy!' it squeaked. 'Take Donny to see gee gees.'

For a moment Dana simply could not take it in; then realisation dawned and a furious rage consumed her. They had supplanted her with this mewling brat! She took one step into the room and met the child's inquisitive gaze and suddenly, as suddenly as it had come, her rage and jealousy vanished like frost in June. She had often longed for a brother; now it seemed she had one. She smiled at the baby, for he was little more, and to her delight he smiled back. But the fat young woman was talking; a nanny, clearly. Feena would need help with the child so long as she was working with Johnny and the horses.

'Now, Mrs McBride, I know full well what you're going to say to me, but he can't get his little tongue round de word hosses so I lets him say gee gees,' the girl said. 'After all, Mrs M, he's barely eighteen months and babbies the world over calls 'em gee gees.'

Dana looked from her mother to the child and read pride and apprehension in Feena's dark eyes. She began to say that the boy was beautiful, that she envied Feena, when he held out his arms to her and she took the wriggling, chattering bundle from the girl and kissed his pink cheek. 'Hello, little brother,' she said softly. 'Well, who'd have thought it?' She turned to her mother, who was smiling now, though tentatively. 'Oh, Mammy, what a wonderful surprise! This little fellow is lucky, so he is, as lucky as I was – and Con, of course – because he'll be brought up at Castletara. He's a link between Con and myself too; a half-brother to us both. What does Con think of him? I bet he adores him!'

'Well, young men aren't much interested in babies, except when they're their own get,' Feena said. 'We named him for your father, Dana – he's Donovan Liam McBride. Isn't that what Don would have wanted? And now the two of you have met, you can be really useful, my darlin' girl. Maureen – this is Maureen, Donny's nanny – is scared of horses but a great hand wit' washing nappies. So she can get on with that while you bring the young gentleman down to the school. To watch his mammy ride the gee gees,' she added, pulling a face at her small son. He promptly scowled at her.

"Osses,' he said. 'Mammy say 'osses.'

'Well I never did!' Feena said gaily as they crossed the stable yard and headed towards the ménage. "Osses is what it will be from now on and what a good thing the rain has ceased, though we've a covered school now which we use when conditions are too bad for the outdoor one.'

Presently mother and daughter parted and Dana settled down to watch Feena showing off the paces of three beautiful hunter-chasers, but all the time her mind was busy with Con's whereabouts, for she had seen neither hide nor hair of him. When Johnny appeared with the buyer Feena had obviously told him that her daughter had returned as they tacked up the first beast, for he came and joined her by the rail, introduced her to Mr Mason and as soon as the other's attention was diverted by the arrival of the first horse leaned over and gave her a quick, embarrassed kiss on the cheek. 'Sorry I am for what I said all them years ago,' he whispered. 'Con lit into me something cruel for the way I behaved but I thought you knew me well enough to realise that I could lose me temper and say things I didn't mean. Never mind, eh? You're back and all is forgiven; that's right, isn't it?' He poked a finger into his son's plump little stomach. 'Who's come to see the gee gees, eh?'

"Osses!' his son said reprovingly. 'Donny see 'osses.'

Johnny laughed indulgently and Dana thought how nice it was that he clearly adored his little boy. She remembered he had been severe with Con, but he had had to be both mother and father to his firstborn. This child seemed more like a grandson and would no doubt reap all the attention and affection which Johnny had been unable to show Con.

Each time her mother disappeared to hand her mount over to old Tom, Dana expected Con to come through the gate, but only her mother was riding today. Con must be busy seeing to the other animals, Dana told herself, but it was not until the customer had left, so satisfied that he intended to buy all three mounts, that Dana was able to ask about Con's whereabouts. He had not come in for his lunch and, stranger still, no one had commented on his absence. Finally, lunch over and the deal concluded with a handshake – and no doubt a large cheque – Dana was able to satisfy her curiosity. She and Feena were alone in the kitchen, Feena washing up and Dana drying, both chatting about almost anything other than Con. Finally Dana realised she would have to put the question direct and proceeded to do so. 'Where's Con?' she asked bluntly. 'I thought he'd be showing at least one of the horses.'

Feena's eyebrows shot up. 'Don't you know? I made sure Con would've got a message to you somehow, though come to think of it I don't know how since the only address any of us have had was that Willows place which returned all our letters. Well, about eighteen months ago Con took a trip to Germany to look at a couple of fine stallions. As you know, we don't go in for heavy breeds and these were massive chaps, which we thought would maybe improve our stock if put to the right mares. But Con came back full of what he had seen and all his talk was of the German war machine; he scarcely mentioned the stallions save to say he'd not bought, but he described everything he'd seen in Berlin.

If anyone but Con had told me such dreadful things I probably wouldn't have believed them, but you know Con.' She smiled at Dana. 'Never a chap to exaggerate, he'd be more apt to play it down if anything. Well, it was his visit to Germany and his conviction that war was coming which sent him over the border to Northern Ireland, where he applied for the Royal Air Force and was accepted. He's a fully trained fighter pilot, has been for six or nine months now, and I think he's aiming to go as high as he can get in the service, though when peace comes I hope he'll return to Castletara, his daddy and meself.'

Dana forced her numb lips into a smile. The news had shocked her to the very roots of her being, because she had never even imagined Castletara without Con. He was in every recollection of her life here, starting when they were both little more than toddlers. She remembered an occasion when they had had a dispute over a fine scarlet ball. Con, being the stronger, had given her a shove, so that she ended up in a pile of manure, squalling indignantly and demanding Con's blood. Then her father had appeared, laughing, and plucking her from the manure had dusted her down. 'No, I shan't skelp the lad for teaching you you're not the cock o' the walk,' he had said. 'And neither shall his own daddy. Take defeat wit' a good grace, me little love.'

Con had grinned up at Donovan McBride and then thrust the ball into Dana's hands. 'Sorry I shoved you, alanna,' he had said cheerfully. 'Now let's take the ball on to the lawn where there ain't no horse muck.'

That had been just one incident of many. Children's parties, trips to the seaside, learning to row a coracle on the nearby lake, then visits to the cinema in town, shopping expeditions and helping in the harvest fields when they were older, and always, always, horses. Stallions, mares, colts, fillies and foals, a constant procession of them to be watched and loved, tacked up, ridden and rewarded, and always she and Con together, closer than brother and sister, seldom at odds.

But she'd been silent for too long. Feena was staring at her over the pile of plates she was about to replace on the Welsh dresser. 'Dana?' she said anxiously. 'You've not seen him for three whole years and you've not tried to get in touch. My dear child, you could've written to him at any time during those three years. You've made it pretty plain that you've been assuming he was still here; why didn't you at least send him a note? Put yourself in his shoes for a moment. You'd left here after a blazing row; you wrote to him once, a very stiff and starchy letter giving him an address which proved to be useless. You must've had other addresses to which he could've sent letters . . . you've just told me you share accommodation with your friend Polly. Why did you not send Con that address? You can't blame him if he thought he no longer mattered to you and turned to other friends.'

'Other friends?' Dana could not help her surprise and dismay showing. 'But Con and I didn't need anyone else whilst we had each other.' A dreadful thought struck her. 'Are you trying to say he's got a girlfriend?'

'Yes,' Feena said baldly, and now when she looked at Dana there was a gently mocking smile on her face. 'Did you think he was the sort of man to pine over one girl when the world is full of pretty women? You underestimate him, my dear. He's had at least a dozen girlfriends

– well, maybe I exaggerate, but he's been serious enough with three or four of them to bring them home from time to time.'

'I see,' Dana said quietly. 'I suppose he's not – not actually married? Of course, if he is . . .'

Feena laughed and reached out to take her daughter's hand. 'Are *you* married, alanna? For all Con knows you might have a couple of kids by now.' She laughed again. 'For all I know you might've made me a grandmother. Oh, how Johnny would hate being married to Granny McBride!'

Dana tried to join in her mother's laughter but it was difficult. All she wanted was to get away like an injured animal and lick her wounds, but she must not let Feena realise how the news of Con had affected her, so she lied boldly. 'Oh well, I suppose I must confess that Con isn't the only one. I've had three or four boyfriends in Liverpool myself and one of them is pretty serious. His name's Ralph – Ralph Freeway – and he's part owner with his brother Jake of the Freeway Cinema where I work. He's joined the air force, just like Con, and wanted us to get engaged before he was sent abroad for training, but I wouldn't. I wanted to see Con first; a pity that's impossible but he's clearly not pining for me any more than I'm pining for him. So when I go back to Liverpool I'll agree to the engagement and next time I come home I will bring Ralph, because you simply must meet him. You'll love him, Mammy, honest to God you will.'

'If you say so, alanna. But only a moment ago you were saying words to the effect that you and Con had a special relationship, and now you say you're getting engaged to some young man you've never mentioned before. Are you sure . . .'

'Yes I am sure,' Dana said swiftly, pinning a bright smile to her lips. 'I've always thought of Con as a brother; that was why I was so upset that he seemed to have forgotten me. I know brothers and sisters don't always get on but Con and I scarcely ever quarrelled. So we'll dance at each other's weddings and no doubt when the war's over and we both come back here with our partners, I'll talk girl talk with her and Con and Ralph will drink Guinness in the village and discuss the war and the air force and all the other things men talk about when there are no women present. But in the meantime, if you'll be good enough to give me Con's address I'll drop him a line apologising for the way I've behaved.' She gave a rather artificial little laugh. 'I owe him that much. Unless you think he'd rather I didn't even write?'

Feena stared at her daughter, clearly nonplussed by her words, and when she answered it was slowly. 'Dana, my love, Con has asked us not to pass his address on. For a short time he went out with Sinead McCulloch but she began pressing for marriage and telling folk in the village that he'd given her a ring. Con said he'd got no intention of marrying anyone, but things were quite difficult for a while. And when young Grainne took a shine to him and began writing him love letters it was the last straw. He told us not to pass his address on, and we haven't, but I'm sure he didn't mean that to include you.'

'Oh, it doesn't matter; I wouldn't like dear Con to think I was pursuing him,' Dana said. 'What it is to be a good-looking and popular young man, eh, Mammy? Forget it. Only when you write do tell him how sorry I am for the quarrel, and horrible Mrs Haggerty sending his letter back. And now let's go and take a look at the rest of the horses.'

She got to her feet as she spoke and headed for the back door, taking her coat off the peg and putting it on, but Feena, following suit, shook her head. 'I shall do no such thing, Dana. You must write a letter – with your address on it, of course – and I'll enclose it with my own. Then the choice will be Con's. He can write direct to you at whatever address you give and I'm sure he'll do so. But he's abroad at the moment, in France I believe, so don't expect an immediate reply.'

'Right,' Dana said as they crossed the stable yard. 'By the way, Mammy, what's happened to the O'Learys? The lodge was so clean and tidy I almost thought I was in the wrong place. Don't say you've given them the sack after all these years?'

Feena laughed at the mere suggestion. 'No, of course not; your father would never have permitted such a thing, and both Johnny and myself always try to do what Donovan would've wanted. The fact is that Mary McKenna – who was Mary O'Leary – came home to live with her parents after her husband ran off with some young fancy piece he met on a visit to Dublin. She's a nice young woman – well, she's not that young, she must be forty – and a stickler for cleanliness and hard work. She keeps the lodge immaculate and we employ her up at the castle three mornings a week, which gives her some money of her own. But you'll meet her, no doubt, before you have to rush off. How long can you stay, love? After all, you've already told me there are plenty of jobs in Liverpool now England's at war, and obviously whilst you're with us you won't need to be spending much. In fact we'll pay you if you'll exercise the horses for us.' She smiled lovingly at her daughter. 'I wish you could stay for ever, my little darling, but it's up to you. It's a decision only you can make.'

But here she was proved wrong, for within a week of Dana's arriving at Castletara the British government made another announcement, having clearly realised their mistake. All places of entertainment were to be opened once more, and that of course included the Freeway Cinema and its popular cafeteria. Dana, listening to the wireless, could only pull a rueful face and tell Feena and Johnny what they must have already guessed: she would have to go. Jake would be hard pressed to get the cinema opened up with more than half his staff missing, and the cafeteria would remain closed until Dana was in charge once more.

Resignedly, Dana said her farewells, carried her haversack downstairs and piled into the old Morris in which Johnny would drive her to the station. She had put all her belongings on the front passenger seat so that she and Feena might sit side by side in the back, discussing how soon Dana would be able to return to Castletara. Feena wept when the train drew in and many promises were exchanged, some of which might actually be kept, Dana thought, as she waved to the two figures gradually growing smaller as the engine speed increased. When they had quite disappeared she sat back in her seat in the empty compartment and allowed herself the luxury of a hearty bout of tears. She had written an abject apology to Con telling him that she would stay at Castletara for at least a month, but this had proved impossible and because of her obstinate refusal to let her mother give her Con's address against his expressed wishes she would have to wait for his reply. She had managed to gather that, in this case at any rate, abroad meant France, which was not so very far away. So she comforted herself with the hope that he would write back, believing her to be at Castletara, and that Feena would redirect his reply to Temperance Court as soon as it was received.

Chapter Thirteen

'Are you ready, Dana?' Polly's tone held an edge of impatience. 'You'd best get a move on. You know how fussy Jake is about opening up on time.'

Dana, emerging red-faced from the bedroom, sighed but took her coat from its peg and began to put it on. 'Friends who've gone into the forces complain about being tipped out of their beds every morning at some ungodly hour, but thanks to staff shortages I reckon we're even worse off,' she said bitterly. 'What's the weather like, Poll? Don't say it's raining again!'

'It always rains in November . . . unless it snows, of course,' Polly said placidly. 'Still, the wind ain't nowhere near as strong as it were last month.' She snorted on a laugh. 'Do you remember that feller who came to talk to us about German spies and parachutists descending from the sky dressed as nuns, who got quite a barracking after someone said it were so windy that the nuns' skirts would be blowed over their heads revealing clumping great jackboots and serge trousers? And some wag in the audience said they'd all get blown to Ireland or into the Mersey, they could tek their choice.' She opened the door as she spoke, then groaned. 'Oh, Gawd, it's positively pelting down, and an umbrella would be blown inside out before you could say Jack Robinson. I vote we catch a tram to the Pier Head and then a bus. No point in getting wetter than we have to.'

Dana agreed and the two scuttled, heads down, across the court, under the arch and on to the main road. Polly leaned towards Dana and bawled at the top of her voice, to be heard above the roar of the traffic. 'There's a good queue for the tram, which means one must be due any minute. Though whether we'll get on the first one which comes along I doubt, even though it's dead early. It's all them perishin' factory workers . . . ah, here comes one with another close behind!'

The girls managed to get aboard the second tram, and at the Pier Head they hurried through the lashing rain to where their bus would presently draw in. When it came, there was room for two on the front seat and the girls hurried up the aisle and sat down. Polly glanced at her wristwatch. 'We're going to be early early,' she said cheerfully. 'This bus normally picks up school kids, but of course they've all been evacuated, though I believe some mums are bringing their kids home. Well, you can't blame 'em. We've had none of this aerial bombardment that the government expected, no nuns have come floating down from the sky, no beautiful ladies with very little clothing and German accents have appeared to try and wheedle state secrets out of our chaps . . .'

Dana giggled. 'I heard a kid in the stalls last Saturday saying that they were being asked questions in school as to what they would do if England was invaded. The teacher mentioned these mythical nuns that everyone's been on about and asked the kids what they would do if they saw a nun descending from the sky. Apparently

345

one of the really little ones piped up with: "I'd tell her she must of slipped out of heaven and she'd best change d'rection at once and go back up again afore she was missed!"'

'Ain't kids lovely? But with Christmas barely five weeks away they'll soon stop thinking about bombs or invasions or anything of that nature. I reckon most everyone will bring their kids home for Christmas itself, but if they've got any sense they'll send 'em back to the country afterwards. The Jerries have had their hands full with France and the Maginot Line and subduing the Poles, I suppose, but what they did to Madrid they'll do to England, so we need to be ready, which means keeping the kids safe. So I reckon the streets and the courts will buzz for a couple of weeks and then we'll get our lovely peace and quiet back.'

Dana's eyebrows rose and she wagged a reproving finger at her friend. 'I thought you liked children,' she said indignantly. 'Lovely peace and quiet indeed! Though I admit it will be nice when summer comes not to have to dodge under the lines of dripping nappies criss-crossing Temperance Court. Aha! Our stop's coming up!'

By the time the girls entered the cinema by the side passage they were both soaked to the skin, for it had been impossible to use their umbrellas in the strong wind. They hurried to what Jake referred to as the staffroom and were divesting themselves of their outer garments, squeaking with dismay to find themselves almost as wet beneath, when the door opened and Jake came in. He grinned at Dana, who was wringing her hair out as though it were a dishcloth. 'Well, well, well, do I see two drowned rats before me?' He flourished an official-looking form at them. 'I've been accepted for the Navy!' he said triumphantly.

'I lied about my age, of course, though they don't seem bothered if you're volunteering. But the question is, what'll we do with the dear old Freeway? We're all right for a projectionist and an organist; Mr Levitt is sixty if he's a day and I don't see Reg's age group being called up any time soon, either. I trust you two to manage the place, though you'll probably need some assistance. It's not difficult to keep the cinema itself running smoothly; you've got cleaning staff for the auditorium, I know, Polly, but what about the cafeteria? I dare say several of the waitresses will either go to work in munitions or join the forces; can you manage with the staff you've got, Dana? And can I take it that you'll stay, at least? I know life in the forces must seem glamorous compared to running this place, but owning a cinema is what Ralph and I have always dreamed of doing. Will you promise to stick by me and keep the Freeway open and running smoothly until the war's over?'

Dana promised, and thought it was worth it when she saw the worry leave her employer's face. 'I know we've had difficulty recruiting cooks, waitresses and so on, but that's because we can't offer the same wages as the munitions factories,' she said reassuringly. 'But a manageress gets even more than a girl handling dynamite so if I need someone to cover for me there'll be no difficulty in filling that post once the word gets around.'

Jake grinned at her. 'Good girl,' he said. 'I've got my instructions and will join my ship in Plymouth in ten days. They've sent me a rail pass and detailed instructions, so make the most of me while I'm here. Now, come with me, Polly; I'm going to the office to write to Ralph, to let him know he's not the only one going to fight for his country.'

The day following Jake's acceptance by the Royal Navy, Dana received the long-awaited letter from Con. It came at breakfast time whilst the girls were eating toast, and it came in the same post as one from Ralph, which Dana opened first because all of a sudden she was terrified by what Con's letter might contain.

Ralph's letter was a cheerful, rambling description of his voyage out to South Africa where he and his fellow would-be pilots were to train on ancient Tiger Moths. He also told of parties given by the friendly local people, and reading between the lines Dana concluded that the South African girls, generous to a fault, were only too eager to give these young heroes whatever they wanted.

Dana grinned to herself. Good for you, Ralph, she thought. Don't you worry about me, because you never pretended anything but friendship, and God knows it's all I ever felt for you.

But Con was different. She opened the letter with shaking fingers and was tempted to make some excuse and carry it through into the bedroom where it might be read in private, for it was long – she counted five thin sheets – and whatever Con said she would need time and quiet to assimilate it. She was about to get to her feet, murmuring an excuse to leave the room, when she caught Polly's eye, and thought better of it. She gave her friend a watery grin, and waved the envelope. 'It's the one I've been waiting for. It's from Con.'

'Oh ho!' Polly said brightly, eyeing the number of sheets in Dana's hand. 'Looks like he's written a novel

– well, a novelette at any rate – so you'd best get reading or we'll be late for work. Want to take it through to the bedroom, so you won't be disturbed by the row I make crunching toast?'

Dana gave a rather artificial laugh. 'No need for that; although it's quite long I don't suppose it'll take me many minutes to read,' she said airily. 'Make me another round of toast, there's a pal. And you can top up my tea if there's any more in the pot.'

'Righty-ho,' Polly said breezily and began to potter about whilst Dana settled down to read her letter. It began conventionally enough.

Dear Dana,

Thank you for your letter. I have to admit it came as quite a surprise after so long; believe it or not, I did not even recognise your writing, though I suppose that shouldn't have surprised me since until the day you left Castletara we were seldom apart long enough to write to each other. In fact I don't think I ever received a letter from you until the one which was pinned up on the board in the mess a few days ago.

I'm glad you went back to Castletara and are once more on good terms with Feena and my father. I agree that Donny is a dear little boy though I've only met him a couple of times. Also, it is nice that you have a good job which you enjoy. How strange that you should have taken to catering; from my recollection you seldom cooked or did any sort of housework, your interest being mainly centred in the horses. However, people change. I've changed myself; had to do so. I'm sure Feena told you how I searched for you after you left; unsuccessfully, of course. It never crossed my mind that you might leave Ireland, far less that you would settle in a big English city like Liverpool. What a fool I was! I've always thought of you as a country girl but it seems I was wrong. I was wrong about a lot of things. Forgive me, but there is a hard streak in your nature which I had never suspected. I honestly thought I meant a lot to you, almost as much as you meant to me. When your letter arrived – aha, I'd forgotten that you did write – it was so stiff and cold that I could not bear to share it with Johnny and Feena for several days. Was that the reason why our letters begging you to come home were returned as 'not known at this address'? If so then the fault was mine and I'm sorry for it.

However, I digress. I'm glad you've written explaining your circumstances, but there was no need for you to apologise. There were faults on both sides – on all sides I suppose I could say – so I will apologise for my part in the misunderstanding. As you can see from the date on this letter I have taken time to reply at some length to your suggestion that we should correspond. To be frank, Dana, I don't think it a good idea. Even remembering how I felt when you first ran away is too painful to contemplate. Going through it twice . . . well, I refuse to consider it. It would be like returning to plunge into a burning building a second time and if you think I'm being absurd and exaggerating I'm sorry, but that's how I feel.

Oh, Dana, this is as hard for me to write as it may be for you to read, but I can't and won't go through it again. It's taken me a long while, but I've made a new life for myself. I have new friends, some of whom are my fellow officers, others not. I'm sure you, too, have new friends and will not miss me. I tell myself we were not just friends but more like brother and sister, so I ought to be able to exchange letters with you, but I find I cannot. I'm really sorry and perhaps one day I'll feel differently but for now at any rate we must both concentrate on our role in the war.

I'm sorry.

Your friend Con.

Dana had started to cry halfway through the letter and was in full flood by the time she reached the end. Con, who had loved her like a sister apparently, had been so badly hurt by her behaviour that he no longer wanted to receive letters from her; her suggestion that he might call in Temperance Court were he ever to visit Liverpool had been completely ignored.

'Dana?' Polly spoke hesitantly. When her friend continued to sob, she pulled a handkerchief from the pocket of her skirt and, leaning across the table, thrust it into her hand. 'Don't tell me; he's been and gone and got married,' she said with an obvious attempt at lightness. 'And what's more he won't accept your apology and says you ought to be beaten like a drum. That right?'

Dana shook her head, mopped her streaming eyes, and blew her nose resoundingly. Then she pushed the rather crumpled pages across to her friend. 'It's worse than that. Much, much worse,' she muttered. 'He doesn't want to write; he says . . . oh, you read it, Polly.'

Polly, who had been staring at the letter as though it might leap from the table and bite her on the nose, tried to spread out the first sheet and muttered a curse as she smeared teardrops. 'Right you are, but whilst I read it you'd best go and give your face and hands a wash and pull yourself together,' she said, speaking briskly though not unkindly. 'Honestly, Dana, for a girl who never shows emotion you can't half cry! This letter is almost as wet as you are.'

Despite her misery, Dana could not help smiling. She, who prided herself upon never crying, had apparently shed a positive river of tears, for now that she looked at Polly's handkerchief it was soaking. She began to apologise, to say she did not know what had come over her, but her voice came out as a croak and instead of the words she had intended to say, far more truthful ones emerged. 'It's a beautiful letter, a far nicer letter than I deserve,' she muttered hoarsely. 'Con's forgiven me, but I don't think I shall ever forgive myself.'

Polly, head bent over the letter, looked up for a moment to jerk a thumb in the direction of the door. 'Go and wash your face and brush your hair; put on a clean blouse if you've got one and then come back and we'll talk as we walk down to the tram stop,' she commanded. 'I know you've had a nasty shock, I know you're very upset, but that's no excuse for turning up late. Jake's an awfully good boss but he is strict on timekeeping, so you'd better pull yourself together. Off with you!'

Dana, gulping, obeyed, and soon the two girls, both neatly dressed and dry eyed though Dana's lids were still swollen, left Temperance Court and headed for the tram stop. As soon as they reached the main road, Dana turned a questioning face to Polly. 'Well? If you'd received a letter like that I bet you'd have cried!'

Polly nodded. 'Course I would, but if you don't mind me saying so, Dana, you deserved that letter. You didn't realise that a feller can be as badly hurt as a girl in the same position. Remember Caitlin? Oh, I know you'll say it's different, but you jilted Con the way Padraig jilted Caitlin. If someone as light-minded and silly as Caitlin can run away from a happy home, good parents and lots of money because she's been let down, then you must admit being jilted is a painful thing.'

'Yes, but I didn't jilt anyone,' Dana said stubbornly. 'And Con wouldn't agree that it was wrong of Feena and Johnny to get wed. He laughed at me, told me to grow up, took their side against me . . .'

'And wasn't he in the perishin' right of it?' Polly pointed out. 'Look how happy your mam is with that Devlin feller! Look how prosperous the estate is and the stud an' all. And did you honestly expect Con to side with you against his own father? Why, Dana, even you knew they were in love! And what good did running away do? It didn't change things. They went ahead and got married and are happy, whereas you have had to struggle just to keep your head above water.'

'Well, yes, but it's Con we're talking about, not me,' Dana pointed out. She spoke rather stiffly, for it was a strange thing for her to be told off by Polly. Usually it was the other way round. 'All right, all right, you've proved your point. I behaved very badly and Con suffered far more than I did as a result of my running

353

away. But surely I should be allowed to be his friend once more so that we can at least exchange letters?'

At this point they had reached the end of the tram queue and the two girls in front of them, recognising Dana from the cafeteria, turned and began to chat, so that it was impossible for Polly and Dana to talk confidentially until they left the tram at the Pier Head and caught the bus which would take them to the door of the Freeway Cinema.

Once ensconced in the bus, however, they were able to resume their conversation in relative privacy. Dana turned to Polly. 'Well? What harm would it do to exchange letters, maybe even to meet up now and then? Three whole years have passed since I ran away from home and as you say they've been hard years, for me at any rate. I ask you, Polly, am I likely to run away again? Of course I'm not. All I'm asking is to be allowed to keep in touch with Con. Feena writes to me and Johnny usually adds a few lines to the letter, so why shouldn't Con?'

Polly sighed. 'Sometimes you're as thick as pea soup and as pig-headed as – as a pig,' she said. 'It's because to Con it would be like picking open an old wound; can't you see how painful . . . oh, God, don't start howling again or they'll likely turn us off the bloody bus. What's up this time, anyway?'

Dana had dived into her handkerchief but now she raised a tear-blubbered face to her friend. 'It's because I know you're right and I suppose Con's right as well,' she said miserably. 'But knowing Con is out there somewhere and I can't even write him a letter makes me feel like a snail torn out of its shell. Oh, Poll, don't you think I might write anyway? He can't stop me, after all. And plain politeness might make him reply so that at least I would know he was still alive.'

But Polly was shaking her head. 'That's the way to get really hurt,' she observed wisely. 'Remember, queen, he is now in possession of your address; even if you were to move he knows he could send a letter to Castletara, secure in the knowledge that Feena or Johnny would make sure that it reached you. You really must learn not to hammer on a locked door. Your Con says in his letter – and I agree it is a beautiful letter – that you have both made new lives for yourselves, and, darling Dana, you have to accept that because of what you did you are no longer a part of his life. Go along with it, and maybe you'll get him back one day. Fight it, refuse to listen to what he's saying, and you've lost the battle.'

Dana thought this over, and just as the bus came to a juddering halt outside the Freeway Cinema she nodded her head. 'All right, I'll just write a couple of lines saying I understand. I won't say anything that needs a reply, I promise; in fact, you can write the letter for me and I'll copy it out word for word. Agreed?'

Polly nodded and jumped to her feet to join the queue of passengers waiting to leave the bus. Neither girl spoke again until they were hurrying down the side passage which led to the staff entrance, and then Dana said, 'Polly Smith, you're years younger than me and not nearly as clever, but you've got something I don't seem to possess, and that's common sense. And now we won't mention Con again until you write that letter for me this evening.'

Polly agreed to this and showed Dana a cheerful and optimistic face whenever their paths crossed in the course

355

of the day, but though she did not intend to show it her heart bled for her friend. The image of a snail torn from its shell haunted her, and though the letter to Con which they dispatched the next day was both short and to the point, Polly longed for the young man to reply, to give her friend at least some hope of an eventual reconciliation. Both she and Dana hurried to meet the postman for the next couple of weeks, but no reply came. And perhaps it's for the best, Polly told herself as she sorted the letters. Perhaps snails can grow new shells if they are forced to do so.

'Pass me the glue.'

Dana and Polly were sitting one on each side of the kitchen table, making paper chains and other decorations, for Christmas was now only days away and everyone was determined that, rationing or no rationing, they would enjoy themselves to the full. So Ernie and Jake had been invited to share a chicken dinner, and Jake had reciprocated with an invitation to come to the small house he and Ralph had shared for a celebration supper. 'Ralph's not allowed out of the training centre so there's no chance of his joining us,' he said regretfully. 'But I dare say we'll manage to enjoy ourselves well enough, and Ernie must come too, of course.'

Now Dana clicked her fingers impatiently. She was making paper chains from old cinema posters which she had cut into strips, and Polly was painting the tips of fir cones with silver glitter. Polly looked into the glue pot then shoved it towards her friend, saying as she did so: 'Sorry, queen, I've used the last and the silver glitter's run out too, so shall we call it a day? If so I'll put the kettle on and make our drinks.' She glanced up at the clock on the mantel and whistled beneath her breath. 'Phew! It's quite late enough to leave off working. We'd best talk about what presents we need to buy for everyone, 'cos there's queues for everything these days.'

'You're right there. I've bought Mam and Johnny's present but I've got nothing yet for Donny. Tell you what, Polly, you know a lot more about kids than I do, so you can tell me what would be a suitable present for a little boy of Donny's age. Until the war sent them all off into the country Temperance Court buzzed with kids and you knew them all. I'm ashamed to admit I couldn't have named one of the scraggly little brutes, apart from the chap who whacked a cricket ball through our living room window. He was Jackie Wilmot, I know that much.'

Polly chuckled. 'I bet he remembers your name an' all, as well as the clack round the head you gave him,' she said.

Dana laughed. 'Good thing I'm not planning a family of my own yet. But I'd like children one day.'

Polly laughed too. 'A good thing indeed,' she said. 'Ernie and I don't mean to have kids until we're quite old – mid-twenties at least, Now, let me think; you say your little brother isn't yet two. Wooden toys are always popular, but I happen to know someone who's trying to sell a model train set. Now that's a present and a half; it'd keep him occupied for hours, give your mam a bit of a break. How old is she anyway?'

'She's forty-three or four; what's wrong with that?' Dana asked aggressively. 'You don't have to be young to have a baby, you know.'

'What a twerp you are, taking offence over a simple

question,' Polly said, imitating Dana's scowl. 'If you think it's rude to ask a daughter her mother's age, then you're even dafter than I thought! It's just that babies are hard work, even for grandmothers.'

Dana jumped up as the kettle began to hiss. 'I'm an idiot, always was, always will be,' she said contritely. 'How much is your friend asking for that train set?'

'I'll find out,' Polly said equably. 'And now I'm taking my cocoa to bed. I'm fair wore out; it's been one hell of a day.'

Dana had had a busy but productive day, for one of the old ladies who sometimes came up to the cafeteria whilst waiting for her bus had looked out an old recipe book she had used during the last war. 'Rationing were bad enough,' she had told Dana, 'but shortages were the worst. It were all right for rich folks, of course, same as it always is. They could pay for steaks, sides of bacon, trays of eggs and bags and bags of sugar, but for the rest of us it were make do and mend, and that included foodstuffs of course. Us poor folk passed our recipes around, so if one woman made a good fruit cake which were mainly grated carrot and another boiled bones for stock and made a pie what tasted like heaven it was soon being copied by half Liverpool.'

Dana had thanked her, not believing she would find the old exercise book at all useful, but flicking through it whilst she waited for the evening rush she had realised she was mining gold. From Mrs Batley's Christmas cake made without dried fruit, marzipan or icing to a steak pie made entirely with vegetables and stock, the book would be invaluable when she was only able to use ingredients which could be obtained from British sources.

Thinking of this kept Dana awake for quite some time, but suddenly she found herself crossing the courtyard at Castletara and heading for the stables, knowing that Con was ahead of her and already saddling up both the tall chestnut gelding, Troubadour, and her own sweet-tempered but frisky gray.

As she crossed the paving she looked around her. It was early in the morning, for the sun was only just edging up over the distant hills, but she could feel its warmth, faint but delicious, when she turned her face up to the sky. Feeling contentment and a sort of lazy anticipation – for she and Con would be hacking out, riding for pleasure, since neither of them would have dreamed of selling their darlings – she pulled open the stable door and slid inside. The warm sweet smell of horses and hay met her and she drew in a deep, ecstatic breath. Lovely to have a day off, for much though she enjoyed the work of the stud it would be grand to ride knee to knee with Con, chatting idly of anything that occurred to them, not bothering to kick her mount into a canter and then a gallop but merely enjoying the creak of leather and the feel of the reins in her hands.

'Con?' He was just lifting her saddle off its peg and turned to greet her, and for a moment, inexplicably, she felt a stab of such sadness that she gasped, but before she could analyse the feeling it was gone and she was happy once more. 'Oh, Con, you've already started to saddle up. Shall I do Troubadour?'

Con placed the saddle in position and started to tighten the girth, and Cloudberry, the gray, began to puff herself out. Dana giggled as Con dug his knee into the mare's round belly, causing her to exhale indignantly. Then he offered the reins to Dana. 'I did him first. Just get hold of these reins and take her into the yard and we'll be up and off before you can say knife.'

'And before Feena or Daddy can change their minds about our day off,' Dana said, smiling to herself. They led the horses out of the stable, mounted without using the block and headed for open country, since, as Con was quick to explain, neither horse had been ridden for several days and would be all the better for a gallop on the downs to shake the fidgets out of its legs.

Dana agreed eagerly and suddenly they were on the downs and the horses were competing to see who could get ahead, necks stretched, eyes wide with the excitement of the race, whilst Con and Dana shouted encouragement, laughed, and when at last the beasts slowed patted sleek, sweating necks and praised each other's mounts. Then they were in a lane, riding between high banks upon which grew hazels, their branches meeting in places over the rider's heads. Con reached up and snatched a handful of nuts, cracking one open with strong white teeth and offering the kernel to Dana; she took it, but said he was not the only one to find free food. Bending down, she began to pick a handful of the little wild strawberries, realising with only the faintest surprise that to find ripe nuts and ripe strawberries at the same time was, to say the least, unusual. She turned to Con and he was smiling at her, but suddenly she read sadness in his smile and even as she held out her handful of berries they disappeared. Startled, and suddenly more than a little afraid, she saw that the day had turned grey and the sunshine had disappeared. Had Con taken the berries? But before she could even ask him he had put a detaining hand on her reins, pulling both their mounts to a halt.

'What's the matter, alanna?' he said softly. 'This is our day off. You're supposed to be enjoying it, not worrying about wild strawberries or hazelnuts.'

'But – but they shouldn't come together,' Dana stammered. 'Strawberries are spring and nuts are autumn. How come we're gathering them at the same time?'

Con's smile this time held nothing but a sort of gentle, mocking amusement. 'Why, hadn't you realised? This is just a dream,' he said matter of factly. 'And it's got to last us for a long, long time, dearest Dana. A long, long, long, long . . .'

'Don't go, Con! Oh, Con, don't go!' Dana begged, her voice rising as her eyes filled with tears. 'What do you mean, it's got to last us for a long time?'

But the scene was fading and Con was growing misty, though when she reached out and grabbed his hands he seemed, for one moment, as solid as she. She gripped his fingers fiercely, repeating the words he had uttered, but then she was awake in her own bed and the church clock was striking the quarter.

Chapter Fourteen

Thoroughly awake now, Dana touched her cheek and was not surprised to find it wet. What an extraordinary dream! It had been so real, and so delightful, until the moment when she had bent down to pick the wild strawberries. And Con had been so real, not angry with her, not even disappointed in her, but simply accepting her for what she was: his loving companion. Lying there in the dark she tried to make sense of what he had said; that this meeting – had he meant a meeting? – would have to last them for a long, long time. But why on earth was she worrying? It was a dream, damn it. Dreams are neither logical nor real. If only she had thought, she would have realised earlier, when they had suddenly arrived at the downs without threading their way through lanes and across meadows. And they had reached the lane leading back to Castletara in an equally unreal fashion. She was being a complete fool. The truth was, she had longed so passionately for Con to reply to her last letter that he had forced his way into her sleep, upsetting her as his letter had upset her. She really must do as he said: put him out of her mind, forget him completely and get on with living her own life. But it occurred to her that though they might not plan to meet, meetings can happen unintentionally. Next time she returned to Castletara Con might already be there, on leave from his airfield and giving a helping hand. As for dreams, who was he to say that they could not meet again in dreams? I'll jolly well dream of him if I want to, Dana told herself crossly. I can dream about anyone if I set my mind to it; bloody Conan Devlin is no exception! And on the thought she turned her head into the pillow and surprised even herself by falling immediately asleep.

She did not dream.

Christmas was over and Dana was back in the cafeteria preparing for the rush of customers who always arrived as soon as the main feature finished. She looked up as the swing doors were violently opened and Ernie burst into the room.

'Hey, Dana! If I get fish and chips can I come to supper with you and Polly? They've made me up to supervisor at the perishin' factory, which means a rise in pay of ninepence an hour, so I want to celebrate.'

Dana, who was making a big pile of Spam and HP sauce sandwiches, stopped work to go over and give him a congratulatory handshake. 'Well done, old Ern,' she said, beaming at him, for she was well aware of how he longed to be able to sport a uniform and talk of his war service. But sensible Ernie was making the best of it and she knew he must have worked like a dog to get promotion. 'Won't Polly be tickled pink, though? Perhaps the two of you might get married even sooner than you'd planned; why not? You'll both be earning good money—'

'That's it!' Ernie said excitedly. That's what I'm going

to suggest to Poll when we meet this evening and I tell her about me promotion. But right now I'm going to buy me sixpenn'orth of dark.' He sighed dramatically. 'Polly's usheretting in the circle tonight, isn't she? If it's a quiet night we'll mebbe have one of the double seats to ourselves. Ooh, that'd be grand, that would!'

'It would probably lose Polly her job,' Dana said severely, but with twitching lips. Ernie had been courting Polly for a while now but Dana knew he would never overstep the mark. He had once told her that Polly was too precious for such things, and besides, she deserved to have all the pomp and splendour of a white wedding even though, if they married in wartime, she would have to buy a second-hand dress from Paddy's market and probably sell it back immediately after the ceremony.

'Only joking,' Ernie said now, grinning. 'See you later then, Dee.'

It was another couple of hours before the two girls finished work that night and they were glad of Ernie's escort, for Liverpool was a busy port and there were always seamen coming ashore and hoping to meet a young lady who, for a small sum, would become a 'friend' for an hour or two. In Ernie's company, however, they knew they would be unmolested. Polly had been delighted with Ernie's news, though she said that a rise of ninepence an hour did not seem a great deal when you considered the responsibilities of the supervisor's job. The three of them walked along, chatting idly, and presently caught a tram going in the right direction. They were soon at the front door of the flat in Temperance Court, and when they had let themselves in to the hall Polly immediately dived into the wire basket beneath the letter box to sort out their post from that of other tenants. Because it was so late, however, the only mail left in the box was for the girls. Polly scooped it up, gave a little squeak of satisfaction and handed Dana two envelopes. 'Two for you and one for me,' she said gaily, inserting her key into their lock and thrusting the door open. 'Gosh, them fish and chips smell so good I swear I could eat the lot, newspaper an' all.'

Dana bustled into the room, which was deliciously warm after the icy breath of the December wind, and opened up the front of the stove so that the room grew even warmer. Then she went to the Welsh dresser, got down three plates, cutlery, salt and vinegar and set them out on the kitchen table whilst Ernie pulled the kettle over the flame and began to warm the pot. 'I'll brew the tea . . .' he was beginning when he noticed Polly staring at the envelope with her name upon it as though it were a poisonous snake about to strike. 'What's the matter, Poll?' he asked curiously. 'Hopin' if you stare hard enough you'll see straight through the envelope, is that it? It 'ud be a lot easier to open the perishin' thing.'

Polly pushed a finger tentatively under a corner of the flap and then turned to Dana. 'Who's yours from, queen?' She leaned across to peer at the envelopes which her friend had tossed down on the table. 'Aha! Sherlock Holmes Smith will tell you without so much as laying a finger on your letters. The one in the white envelope is from your mam and the one in the blue envelope is from Ralph. Sherlock Holmes Smith reckernises the writing.'

Dana nodded. 'That's right,' she admitted. 'But why don't you open yours, Poll? It looks kind of official. Put me out of my misery, girl, for as you well know I'm curious as a cat.'

'Oh, shut up jabberin' and butter some bread to go with the fish and chips,' Polly said. She put her hands to her warm cheeks. 'I don't think I'll open my letter just yet. I'll wait till Ernie's gone home.'

'People who are going to marry one day don't keep secrets from each other,' Ernie said reprovingly. 'Now I'm a man of substance, our Polly, I don't see no reason why we have to wait for the war to end. What with kids being evacuated and factory workers moving out of the city to be near their work I reckon we could afford to rent a couple of rooms, or even a little house. What say we give it a go, queen?'

But Polly had opened her letter. She stared at the first page, for there were several, and Dana saw her lips moving as she read the contents to herself, saw also her cheeks begin to flame with excitement. Then she flung her arms round Ernie's neck and gave him a kiss, flourishing the papers under his nose as she did so. 'Oh, Ernie, ain't I the cleverest gal you ever did meet?' she said exultantly. 'Remember when the government closed all the cinemas and that, and Dana and meself were out of a job? Well, I applied to join the WAAFs, had me interview and passed me medical all right, but of course there was a rush of girls wanting to join so we were told there might be a bit of a wait before we were either accepted or rejected. And I'm accepted, got me rail pass an' all, and I'll be off to the training centre next Monday week!'

Dana gasped, a hand flying to her mouth, and was hard put to it to hide her very real dismay. It had never occurred to her that Polly might volunteer for one of the services, and even had it done so she would not have thought her friend would have been accepted. She was so small and slight, looking more like a twelve-year-old than a young woman. But it would not be tactful to say so. Instead, she conjured up a delighted smile. 'Oh, Polly what wonderful news, but *how* we shall miss you! It'll be awful trying to manage the Freeway without you, but even worse here, in Temperance Court. Indeed, if it wasn't for my promise to Jake, I'd follow your example and— Whatever is the matter, Ernie?'

Ernie's face had turned plum-coloured, and to Dana's considerable distress she saw a tear trickle down his cheek, to be impatiently brushed away. 'The matter? What the devil do you think is the matter? I'm a feller, I am, fit as a bleedin' fiddle, strong as a perishin' ox, yet the buggers have turned me down, not just once but three effin' times, and now this – this little blonde nothin' goes and gets took on by the bleedin' WAAF! There's me, proud as a bloody peacock over bein' made up to supervisor, with an extra ninepence an hour an' all, about to say we'd get married on the strength of it, and – and . . .'

Polly looked as dismayed as Ernie clearly felt. 'I'm – I'm that sorry, Ernie. I forgot you'd been turned down,' Polly said, and Dana reflected that her friend had spoken with even less tact than usual. 'I expect it's because they don't have nearly as many women volunteers as they do men. But surely you can see it's good that they want me? I may be a little blonde nothin', like you said, but somebody thinks I'll be useful,' she finished, some bravado entering her tone.

Dana began to speak, to say that she was sure Ernie had not meant to call names, but he overrode her, his eyes flashing indignantly, his face still red with both temper and disappointment. 'Awright, awright, I shouldn't of called you names,' he said grudgingly. 'But you shouldn't of applied to the air force without telling me.'

But now Dana could see by her friend's pink cheeks and sparkling eyes that Polly's blood was up. The younger girl stamped her foot and put both hands on her hips, glaring at Ernie as though he were a German storm trooper about to attack her. 'Oh yeah, Mr Wonderful? And just what would you have done if I had told you I'd applied? Answer me that! I suppose you'd have gone to the recruiting office and crossed me name off the list. Well ha bloody ha, a fat lot of notice they'd have took of you. I've signed on, I tell you.'

Ernie snorted. 'Oh, signed on, have you? Then you can bloody well sign off,' he shouted, apparently forgetting that his voice was probably audible all over Temperance Court; and if so this entire conversation was being eagerly overheard by any residents still up at this hour. 'You can get down to that recruiting office first thing tomorrow morning and take your name off of the list! Say you done it without your feller knowing; that'll fix it.'

Dana stared from face to face, reflecting that they looked like a pair of indignant terriers cheated of a rat. Ernie's fair hair stood on end, his hands were clenched into fists and his face was still scarlet, whilst Polly's face was rapidly beginning to resemble his, in colour at least. Dana stopped buttering bread and shouted at her companions to shut up. Too late, of course, she told herself ruefully, but at least if it came to blows, which looked likely, Polly and Ernie would not have an audience listening to their every word.

However, it seemed the mere reminder that they might be overheard had been enough to bring the combatants down to earth, though not, alas, to end the dispute. Polly was still defiant, Ernie still insistent that she should say she had changed her mind, and presently Dana decided that she would have to take sides, though reluctantly. The couple were still swapping insults – Ernie was a pig-headed bossy beast, Polly a stubborn stupid kid – when Dana's voice rose, shouting them both down. 'Polly, Ernie, behave yourselves! Squabbling like a pair of kids in a kindergarten is all very well but I'm afraid, Ernie, that Polly has a point. She signed on, passed her medical and her interview and has been accepted as a member of His Majesty's air force. She can't simply change her mind, nor let you change it for her. And as for her not telling you she'd applied . . . well, you've rather proved her point, haven't you? You would have kicked up an enormous fuss . . .'

'No I wouldn't, because I'd never have believed for one moment that she'd be accepted,' Ernie said unwisely. Polly gave a gasp of outrage, bounced across the few feet which separated them and punched Ernie on the nose with enough force to send him staggering backwards. He crashed into Dana's table, sending bread and butter, battered fish, chips and the bottle of vinegar flying, and added to his unpopularity by bleeding over everything from his poor injured nose.

Polly, clearly aghast by what she had done, began to

369

try to apologise, but Ernie was having none of it. 'Say what you like, that was an – an unprovoked attack,' he said stiffly. 'I didn't do nuffin', so you can bloody well clear up the mess you made, Polly. I'm off.' And before either of the others could stop him he had slammed out of the kitchen and they could hear him clattering across the cobbles and disappearing into the blackout.

Left to themselves the two girls stared rather helplessly at the chaos surrounding them, then without exchanging another word began to clear up. Polly collected the ruined fish and chips, offering rather timidly to save any food which was not spotted or streaked with Ernie's blood, but Dana, with a shudder, refused this well-meant offer.

'I'm afraid it will all have to go into the bin, because they truly aren't fit for human consumption,' she said firmly, ignoring Polly's muttered reminder that there was a war on. 'Fetch the jam out of the pantry, Poll, and I'll cut some more bread and butter. It's a pity about poor Ernie's fish supper, but we've got bread and jam, which will have to fill the chinks. There's plenty for all three of us, if Ernie deigns to return after what you did to him.'

Polly gave a rather watery giggle. 'Since it's already eleven o'clock – no, a quarter past – I can't see him coming back tonight,' she observed. 'But I'll bet my bottom dollar that he turns up at the Freeway as soon as his shift finishes tomorrow, full of apologies for all the horrible things he said. Oh, Dana, I swear I didn't mean to clout him on the snitch . . .'

'I'm sure you didn't,' Dana agreed readily, 'but it's a good thing he's been brought up never to hit a lady because for one minute, just before the blood started to flow, I thought I read retribution in his eye. But I am sure you're right and he'll come round just as soon as he can.'

But Dana was wrong. Three days passed and both Dana and Polly were beginning to get seriously worried. On the fourth day, Polly screwed up her courage and rang Ernie's factory from the call box on the corner. She could not speak to Ernie himself but left a message which the girl on the switchboard promised faithfully to pass on. All Polly said was: 'Missing you. Come to supper tonight after the Freeway closes.' She had wanted to add 'It won't be fish and chips!' but Dana had dissuaded her.

'You may still think it's funny but I expect Ernie's nose is still the shape and colour of a ripe tomato, and if you ask me he's probably sporting a black eye as well. I expect he'll want to be able to look dignified when he sees you next.'

Polly had looked aghast. 'A black eye?' she quavered. 'Oh, Dana, will he ever forgive me?' But when the girls arrived back at Temperance Court that evening they saw him in the faint moonlight, standing by the front door and clutching a large, newspaper-wrapped parcel.

Polly, still conscience-stricken, began to apologise for the happenings at their previous meeting, but Ernie took the key from Dana in a masterful manner, unlocked the door and ushered them into the kitchen, then lit the lamp. As Dana had foretold, there was purplish bruising beneath his right eye and across his cheek, but his smile, as he unwrapped the large parcel of fish and chips, was triumphant. 'Shurrup, our Polly, and let a feller get a word in edgeways,' he said genially. 'I've got an announcement to make.' He pushed Polly into a chair and waited whilst Dana, too, sat down, then cleared his throat and puffed out his chest. 'You ain't the only one what's going to fight for her country, Polly Smith,' he announced. 'I've been and gone and joined the merchant fleet, without havin' to answer one question concernin' why I wheezes when I has to run half a mile. So what do you think of that?'

For a moment both girls were too stunned to speak. Then, quite unexpectedly, Polly burst into tears, jumped up from her seat and flung her arms round Ernie's neck. 'You mustn't, you can't, I won't let you,' she wailed, tears spouting from her eyes like fountains. 'I were talkin' to Tommy Finch what lives two doors down and he were telling me about something called the wolf pack, what the Germans have got skulkin' under the Atlantic. He says they torpedo our merchant ships 'cos it's like it used to be in the old days . . .' she turned tear-drenched eyes upon Dana, 'you know, the king's troops or whatever would lay siege to a town and try and starve 'em out. That's what this here wolf pack will do – attack the ships bringin' supplies from America to try to starve *us* out. And o'course the men on the ships will either drown or be killed by the wolf pack when they's strugglin' in the water. Oh, oh, oh, it's all my fault. I wish I'd never joined the perishin' WAAF, 'cos then you'd not of even thought about goin' to sea! Oh, and there's aircraft what'll bomb the ships to stop them gettin' through with grub and guns . . .'

But at this point Dana thought it best to intervene, for she had seen the colour drain from Ernie's face and a look of considerable trepidation appear in his eyes. Hastily, she got to her feet and tapped Polly's shoulder, and then, when Polly did not respond, she tugged her friend free from Ernie's embrace and spoke sternly. 'Polly Smith, how dare you say such stupid things! Do you think the Navy are sailing across the Atlantic just for show? Haven't you heard of convoys? Our fighting ships surround the merchant shipping and keep it safe. They've got things called depth charges which blow submarines apart, and of course if the Jerries are lucky and score a hit on one of our ships, the fellers take to the lifeboats and are picked up and brought back to port by their rescuers. So, though what Ernie will be doing is just as brave as though he were in the Royal Navy and not the merchant fleet, he'll be fine, honestly he will.'

'Oh,' Polly said doubtfully. She rubbed at her tear-wet cheeks. Then a fresh thought occurred to her and the tears welled up again. 'Oh, but if I'd known Ernie was going to sea, I'd have applied to join the Wrens. I might even of got on the same ship as him!'

'No you wouldn't,' Dana said hastily, grinning at Ernie, who was once more looking both proud and happy. 'Wrens don't go to sea, WAAFs don't fly in aeroplanes and Ats – they're the army girls, the ATS – don't get issued with rifles or – or bayonets. And now let's start on the fish and chips before they go cold and greasy.'

Once in her own bed that night, however, Dana gave her future serious thought. All around her, women were joining one or other of the forces and she realised that she longed to be one of them. Uniforms apart, the Land Army definitely beckoned. She knew farming, could drive a tractor or manage a team of horses on the plough, and do many other things which farmers and their wives and children learned as a matter of course. But she had given Jake her word that she would look after his precious cinema, and though the prospect seemed horribly dull when compared with the excitements of life in any of the forces, she did not feel she could go back on the promise which she had given to Jake so easily, and with so little thought. It was all very well telling herself that circumstances altered cases; her one attempt at finding someone to cover for her as manageress of the whole cinema had nearly ended in disaster. She had seen half a dozen applicants, most of whom were elderly and seemed to consider that working for a woman was something they preferred not to tolerate. The man she had eventually appointed, however, seemed perfect for the job. He was in his forties, handsome and self-confident, and had managed one of the big cinemas in London before returning to his Liverpool home to keep an eye on his elderly mother, left a widow after his father's death. Jimmy Strange did not object to taking orders from a woman, agreed with her choice of films and seemed willing to muck in, doing any job that needed an extra pair of hands from waiting on in the cafeteria to selling tickets, ushering folk to their seats, or selling ice cream, popcorn and chocolate bars during the interval.

He had been with them a month when Dana, checking the books, noticed discrepancies which should not have been there. Frowning, she checked the sums taken against the tickets sold, and her heart sank like a stone. Jimmy was so good at his job, so cheerful and efficient! The staff liked him to a man – or rather to a woman – and his willingness to ease the load, which Dana sometimes felt almost crushed her, had been a tremendous bonus. Ask Jimmy to work a double shift, see him in the kitchen poaching eggs whilst one of the waitresses made toast, come across him in the auditorium clearing the ice cream wrappers and popcorn bags which careless customers had abandoned as they had left, and you had to admire him.

Dana, having noticed the disparities, mentioned them to Jimmy, who said apologetically that, because the job was so new to him, he had undoubtedly made mistakes. This had relieved Dana's mind considerably. She felt that to lose his help would be more than she could bear, and so they had soldiered on. Indeed, Jimmy might still have been working at the Freeway – and creaming off money in a dozen different ways – had one of the customers not lost a gold watch. She was an old lady and it was an antique fob watch valued by its owner for sentimental reasons as well as its worth, which was considerable. Jimmy had been helping the cleaners to get the auditorium cleared and had lined the cleaners up, demanding sternly that they turn out their pockets. They did so willingly enough and Jimmy was just dismissing them and telling the tearful old lady that she must have lost the watch somewhere else when Dana appeared on the scene, demanding to know what was going on. Jimmy told her, and was repeating that the watch must have been lost elsewhere when Dana, standing by him, saw that his right hand was plunged into his pocket. Without giving herself time to consider, she grabbed his wrist and jerked his hand out of its resting place, bringing with it something which shone and sparkled as it flew into the next row of seats.

Speechlessly, Dana stared at the man she had both liked and trusted, and he stared back as boldly as though he had never seen an antique gold watch, far less had it

375

in his pocket. 'What did you do that for?' he asked in an injured tone. 'I were just about to give it to the lady when you snatched it from my hand and chucked it into the next row of seats. I'm surprised at you, Miss McBride; anyone might have thought I meant to steal the perishin' thing, which probably ain't worth tuppence.'

Dana reached across and picked up the watch. She was burning with anger but realised that there was only one thing she could do. She handed the old lady her property, then turned to Jimmy Strange. 'Well, Mr Strange, I dare say it will be no surprise to you to learn that I've had my suspicions of your honesty for some time. You think you're very clever, but you weren't clever enough to cook the books so that I wouldn't notice. Don't come in tomorrow – or ever again for that matter – and don't expect a week's salary in lieu of notice. I'm pretty sure a solicitor would say you should be prosecuted, but I don't have the time for such goings on.'

Jimmy Strange stared at her. 'Just you watch yourself, you jumped-up ginger-headed little bitch,' he said, and afterwards Dana thought that the worst thing was that he kept his voice low and even pleasant, though the words he spoke were full of malice. 'You can keep your effin' job. I wouldn't work for you any longer if you were to pay me a hundred pound a minute, and you won't find it easy to replace me 'cos I'll put the word around, so I will. Half the staff'll leave 'cos they'll know you set me up, and t'other half – the half what stays – ain't worth spit.'

He spat on the words and the cleaning staff, mostly elderly ladies, who had been listening, fascinated, to the conversation, blinked. After a moment the oldest and most vociferous of them, a Mrs Butterworth, surged forward. 'Why you nasty, thievin' little bastard,' she said indignantly, pointing at Jimmy. 'One or two of us has had our doubts about you and now we know we was right. The usherettes have missed popcorn and chocolate bars; they thought it were the delivery company and accused the chap on the van of short-changin' us, but there were those among us – me for one – what thought otherwise.' She turned to Dana, 'You tell the scuffers, Miss Mac! He'd of stole that watch if you'd not acted quick. You go and get the scuffers whiles me and me mates hang on to him.'

Dana had turned to the man beside her, but he had gone. The last she saw of him was his dark figure legging it to the exit.

Remembering the incident, and how unhappy it had made her, Dana sighed to herself. When she had eventually discovered the extent of Jimmy Strange's perfidy she had determined to pay back every penny and had done so, despite the fact that Jimmy's little excursions into dishonesty had made up to quite a sum. All the staff had been wonderfully supportive, and Polly, dear Polly, had insisted on paying her share of what they referred to as 'Jimmy's debt', because she said she had suspected him from the first – too smarmy, too eager to please, too perishin' hard-workin' – of not being what he seemed, but had done nothing about it.

But now the debt was paid, Polly and Ernie had gone their separate ways and the cinema was doing even better than it had in Jake's day. With the help of the cookery book from the Great War, Dana's offerings in the cafeteria were much admired and extremely popular. Customers often queued for tables, sometimes even people who had not attended the cinema performance, and Dana paid in at the bank two or three times a week, because the Jimmy Strange episode had taught her a valuable lesson. Dishonesty comes in various guises, and to keep more money than was necessary on the premises could be to put temptation into the way of someone who would not turn thief for a few shillings but might do so for a few pounds.

Time passed. Polly left for her training centre and wrote to Dana two or three times a week; she was very happy. Ernie joined his ship the *Sarah Jane* and wrote to Polly almost every day, though he was only able to post the letters on his return to port. Naturally enough, Polly relayed the information Ernie gave her in her letters to Dana, and Dana, writing back with stories of nights spent fire watching and days spent cooking, cleaning and doing the cinema's books, felt tempted to invent, for hers was dull work, no matter how you looked at it. And lonely. Very soon after Polly's departure, Dana realised that she had never been so completely alone, save for the short period – a matter of weeks – between Caitlin's leaving Temperance Court and Polly's moving in.

What was worse, she and only she was in command. After the awful experience with Jimmy Strange she had determined not to employ anyone else in a managerial position who might take advantage of the easy way she had always run things. Besides, as the war progressed she became a fire watcher, an air raid precautions warden, and anything else which would help when air raids began. No one doubted that eventually this would happen all over the country, though at present the

Luftwaffe were concentrating mainly on London and the south.

'But they'll soon get our measure and come up to ports such as Liverpool and Barrow-in-Furness,' Ralph said in one of his letters. 'A good job there's a nice deep shelter only twenty yards or so from the Freeway; mind you go there as soon as the sirens sound.'

Since the sirens sounded mainly at night, and at night Dana was in the city centre fire watching, the shelter was of little use to her or to the patrons of the Freeway, long since dispersed in the home-going crowd, but she did not say so to Ralph. Instead she wrote funny, cheerful letters, knowing he enjoyed receiving them and wishing desperately that she could send the same sorts of epistles to Con. This, however, was impossible, since he had never replied to the letter she had sent in response to his own long and painful one. She got news of him through Feena and Johnny and hoped that he heard of her by the same circuitous route; if he wanted to, that is. Alone in her position as manager of both the cinema and the cafeteria, alone in her rooms at Temperance Court, Dana soldiered on. She wrote to Jake, telling him she felt a fraud because she was neither in the forces nor making munitions, but she never suggested that she might find a replacement for herself, or that she might abandon her post. Jake was in the thick of it, and his replies to her letters revealed how he longed to hear every detail about the Freeway. His plans for the cinema when the war was over were a trifle grandiose, but Dana took them with a pinch of salt. She guessed he was just dreaming, and everyone deserved their dreams, so she never said anything in her own letters which might bring him down to earth.

If I do happen to meet someone who could take my place and manage the cinema alone then I do believe I could find a second person to cope with the cafeteria, Dana told herself in bed one night, letting herself relax and turning her pillow so that the cool side was against her cheek. If I could do that then I really might abandon the cinema and join the Land Army. Oh, what bliss it would be to smell fresh air and green grass instead of dust, plush seats and celluloid! But that time had not yet come and right now, she told herself firmly, she meant to go to sleep and dream of Castletara and Con.

In fact, so tired was she that she dreamed of cinemas, and cooking, burning in her dream a great many cakes, and having to promise an indignant Jake that she would not only pay him for all the ruined ingredients but would make the cakes again the very next time she had a day off.

In the morning, still groggy with sleep, she actually thought the dream a reality, and was planning how she could possibly obtain cake ingredients when rationing – and shortages – made every ounce of sugar or flour precious, when the truth dawned and she gave a snort of amusement. It had only been a dream, and she had best get washed and dressed or she would miss her tram and be late for work – almost as blameworthy as burning a bunch of fancy cakes!

Chapter Fifteen

June 1940

Dana was cooking for the cafeteria when the knock came at the door. Sighing, she was about to dust off her hands and answer it when the door was pushed open and Ernie's grinning face appeared in the aperture. 'Hi, Dee!' he said cheerfully. 'Didn't expect to see me, did you? I thought I'd pop in just so's you could drop our Polly a line, let her know I'm still in the land of the livin' so to speak. All right if I come in?'

'Course it is, and it's wonderful to see you,' Dana said at once. 'We've been worried about you, though of course we realised you'd had no chance to write home. I take it you've been involved in this rescue thing that everyone's talking about?'

'That's right; the old *Sarah Jane* was one of the ships sent to Dunkirk to get the BEF back from the continong, but the troops are all home now – well, all the ones who made it to the beaches – so as soon as the old girl is patched up we'll be off on another Atlantic run.' He came right into the room as he was speaking, put the kettle on and peered inquisitively at the paraphernalia of baking spread out all over the kitchen table. 'Have you taken in lodgers or something? There's enough food here to feed an army!'

Dana laughed. 'No, no, I'm still on my own, apart from when Polly is on leave of course. I'm baking for the cafeteria; just scones and stuff like that. But I'm making a mince and onion pie, so if you'd like to share it you can stay for lunch. And whilst the kettle's boiling you can jolly well be useful. There's a bag of peas in the pantry waiting to be podded . . .'

'Peas!' Ernie's eyes glistened. 'Cor, that'd be a treat and a half that would. We don't get much fresh food of any description whilst we're at sea, which is most of the time of course. We've just come back from America with a load of grub, weapons and so forth, and some stupid clerk made a mess of revictualling us. We ran out of food just off Ireland except for half a bag of spuds, so even the thought of fresh peas sets all me juices goin'.' He emerged from the pantry with the bag of peas, shed his jacket and sat down opposite Dana. 'Mind if I eat a pod or two?'

Dana was beginning to say that he could help himself when her eyes widened and she peered more closely at her companion. 'Ernie, you're wounded! And that bandage is all bloodstained. Whatever happened? Do you want a fresh dressing?'

Ernie, grinning bashfully, shook his head. 'Nah, it's fine,' he said airily, and then, apparently seeing the concern on Dana's face, continued, 'It ain't nothin' really, only a scratch. Someone said the dockers – the thieving buggers – had left some pineapples down in the hold, and of course there was a rush to be the first to get 'em. Me and a mate made for the companionway at the same moment, and I caught my arm on a nail sticking out at the side.' He grinned as Dana laughed. 'But don't you go tellin' nobody 'cos everyone thinks I got it in mortal combat. Poll writ to you lately? Last time I heard from her she was waiting for her posting. Could be anywhere in Great Britain, she said; fancy that, hey? I can just see our Poll eatin' haggis and wearin' a kilt.'

'She'd not had the posting last time she wrote,' Dana told him. 'I'm hoping she'll come in this direction so we can meet occasionally. I suppose I could telephone her – I've done it a couple of times – but it's not really very satisfactory. She's awfully shy on the phone; first of all she shouts and then I ask her questions and there are these long pauses. I'll tell her that you're safe and that your ship was one of the ones getting the BEF to safety, though.'

Ernie, expertly podding peas, nodded his agreement. 'Ta, Dee. As for callin' her station, I ain't comfortable on the phone either,' he acknowledged. 'But tell me where you got these peas from. Fresh veggies and fruit is like gold dust, so how come this here bag is bulging with pods?'

'I've a pal with an allotment just a bus ride from the cinema; he's agreed to go shares with his produce if I help with the heavy digging, planting and weeding.'

'Cor, Dee, that 'ud be great, especially the peas,' Ernie said enthusiastically. 'Who's the feller? Ought I to tell Ralph? He might not be all that pleased.'

'Tell anyone you like,' Dana said rather crossly. Ralph, she knew, was writing to a South African girl and hoped to marry her once the war was over. But there was no point in telling Ernie that. Because she and Ralph exchanged letters, everyone took it for granted that they were a couple, which was downright daft, since she wrote to Jake as well without anyone getting the wrong idea. She supposed it was because Ralph was younger than Jake and had taken her out a few times before the war had started. Now, she looked consideringly at Ernie before answering. 'But don't go getting all excited. My pal is old Mr Levitt the projectionist – Bruce's replacement. I'm sure you remember him.'

'Oh aye,' Ernie said, losing interest. 'Okay if I just nip round to see me old boss, the feller who made me up to supervisor at the factory? Then I'll be back here, fair dribblin' at the thought of your cooking.'

When Ernie had gone Dana's thoughts flew to the rescue work upon which he and others had been engaged. Was it really a triumph, or was it, in fact, a miserable retreat? Mr Churchill had called it 'a miracle of deliverance' and also 'a colossal military disaster'. Which was it? She supposed that it was a mixture of both, but now that the troops were home they would be on hand to tackle an invasion if such a thing were to happen.

If only I could help, she thought miserably, cutting out scones and sliding them on to a baking tray. If only I wasn't tied to the Freeway by my promise to keep it running for Jake and Ralph. How she envied Polly! The air force had taught her friend to drive, and to maintain whichever car she was given. Polly was entirely happy, whether driving the gharry to pick up troops having time off in the nearest town or at the wheel of a staff car, with a wing commander sitting behind her, either stiff and starchy or young and friendly, she did not much mind which.

I've driven a tractor since I was ten or twelve; I'm sure I'd learn to drive in no time at all, given the opportunity, Dana thought enviously. But though it would be nice if things were different, I really am doing useful work. I'm giving entertainment and relief to a great many people by simply keeping the Freeway open, and I'm feeding people for a reasonable cost whenever they're prepared to climb the long flight of stairs up to the cafeteria. Perhaps one day . . .

But a glance at the clock told her to rescue her scones, just as the door shot open and Ernie bounced into the room once more. 'Told you I wouldn't be two ticks,' he said breezily. 'What's showin' at the Freeway this evenin'? Usually our turn-round at this end is so quick we scarce have time to make a phone call once the dockers have shifted our cargo.'

'It's a comedy, with Walter Pidgeon and Deanna Durbin,' Dana said at once. '*It's a Date.*'

Ernie sniggered. 'I haven't even asked you yet,' he said, grinning. 'We don't want to make Polly jealous, do we?'

'It's the title of the film, as if you didn't know, and if anyone ought to be jealous it's you,' Dana said rather unkindly. 'While you're crossing the bounding main with a load of other seamen Polly's driving handsome officers around in her staff car and probably getting asked out ten times a day.'

She expected Ernie to scoff at this and felt guilty when she saw his expression change to a look of real worry. 'I hope to God you're wrong,' he muttered. 'But she looks so cute in her uniform . . . oh, I dunno . . .'

'Oh, Ernie, for goodness' sake! I was only teasing, the same as you were when you asked about Ralph,' Dana said quickly. 'Polly's a one-man woman; she loves you and means to marry you whether you want her to or not, so for heaven's sake stop worrying.'

'Right,' Ernie said, though he did not sound particularly convinced. 'My, that mince and onion pie smells good! Tell you what, I'll nip down to the corner shop and buy a bottle of Corona to go with it.'

'That'll be grand,' Dana said. She hesitated, then continued, 'I'm really sorry I teased you about Polly and her officers. Please forget I said it, because playing an underhand game is the last thing Polly'd do.'

That evening, Ernie watched *It's a Date* from a seat in the circle and Dana, who was acting as usherette, watched it for the third time in a week from the stalls. The moment the National Anthem finished she nipped up the stairs to prepare for the evening rush, and when Ernie reappeared she insisted that he should have poached eggs on the house. He told her that the *Sarah Jane* would be sailing in the early hours of the next morning and since Dana would be fire watching they said their goodbyes on the pavement outside the Freeway, both promising to write, though Dana was well aware that Ernie's letters were more like scrappy notes. However, he shook her hand on parting, thanking her both for her company and for what he described as all the delicious grub. Then he hurried off to rejoin his ship, and Dana went home to write a letter to Polly, telling her that her young man was safe and would be writing himself as soon as he had the opportunity. It was well after midnight when she finally sought her bed, and if she dreamed at all she had no recollection of it when day dawned.

Almost a year after the BEF had been brought home, Dana went back to Temperance Court after a sixth night of horrendous raids upon the city.

The Luftwaffe had indeed got their measure and attacked with a vengeance. Dana had been fire watching on the roof of a large warehouse and remembered how the previous May they had blessed the weather gods for sending a flat calm and almost no breeze to aid the BEF's evacuation. Now, the clear skies and good visibility were on the enemy's side. Of course the ack-ack batteries and the Spitfires had done their best, but the sheer volume of heavy bombers droning over the city had continued their attack until the people on the streets, the home guard and ARP wardens, had not known which way to turn. Dana thought that the wonderful weather they were enjoying was the reason for the heavy raids which the Luftwaffe had flown to such terrible effect. After wearily crossing the court and fumbling her key into the lock, her first action when she entered the kitchen was to put the kettle on, and her second to glance at the clock on the mantel. Good! She would have a cup of tea and then go to bed for a couple of hours, for it was generally understood that shops, cinemas and theatres would open a little later than usual after such heavy and relentless bombing. She drank her tea and crawled into bed but found she could not sleep. A thousand worries chased themselves round and round inside her head. Friends in other parts of the city might be dead or badly injured and she would know nothing about it until the lists were posted. There were friends in other towns and cities too, for she supposed that Liverpool was unlikely to be the only place targeted by the Nazis. The south coast ports were regularly attacked, for France had fallen the previous year and the bombers no longer had so far to fly to reach their destination.

Dana tried turning her pillow, counting sheep, even counting racehorses, but nothing worked, so she slid out of bed, dressed herself, grabbed some bread and jam from the cupboard and set off for the Freeway. There was always work needing doing at the cinema so she might as well get on with it. Once outside in the gentle sunshine, however, she wavered for a moment. It would be lovely to catch a bus and go out to the allotment, which was now hers and hers alone since Mr Levitt had moved in with his granddaughter, who lived quite near the Freeway. The young woman had a small cottage with a big garden, and this kept her grandfather quite busy enough without the additional work of the allotment. Dana had taken it over and enjoyed her time spent there, finding even the hardest work relaxing when compared with managing the cinema as well as the cafeteria.

Emerging from the court, she was heading for the tram stop when she suddenly remembered it was very unlikely that any trams would be running. The metal rails were splintered and broken, rearing out of the roadway like angry snakes. Bomb craters were everywhere, buildings vanished completely or reduced to a mere heap of rubble, and people looking dazed and grey as they wandered about, unable to recognise what had once been their homes.

After she had walked a fair distance, however, a bus overtook her and in response to her frantically waving hand drew up alongside. She asked the conductor where he was bound and heard with relief that the vehicle would take her to within a few hundred yards of the cinema. Thanking her lucky stars that the Freeway was closer to the suburbs than the city centre, she collapsed into her seat, voicing the thought as she paid the conductor that surely the bombers would bypass them tonight, since there could be very little left to destroy. The docks had been heavily hit, the Mersey was full of sunken shipping and the warehouses which had contained the food the country so badly needed were still blazing. Dana and the conductor agreed that they would all be the better for a night's rest – they were fellow fire watchers – and then the conductor dinged his bell, the bus swerved to the side of the road and stopped, and Dana climbed down.

She nearly walked passed the Freeway Cinema. It was just a mound of cream-coloured bricks with a great crater in the middle; it had clearly taken a direct hit. For one moment Dana simply stood there staring, swamped with pity and guilt. She had longed to be free of her promise to Jake, but not this way. This was financial disaster for Jake as well as emotional disaster, for he had put all his affection, all his plans for the future into the Freeway Cinema, and now it was nothing, might never have existed.

Dana felt a great sob rising in her throat, but she forced it down though she could not stop the tears from coming to her eyes and welling over. I'd like to kill the blighters who did this, she found herself thinking as she turned away from the ruin that had been both her work and her charge. But at least I'm free now to do whatever is most useful, whatever will hurt the enemy most. I'll go home right away and see if I can find someone who will take me into one of the forces. They will probably find out that I have worked in catering and put me in the cook-house, but if that helps the war effort I won't moan, I'll just get on with it. And as soon as I've been accepted I'll go round and see our landlord. I suppose he won't let me keep the rooms on once I'm in the forces because of the folk bombed out, but old Mrs Butterworth who cleans – or rather used to clean – the Freeway has said more than once that she's got a spare room with a bed in it which I'm welcome to use if I can't get back to the city centre after my shift. I'll take her up on it when I get leave and can come back to the city.

Dana went over and was about to give the nearest pile of bricks a little pat for old times' sake when she heard a shout. Two wardens were coming up the street armed with lengths of the white tape with which they cordoned off dangerous bombed buildings. They gestured to her to stand back and began their work, and Dana, who had opened her mouth to explain that this building had once been her workplace, closed it again. Then she turned and headed for the nearest bus stop.

It took time; everything, it seemed, took time during the war, but eventually Dana was accepted by the Land Army. Her uniform and rail pass arrived, and a letter telling her to report for duty at Tullimore's Farm the following Wednesday. Dana, reading the letter, smiled to herself. The very fact that they wanted her to start on a Wednesday instead of demanding that she arrived earlier in the week meant that the authorities were at last coming to terms with the facts of life. All travel was both difficult and tedious, but cross-country travel was the worst of all. If she wanted to be certain of arriving at this farm the following Wednesday then she had best set out on Tuesday.

This gave her three days, if you counted Saturday and Sunday, in which to plan her move. Remembering old Mrs Butterworth's frequent offers of a bed should she find herself unable to reach home during the heavy raids, she applied to the old lady for a more permanent arrangement. She explained that though she would be away most of the time she was bound to get leave occasionally and would want to return to Liverpool. She had heard from various sources that the ferries between Holyhead and Dublin were still sailing, so though she might spend at least some of every leave in Liverpool she fully intended to get on a train for Holyhead just as soon as she got sufficient time off for a visit to Castletara to be practical. She did not tell Mrs Butterworth any of this, however, since she had no idea whether she would be allowed to leave the country. But she told herself that Ireland was neutral and set off on her journey to Tullimore's Farm around lunchtime on the Tuesday.

Chapter Sixteen

August 1941

The train seemed to stop frequently – she had no fewer than seven changes – and on Tuesday night she slept in a chilly waiting room on a tiny station whose name had been blacked out on all destination boards. She was not alone; two seamen heading for Great Yarmouth and a pretty little WAAF, already late and worrying herself sick, also curled up on the hard benches, waking every time a train shrieked its way through the station and cursing the drivers who hooted merrily as they passed through. She reached Norwich Thorpe station, which was as far as her train would carry her, quite early on Wednesday morning, waved her rail pass at station staff and was just in time to leap aboard a local train bound for the nearest station to Tullimore's Farm. She was accompanied on this last leg of her journey by another girl, a very pretty girl, for though her uniform was as bizarre and ill fitting as that which graced Dana's lanky form she wore it with such an air that it looked quite acceptable. She told Dana that her name was Vera Potter and that she too was bound for Tullimore's.

'Someone's supposed to pick me up,' she said, when they arrived at the station whose name was on the rail passes. She stared around her at the empty platform and the empty road outside. 'Mind you, they told me I'd not get here until the five ten, but the perishin' train was early for once. Who's meeting you?'

'Dunno; no one, I don't think,' Dana said doubtfully. 'There was a porter here a minute ago bawling out the name of the station. If we ask him how we get to Tullimore's Farm, no doubt he'll point us in the right direction. There's no taxi, but surely there will be a bus?'

There was. The porter, rousted out of his snug little ticket office, said that the twice daily bus would be along in a moment and they must ask to get off at Tullimore's Corner. 'Simple!' Vera said as she and Dana lugged their kitbags out of the station and into the dusty country road. 'Weren't we lucky though, Dana? If the bus only comes twice a day, we might have had to wait hours and hours. Cor blimey, what a terrible thought, 'cos there isn't a pub or a bakery for miles, from what I can see, and I've not had a bite since yesterday evening.'

Dana agreed that they were indeed lucky, though she thought privately that, the station being a little way outside the village, they might presently find themselves in a more built-up area, and this was speedily proved to be true. The village was small, consisting of perhaps a dozen cottages, a pub called the King's Arms, a smithy, what Dana took to be a general store, and a bakery with a sign outside announcing that it doubled as post office and telephone exchange. The girls got a good look at the village since the bus stopped here, to take on board not passengers but various parcels and packages, including an extremely lively and aggressive young goat and a basket from which two hens popped inquisitive heads. Dana beamed at her companion, loving every minute.

This was so like Castletara! Many a time Dana had caught the local bus into the village with a couple of broody hens wanted by a neighbour squashed into a basket on her knee. When she and Con were young they had walked to school in good weather and caught the bus in bad, and she had no doubt that, later in the day, this very bus would be ferrying schoolchildren from the village to their homes in some remote part of the country-side.

She was explaining all this to her companion when the bus juddered to a halt. The conductor, who had been filling in a form and anxiously counting the money in his bag, got laboriously to his feet. He was a thin, grey-haired little man of sixty or so, and as the bus stopped he beckoned to the girls, giving them a wide and toothless smile as they approached him. 'You asked for Tullimore's, ain't that right, my women?' he asked genially. 'Well, if you foller that lane you can't make noo error.' He eyed their brogues doubtfully. 'Thass a rare shame you in't wearin' wellies, 'cos the lane lead over the marsh and we've had a deal o' rain lately.' He snorted. 'Typical August weather in these here parts. Still an' all, thass oonly half a mile so you'll soon be settin' down to a noice cuppa and a slice o' Mrs Tullimore's apple cake.'

The girls jumped down, waved to the bus and set off along the lane, trying to avoid the deepest puddles, though with very little success. At this point the track was thickly hedged and also ditched, but presently they emerged on to the marsh, which appeared to stretch as far as the eye could see. Dana would have plodded on, but Vera caught her arm. 'Where's the bloody farm?' she said, her tone incredulous. 'You can see for miles, so we ought to be able to spot a building easily.'

Dana laughed. 'Country folk have strange ideas about distance,' she told the other girl. 'Besides, no one could grow any sort of crop, not even sugar beet, in a marsh. I reckon we've a good way to walk before we reach Tullimore's, and when we get there there will be fields and hedges and all sorts.'

Vera pulled a face and gave an eloquent shudder. 'I'm a city girl, I am, and this perishin' marsh scares me stiff. I mean to apply for a transfer just as soon as I can get paper and pen,' she said, slowing her pace to a snail-like crawl. 'After all, I'm a perishin' volunteer; it's not as though I were conscripted. So if I don't like it here I shall move on.'

'Oh, don't be such a ninny,' Dana said scornfully. 'And if you did move on, which I don't think the Land Army would allow, you might find yourself even worse off. Give it a chance for heaven's sake, and keep walking. I know this lane's pretty muddy but at least it's not as muddy as the marsh.'

Vera sniffed but quickened her pace to keep up with her companion, and sure enough, after they had walked well over a mile, the marsh disappeared, to be replaced by enormous fields, hedged and ditched. The crop, which the girls guessed must be sugar beet, was already at knee height and clearly being harvested, though they could not as yet see any sign of life. Shortly after this they saw trees, and through the leafy branches a house. 'There it is: Tullimore's Farm, our future home,' Dana said, trying to infuse her voice with enthusiasm, though in fact as they drew nearer she thought that despite the many trees surrounding it it looked a grim place. Between them and the house was a large pond surrounded by reeds, with willow trees bending over the still water as though anxious to see their reflections in its dark depths. Dana repressed a shudder. She was not normally imaginative, but the sight of the black water, the bulrushes and the reeds made her remember the book by Mary Webb and the poignant picture the author painted of Sarn Mere and the pathetic little figure of Jancis carrying her baby as the girl walked slowly into the dark mere, until the water closed over their heads.

Her companion seemed to find the water eerie as well, for she clutched Dana's arm, saying tremulously: 'Is that there lake thing what they calls a Broad? Oh, Dana, I'm that scared I'd run off home for two pins. I reckon you could drown in there if you was to miss your way on a dark night.'

Dana, who had been thinking exactly the same thing, pulled herself together. 'Of course it's not a Broad, it's just a pond,' she said reassuringly. 'And as for walking into it on a dark night, how would you get through the reeds and the bulrushes?' As she spoke a flotilla of ducks spotted them and came quacking towards them, accompanied, to Dana's dismay, by several very much larger birds which she recognised as geese. The birds made their way through the reeds and Dana, who had been about to say that only ducks could get in and out of the pond without flying, remembered incidents from her own home and grabbed her companion's arm. 'Geese! Run like hell!' she shouted, suiting the action to the words. 'You aren't going to drown, but if we don't get out of their territory our bums will be black and blue.

Geese are better than guard dogs and they can peck harder than you'd believe. Don't look back, just run.'

However, the geese knew where their territory ended, and twenty or thirty yards from the pond they ceased their pursuit and waddled back the way they had come. Dana looked at her companion and could not suppress a laugh. Poor Vera was puffing breathlessly and staring round her as though at any moment some huge creature might appear from the trees which crowded close to the poorly maintained drive. 'I wish I'd never come,' she whimpered. 'What would them geese of done if they'd caught us?'

'I told you; they'd peck any bit of us they could reach. But they only do that to strangers, which we shan't be for very long, of course.' Dana hoped that Vera had not noticed that she was crossing her fingers behind her back, for all the geese she had ever known had attacked anyone they considered threatening. Still, one grew used to them, as she and Vera would have to do.

Despite Vera's nervous fears, they reached the farmyard without any further alarms, crossed the muddy puddles and knocked boldly on the back door. There was a considerable pause before it was answered, and then, just as Dana had put out a hand to grasp the doorknob, it shot open and a woman's face appeared.

'Good afternoon, Mrs Tullimore. We're your new land girls. May we come in?' Dana said politely, and the woman grunted and moved aside.

'I were told you'd be comin' tomorrer,' she said. 'I thought you'd go to your lodgings, settle in there afore coming on here.'

The girls stared at each other. Lodgings? There had

been no mention of lodgings in their instructions. And just where were they supposed to lodge, anyway? They had caught a bus from the nearest village to the end of the lane and had then walked for the best part of an hour over flat and muddy countryside. If they were indeed meant to live so far from their place of work they would have to have bicycles or a regular lift from a friendly villager, otherwise they would spend a large proportion of their time getting to and from the farm. Poor Vera, clutching her kitbag and gazing timidly round the large kitchen, was clearly in no state to question Mrs Tullimore's words, but Dana knew that if she did not make the situation clear at once she and Vera would find themselves most uncomfortably situated. She spoke up firmly, as though to an employee rather than an employer.

'I'm very sorry you've been misinformed, but there is nothing in our instructions concerning lodgings. Why, it would take us half our working day just to get to and from your farm, and in really bad weather we wouldn't be able to report for work at all.' She looked around her, at the large stone-flagged kitchen and the equally large cooking range, the big table and the quantity of chairs surrounding it. 'Judging by the number of chairs, you must have other land girls. Do they lodge in the village? I imagine not.'

The woman glared at her balefully. She was tall, taller than Dana herself, and hatchet-faced. Her small mouth, which appeared lipless, tightened at Dana's words and her tiny black eyes sparked dangerously. 'We've one other girl; she live in,' she admitted after a pause so long that Dana was beginning to fear she did not intend to answer. 'Her name's Elaine and a fat lot of use she is, idle trollop.

But I'm tellin' you, there ain't no room for a couple more; you'll have to lodge out. As for arrivin' late, if you do that you won't get no wages.'

Dana snorted. By now her blood was up, and a glance at Vera showed that her companion was equally irate. Good, because it might take the pair of them to worst this horrible woman. 'This appears to be a very big house,' she said coldly. 'Are you trying to tell me that you've no empty bedrooms? I think, if you don't mind, we'll take a look around.'

The woman bristled, clenching her long thin fingers into fists. 'You'll do no such thing . . .' she was beginning, but Dana had slung down her kitbag, Vera had followed suit, and they were already heading for the door which must, they realised, lead to the rest of the house. They were actually halfway up the first flight of stairs when the woman shouted at them to stop and, when they did so, said grudgingly, 'You can join Elaine in the attic; I was forgettin' that there's room in there for several, so don't you go meddlin' with any other doors. Go straight up the attic stairs. It's a wretched nuisance, because there's only the one bed up there, but it'll give you and your pal something to do for the rest of the day. You can carry the old iron bedstead and the mattress that's in the third room on the left up to the attic.' Her eyes flickered over them with loathing. 'You looks strong enough for that, at any rate.'

'If there's a bed and presumably furniture in the room third on the left why can't we sleep there?' Vera asked suddenly. 'Attics is cold in winter and hot in summer – I should know – so why not let us have a room on the first floor?'

This time there was an even longer pause before the farmer's wife spoke again. 'It ain't convenient to have young girls sleepin' on the same floor as married folk; besides, my husband snores. And what about when my son come home, eh? No, if you won't get lodgings in the village it's the attic or the cow byre, take your choice.' And before either girl could say a word their unwilling hostess turned on her heel and clattered down the hall, slamming the kitchen door when she reached it with enough force to crack its hinges.

The girls took advantage of Mrs Tullimore's absence to do exactly as she had forbidden and have a good nose round all the rooms on the first floor. There were seven bedrooms, most quite large and commodious and all bar two obviously unused. The Tullimores' own room had so much furniture in it that the girls thought the couple must dress and undress in some other place, otherwise they would be constantly barking their shins and cracking their elbows on the occasional tables, chests of drawers, wardrobes and similar objects that cluttered the floor. Most of the stuff was old, the upholstery moth-eaten or riddled with dry rot, so that even moving it might prove hazardous. The only thing of interest was a photograph of a young man in RAF uniform with his forage cap set on Brylcreemed hair and a slight smile – shy but proud – on his lips. This was clearly the Tullimores' son, who from his photograph looked a nice enough lad, and when they reached his room Dana thought he was probably as glad to get out of the farm as they would have been, for from every available space model aeroplanes soared. Some were strung on fine cotton from the ceiling, others stuck to the walls and windows. He had two bookshelves, one crammed with technical tomes, the other with the usual boyish fiction: Henty, Kipling, Maxwell Scott and Frank Shaw.

The girls stared, then backed out of the room, closing the door quietly behind them. 'Poor devil; what he must have suffered livin' in this hellhole and dreamin' of escape, though I dare say he didn't think escape would come in quite the way it has,' Dana said softly as they headed for the next room. 'I dare say the old crab didn't think of it, but there's no way we could possibly get that huge old bedstead up the attic stairs, so we'd best look around for a couple of camp beds. And while we're about it, we'll nick a washstand and a couple of chests of drawers for our stuff. I wonder what time this Elaine gets back?'

'I wonder where she is now, for that matter?' Vera puffed as she and Dana manoeuvred a large chest of drawers up the narrow stairs. 'What a surprise she'll get when she sees us !'

'Yes, I dare say, but she must be a bit of a wet weekend,' Dana said as they reached the attic. 'If she'd had any gumption she would have nicked some of the furniture from the proper bedrooms and brought it up here instead of laying her clothes out on the dusty floor and washing downstairs in the kitchen.'

'Don't be so critical, Dana. How was she supposed to move any of this awful old furniture without someone to give a hand?' Vera said reproachfully. 'I wonder where she got the camp bed from?'

They were soon to discover, for in one of the bedrooms they found a good deal of camping equipment and triumphantly provided themselves with a camp bed and a sleeping bag each. Their hostess was supposed to supply them with bedding, but they guessed that they would have to fight for every extra blanket, no matter how icy cold the weather might become.

When they had made the attic – which was huge and ran the whole length of the house – as comfortable as possible, they returned to the kitchen, just as the back door opened and a small, slender girl with wide blue eyes and soft fair curls entered the room, just ahead of two very elderly farm hands. All three were clad in breeches, oilskins and big wellington boots, and Dana guessed it had started to rain again, for all three took off their boots, placed them in a row by the back door and then shed their oilskins, shaking them vigorously into the yard before hanging them on the pegs above the boots. Dana heard Mrs Tullimore's grumbling tones begin and spoke loudly. 'Good afternoon one and all, or should I say good evening? I'm Dana McBride and this is Vera Potter and we're the new land girls.' She grinned at Elaine, pretending not to notice how the other girl's eyes filled with tears. 'And you must be Elaine, but I'm afraid these two gentlemen weren't mentioned when Mrs Tullimore welcomed us to her home.'

The fair-haired girl held out her hand, which was vigorously shaken by both Dana and Vera. Then she turned to the two old men. 'This is Mr Grundy; he's a marvel with horses. The ground gets so boggy the tractor isn't much use most of the time. And this is Mr Miller, who does just about everything. He milks the cows, tends the pigs, drives the tractor in summertime and is a master hedger. They're both trying to teach me so's I can be useful . . .' she grinned shyly at the two old men, who were grinning toothlessly back, 'but it's uphill work, isn't it, chaps?'

Both grinned and nodded, the older of the two – Mr Grundy – saying placidly that she were a grand girl and doin' her best, and then Elaine and the two old men sat themselves down at the table and Elaine beckoned the two newcomers to follow suit. 'When we're working a good distance from the farm, we take what they call a packed lunch,' she whispered, 'but often it's just a cut off the loaf and an apple. So when we come in, 'cos it's too dark to work out any longer, the missus – that's what the fellers call her – is supposed to provide us with a high tea. We have to hand over our ration books, you see, and of course there's no cooking facilities in the attic, which is where I sleep, so it's Mrs Tullimore's grub or nothing. Are you two in lodgings? They said I must live out, but the village is so far . . .'

'No, we're living in, for the same reason,' Dana said quickly. She lowered her voice. 'We've taken some furniture up there as well as camp beds and sleeping bags. We took up a washstand as well . . .'

'Ooh, if she finds out she'll go mad,' Elaine whispered. 'I'm supposed to wash in the kitchen, but of course it's not ideal and an all-over wash is out of the question, unless you use the tin bath in the washhouse. You can fill the copper and light the fire underneath it but it's awful difficult to get the temperature right; you come out either looking like a boiled prawn or shivering with cold. But with the three of us we ought to manage something.'

At this point the farmer's wife approached them, slapped half a dozen plates down on the table and began

403

serving the boiled potatoes, boiled cabbage and boiled carrots, splash of gravy and tiny square of fatty bacon which was apparently their hostess's idea of a sustaining meal. Dana stared at her plate, then around at the other diners. The old men were shovelling food into their mouths as fast as they could and for the first time it occurred to her that they must live somewhere; would it not have been possible for them to find room in their cottages for three not very large land girls? She whispered the comment to Elaine, who shook her head decidedly. 'Their cottages are in a dreadful state: leaking roofs, earth floors and tiny,' she said. 'Mrs Grundy has a daughter with three or four young children all living in her cottage – no husband, of course – and Mr Miller's wife suffers from chronic arthritis and spends a great deal of time in bed. They're two room cottages: a live-in kitchen and a bedroom. So you see no one could possibly expect them to take in lodgers.'

'Right,' Dana said decidedly. She looked at the food on her own plate and those of her two companions, then considered Mrs Tullimore's still empty dish and raised her voice to its normal level. 'And what might you be having for high tea, Mrs Tullimore? I dare say it won't just be vegetables and a square inch of fatty bacon.'

'That's no affair of yours, Miss Long Nose,' Mrs Tullimore said sharply. 'Eat what you're give or you'll get nothing, I'm warnin' you.'

Dana sighed. She would have liked to pick up her plate and hurl it and its contents out into the yard, but the truth was she was hungry, really hungry, and the vegetables smelled good. 'Very well; because you didn't expect us we shall have to make do with what you've provided, but in future we shall want to make sure we're getting our fair share of anything that's going,' she said firmly. 'We saw ducks and geese as we came past the pond and there were hens flapping and pecking all over the yard. I know most of your acres are turned over to sugar beet, but I'm not entirely ignorant of farming matters, you'll be sorry to hear. I recognised plum, apple and pear trees in an orchard, you yourself referred to the cow byre and I heard pigs grunting as we crossed the yard, no doubt hoping they were about to be fed. So you see, I can tell you aren't short of food, you just prefer to keep it for yourself.'

Mrs Tullimore, red in the face and tight-lipped, was swelling up like a balloon when the back door opened and her husband entered. At least, Dana assumed it was her husband, but he was a very different kettle of fish from his wife. She thought he must be six foot five or six, and he was as broad as he was long. He hung up his tweed cap and oilskins and turned to stare at the newcomers. Although he was nothing like his wife in appearance, however, Dana soon realised that he was cut from the same cloth. He was greedy yet mean, seldom eating when the rest of them did but always sending the workers off about their business before he and his wife had their meal. Elaine told them that Mrs Tullimore would bring forth from the depths of the oven huge succulent joints of lamb or pork, great golden-crusted pies or delicious fruit crumbles, but none of these delicacies were ever offered – or indeed openly shown – to any of the farm workers. The old men took it for granted but Dana, Vera and Elaine realised they would have to grow both forceful and deceitful if they were ever to get a decent meal, and that night the three of them sat up in their far from cosy camp beds and plotted. Before it was time to sleep, they had decided they would threaten the Tullimores with the authorities, and would if necessary tell tales to the Ministry of Agriculture and Fisheries, for it was perfectly obvious that the farmer and his wife did not declare half the food they produced.

'Of course they'll guess it's us and will be even nastier as a result,' Dana warned her companions. 'But it'll be worth it if we get some decent grub. After all, the work's hard and pretty unrewarding, we're icy cold in that bloody attic – no, I won't apologise for swearing, Vera, it is a bloody attic – and we're starving hungry and fed on kitchen scraps most of the time, whilst the Tullimores live on the fat of the land. If that's justice then my name's not McBride!'

In fact the mere threat of carrying tales to the Min of Ag was enough to change things to a certain extent. Grudgingly, and with many a bitter remark, Mrs Tullimore doled out a small amount of acceptable food to the girls each day, though it was always the fattiest part of the joint, the wing rather than the leg or breast of a bird and the sausages containing the most bread, having been made at the end of the batch.

'It wouldn't be so bad if she wasn't such a good cook,' Vera moaned one day, when the girls had been at the farm for fifteen months, and were growing used to the hard work, relieved only in that in the winter months at least they were free to go to any dances to which they were invited at nearby RAF stations, it being, despite double summertime, too dark for work after about four o' clock. Every time they were told that a gharry would pick them up in the village street at such and such an hour, Dana hoped desperately that on arrival at the RAF station she might see that familiar dark head, that whimsical lopsided smile, and know that she had caught up with Con at last. In fact, she saw Con everywhere. She went into Norwich with a crowd of girls to see a film at the Haymarket and saw him in profile sitting two rows ahead of them. But when the lights went up this Con was fair-haired, with eyes rather too close to his nose for good looks. At other times she saw him across the dance floor, or on a railway station waiting to board a train, but it was always a Con lookalike and never the real thing. She knew he was on a bomber station, knew that Feena would forward any letters she cared to send, but her mother had promised not to give her Con's address and Dana would not ask her to break her word.

Often and often, particularly when she was hoeing sugar beet, a task much hated by everyone, Dana heard the roar of engines overhead and looked up to see the Wellingtons, Halifaxes, Hampdens and Blenheims on their way home from a night flight to Germany. The Americans had been in the war since December 1941 when the Japs had attacked the American fleet in Pearl Harbor, but the Yanks flew day missions, leaving the night hours to the Brylcreem boys, so when she heard the bombers returning she would imagine Con sitting in the pilot's seat and longing for the moment when he would land, go to headquarters for debriefing and then grab a meal of some sort at the cookhouse before falling, exhausted, into bed. Sometimes, she hoped that he might look down on the sea of beet and mud beneath him and wonder if one of the tiny stick figures toiling away below could be his old playmate. She knew he knew she worked as a land girl, because she had asked Feena to tell him her whereabouts and what she was doing. Feena had promised to do so, and Dana knew her mother would keep her word. Occasionally Feena passed on some of Con's news, though she was always careful never to reveal the name of his station. At first he had piloted Wellingtons – Wimpies, the men called them – and then had transferred to Manchesters for a short while, though now it seemed he was on Lancasters, regarding them as in a class by themselves.

When she had first gone to Tullimore's, Dana had been as ignorant as either of the other land girls about the great planes which droned overhead, but because of Con she began to be interested, to read everything she could on the planes he flew, and, eventually, to recognise each one by its engine sound even when it was above the clouds, too high for a visual sighting.

It was a cold day in mid-November and Dana and Elaine were cutting sticks of sprouts to be sent to market the next day when Elaine came out with a curious question. 'Dana, I've often wanted to ask you. What sent you into the Land Army and out to this godforsaken spot? Oh, I know the cinema you managed was destroyed in the blitz so you had no job, but that could happen to anyone. It sometimes seems to me you're punishing yourself; surely you're not feeling guilty because your friend Jake trusted you to keep his cinema safe? I mean, that's absurd.'

'Punishing myself? What on earth do you mean?' Dana asked, genuinely puzzled. 'If you ask me, we're all punished by the perishing Tullimores!'

'Well, perhaps that was a bit strong,' Elaine admitted, colouring slightly. 'But when a good-looking bloke asks you to dance . . . well, you sort of hold yourself away from him, and hardly open your mouth. There's that dark chap with the shrapnel wound on his forehead who always makes a point of dancing with you, but you freeze him off . . .'

'I do not,' Dana said, now annoyed as well as puzzled. To be sure, she had no desire to 'get involved' as she put it to herself, but other than that . . .

'You do,' Elaine insisted. 'And you don't make the best of yourself, you know you don't. Why, Vera's a first-class hairdresser, got paid a huge wage in a big London salon when she was in civvy street. But though she's offered to cut and shape your hair a dozen times, you've always said it wasn't worth her trouble. And then there's your clothes . . .'

'Oh, don't start,' Dana said wearily. 'There's a war on and we can't pick and choose. It's number ones or dungarees.'

'Yes, but when the rest of us go to a dance we're all turned out neat as new pins. If we've got any makeup we wear it, we iron our clothes so that we look as well turned out as any WAAF or Wren, and we wear our own decent shoes rather than those great clodhoppers provided by the Land Army. But you simply refuse to make the effort, and if that's not punishing yourself I don't know what is.'

'I hear what you're saying, but you must have heard the expression "you can't make a silk purse out of a sow's ear",' Dana said, grinning. 'Do try and get it into your thick head, Ellie, that I'm not on the catch for a feller.

409

When the war's over I'm going home to Ireland; there are plenty of blokes over there who won't care if I wear wellies to bed! And until then I'm quite happy to sit back and watch you women fighting over any chap that's going.'

There was a short silence. Dana cut three more sticks in rapid succession and chucked them into the big basket which, when it was full, she and Elaine would carry back to the edge of the field so that old Mr Miller might add the sticks to the ones already aboard the farm cart and return with his load to Tullimore's. As Dana turned back to her work, Elaine took a deep breath and spoke again. 'What about that fellow you've mentioned once or twice? Con, isn't it? I know he's in the air force and I suppose he must be abroad since you never arrange to meet, but why don't you write to him, Dana? Oh, I know you do write letters, but why doesn't he write back? Most of your post – in fact all of it, come to think – is internal.' She waited for a moment, but Dana said nothing. 'Look, I know it's none of my business, but you aren't very happy, are you? And if you are punishing yourself, it's about time you stopped. I guess this guy, this Con, has found himself a girlfriend, and you're hurt, naturally, but it happens to all of us, you know. Fellows discover a girl they prefer to the original one, or they get killed, which is worse. Their girlfriends stop caring about their looks, they think their lives are over, but after some weeks, or even months, they begin to pick up the pieces, to live again. They get out the old warpaint – if they're lucky enough to have lipstick, powder and that – and tidy up, go to the dances, find another boyfriend . . .'

'Well, I don't want *any* boyfriend,' Dana said, chopping

at a particularly obstinate stalk and wiping the rain off her face with the back of a muddy hand. 'I don't even want Con any more.' She straightened and looked Elaine in the eye. 'Con dropped me ages ago; we mean nothing to each other now.'

'Then if that's true, it's about time you pulled yourself together and forgot him,' Elaine said bluntly. 'You're both Irish, I take it? From the same village, or the same area at any rate? Well, what will happen after the war, when the two of you go home? He'll probably have a nice little popsie, but what will you have? Nothing. Not even your looks, unless you get your finger out and start trying.'

Dana stared at her companion, eyes widening with horror. 'Do you know, I've never thought of it like that,' she said slowly. 'And you're right, Elaine. Con's most awfully attractive; he still writes to my mother and has actually gone home a couple of times, though of course it has to be on the sly and out of uniform. Mum tells me he's had a good few girlfriends but seems to have settled for one called Mirabelle.' She sniffed disdainfully, 'A stupid name for a stupid girl, but if that's what Con wants . . .'

'If that's what he wants, then you'd better start smartening up and stop going around like a perishin' scarecrow,' Elaine said cruelly. 'Tomorrow's our day off. I told Vera I was going to talk to you and she said if you were agreeable she'd start on your hair tomorrow morning, early. We'll all help, because everyone's fond of you, Dana, and we hate to see you looking so miserable.' She grinned at her friend. 'And it doesn't do us any good with the fellers to have a pal with a face like a wet weekend. They're afraid that if we suggest going

411

out in a foursome they might get landed with you,' she added, twinkling.

Dana scowled, then gave her a shove. 'All right, all right, I take your point, and I'll be grateful if Vera really will do my hair because it's so long I'm always afraid it will get caught up in the farm machinery.'

There were now five land girls sleeping in the attic at Tullimore's Farm, five young women queuing for the washstand in the morning, five eager appetites waiting for a meal to be served up in the farm kitchen. Despite the increase in their numbers, however, things had not improved much. Mrs Tullimore still had it in for Dana, who had become the spokesperson for the whole group. The farmer's wife always referred to Dana as "Miss Long Nose" and argued over every single point she raised, but though the food was of the plainest Dana made sure they all got their rations and quite often a bit over; otherwise, she told the farmer's wife, she would inform the Min of Ag that the big old sow known as Crusher had actually given birth to eighteen piglets and not fifteen, or that the hens had laid a great many more eggs than had been sent off to market. So things could have been worse, Dana concluded, throwing the last stick of sprouts into the basket. 'We'd best get this lot over to the gate,' she said, seizing the handles at her end and watching as Elaine followed suit. 'But what Vera thinks she can do with my ginger frizz I can't imagine, and all the powder in the world won't disguise the fact that there are ten million freckles on my face!'

Next day the beautifying of Dana began. Vera, cutting great swathes of Dana's hair and watching them drop to

412

the attic floor, told her client severely that she should not refer to, or even think of, her hair as "ginger frizz". 'You're so indifferent to what you see in the mirror that you simply have not noticed your hair colour is darkening with every year that passes,' she said severely. 'I think I'd describe it as auburn, though in the summer it's lighter, of course. And as for your freckles, they are most certainly not all over your face. They're just a band across your nose and your cheekbones, little golden freckles which would not even be visible beneath a light dusting of powder. And if you could just lay your hands on some lipstick . . .'

'Yuck!' Dana said, revolted. 'My lips are quite red enough, thank you very much.'

Vera lifted Dana's hand and groaned. 'Look at your nails! Well, you'll have to soak them in warm soapy water and then scrub the filth off. Sally is ironing your white shirt and Fenella is putting a stitch in the seat of your breeches so they won't look as though they're about to descend to your ankles whenever you do a quickstep. And dear little Elaine is lending you her new shoes; it's a pity they have to be lace-ups, but they're a good deal daintier than our working brogues.'

It took all day, but by the time the five girls stole down to the forbidden parlour and gathered round the mirror, the transformation was complete. Dana said exultantly that her own mother would not have recognised her. She had approached the glass with as much caution as she would have shown had she suspected it might leap from its frame and bite her, and she was almost speechless when she saw a slim and undoubtedly attractive girl staring back at her. Instead of the great mass of untidy reddish frizz, this girl's head was covered in feathery auburn curls, and her greenish hazel eyes, framed by the long lashes which Elaine had darkened with boot polish, looked huge. Despite Dana's squeals of protest, Fenella had produced a pair of tweezers and plucked her eyebrows into two delicate wings, and these too had been darkened with boot polish. Sally had lent her a little face powder to hide her freckles, and she had submitted to wearing a pair of clip-on earrings, imitation emeralds which matched and accentuated the colour of her eyes.

There was a breathless silence whilst all five girls critically examined the changes which had been wrought, and then Vera spoke. 'You'll slay 'em,' she said exultantly. 'I knew the hair would make a difference, but I had no idea how much! Oh, Dana, if your feller was to see you now . . .'

Dana sighed, then turned reluctantly away from the mirror and headed for the kitchen and the meal which should be on the table. 'I don't have a fellow, but I mean to get myself one,' she called over her shoulder. 'I'll teach bloody Con Devlin that he was a fool to cast me off!'

They entered the kitchen in a body to find Mr Grundy and Mr Miller already seated at the table, whilst Mr Tullimore was washing up at the kitchen sink and his wife was at the range, stirring an enormous pot. This indicated that they would all share the meal and that meant it would be a good one, for the farmer and his wife never stinted themselves. The two old men looked up and greeted the girls, then stopped short, openmouthed. It was clear that they scarcely recognised Dana. Mr Tullimore turned away from the sink, dried his hands on the roller towel which hung on the back door, and frowned at her. 'Mrs Tullimore han't told me we had company,' he said, and Dana, unable to stop herself, gave him a broad grin.

'I've had my hair cut, Mr Tullimore,' she said cheerfully. 'We're off to a dance at the American airbase later on so it's best bib and tuckers presently.'

'Oh aye?' the farmer said uncertainly. 'What else ha' you done, my woman? 'Cos it ain't just your hair. There's suffin' else different.'

Dana opened her eyes very wide at him, hoping the boot polish would not begin to run and give her away, but before anyone could comment Mrs Tullimore was doling out stew and dumplings and all conversation ceased in delighted anticipation of the treat to come, for though Mrs Tullimore had many faults, she was an excellent cook. She worked her way along the table without once raising her eyes from her work, and Dana noticed that by some mysterious sleight of hand she managed to keep most of the meat for herself and her husband. Then the woman must have noticed Dana's gleaming head, for she stopped with her ladle in mid-air. 'What have you done to yourself, Miss Long Nose?' she asked nastily. 'Not hiding behind that bush of ginger hair any longer? Heh heh heh, a right sight you look!'

Dana knew how spiteful the older woman could be, but still felt a tide of warmth creeping up her neck. Did she look an awful sight; a freak, in fact? But almost immediately there was a chorus of disapproval aimed at the farmer's wife to which even her husband added his voice. Various remarks were made, all of a complimentary nature, and Dana smiled serenely, reassured when Mr

Tullimore joined in the praise that she had not made a fool of herself: the new style really suited her. And this very evening she would push Con to the back of her mind, even if she could not forget him altogether, and give other fellers a chance.

When the gharry decanted them at the station which was hosting the dance, Dana clutched Vera's arm for a moment, trying to make herself look less conspicuous. She was taller than most of her contemporaries and tended to slouch to hide the fact, but now she remembered how hard the girls had worked to improve her appearance and, straightening her shoulders, stood tall. Vera patted her hand approvingly. 'Good girl. Now don't forget – you're going to slay 'em,' she said. 'Be especially nice to the chap with the scarred face; he always asks you for a dance and I don't mind telling you, my old darling, that you've not given him much encouragement. But tonight you're Cinderella after the transformation scene, not before.'

Dana giggled as they joined the queue to leave their coats on the pegs behind the counter. The dance was being held in the mess and refreshments would be provided for a nominal sum, though only beer would be available and not the more potent spirits. Men outnumbered girls by two to one, and it was not unheard of for tipsy disagreements to become drunken brawls once the combatants left the mess to return to either their billets or the waiting gharries.

There were hard little wooden chairs set out around the walls of the large room, but scarcely had Dana and Vera seated themselves when the gramophone was switched on and a lively tune began to play. 'Quickstep,' Dana muttered. 'Or is it the foxtrot?' She sighed, eyeing her friend mournfully. 'Oh, Vera, this is the part I hate most! Have you ever been to a cattle sale? Well, if you had, you'd understand how I feel. They lead a cow into the ring and all the farmers stare and then the bids start rolling in – or not, as the case may be. A poor beast raises little interest and that's exactly how—'

She was interrupted. The young man with the scarred face did not seem to be present and the man who was smiling down at her was a stranger. He had light brown hair cut very short and when he smiled he showed very large, very white teeth. 'May I have the pleasure of this dance, ma'am?' he said in a soft drawl, his very dark eyes fixed on Dana's face so there could be no doubt as to whom he was addressing. As she got to her feet, Dana saw the flash on his shoulder; so he was a Canadian! She was glad she had realised it; she knew from past experience how it annoyed Canadians to be taken for citizens of the US of A.

As she slid into the Canadian's arms he smiled down at her. 'I'm Hank Theaker – Flight Lieutenant Theaker if you want to be formal. And you are . . .'

'I'm Dana McBride, and as you can probably see from my oh-so-smart uniform, I'm a land girl,' she told him.

The Canadian whistled under his breath. 'I did wonder why you came to a dance in breeches,' he said, and Dana could hear the suppressed laughter in his voice. 'I have to warn you I'm no great dancer, though I'll try to avoid landing my eleven stone on your feet. But the minute I saw you I decided I wanted to get to know you . . .'

He twirled her round as the music came to an end and

Dana was just congratulating herself on her new appearance, which certainly seemed to have paid off, when he added: 'You were the only girl I could see who didn't make me feel like Gulliver among the Lilliputians! I'm six foot four, which is kinda tall even at home. Are you from round here? No, don't tell me, let me guess! I'll put money on your being Irish; I don't know if you know it but Canada is full of Irish cops with names like O'Hara and McIntock. Am I right?' As he spoke he was leading Dana towards the long counter which had become a makeshift bar. 'Going to let me buy you a beer or a soft drink? And there are some really good little pies with some sort of plums inside – damsons, I think they're called – so if we're quick we might manage to grab a couple.'

Dana said that a soft drink would be fine and looked round, thinking she really should join Vera and the other girls, but they had already scattered so she followed Hank meekly and perched upon one of the two vacant chairs in the corner he had chosen. They began to talk, and perhaps because he, like herself, was not a native of this land they soon became easy with one another. Dana, who had never managed to talk freely about her home in Castletara, found she could do so with Hank. She even told him about Con, admitting ruefully that their friendship was now a thing of the past, and the tall Canadian put a large hand over hers and gave it a consoling squeeze.

'War breaks up marriages, let alone friendships,' he told her. 'I was married; would be still except that Mary Lou filed for divorce, saying that I'd ill treated her and then abandoned her to live with my parents on our farm on Prince Edward Island.' He sighed, and pulled a rueful face. 'I promise you, Dana, that none of it was true, but in a way I couldn't blame her. She'd met someone else, a fellow who ran his own successful business, probably earning as much in a month as I do in a year. I didn't contest the divorce – my mom and pop advised me not to do so – so now I'm fancy free, except that I find it hard to believe my marriage is over. If I'd been home . . . but I wasn't, so no use repining.'

'No use for me either,' Dana admitted. 'I abandoned Con and my home, went without even leaving an address. Con joined the air force and my mother tells me he has found consolation with somebody else. So you and I are in the same boat.'

The Canadian nodded. 'Gee, I couldn't put it better myself. But it's not a bad boat to be in, or it won't be so bad now we've met.' He cocked an eyebrow. 'Any chance of meeting again? I've got a fourth share in an old jalopy so I could pick you up any time you're free and we could do the town. Or just meet for a chat,' he added wistfully. 'Me and my crew were only posted here a month ago and don't know a soul apart from a few others on the station. It'd be grand to have a pal to go around with. What do you say, honey?'

'Isn't it a bit soon? We've only just met,' Dana said doubtfully, but inside her heart was singing. Already she realised she liked Hank a lot, and anything which took her mind off the loss of Con was welcome. She looked across at the Canadian and saw the same expression in his eyes which she guessed was in her own. She smiled at him. 'Though why not?' she said lightly. 'I'm free evenings, because no one can do much on the land after dark. I won't pretend the Tullimores are nice welcoming people, because they aren't. They're mean, bad-tempered and demanding, but since we shouldn't be spending time at the farm that won't matter. So yes please, Hank, come calling whenever you're not flying.'

Over the next few weeks Dana learned a great deal about her new friend. He had an elder brother who had not taken to farming life and owned a large hardware shop in the nearby town. Hank himself had come across to Britain and joined the Royal Air Force back in 1938, since he had learned to fly light aircraft at college and, seeing that war would come, had decided to get himself properly trained for it. He was a keen sportsman, an excellent shot, and loved fishing, whilst at home he was a member of an ice hockey team, a sport he missed sadly but meant to take up again when the war was over. He told Dana that as a boy he had wanted to join the Mounties – the Royal Canadian Mounted Police – but had felt he could not leave his parents' farm once his brother had defected to the town.

Life for Dana began to improve with every week that passed, except, of course, that she now worried over Hank's safety as she still worried, in her heart, over Con's. But Hank's loving admiration was balm to her wounded spirit and Vera remarked how much happier her friend had become since meeting the Canadian.

Dana agreed that this was so, but kept to herself one reason for allowing Hank to get close in a way which no one but Con had ever achieved. It was because, a week after the dance at which they had met, she had learned why the young pilot with the scarred face had not been present. His Wellington had been hit as it delivered its bombs to the target, and though others in the flight had seen two parachutes loom and begin to descend earthwards, they thought that both airmen had been deliberately fired upon by the ground forces. Since no word had come of their capture it was taken for granted that the entire crew was dead, and Dana felt miserably guilty. She could have been nicer to the scarred young man; he had only wanted friendship, after all, but she had denied him even that, and now it was too late. So she gave Hank the warmth and affection which the scarred young pilot had never received, or not from Dana at any rate. She said no word of this to anyone, and very soon such a confession was unnecessary. She liked Hank for himself, and when he talked of taking her home to Canada after the war she went along with it. Why not? A new life in a new country was not such a bad idea, after all.

Chapter Seventeen

A year passed: Hank and his crew were posted to Cumbria and Dana and he exchanged letters and phone calls, as did Dana and Polly, though the two girls did not meet, since Polly was now stationed in Scotland. Polly had a week's leave over the Christmas of 1943 which she hoped to spend in Liverpool with Ernie, but this proved impossible. Two days before her leave started the *Sarah Jane* and the rest of the convoy would set out across the Atlantic Ocean, heading for America to pick up the supplies, so desperately needed, which would be available to them as soon as they docked in the United States. Polly told Dana exactly how things stood.

'I've got a week's leave and there's no point in going back to Liverpool, even though air attacks are rarer than they were,' she said. 'Any chance of me coming to you? If one of the other land girls is going home for Christmas couldn't I sleep in her bed? And the air force will give me a ration card which I can pass on to the farmer and his wife, if that would make me more acceptable as a guest.'

Dana, who had had to walk through a snowstorm to reach the telephone box in the village, gnawed her lip. 'Don't worry about the ration card; the old devil always manages to put food on the table, and now that there are five of us she has five extra ration books. The trouble is, Poll, she absolutely hates me – well, she hates us all, but she hates me most – and that means she'd say you couldn't come out of sheer spite. But there's a pub in the village – it's called the King's Arms – and they do take folk in from time to time on what they call a bed and breakfast deal. I could book you in there for half a dozen nights, and we could split the cost. The only thing is, what would you do with yourself all day?'

Polly was beginning to reply, optimistically, that she was sure she could find something to occupy her when she had a bright idea. 'I remember you saying last year, Dee, that at Christmas the farm was pretty well dead, with very little work to do,' she pointed out. 'Why don't you take a week's leave, the same as me? If you could find us a cheap hotel or boarding house in Norwich we could have a grand time. We could explore the city, go to the cinema and the theatre, visit museums and art galleries; oh, we could do all sorts! And so far as I can recall, you've not had a day's leave since you started there in the summer of 'forty-one.'

'Gracious, you're right,' Dana said, much struck. 'I keep thinking I'll wait until things are quiet and then try to get across to Ireland. Just for a few days, you know, because I'm missing all my little brother's childhood and of course it would be heavenly to see Castletara, Mammy and Johnny Devlin once again.'

'And there's always the chance that Con might be there,' Polly said, highly daring, but Dana demurred.

'No, I told you that he was no longer a part of my life, and I meant it. If we met we'd be polite, but after all this time we'd be strangers to one another; he might not even recognise me! I'd like to take Hank back to Castletara with me, introduce him to Feena and Johnny and the little lad, but it would be rather dodgy since he's a Canadian as well as a flight lieutenant. Ireland *is* a foreign country no matter how you look at it, and he can't afford to get wrong with either our authorities or his own, so I've more or less put a return visit for myself on hold.' She lowered her voice. 'There's rumours round here about an invasion . . .'

Polly cut across her at once. 'Perishin' walls have perishin' ears, careless talk costs lives, be like Dad, keep Mum . . .'

'All right, all right, I get the message,' Dana said, giggling. 'We'll talk when we meet. Oh, Polly, it will be grand to see you again after so long!'

Despite Dana's fears that the Tullimores would try to prevent her from taking a week off to see her friend, this did not prove to be the case. Young Reggie Tullimore announced that not only was he coming home for Christmas, but he would be bringing a couple of pals, and the Tullimores promptly decided that life would be easier if all the girls took that week off. Delighted, everyone made their plans, and on 23 December a chattering, laughing little group descended from the platform at Thorpe station to go their various ways. Dana was secretly delighted as she stood by the doors which led to the buffet to see Polly give her a quick indifferent glance and then walk straight past her; in fact she had to grab Polly's arm before her friend recognised her.

The two girls laughed and clung, then went into the

buffet for watery coffee and a ham and pickle sandwich, for their lodgings were on Riverside Road, a very short walk indeed from the station, and the landlady worked at a munitions factory on day shift so would not be home to let them in until after five o'clock.

Outside the station buffet snow began to fall, and inside it grew colder every time a would-be customer pushed open the door. The two girls stuck it for a while but then Dana picked up her kitbag, slung it over her shoulder, and beckoned Polly to follow her. 'It's stopped snowing, and the river has willow trees and a path alongside the water,' she told her friend. 'If you can put up with the cold, at least we can talk there without fear of being overheard. And I'm longing to know what you've heard about you know what.'

Polly laughed but got to her feet at once. 'It can't be much colder out there than it is in here, every time the door opens,' she observed. 'Lead the way, Miss McBride!'

And presently they were on the towpath, and were at last able to speak freely. 'Everyone's talking about an invasion, just like they did at the beginning of the war, only this time it's us invading them and not vice versa,' Dana said. 'Remember how we were told to "keep an eye on the sky", where we would see paratroopers dressed as nuns floating down to earth? I used to keep an old kitchen knife in my pocket whenever I went out walking, but whether I should have been strong enough – or wicked enough, I'm not sure which – to plunge it into the heart of a descending German I rather doubt. I've heard the air force chaps talking in the King's Arms but there's been no talk of invasion from the sky this time; this time it's—'

Polly's hand shot out and cut Dana's words off in midstream.

'You aren't supposed to know anything about it, and nor am I,' she said reproachfully. 'Tell me about Hank – I take it he's a flyer? I know he's Canadian, and a great many of his fellow Canadians are over here at the moment. We meet 'em all over; grand chaps for the most part.'

For ten minutes or so the two girls walked briskly along the towpath, their eyes on the fast-flowing Wensum and the willows on the opposite bank, leaning over the water as though to admire their reflections. Dana guessed from her friend's demeanour that she had something to say which was too important to be hurried, so she asked no questions but bided her time. Knowing Polly as she did she guessed she would not have to wait for very long, and sure enough Polly gave her a quick glance and was just beginning to speak when the snow started once more. It wasn't much at first but it soon became clear that this time it did not intend to stop. Furthermore, a nasty wind got up, and with one accord the girls turned back and began to hurry towards Foundry Bridge.

'It's no use trying to talk,' Polly shouted. 'Oh, damn it, we were better off in the buffet, but you know Norwich better than I do. Isn't there a quiet little café where we could talk without being overheard? I was posted pretty near here just before you joined the Land Army, but we only came into Norwich twice and then the gharries left us on Castle Meadow, which is nowhere near the station.'

'There's a fish and chip shop not far from here,' Dana began, and then inspiration struck. 'I know! There's a sort of shack place about a hundred yards or so from

Foundry Bridge. It's quite near the river and they do a pretty good pot of tea and slices of buttered toast for one and six, and in this weather it'll probably be deserted.' She grinned at her friend through the now fast-falling flakes. 'Will that suit your majesty?'

Polly confirmed that it would be fine and ten minutes later the two of them were shaking the snow off their coats and hats – Dana's hat had caught enough in its wide brim to make at least two good snowballs – and settling themselves at one of the small tables. The place was empty save for a large woman who leaned her elbows on the counter and addressed them in a jovial tone.

'Whass your pleasure, young ladies? Don't go sayin' bacon sandwiches, 'cos we're clear out of bacon, and the fancy cakes what I make when I can get hold of dried fruit went by mid-morning. But of course there's plenty tea in the urn and there's toast, or a nice jam sandwich. There's even one of them there Cornish pasties if you've a fancy for suffin' hot.'

The girls settled for tea and toast, and having provided them with both the woman went back behind her counter, turned up a small wireless set, and got out her knitting. The girls had seated themselves as far from her as possible, and now Dana leaned forward eagerly. 'Well? Come on, Poll, what is it you've got to say? I can tell there's something.'

Polly put down her toast and leaned forward. 'Me and Ernie are sick of waiting to get married, so we've set a date for this coming June,' she hissed. 'I've gorra friend in the WAAF – Wendy Burrowes – what got married before the war. She kept her wedding dress in a linen bag all done up with moth balls so's it wouldn't be

427

spoiled, 'cos she has a younger sister and she thought maybe the girl might want to get married herself one day and might need the dress. Only thing is Wendy's about my size but her sister just growed and growed and now it won't fit her at all – the wedding dress, I mean – so Wendy's give it to me.' She sighed romantically. 'It's a dream of a dress, honest to God it is. I showed Ernie – I know it's supposed to be unlucky but I think that's only if you're wearin' it at the time – anyway I showed it to him and he said we should set a date for our wedding 'cos we were both sick to death of waiting. We decided on the twenty-first of June because that's Ern's birthday and he reckons it's always sunny and bright, besides being the month that strawberries are ripe . . .'

'Oh for goodness' sake get on with it!' Dana said impatiently. 'So you've settled on a wedding date at last; I really don't blame you . . .'

Polly scowled at her. 'Shurrup and listen, can't you?' she said crossly. 'Only when Ernie told a feller on his ship what knows a thing or two about who will be where and when, he advised Ernie agin it. He said that due to unforeseen circumstances he didn't think anyone would be granted leave at that particular time and when Ernie pressed him, he said it were all very hush-hush. Everyone's going to be rare busy was all he'd say, so I asked a few questions too and the general feeling was the same in the WAAF as it was in the merchant navy: that we'd chose a real bad month for to get wed. I suggested to my wingco that maybe we'd best plan on an autumn wedding, and he looked real awkward and said if I'd take his advice I'd forget nineteen forty-four altogether and start planning for nineteen forty-five.'

'Gosh! Then from what you've told me I reckon the folk in the know think the invasion will start this coming summer,' Dana said, keeping her voice low. 'Of course I've heard rumours – everyone has – but this sounds like the real McCoy.'

'It is,' Polly said, nodding. 'So Ern and I talked it over on the telephone, making sure we didn't give no secrets away, mind you, and decided we'd be safe enough to get wed the followin' June; same date as before only a year later. If the war's over by then – and the chaps in the know seem to think it will be – then everything will be just right. I've got me dress so I shan't have to wear uniform and we'll find a couple of rooms in Liverpool which will do until we've saved up enough money for a real home of our own. But the main reason I wanted to talk to you now, Dee, is because I want you to be my bridesmaid. I had thought to ask you to give me away but my wingco offered – he's awful kind – so I knew you'd understand that I couldn't possibly refuse him. He's going to let us use his cottage in Devon for our honeymoon; ain't that just wonderful? So if you'll say you'll be bridesmaid I'll be that made up I'll dance all the way up the aisle.'

Dana chuckled appreciatively. 'It's sweet of you, alanna,' she said. 'And I'll be honoured, of course. But unless I've been demobbed by then I'll still be in breeches and my funny hat. Don't you think that would rather put a damper on the proceedings?'

Polly laughed too. 'So it might, except that Wendy had a dress made for her chief bridesmaid what's just about your size. Wendy's bridesmaid was a tall, skinny girl, just like you – and though the dress was pale pink to start with, it's got somewhat faded over the years and is now a sort of magnolia colour. Honest, queen, it will suit you down to the ground. Promise me you'll be my bridal attendant! I shan't feel properly married if you won't.'

'Of course I will,' Dana said at once. 'I'll be honoured. And now that's settled we can talk about other things. You've never met my Hank. However, that omission is about to be remedied; he's got a forty-eight coming up in two days and I've promised to meet him off the train which gets into Norwich Thorpe at ten forty. He'll buy us lunch and you'll be able to meet him.' She chuckled. 'You'll get to know a lot about his home, I fear, because his family own a farm on Prince Edward Island and he adores the place and loves talking about it. Unlike you and Ernie, we've always meant to get married when peace breaks out and not a moment before.'

'Oh, Dana, we could have a double wedding!' Polly said excitedly. 'Now that the bridesmaid's dress is faded it looks just like a wedding dress. Because of the time of year we could both wear a wreath of little white rosebuds in our hair and carry a bouquet of summer flowers. Oh, do say you will! It would make the day perfect.'

Dana laughed but shook her head, 'No, no, one's wedding day is something to remember for the rest of one's life and the bride is – must be – the centre of attraction. Tell you what, though; if you're marrying on the twenty-first of June, we'll marry the following day so that you can come to my wedding before going off on your honeymoon.' This was agreed, and having settled all the salient points the girls proceeded to have a most enjoyable leave. Polly was unable to resist asking Dana whether she had yet managed to get in touch with Con because, as she pointed out, when the war ended they would surely both return to Castletara and it would be awkward to meet for the first time after so long.

Dana, however, brushed this aside. 'Don't forget I shall be a married woman about to set off with my husband to a new life in Canada,' she said gaily. 'Didn't I tell you I went back for a crafty weekend last autumn? Feena and I discussed the situation and Feena said she had implored Con to come home whilst I was there so that we could become aquainted once more. I don't think it would have worked but since Con couldn't get leave Feena had to scrub the whole idea. She has explained to Con that I'll be marrying Hank as soon as peace breaks out and apparently Con will be marrying his Mirrie round about the same time. They will go back to Castletara for a while and Feena and Johnny will probably take them into partnership. Feena says they will send me my share of the profits twice a year so that even when I'm in Canada I shall have a certain independence. It's good of them, don't you think? I mean, I shan't be doing any of the work, so why should I get any money? But that's the way it has been arranged, and everyone thinks it's fair.'

The day of Hank's arrival was heralded by a blizzard, so once more Dana and Polly fled to the buffet though this time with a tall, soft-spoken Canadian airman as their companion. Despite the fact that due to the fearful weather conditions Hank's leave was cut short, Polly did manage to get to know the Canadian and liked him, though she still thought secretly that no matter how delightful Prince Edward Island might prove to be it could never hold the place in Dana's heart occupied by Castletara and Con. But that was Dana's business, and besides, since Con planned to marry his Mirabelle it seemed pretty clear that even if Dana were secretly pining for him – and she showed no sign of it – Con himself had definitely put Dana completely out of his mind. So Polly turned her thoughts to her own affairs. Back at her station she was far too busy even to think much about her own wedding, far less Dana's. The two friends kept in close touch however, mostly by telephone and letter, and when peace was declared and Churchill announced that 8 May 1945 would be Victory in Europe Day they returned to Liverpool to join in the celebrations.

The preparations for Dana's wedding had had to be put on hold, since the Canadians and Americans were being repatriated. Dana and Hank bade one another an affectionate farewell, Hank promising faithfully to return as soon as was humanly possible. 'Trust me to take care of you,' Hank said earnestly, as he queued to get aboard the ship which would take him home. 'I guess we'll marry in Castletara so's you can have your people to share your day, but as soon as we're settled I hope Feena and Johnny will make tracks to Prince Edward Island so's they can meet my folks. They'll get along just fine, I know it.'

And then it was Polly's wedding day. Both girls had been demobbed and were relishing their new-found freedom, though they had had to move in temporarily with friends in Temperance Court, having nowhere else to go until Polly and Ernie were married and took possession of their new flat. So it was in the Hodgkins' spare bedroom that the two girls got ready for the most important day of Polly's life. They began by trying on their dresses and ended by talking over old times and old ambitions, sitting on the bed they had shared the previous night and remembering everything from the dreadful time they had had under Mrs Haggerty's unpleasant rule to the kindness of the Freeway brothers and the excitements of running a cinema and cafeteria together for the first time. Jake had been killed in 1943 and Ralph, as they had expected, had gone back to South Africa where he had used every penny he possessed to buy not a cinema but a flower farm. He had been invalided out of the air force after he had been badly injured when his Mosquito had crashed, so now, when others were just beginning to relish their new-found freedom from rules, regulations and uniforms, Ralph was already harvesting his first crop and enjoying the thrill of being a husband to Sally-Ann and father to the three-month-old Jake, named of course for Ralph's beloved brother.

'If it hadn't been for the war, I wonder if you and Con might have made up your differences and become friends – or even lovers – once more,' Polly said thoughtfully, glancing in the mirror to make sure her coronet of white rosebuds was straight. She smiled at her friend. 'Once you would have jumped down my throat simply because I had dared to mention Con's name. Now you've come to terms with what's happened and are happily living your life without your old childhood friend. Does he know you're getting married? Has he sent good wishes – or bad ones for that matter – to be read out on the day? Or has he decided to ignore the whole thing?' She watched her friend closely, but Dana's face gave nothing away.

'I dunno. Feena just said he was getting married as well and would return to Castletara, for a while at any rate. It would have been nice if he could have brought himself to admit our quarrel was a foolish one, but—'

'Polly? Dana? What the devil are you two girls a-doin of? Don't you know what the time is? That there feller in uniform what's going to give you away – heh heh heh – come down from the hotel five minutes ago and he's a-settled in my parlour tryin' to stop the kids from muckin' up his uniform.'

Polly jumped guiltily to her feet. 'We'd best be going. The car will be arrivin' any minute and I bet Ernie's already in his number ones and standing up by the front of the church as frightened as a codfish.'

Dana giggled and dug her friend in the back. 'Just how frightened is a codfish?' she began, but Polly was already at the foot of the stairs, flinging the parlour door open and apologising to Wing Commander James for her tardiness.

'But we're ready now. The car will arrive any minute so we might as well walk through the arch; then he won't have to turn round.'

Polly's dress had a short train, and in view of the state of the cobbles Dana bent to pick it up and held it a foot above the ground as the driver jumped out of the car to hold open the door for the wedding party.

As always happens when a girl is wed from one of the courts, every inhabitant from the oldest to the youngest crowded round to wish her luck and wave her off. They waved at Dana too, knowing that she herself would soon be married, knowing also that she had once lived in the court, and Dana waved back, trying to quiet the silly little voice inside her which was saying that she did not want Canada or Hank's farm or Hank himself. She wanted . . . what did she want? Not Con, not her old life at the Freeway Cinema, not . . .

Then she pulled herself together, gave herself a shake. It was too late for regrets, she told herself firmly. Live the life you've chosen and stop whining, Dana McBride!

Con stood by the rail of the ferry heading across the Irish Sea, bound for England. It felt strange to be coming to Liverpool, because in his mind it was the city he should have searched first when Dana had left. What a fool he had been! He should have realised she would want to get away from himself, from Feena and Johnny, from Castletara . . . and more than that, she would want to get away from Ireland itself. He had considered London, but thought it too far and probably too expensive, so when he did try England he had searched the small provincial towns, never even considering that she might stop at the port in which she landed. If he had known about Caitlin, how she and Dana had clung together, two runaways wanting to prove themselves independent persons before even thinking about returning to the land of their birth, then he would certainly have searched Liverpool. Even in his self-disgust, however, he had to grin at the thought of Dana working in a commercial kitchen. She had always been a tomboy, a lover of the outdoors. Feena had had a job even to get her to keep her own room tidy, and as for cooking! He chuckled to himself. Most of what she cooked she burnt, and whatever she didn't burn arrived on the table half raw. His father and hers had often teased her, saying she would

435

make some man a terrible wife. But Dana had just tossed her red head and said she meant to marry a man who could afford a cook; her place was outdoors, and preferably with the horses.

'Mind your back, sor. We'll be dockin' in ten minutes and you won't want to get your decent suit covered in dort, 'cos we've a load of grand Irish spods to get down the gangway as soon as we dock.'

Con muttered an apology and moved further along the rail. He was here on impulse and was already regretting it, but when Feena had told him so off-handedly that Dana was getting married to some Yank or other he had seen at once that it was an opportunity to take a look at the girl he had once loved without her seeing him, or even knowing he was nearby. She would be far too busy with her new husband to notice Con Devlin, he told himself.

Accordingly he had boarded the ferry, first ascertaining at which church the girl from Temperance Court was getting married, and then whereabouts in Liverpool said church was situated. He had not asked Feena or Johnny for such details, since he could imagine what false hopes this would raise in their breasts. Instead, he had said he needed to visit a member of his crew who was trying to rent some rooms near the factory in which he had obtained a position. Unfortunately, the owner of the rooms seemed determined to let only to the Angel Gabriel or someone of similar ilk, so Freddy had written desperately to Con, his old squadron leader, begging for a reference. Con had forwarded the reference but had said he would come over in person and make sure that the landlord knew how fortunate he would be to have Freddy and his new wife as his tenants.

He meant to go there, too. But first he would take a look at Dana in her bridal finery. Seeing her the property of another man, and happy, he told himself that he would acknowledge at last that they would never have suited, were poles apart. Then he could start to live his own life, as everyone was always urging him to do, as indeed he knew he should.

He reached the church, checked that it was the right one, joined the crowd which had already collected. 'When's the bride arriving?' he hissed to the young woman nearest him and she turned, eyeing him up and down before replying.

'They're in already, all of 'em, bride, groom, best man an' all,' she said, having to speak loudly to be heard above the hum of the crowd. 'Ooh, ain't it grand to see a real weddin' for a change, instead of all that austerity stuff! She's in white, of course, wi' rosebuds in her hair and holdin' a bunch of 'em, a bouquet they calls it. She's gorran attendant what held up her train goin' in . . . but you'll see for yourself any time now. Here they come!'

They came out of the shadowy porch into the bright morning sunlight. Con stared and stared, whilst his heart bounced and leaped and his breath came short. He had been told Dana had changed, yet he could see no difference from the red-headed, freckled-faced kid he had once loved. She was exactly the same! He began to push his way through the crowd, his eyes fixed on the tall, slender girl in the long white dress, whose hand was tucked confidingly into the elbow of a well set up man in air force uniform. He never even saw the small blonde nor the fair-haired man whose arm she clutched. He had eyes only for Dana, and as he neared the couple Con realised that the man with his old love wore the insignia of a wing commander, that his hair was greying at the temples, that he was old enough, dammit, to be her father!

Fury and jealous rage gripped him. He began to push his way through the crowd and the movement must have caught Dana's eye for she turned, sliding her hand out of the officer's arm, and then her eyes met Con's. She shrieked, gathered up her long skirt and headed for him like an arrow from a bow. Watchers were pushed to one side, a child got trodden on and yelled indignantly, but Con had her in his arms and was shaking her, shouting at her, saying that he would thank that dirty old man to find someone his own age because Dana was his . . . his . . . his!

'You shan't be married! It will have to be – to be cancelled. Annulled! You're mine, you always were mine, and nothing's changed!' Con shouted. 'Tell your fancy man it was all a mistake; you're a part of me and I don't mean to let you go! We're going back to Castletara, where we belong, the pair of us!'

Dana snuggled against him, feeling a laugh and a sob together bubbling up within her. 'I'm not married,' she whispered into his neck. 'It's my friend Polly's wedding. Oh, Con, I've spent the last nine years running away, but that's all over now; and you've not said you love me, not once!'

Con laughed, but there was a catch in his voice when he spoke. 'I love you, Dana McBride,' he said. 'Will that do?'

ALSO AVAILABLE IN ARROW

The Lost Days of Summer

Katie Flynn

Nell Whitaker is fifteen when war breaks out and, despite her protests, her mother sends her to live with her Auntie Kath on a remote farm in Anglesey. Life on the farm is hard, and Nell is lonely after living in the busy heart of Liverpool all her life. Only her friendship with young farmhand Bryn makes life bearable. But when he leaves to join the merchant navy, Nell is alone again, with only the promise of his return to keep her spirits up.

But Bryn's ship is sunk, and Bryn is reported drowned, leaving Nell heartbroken. Determined to bury her grief in hard work, Nell finds herself growing closer to Auntie Kath, whose harsh attitude hides a kind heart. Despite their new closeness, however, she dare not question her aunt about the mysterious photograph of a young soldier she discovers in the attic.

As time passes, the women learn to help each other through the rigours of war. And when Nell meets Bryn's friend Hywel, she begins to believe that she, too, may find love . . .

arrow books

You are my Sunshine

Katie Flynn
Writing as Judith Saxton

Kay Duffield's fiancee is about to leave the country, and her own duty with the WAAF is imminent when she becomes a bride. The precious few days she spends with her new husband are quickly forgotten once she starts work as a balloon operator, trained for the heavy work in order to release more men to fight.

There she makes friends with shy Emily Bevan, who has left her parents' hill farm in Wales for the first time; down-to-earth Biddy Bachelor, fresh from the horrors of the Liverpool bombing, and spirited Jo Stewart, the rebel among them, whose disregard for authority looks set to land them all in trouble.

arrow books